THE FORGER AND THE DUKE

MISTY URBAN

OLIVERHEBERBOOKS

CHAPTER ONE

CORNWALL, 1770

M ost people begin the day that will change the course of their lives entirely unaware of what is to come.

But Amaranthe Illingworth anticipated a great event when she set out that morning from her cousin the baronet's home in Haye. She drove herself toward the market town of Callington in the trap she had learned to hitch herself, needing only the help of the baronet's stable boy to fasten the sturdy cob into his traces. Traffic on the dusty road was light, a few farmers heralding sheep, while the ladies from West Haye, heading to the shops, hailed her with smiles and waves. In her green riding coat and the smart Joan cap with its frill of muslin about her face, Amaranthe supposed herself exactly the sort of person who deserved to possess a rare, priceless, and irreplaceable manuscript.

The sun of a warm spring day shone on her head, and fortune smiled as well, for there were no other customers to take precedence as Amaranthe stepped into the bookshop beneath the musical jangle of the bell above the door. Mr. Finney, the proprietor, bustled out from the back room to greet her and obligingly cleared a space on the shop counter as Amaranthe set the leather valise atop it. He unrolled one of the parchment scrolls and nodded with approval at the dense rows of tiny black script that covered the page, here and there highlighted with red.

"Miss Illingworth, you have the neatest hand I can conceive. What a boon you would have been to any medieval scriptorium," Mr. Finney said.

Amaranthe laughed. "Perhaps so," she said, "saving that I would have been barred from the company of monks, given the unfortunate attribute of my sex. These are acceptable, then? I used my own recipe for iron gall ink, which—" She held up a hand to ward off Mr. Finney's immediate demand— "shall remain my own little secret, for now."

While there was no binding agent superior to gum arabic, Amaranthe had found with much experimentation—and occasionally irritating the cook—that using vinegar and a touch of indigo extended the life and quality of her ink. She meant to guard this secret jealously, as having a superior ink would help secure her reputation as a copyist.

"And I used mercury sulfide for the vermillion," she confided, pointing to a line of script. "So that color ought to stay fast as well."

"As like to the original as it is possible to be." Mr. Finney rolled the document with care. "I shall have these pages framed and sell them to antiquarians and visitors. It's not every town can boast a place in the Domesday Book. Would you like a folio for your own?"

"I have the page imprinted in my head, I assure you," Amaranthe replied. "Ancient Calwetone housed twenty-four villagers, fourteen smallholders, and eleven slaves. Assessed for thirty ploughlands, half a league each of pasture and woodland, seven cattle, and one hundred eighty sheep, the whole of it six pound's value to King William. If only the Conqueror could see what Callington has become."

Mr. Finney chuckled. "You are a rare find, Miss Illingworth, precisely because you can decipher medieval scripts, instead of merely copying them." He cast a look about the store. "I suppose you wish to discuss payment?"

Amaranthe's breath grew shallow and high in her chest. Finally. After two years of longing, copying pieces at her own expense, and scraping together what pennies she could from the stingy stipend her cousin allowed her. Two years of working long into the night by the cheap tallow candles the baronet doled out to his servants, the acid ink staining her nostrils and hands. Two years of refurbishing Favella's cast-offs so she spent nothing on herself. At last, she had earned her prize.

Her vision danced as Mr. Finney draped a small cloth over the counter and a few dust motes rose into the air, sparkling in the sun slanting through the shop windows. Her blood sang. She felt as Adam must have when his Creator revealed the creature He had made for his companion. But this creation was perfect.

The book was quarto size, regular folio pages folded into fourths, in all not much larger than her hand. In a fashion not now seen it was a girdle book, with a length of leather extending from its cover that could be tucked into a lady's belt as she went about her day. The clasp was not ornate but had kept the pages within from buckling as parchment was prone to do. With more reverence than the vicar at St. Mary's used when distributing holy bread, Mr. Finney opened the three-hundred-year-old cover, and the dark ink and brilliant illuminations shone forth as if the scribe had finished them but moments before.

Amaranthe's blood pounded in her ears. She had worn her

most delicate gloves for precisely this reason, the gloves she would wear to an assembly on the rare occasion she and Favella went to balls. With the lightest possible touch, she turned the pages, marveling at the beautiful script, the fanciful tracery of the initial capitals, the infinitely detailed artwork of the miniatures. It was not among the costliest Book of Hours one might find, but neither was it the poorest. Her throat tightened as she noted the line of pinpricks down each page and the faint grid of ruled lines, the marks of a careful scribe.

She turned to the front where, on the flyleaf, were listed the names of the book's proud possessors, all women. First and faintest was Blanche, Lady Willoughby de Broke. Then there was the elegant hand of Elizabeth, the third Baroness Willoughby de Broke, who had married a man knighted by Henry VIII and buried her treasure in a handy trunk when their monarch broke with the Roman Church. Margaret Greville had signed her book boldly; she had held her barony *suo jure,* in her own right, one of the few English peeresses.

The last name Amaranthe didn't recognize: Marguerite, Lady Vernay. Her research on this point had been unfruitful. Vernay was the courtesy title granted the eldest son of the Duke of Hunsdon, but the current Lord Vernay was a young boy, and of his father the duke's two wives, neither was named Marguerite.

Less of a mystery was why such a treasure had returned to the tiny town of Callington. Lady Blanche's husband, Nicholas Willoughby de Broke, lay interred in their own St. Mary's, and whomever disposed of Lady Vernay's possessions must have hoped the book might fetch a fine price from distant family or curious friends. Fortunately for Amaranthe, no one else, not even the tourists who came to light candles around Sir Nicholas's magnificent effigy, had shown interest in an old prayer book, and Mr. Finney had agreed to let her barter for its purchase.

Amaranthe reminded herself to breathe. Finally, finally, this precious thing was hers. "I shall wish a proper bill of sale be made out, Mr. Finney, so there can be no doubt in any mind that this book is my property."

As the ward of her cousin, made so by the lamentable and unforeseen death of her gentle parents, Amaranthe had no legal possessions of her own, and would not until she achieved the age one-and-twenty and could claim, in her own name, the tiny allowance out of her father's pension that her cousin now commanded for her maintenance. But she could not wait three years for this book. This slim volume would be her guide to improving her copyist abilities, showing her how to draw and ink miniatures and design capitals and borders in the style of the medieval scribes. But more than that, it was the first in the collection she meant to build, a library to rival Sir Robert Cotton's, one that would establish her renown. Miss Amaranthe Illingworth, antiquarian.

And besides, it was a beautiful artifact. The one beautiful thing, aside from her older brother Joseph, that she could love in this world, and call hers.

She wrapped the book in cloth and deposited it in her valise, with no inkling of how lamentably brief her possession of this treasured artifact would be.

The stables were quiet when Amaranthe returned to the baronet's house of Penwellen later that afternoon. She found it curious that Thaker, the stable boy, did not come to meet her, his hands slick with grease from oiling leather and his pockets heavy with dried apples for Morningstar. But the quiet vicarage in St. Cleer that had been her home for the first sixteen years of her life had also been home to a small, fat mare whose care had fallen to Amaranthe, so with the familiarity of long habit she unharnessed the placid cob, brushed and fed him, and was returning the harness to its peg when she heard voices in the building.

"I cannot see what possible interest your condition is to me."

Amaranthe stopped with one foot in midair. Then she put it down carefully. She now understood the expression about one's blood turning cold. The tone of the baronet's voice told her she must not make a noise.

"Now what can ee mean? The cheel is yours and ee do know that, aye?"

That was the voice of the new maid, Eyde. She'd come from the village of Laneast, one of many offspring of a manganese miner, and entry into service was quite a step up for her. She'd struggled to adjust to the big house and Favella's exacting standards.

What child did she speak of? Reuben and Favella had no issue.

Reuben's tone was icy. "Allow me to remind you that my lady will not tolerate a maid in the family way, and neither will I."

A pause rolled out. Amaranthe heard breathing. Her own, but perhaps the girl's also. The air glittered with sharp points of light.

"*Areah!*" the girl cried. "I knowed ee'd come over so, I *knowed* it, and still I let ee—" The words stopped, a muffled sound following. A sound like her parents had made in the grip of their fevers, a wounded creature keening with pain.

"Cease your screeching," the baronet said shortly. "I will not have you in my house until you rid yourself of this unfortunate development."

"Rid me—rid me!" The girl gasped. Amaranthe shivered at the agony in her voice. "Ee shall give me a coin or three to turn me off, then? I've not a penny for my pocket!"

"You dare ask me for money!" Her cousin's cold fury was worse than any roar. "Your morals are as light as your skirts. Consider yourself released from my employ." He added with a sneer, "Slattern."

Amaranthe's mind refused to order the facts. Eyde, it would seem, was with child. But for Reuben, wed to pale, fretful Favella, to be father of this babe, and not acknowledge it? True, a bastard child could not inherit his house and lands, but to turn Eyde off entirely—this was a malice she would not have thought even Reuben possessed.

There was a suck of air, as if her cousin drew on a cheroot. It would be in line with his arrogance for him to smoke in the stables, a building which could easily catch fire. But it was Eyde, sobbing.

"I've nowhere to go. No one a' will take me."

"That," said the baronet, "is likewise your problem. Not mine."

Amaranthe couldn't distinguish the sounds that followed. A cry, cut off as if bitten, the hiss of sliding leather, then a familiar snap. At a howl from the girl, Amaranthe rushed forward.

Eyde knelt in the tack room, her skirts stirring the dirt and hay upon the floor, her arms flung up over her head as the baronet slashed the short, sharp horsewhip toward her head. Amaranthe's heart stopped beating for a moment, though that didn't stay her steps. Her life as a rector's daughter had been so gentle, and she knew only tenderness from her parents. It had been a sobering education when she fell under her cousin's wardship and learned a man could be capable of gross indifference to his fellow creatures, as well as insolence and casual cruelty.

Before she knew how she'd arrived there, she stood between Eyde and the baronet, her hands raised, her voice a shriek unfamiliar to her own ears.

"Cousin! Stop, I beseech you."

The baronet's lip curled and with an angry, contemptuous stroke he brought the whip down on Amaranthe. The braided leather laid a trail of fire across her forearms and wrists, and the cluster of beads at the tip shredded her fine gloves. Amaranthe sucked in a breath of outrage and true fear.

"She came at me. I've a right to protect myself," Reuben snarled.

"But if you beat her, she might lose the babe." Amaranthe's hands burned as if she'd touched acid, and her cousin's scowl was terrifying. She understood now. He had done something base, and he did not want to be discovered in it.

"'Twould be a solution for us both," Reuben answered.

The baronet was not a handsome man. Her elder by more than a decade, born the heir of an eldest son, he had always been condescending. Amaranthe knew from two years of living beneath his roof that he was a man who valued little beyond his own pleasures and the respect he felt due him. But she had never, until now, known him to be so completely deprived of morals.

"Favella will have fits when she learns you did this."

The words slipped out before she could consider the wisdom of mentioning the baronet's wife. Favella, the one thing in the world the baronet cherished, was delicate and excitable, and not upsetting Favella was the axis about which the household rotated. Favella's need not to be vexed was one reason that much of the housekeeping, visiting, and other duties of the house had fallen on Amaranthe. But for her cousin to defile the marital bed—

The baronet's face reddened, his lips in an ugly twist. "Favella isn't to hear a word of this." He glared at Amaranthe and then Eyde, who flung her arms around Amaranthe's knees and clung for dear life.

"I don't see how she cannot," Amaranthe blurted. Eyde's condition couldn't be hidden if she stayed in their service, and Amaranthe couldn't let the baronet toss her out. Eyde's family hadn't been able to support the girl alone; how could they feed two more mouths? They were more likely to send her away. Illegitimate children had no place in the world.

Her cousin's face turned calculating, and he stepped forward and grasped her hand. Amaranthe sucked in her breath as his grip pinched where the burning lash had fallen. Her palm stung.

"You forget yourself, cousin." Reuben's breath was foul, and she saw rot in his teeth as he bared them at her. "I have been lax with you, I see. Letting you take advantage of my good nature."

That was a jest, surely. Her cousin kept most of her allowance for himself. He watched every pat of butter she put on her bread, every lump of sugar she carved off the loaf for her tea. He read the letters that came and went from her brother at Oxford and her friends from school. She'd had to leave Miss Gregoire's when her parents died because Reuben would not stand her tuition.

The baronet pulled Amaranthe toward him, and she turned her face aside as he leaned close, his chuckle wafting onions and sour beer in her face. She breathed through her mouth, trying not to gag with disgust and terror.

"I think, *dear* cousin, it is time you began earning your keep."

"I already do everything a wife does," Amaranthe lashed out, not looking at him. She feared she might faint from the humiliation of being treated so.

He sneered and tugged her arm, trying to pull her against his fleshy stomach, his fleshy thighs. "Not everything, cousin. But perhaps you should. It might teach you a lesson about who your master is."

Amaranthe bit down on her lip so she didn't whimper. She was innocent, but she felt her innocence being shredded like rags. Her cousin had done something vile to Eyde, and now he meant to turn his attentions on *her*.

"Let me go." Amaranthe drew her arm up and twisted, breaking his grip.

He stepped back, but his expression didn't falter. "Make no mistake, *cousin*." His leering gaze traveled down her neck and over her bodice. The smart riding jacket, Favella's castoff, suddenly felt filthy against her skin. "You and I will reach a new understanding about your freedoms beneath my roof. You have lived on my generosity long enough."

He didn't spare a glance for Eyde as he strode away, dropping the whip on the floor. Amaranthe was tempted to pick it up and throw it at him, but it would serve no purpose. She extended a hand to help Eyde to her feet and winced as Eyde gripped the welts on her palms.

"You cannot stay here at Penwellen, Eyde." Amaranthe tried to keep her voice from breaking with despair. "Do you have someplace to go?"

Eyde's face crumpled. "Me mum's whimmy at er best, and me da—ee'll do whip me proper." She wiped away tears. "Miss. Ye can't stay here neither. He won't be said nay."

Amaranthe shuddered and pushed away the dark image Eyde's words conjured. She'd be whipped to ribbons before she took the risk that her cousin would force himself upon her. "It seems we're both leaving Penwellen, then. But where are we to find aid?"

Amaranthe had no coin; she'd given her last farthing to Mr. Finney. She didn't dare step inside the house. Favella would fly up in the boughs at the sight of her, dirty and bleeding, and Reuben would deny any accusations. Best to get away quickly and send for her things later. But where to go? Her chest squeezed with panic.

Her brother, Joseph, lived in tiny rooms at Oxford. His stipend barely kept him; it could not accommodate a sister and a maid. Her father's relatives had sent her to Reuben; they would refuse to support her. Her mother's few remaining friends were poor and frail. But how was she to flee to a strange place, alone and unaided, and what employment was she fit for, eighteen, gentle-born, with a Cornish girl in her keeping who would never be able to find work with a babe in arms?

No one in Haye or Callington would hide them from Reuben. The baronet might not be admired, but as her legal guardian, he had every right to demand Amaranthe's return. No one she knew here could protect her. The nodding acquaintances she had made, aside from Mr. Finney, were Favella's friends, and so was the rector's wife.

Amaranthe spared a pang for the thought of Mr. Treen, the man who had taken over the printer's shop in Callington. He was handsome and courteous and while all the girls giggled at him, Amaranthe had thought that once or twice he had looked appreciatively on her. But an acquaintance so slight could not be called upon to intervene between her and a man of the baronet's standing. She must think how to get herself and Eyde to safety, and survive along the way.

No good calling Thaker for assistance; the boy did not hear. He'd help if he could find them, but he had an uncanny way of keeping himself from the baronet's path. She would ask at the kitchen door for Cook to wrap them some bread and cheese, and perhaps fetch Amaranthe's cloak. At least she had not yet taken her book to the house. She still had her most precious possession. It would break her heart to part with it, but she could ask Mr. Finney to return her money. Or, at worst, sell or pawn the book elsewhere for a roof over their heads.

The trap stood parked in its customary place, the pole resting against the ground. The well and the seat sat empty.

The valise was gone. Reuben had stolen her book.

A red wave of fury washed over Amaranthe, followed by an icy rage. That gesture alone—that he would rob her—told her more than anything else he would not be reasoned with. She must flee if she meant to keep her virtue and possibly her life. The welts on her hands burned as she clenched her fists.

After a quick, hurried exchange with the cook at the kitchen door, the two women had their cloaks and a small basket of food, but little else.

"Where do we two go, then, miss?" Eyde whispered, wide-eyed.

"We shall go to my old schoolmistress at Bath. Miss Gregoire will surely help us."

Amaranthe eyed the sunny sky, that warm, deep-washed blue that belonged only to the south of England. How cruel that such a sun would shine on a day that had taken everything from her, but perhaps God in His mercy would grant them fine weather for their travels. They would catch a farmer's cart where they may, but most of the path would be spent walking. With a young girl several months pregnant and Amaranthe in her worn half-boots.

"Upcountry," Eyde said apprehensively. Anywhere beyond Cornwall was a wild, uncharted country to the Cornish natives.

"Somerset," Amaranthe confirmed. She took the girl's arm and they set off north.

She wouldn't miss Favella. She wouldn't miss anyone here save Thaker and Mr. Finney. She was glad, in a way, to rid herself so resolutely of her poisonous cousin. But what would happen to her and Eyde, if they survived the journey and the footpads and highwaymen along the way, she couldn't begin to say.

All that she'd miss was her Book of Hours. She would come back for it. Someday she would confront her cousin and she would win back what he had taken from her. He could strip her of everything, home, possessions, income, pride, but he could not have her dream of her future. She would not allow him to take that.

CHAPTER TWO

SIX YEARS LATER: LONDON 1776

"You want to ship off to fight in the American colonies now? Who put this bugbear into your brain?" Viktor Vierling lowered one side of his morning paper to stare across the booth at his friend, Malden Grey.

Mal stared back. "It's something to do."

Something active and decisive, with a defined aim in mind. His life was badly missing definitive action at the moment.

"I could afford to buy a cornetcy in the cavalry when my quarterly allowance comes through," Mal said. "Sail out with Burgoyne and his Hessians to Quebec." He pointed to the headlines on Vierling's paper, the news borne on all the printed matter being passed about, and argued over, in the small, noisy coffeehouse.

"With your rotten luck, you'd be killed by some rebel patriot popping from behind a hedge to shoot at a redcoat. Or worse, by some camp disease that turns your guts to water. Who will support your aunt and uncle when you take a musket ball in the belly?" Viktor demanded.

"They could sell my commission, I should think."

"Who would look after the ducal children?"

Mal shifted against the high, hard back of his bench seat, which separated their table from the one behind. "The duke's children have a stepmother. She ought to be looking after them."

Viktor turned a page of his paper. "It's a month aboard ship to sail to Halifax. Have you forgotten Gibraltar?"

Mal winced. As a wild young lad he had signed up as a midshipman to fight in the Seven Year's War. One voyage to the Mediterranean spent puking out his innards had put paid to the notion that he would ever become an able seaman.

"Are there any vacancies in your troop?"

Viktor was a member of the 2d Horse Grenadier Guards, part of the British Household Cavalry. Guarding the King's interests at home was a noble enough duty, though many of Viktor's German countrymen, as well as any other European troops the King could recruit, were being sent to the Americas.

Viktor lowered his paper again and considered Mal across the rough wooden table. "I could try. They like their guards tall and strong enough to heft the equipment, so you'd suit. Have you thought about the Corps of Engineers? You'd enjoy blowing things to rubble."

"I considered it, and the training would be here in Woolwich. But it would be back to Gibraltar to work on the fortifications, and I'm not known for my sea legs."

"You've given up hope of being called to the bar, then," Viktor said.

Mal stared into the gritty dregs of his black, bitter coffee. His future looked equally dark.

Around them, the fellow patrons of the coffee shop carried on lively conversations about politics and military strategy. One portly gentleman in a bright orange waistcoat and periwig, with a gold-tipped walking stick and a mongrel dog curled at his feet, shouted that the British victory in the Battle of Quebec would turn the tide against the pesky rebels. The Battle of Bunker Hill last year had proven how costly it would be to bring the rowdy Americans in line, but the buzz of conversation was over what France would do, having lost a great part of their own American possessions to Britain in the last Treaty of Paris. Every strategist in the coffee shop had a different, dire prediction.

Mal didn't long for military action; he was a thinker, not a soldier. But his latest plan for supporting himself in the law, after a roster of other failed ventures, was not offering much in the way of advancement.

"The Benchers called that beef-witted Froggart to the bar before me," Mal said. "He's not been in the Middle Temple nearly as long as I have, and I doubt he's opened a single book. But a barrister he shall be now, with his wig and robes, because he attends more meals and licks the boots of the judges."

"Which you won't do." Viktor shook his head. "Yours is the most dastardly luck, old man."

Mal downed his coffee, all but the grounds, and signaled for another cup.

Malden Grey had grown up under the curse of bad luck. Indeed, he was known for it.

It began when his mother, the daughter of a Bristol haberdasher, allowed herself to be wooed to ruin by a silver-tongued gentleman traveling through the West Country on holiday. She gave her hand and her virtue to the scoundrel and was left in tears when an irate duke came to recall his heir to his duties. Marguerite died when Mal was young, and when the parish couldn't produce any record and her kin could find no trace of her marriage lines, there was no recourse but to declare him illegitimate. Malden lived his life under the cloud of being a bastard.

He had been raised by his aunt, his mother's sister, who married an innkeeper, a jolly man named Littlejohn. When Mal was a lad, Littlejohn was trampled by a neighbor's bull and his broken leg taken off to save his life. Mal had not been ill-treated in their home, but he worked hard for his keep, running for his uncle and their many guests, with little to look forward to in his future but a life of continued drudgery.

Then out of the blue, his father, the new duke, located Mal, acknowledged him, and paid his tuition at Winchester. In rebellion to his father's wishes Mal tried the navy, carpentry, and a post as a turnpike toll collector—all endeavors with unfortunate ends—before he agreed to take a degree at Cambridge. Neither medicine nor the priesthood suited him, so he'd settled on the law, an occupation conducive to the life of a young gentleman at liberty in London.

But after his active, hardscrabble upbringing, Mal found he wasn't built for a life of leisure. He could drink himself under the table each night with his fellows, spend mornings in the coffee shops arguing politics and his afternoons in the Temple Hall hashing out finer points of law, then take himself off to the evening's entertainments of theater, tavern, or gaming hell, but it all turned into a dreary round of sameness. He had too active a mind to take pleasure in enforced idleness. If only he could be called to the bar, he was determined to apply himself, rise quickly among the ranks of serjeants, and eventually find a place on a high court, perhaps even the King's Bench. His rulings would be just and fair and wide-reaching, like those of the newly created Earl of Mansfield.

But the Benchers had to call him first, and as always, Mal never knew if his bastardy advanced his cause or hindered it. As the acknowledged throw of a duke he was accepted among the sprigs of the nobility, none of them much concerned about the niceties. But to the moral principles of the gentry and the aspiring *bourgeoisie,* his natural birth was a stain on his character. He might never be deemed worthy of carrying out the cause of justice.

"Some days I wonder if it is luck," Mal said grimly, watching the poor serving boy acknowledge every other bid but his own. "Some days I wonder if it's simply fate. Or if I'm under a curse."

What he most needed was to prove himself a worthy guardian to his half brothers and sisters. The three children of his father's first marriage required a protector now that gout had carried off the 3d Duke of Hunsdon, and Mal didn't trust Sybil, the current duchess, as far as he could throw a cat. The children wanted a clear head and a steady hand to guide them, and Mal was determined to provide that hand. He might speculate about shipping off to the Americas, or another theatre of war, but he'd never abandon his half-siblings. They were his duty, his blood, and they were overall rather likeable people, though he hadn't spent much time with them.

A commission in the Grenadiers suited his requirements. If he couldn't become a barrister, a gentlemanly profession, then a military man could be trusted with the oversight of one young duke and the estate he had inherited.

Mal tapped the paper in Viktor's hand. "I'm calling upon the duke's banker to draw upon my allowance. Care to join me?"

Viktor glanced at his cup. "I haven't finished."

"I'll come find you later, then." After the coffee shop, Viktor would adjourn to his club for dinner and cards, and from there to whatever entertainment was on offer. The duties of the Household Cavalry did not seem onerous, beyond presenting for drills and reviews, prancing about in public places, and keeping oneself in good trim for the uniform. Mal, like Viktor, was tall, well-built, and pleasant to look upon. Surely his bad luck was about to turn.

He found out quite soon that was not to be the case.

Mal strolled down the Strand to Thomas Coutts & Co., nodding at the women who cast him appreciative glances from under their lashes, the young bucks and dandies who hailed him as their fellow. He made his request and lounged against the counter, twirling his walking stick and imagining it a ceremonial sword. The young banker returned from a back room, looking rather sickly, and coughed into a hand with ink-stained fingers.

"Mr. Grey. I regret to inform you that your allowance for the quarter has already been withdrawn."

"I beg your pardon," Mal said, "but this is the first I've presented myself to claim it."

"Nevertheless, the entries indicate the monies have been collected."

The clerk conducted Mal into a richly paneled room with plush carpet and a fragrant oil lamp lit in one corner against the dull grey London afternoon. Bronze fixtures gleamed with polish. The head of the bank, Thomas Coutts himself, sat behind a large oak desk. He was a neat and unpretentious man, known to be efficient and discreet. He was also known, quite surprisingly, to have married a girl who had been nursemaid in his brother's household, and the union was by all accounts a happy one.

Not all women who married far above their station came to ruin and early death, as Mal's mother had. Mal stowed the old bitterness in the back of his mind, where it belonged, and sank into the chair Coutts indicated. His heart sank accordingly at the banker's expression as he opened a leather-bound account book.

"All of it," Mal said with disbelief after the banker had finished. "Every bit of income for the quarter. Sybil's allowance. Mine. The household expenses for Hunsdon House. All withdrawn?"

"All of it," Coutts confirmed with a solemn nod. "The income from the estates, from the annuities, and from the investments." He offered a pained smile at Mal's shocked expression.

"I assure you that the transaction seemed legitimate at the time. We had no reason to suspect that the duke's steward, Mr. Popplewell, was making these withdrawals without authorization."

Without Mal's authorization, certainly, and furthermore without his consent. But he wasn't the legal guardian yet. The bank had no reason to alert Mal to Popplewell's doings, and Mal had no recourse to stop him. Coutts's sympathetic expression told Mal that this wasn't the first time he'd seen a land steward of a wealthy estate empty all the accounts and abscond with the funds.

More than that, who was it all for? Popplewell must have known he couldn't get away with looting the inheritance of such a personage as the Duke of Hunsdon, especially since the duke was still a youth, with the fight over his wardship making its slow and expensive way through the courts.

"Whose is the second signature?" Mal asked. "By terms of the trust, no one person is allowed to draw on any significant sums. It was set up so the estate could not be robbed."

Coutts flinched at the word 'robbed' and peered into his book. Mal guessed what he would hear even before the banker spoke.

"The duchess co-signed on the withdrawals. Lady Hunsdon."

"Sybil," Mal hissed. He rose swiftly.

"Thank you for your assistance, Mr. Coutts. I am sure Mr. Popplewell and the duchess will be able to account for this irregularity. No doubt they mean to tell me they have transferred the Hunsdon funds into some clever and lucrative investment."

"No doubt," Coutts said blandly, rising also. "I am sure it is as you say."

Mal paused, gritting his teeth. It went against the grain to ask for help. He would rather be dragged by wild horses than admit he'd been made a fool.

"I am sure, Mr. Coutts, that I can rely on the discretion of your bank and your employees to ensure that no further withdrawals are made on any of the duke's accounts for the duration." He hoped he had the authority to make such a demand. Coutts knew his guardianship was not yet official, though Mal meant to do everything in his power to make it so, especially now.

"It is an honor to handle accounts for the Duke of Hunsdon, Mr. Grey," the other man said. "You may trust that you are in good hands."

Mal stalked out of the bank, seething. Popplewell would not be in good hands, and neither would Sybil, once Mal found them. Just what were they plotting between them? Popplewell was a shifty sort, the previous duke's man of business, with neither the wit nor the connections to make much of himself. What sort of hold did he have over the duchess to make her concede to his schemes?

Mal headed directly for Hunsdon House, located in a fashionable West End square where the first Duke of Hunsdon, a crony of George I, had claimed a strip of land. Rather than hire a chair, Mal decided his wrath was better served by walking, and it was testament to his glowering expression that, despite the attire marking him as a man of relative means, he was accosted by neither cutpurse nor streetwalker, nor anyone else, as he traversed Haymarket, Piccadilly, Lesser and then Greater Swallow Street into the Palladian environs of Hanover Square.

The knocker was off the door, indicating that Hunsdon House was not receiving callers. Odd; Sybil thrived on social intercourse. She was the kind of woman who couldn't tolerate a moment alone with her own thoughts. Mal rapped on the stout oak portal with his walking stick. No answer. No porter, butler, or underbutler to take his card. No footman who ought to have leapt into the breach if any of the above were neglecting their posts.

Mal inserted his key and pushed open the heavy door. The house was untidy and bare of occupants. There was no swish of skirts as parlormaids hurried around the lower level or chambermaids saw to the rooms above. No tweenie whisking herself out of sight. No distant bustle from the kitchens or the offices on the ground floors, where one would expect tradesmen to be moving to and fro.

No visitors. No guests.

In the duchess's suite, the dressing room stood bare. One wardrobe bulged with last year's gowns and their accoutrements. The other two wardrobes had been picked clean. The duchess's hats were missing. Her shoes were missing. Her jewels were gone.

Mal returned to the front rooms, searching for the back stairs to the nursery and the children's rooms above. Several of the tables in the foyer lacked their usual ornaments. Certain valuable items which had been the source of much pride to previous dukes had vacated their customary places in the formal drawing rooms.

The sense of any human habitation in the house was missing.

It dawned on him with a slow, awful realization, like the cold flood of a rising tide. The children were missing, too.

CHAPTER THREE

The house was quiet, just the way Amaranthe liked it.

In the five years since her brother had graduated Oxford and they'd moved to London, Amaranthe had become inured to the near-constant noise: the clattering of carriages and passing pedestrians, the hawking of street vendors, the cries of the street sweeps and errand boys, the endless traffic and daily commerce of a sprawling, burgeoning, restless city. But part of her missed the deep, endless quiet of the country, and she preferred calm while she worked.

Voices drifted up to her parlor from the floor below, the steady thump of Mrs. Blackthorn at work in the kitchen, Eyde's low murmur as she chatted with the cook, and the small, piping voice of Derwa, Edye's daughter, as she ran back and forth on her errands. Amaranthe liked the soothing reminder that there was someone else in the house, so long as the voices weren't clear enough to interrupt her concentration, since after all it was her labors that supported the household.

After a time, she grew aware of an altercation in the lane outside. Some thoughtless nob had driven his fancy coach into George Court, a passage barely large enough to admit a sedan chair or a wagon. A carter with a load of furniture coming from the Blue Posts, the public house, chided the driver of the coach for such a booby-headed act as to block the conduct of honest business, leading to unkind speculations on the groom's parentage. The groom rallied with suspicion as to whether the carter's business was indeed honest, and as passersby gravitated to the scene, the temperature of the debate rose quickly.

Amaranthe watched with fascination through the large display window in her front parlor. The house was designed to accommodate a shop, and she had leased it for this reason, acquiring it from a watchmaker who had conducted his business on the ground floor and lived in his private rooms above. She was not yet prepared to open her antiquarian bookshop, but she had procured the premises with that aim in mind. The large display window admitted the light she needed, and there were rooms above for her and Joseph and rooms below for the servants and whatever poor souls came to them in need of aid.

"There's to be blood in a moment, right enough," Mrs. Blackthorn commented, and Amaranthe looked around to see that not just the cook but Eyde and Derwa hovered in the parlor doorway, watching the spectacle through the display window with her, as good as a farce or a puppet show at a fair.

Amaranthe put down the small brush with which she was applying gold paint to her parchment. "I suppose one of us ought to go calm the waters, if anyone will listen. Where is Davey?"

The small Welshman was Eyde's husband. They pretended he didn't live with them in George Court so Amaranthe might avoid the tax on male servants, and instead of quarterly wages she paid him piecemeal for errands run and other services performed about the house. He was their butler, boots, jack of all trades, and running footman when called for.

"He popped round to the Blue Posts for our small beer and

the porter you like, mum," Eyde said. "Shall I have Derwa fetch ee?" Despite their years upcountry, small bits of Cornish dialect still crept into Eyde's speech.

"No, because then Derwa might find a playmate, and we won't see her till she wants her supper," Amaranthe answered. She smiled at the small girl who leaned against Eyde's hip. Derwa, who treated Amaranthe more like a favorite aunt than their employer, was the reason she never for a moment regretted their hard flight from Cornwall six years before.

She regretted the loss of her manuscript, daily, but she never spoke of it.

The three women looked at one another in surprise as a knock sounded at the front door. Amaranthe was not out in Society, and so not in the habit of making or receiving the social calls that would have filled her days as Favella's companion were she yet living in her cousin the baronet's house. Any friends she had would send a note in advance so they might be met with some of Mrs. Blackthorn's excellent seed cakes. Amaranthe's clients were arranged through the booksellers she worked with; they were not given her home address. And Sundays were Joseph's holidays from his tutoring post, so they rarely expected to see him at home.

It was not like Joseph to forget an appointment, but then he had been distracted lately; Amaranthe suspected a young woman and not any intellectual preoccupation was the cause. She herself knew what it was to look up from her work to find that hours had gone by.

"Eyde, would you—" Before she could finish Derwa slipped out, grunting as she heaved open the front portal, nearly as heavy as she was. An exclamation of surprise followed.

Amaranthe stifled astonishment as three strange children filed into the room. Aside from Derwa, children were not entities she had much to do with, and these three looked more expensive than most. The two boys wore full suits with coats and waistcoats lined with large silver buttons and white stockings below buckled breeches. The girl, slightly larger than Derwa, was lost in a froth of silver-blue satin. All three looked nervous and miserable.

"We've come to—" the younger boy began, but the elder cut him off.

"We haven't been announced," the youth said with a gravity that made Amaranthe want to laugh.

"I beg your pardon," Amaranthe said, keeping her voice serious so he would not think she was having fun at his expense. "My butler is employed elsewhere. Can you perhaps give your names to my maid?"

"Introduced by the maid?" the youth said in disdain, and an inkling visited Amaranthe as to who these children might be.

"Oh, stuff it, Huey!" the second boy burst out. He held his hand with its folded tricorn cap to his chest. "This is the duke, I'm Ned, and this is Millie. We're looking for Mr. Joseph, please."

The little girl clutching his hand bobbed a curtsey and stared at Amaranthe with a beseeching look.

"I am Algernon Francis Hugh Delaval, the Duke of Hunsdon," the elder boy proclaimed with all the hauteur of the nobility, and Amaranthe had the satisfaction of knowing her suspicions were correct. "This is Lord Edward—" he indicated his brother— "and Lady Camilla."

Lady Camilla executed a deeper curtsey that put her off balance. Lord Edward caught her before she toppled.

"We," the duke continued, "are here to see Mr. Joseph Illingworth." He did not say *please*.

A footman in livery huffed through the door behind them. "Beggin' your pardon, miss, I'm here to announce—"

"We've done introductions already, Ralph," the young duke said. He gave Amaranthe a commanding look.

"I'm afraid Mr. Illingworth is not home at present," Amaranthe said, at a loss what to do with these very proper and unexpected ducal children. "Would you care to leave a card?" That might be going too far. Would a young duke have a card?

"Do you know where he is?" the duke asked, while the younger boy wailed, "We must find him!" and the girl cried, "Not home? But where else could he be?"

"I can send him to Hunsdon House when he returns, if the business is urgent," Amaranthe suggested. "Am I correct that you are his pupils?"

"He is tutor for Ned—Lord Edward and I," the duke said freezingly. "*Not* for Lady Camilla."

Amaranthe glanced out the window and saw the ducal arms on the doors of the carriage blocking traffic in the court. It pulled away while the carter, muttering crossly to himself, set his team in motion, and the passersby drifted off, the entertainment over. Eyde sidled close to Amaranthe, looking at the children's rich clothing with wonder.

"And why should the cheelin be on your doorstep, Miss Amaranthe?" she whispered. "'Oo 'as the charge of een?"

The young duke stiffened and did his best to look down his nose at her. He was nearly of a height to do so. "We have the charge of ourselves, miss."

His lofty proclamation was undercut by the expressions of woe that burst from his siblings. "There's no one at home!" Lord Ned exclaimed, and at the same time Lady Camilla begged, "Oh, don't send us back there! Don't make us go!"

Amaranthe decided it was time to take things in hand. "Come in and be seated," she ordered the trio. "Derwa, you may take their hats. Eyde, you may help Mrs. Blackthorn prepare a tray." The cook had already disappeared, and as the scent of warm yeast floated up the stairs, Amaranthe guessed to what purpose. "I shall send someone round to see if my brother is at his favorite coffee house, and we shall enjoy tea while we wait."

"Tea!" Lady Camilla said gratefully, clasping her hands. "Oh, yes, please."

The young duke stood stiffly. "We should hate to impose—"

"Oh, do stop shamming it, Huey!" his brother exclaimed. "She's got something to eat." He came to inspect the parchment spread over Amaranthe's easel as she began to cover it. "What are you doing?"

"I am gilding the capitals on this folio, and *pray* do not put your finger in my paint! Gold leaf is dear," Amaranthe said testily as the boy prodded her dish with a curious finger. He held up the gilded fingertip, abashed, and Amaranthe handed him the old rag she used to mop up spills. The other children crowded close.

"Are you copying that page? For what possible reason?" the young duke asked.

"I am making a copy of this book at the request of its owner," Amaranthe explained. "It's a medieval prayer book known as a breviary, and it was made for a fifteenth-century French queen. I am copying the prayers and offices, and a painter is doing the miniatures."

"And people pay for such things." The young duke appeared dubious.

"Well enough to support us." Amaranthe cleaned her brush, finding it best not to explain further exactly how she earned enough to support them. Not even Joseph knew the whole of it.

The old pang of loss needled her heart as she looked upon the neat, tight script of the breviary. Every line, every detail made her long for her lost Book of Hours. If only there had been some way she could have searched for it before they fled Penwellen. Reuben could only have stolen it out of spite; she doubted he read Latin even in block print, much less the minis-cule of handwritten Gothic script.

"It's called illumination when it has the gilding like that," Ned announced. Amaranthe shifted his pointing finger away from the parchment before he smeared gold paint in a place it didn't belong.

"It looks just like the Latin exercises Mr. Joseph gives you to copy. I wish *I* might learn Latin," Camilla said.

"You don't, Millie. Cicero'll make you want to gnaw your arm off," Ned assured her.

"Girls don't read Latin," the young duke scolded.

"I do," Amaranthe said calmly. "But this happens to be Middle French. The book was translated into the vernacular, since the queen who owned it likely did not read Latin, either."

She paused in the act of arranging the sliding bar that she used to rest her hand while doing fine work. The young duke turned away, showing no interest in the manuscript, so she pulled the protective sheet over the page, using the bar to keep the fabric from touching the drying ink. Some flaws must be expected in a work made by human hands, and she could explain a smudge to the manuscript's owner when she turned in her commission. But flaws in the separate copy she was making for herself—a duplicate of which the original owner had no knowledge—well, it would not serve for that book to be unreadable.

"Now," Amaranthe said, covering the rest of her paints and tools to protect them from inquisitive fingers, "what business do you have with Mr. Illingworth?"

"We," Ned began, but a glare from his older brother quelled him.

"We will discuss it with Mr. Illingworth," the young duke said with a fierce frown.

Oh, he was high in the instep, blue blood true, Amaranthe

thought, but she was saved from dealing a possibly unwise reproof when Mrs. Blackthorn entered with a tray. Camilla stared at the cook's face, then gave Amaranthe a look of dismay.

"You keep an African, miss? For shame!" she cried. "Slavery is a stain on the British character and ought to be abolished."

"Mrs. Blackthorn is a free woman who earns a wage from me," Amaranthe replied. "A not insignificant stipend, I think, given her talents."

"At least Mr. Joseph eats what I feed him." Mrs. Blackthorn sent Amaranthe a scolding look. She had found safety in Amaranthe's household, in the promise that her secret would not be exposed and she would not be compelled to return to the man who claimed he owned her. Amaranthe agreed with Lady Camilla, and Mrs. Blackthorn, on the subject of enslavement.

"I enjoyed last night's pudding very much," Amaranthe said in her own defense. "Only I am not fond, as you know, of raisins."

She poured tea for the children, filling their cups mostly with milk, and noticed that all three took large helpings of bread and butter. When they were settled with food, Amaranthe went into the hallway where Eyde and Mrs. Blackthorn hovered in concern.

"The children are hungry!" Mrs. Blackthorn exclaimed in a hushed tone. "What should I feed them?"

"Whatever we have," Amaranthe said. "The pudding that is left, meat and cheese, and soup if we have any, or perhaps a thick gruel. They have missed their meals today for certain." She peeked into the room and saw that, in her absence, all three children had taken the liberty of depleting the tea tray.

A wild suspicion stirred her mind. The boys looked neat enough, their clothes fine and correct, but the bow in Camilla's hair had been tied by herself, and she was wearing delicate slippers completely unsuitable for the street. Someone was not properly looking after these children, little lords and lady though they were.

"Eyde, find Davey and have him fetch Mr. Joseph from the coffee shop. He'll be at the Orange or the Smyrna." She couldn't ask Edye to fetch Joseph herself, as a woman wouldn't be allowed to set foot in those male precincts. "We must get to the bottom of what these children are doing here."

Eyde hesitated. "We'll not get our heads combed for having een, will us?"

Lady Camilla daintily licked her fingers, then used them to capture the last crumbs on her plate. The sight tugged at Amaranthe's heart. "I would anticipate a great deal of trouble under normal circumstances, but in truth I wonder if anyone at Hunsdon House knows they're gone."

The moment the cook and maid whisked themselves down the backstairs, the front door burst open. In it stood a man in a towering rage. He was dressed in an elegant coat and breeches, his stockings as white at his cravat, and his face was dark with anger. He glared down the narrow hall at Amaranthe as if he were a giant come to devour her whole.

"Where are they?" he bellowed. "I saw the coach outside. Where are the children?"

"In the parlor, having their tea," Amaranthe retorted. "And who might you be?"

"Their guardian." His irate gaze raked Amaranthe from head to toe. "I warn you, I do not deal lightly with kidnappers. I will have them back at once, or you will bear the consequences, and I warrant you will not like them."

CHAPTER FOUR

"R eally!" Amaranthe said. "I've hardly kidnapped them. You are very much mistaken if you think I have."

Indignation stiffened her spine, but trepidation swirled in her belly. He was very large, and grew larger as he stalked down the hall.

"I'll press charges. Abduction. Blackmail. I suppose you've settled on a ransom? How much do you suppose you could earn for stealing the Duke of Hunsdon and his siblings?"

Amaranthe waved toward the front door, hoping her hand didn't tremble. "You may leave my house this instant, you insulting person!" She might be nervous, but she refused to be intimidated.

"I will find where you've hidden them."

The man advanced, and Amaranthe stepped back, as if they were dancing. He was quite tall, his shoulders treacherously wide. He lifted his chin to glare over her head and Amaranthe noted a strong, square jaw set with determination. He was not the fleshy, soft sort of gentleman she was used to dealing with, the rare times she dealt with gentlemen.

"Hugh! Ned! Millie! Where is she keeping you?"

"In the parlor, Grey," Ned called back in cheerful tones. Camilla's reply, muffled by a mouthful of cake, followed.

The stranger stormed past her and Amaranthe whisked out of his way, certain an explosion would follow if she made the error of contact. Her pulse clattered in her throat like a mouse in the coal bin. He pushed into the parlor, and she scurried after him to shield the easel with her body. The parchment pages were covered with the cloth, but the book from which she was copying stood open. She planted a hand on her hip to broaden her silhouette and keep him from seeing anything.

His attention fastened on the children. The Duke of Hunsdon lowered his piece of bread and butter, but the younger two kept eating steadily. Perhaps they were used to this strange man and his belligerence.

"How did you get here?" the stranger barked. "Account for yourselves!"

"Ralph brought us," Ned said with a guilty expression.

"We took the coach," the duke added, unrepentant.

"But why here?" The man's gaze swung on Camilla.

"We needed help," she said simply, fishing a crumb of cake from her lip with a little pink tongue. "And Mr. Joseph was the only one we could think of."

The man they called Grey flinched at this and turned an accusing stare on Amaranthe. Beneath the scowling brows, his eyes were an unnerving, icy blue. "Where is Mr. Joseph, then? And who is this?"

Amaranthe planted a second hand on her hip in exasperation. "Their kidnapper, of course." How she hated gentlemen with their insolent manner toward those they thought subservient, which was everyone.

He looked to the children for clarification, but they had none. "She was here when we came in." The young duke shrugged.

"His wife?" Ned guessed.

"His housekeeper?" Camilla tried.

Amaranthe bit her lip and crossed her arms over her chest. "The criminal mastermind who is holding you ransom," she replied. "The first step in my villainy apparently being to fill your empty bellies."

The scowl gave way to a look of bafflement. "Then this is the tutor's house? Mr.—Islington."

"This is where the tutor lives, but that is not his name." Amaranthe decided to help him no further. He was above her in rank, but his manners were decidedly shabby.

"Where's Ralph?" the man called Grey demanded.

"Out seeing that the coach isn't stolen before I can spirit the children away in it," Amaranthe replied. "Seeing as how my nefarious plan entails traveling through London in broad daylight in a conveyance with the ducal arms emblazoned on the door. How I wish I had thought this through a bit better."

The stormy eyes narrowed. "All right, Mrs.—Islesworth—"

She kept her arms folded, meeting his stare. "Do you mean to tell me that you pay my brother's salary without knowing the first thing about his circumstances? I would expect you to be a bit more diligent about whom you employ to see to the children if you think to call yourself their guardian."

A look of discomfort replaced the anger with which he'd entered. Amaranthe resisted her natural inclination to soothe. He hadn't earned it.

"So you would be—"

"Miss Amaranthe." Mrs. Blackthorn appeared in the doorway, holding a tray heaped with delicious-smelling bowls and dishes. "If you'll help me pull out the dining table, mum, we can feed our guests."

Mrs. Blackthorn regarded the intruder with interest, observing his smart attire. Her gaze lingered on his face, which could by the strictest definition be called handsome, then she turned to Amaranthe with a grin. "Shall I fetch more tea?"

"I perceive the children's guardian means to collect them, so I expect they'll be leaving soon," Amaranthe replied. The man's mouth twitched with a reply that was drowned out by the immediate and vocal dissent of his charges.

"We'd be ever so grateful if you let us stay for dinner," Ned said at the same time Camilla cried, "Oh, indeed yes, more tea! And any cakes if you have them?"

The man's eyes flicked to the young duke, who stiffened his shoulders, but the way he stuffed the last bit of bread in his mouth betrayed him. "We'll leave if you wish it, Grey," the duke mumbled.

"It appears tea is in order," Grey said grudgingly, and looked about for a chair. As Amaranthe was obliged to attend to the tea tray, the interloper took the chair before her easel, his frame too large for the delicate Queen Anne piece. She prayed he would not knock over one of the pots of color or lean on her canvas and smear the morning's work beyond repair.

His gaze flickered to the prayer book, and he studied the open manuscript as if he could decipher it. Amaranthe clinked the tongs against the china bowl to divert his attention. A man who stormed into her house because he had lost track of his charges couldn't be accused of deep perception, but his clear blue eyes looked altogether too intelligent.

"Sugar?" she inquired with false politeness.

"Sugar is produced by slave-holding plantations in the West Indies," Camilla said around the generous slice of seed cake that Mrs. Blackthorn put before her. "If we were to cease eating sugar, we might at last break the back of that pernicious institution."

"That is true." Amaranthe regarded the liquid in her own

cup as it closed gently around a lump of sugar crystals. In defer-
ence to Camilla she added only cream to Grey's tea.

"I beg your pardon, Camilla, but who has been exposing
you to abolitionist causes?" Grey wanted to know.

He accepted the dish Amaranthe passed to him, but his gaze
was on Camilla as he did so, and Amaranthe startled as his
fingers brushed hers. He had dispensed with his riding gloves,
and she of course was not wearing mittens, which got in the way
of her delicate work. His hands, a man's hands, were firm, well-
shaped, and warm. A familiar pattern of ink stains marked his
fingertips. She couldn't recall the last time a man not her
brother had touched her.

Reuben. Reuben with his insinuating sneer was the last man
who had touched her. A heavy flush moved through her chest as
Amaranthe pushed away the unwelcome memory.

"I don't intend to censure you for your beliefs," Grey added
when Camilla looked wary. "But I would like to know who has
been conversing on these topics around you."

He ought to have known already, Amaranthe thought, but
bit her lip. Rather high-handed of the man to accuse her of
wrongdoing when he was clearly the most negligent guardian
alive. She wondered what sort of activities left ink stains on the
hand of an idle dandy. Writing love letters to various ladies of ill
repute? Scribbling vowels when he dove too deep into his
pockets at the gaming table?

"Mr. Joseph let me read some of the pamphlets his friend
gives him," Camilla confessed. "She is a Quaker. I wish he
might take me to one of their meetings."

"A Quaker!" Grey recoiled. He glared at Amaranthe as if
she were responsible for this. "Pamphlets! I thought he was
teaching the boys Latin."

"It would appear you have not been supervising the boys'
education very carefully." Amaranthe had no idea her brother

was consorting with Quakers, either, but she leapt by instinct to Joseph's defense. "What else has escaped your notice, I wonder?"

He glared at her, his ice-blue eyes narrowing. "What else is there?"

Amaranthe cut two more enormous portions of seed cake and passed them to the boys. She lifted her gaze to meet Grey's glare head-on, waiting for him to notice the obvious.

Clearly the gleam in his disturbing blue eyes was deceptive. No one could be denser than he was.

"Your art is very interesting." The young duke broke the frosty silence. "You are to be addressed as Miss Illingworth, I take it?"

Amaranthe supposed her small parlor appeared quite poky to children used to a ducal home, but it suited her perfectly. She'd lightened the dark, solemn interior of the watchmaker's shop with a bright wallpaper hand-painted with her own design. She'd chosen a motif of scrolled vines recalling the front pages of her lost Book of Hours, to remind her daily of the dream to which she aspired, and the precious book she was resolved to recover. Here and there hung reproductions she had made of various illuminations that struck her fancy in the manuscripts she copied. She altered them as she saw fit and displayed them on her walls the way landed families displayed their ancestors, evidence to future customers of her skill.

She had likewise freshened the upholstery of the delicate Queen Anne furniture with embroidered motifs and marginalia taken also from various medieval manuscripts. The effect called up a lost, dark age of beauty and deprivation with hints of wildness lurking beneath the trappings of civilization. Amaranthe could be certain there was no other drawing room in all of Britain like hers, and the thought pleased her immensely.

"I am Miss Illingworth," Amaranthe answered, "and I am

glad you like my art. These are copies I made from medieval books, mostly poems of romance."

Why she introduced the topic of romance, she couldn't say. The children dutifully regarded their surroundings over their bowls of soup. Their guardian watched Amaranthe.

"You are Illingworth's sister," he deduced.

"How kind of you to notice." She had no idea how to address him. He'd made no introduction to her.

"You look a great deal like him," Ned said.

"So we are often told, thank you."

"He won't let me take lessons with Ned." Camilla frowned.

"How rotten of him," Amaranthe replied. "Does your governess at least teach you on topics you find of interest?"

"I don't have a governess. I have—well, had a nurse."

Grey blinked at her in surprise. "Millie, what happened to your nurse?"

"Gone for days, Grey." Camilla stared back at him with wide eyes. "She got word her da was ill and had to go do for him. She said she'd come back, but..." The girl's eyes fell, and she crammed a slice of cake into her mouth as consolation.

"Who is looking after you, Lady Camilla?" Amaranthe asked softly.

She gulped. "Huey and Ned."

Grey put down his tea. He appeared at complete loss for words. Any aggravation Amaranthe felt over his thick-headedness evaporated at the look of horror upon his face.

"Where are all the servants?"

The children looked at one another, and a long silence ensued.

"How long have you been without proper meals?" Amaranthe asked.

Camilla bit her lip and appealed to her brothers. The young duke stared into his dish of tea. Ned struggled not to cry.

The little girl straightened her shoulders. "Cook left two weeks ago."

"Ralph's run round to the cookshop for us," Ned said, "but now there's no more coin and..." He trailed off.

"There are a great many things missing from the front of the house," Grey said, but his tone lacked accusation. Instead his voice sounded carefully bland. Amaranthe wanted to slap him. How dare he care about ducal furnishings when the children were clearly in desperate straits?

Young Hunsdon shook his head. "That wasn't Ralph who stole Papa's things. I don't think it was any of the others either. Nurse said they wouldn't risk charges, even if they weren't getting proper wages."

Grey no longer looked cavalier. He looked like someone had planted him a facer and laid him out cold. "Popplewell," he said, the way one would utter a curse.

"Who is Popplewell?" Amaranthe asked. Was her brother employed in a house frequented by criminals?

"The land steward for the various estates," Grey said grimly. "He appears to have absented himself from the country, along with—never mind. Where has Sybil been all this time?"

"We haven't seen her ladyship in weeks, sir," Ned answered. "Left with a great fuss and bustle, you couldn't conscience the amount of luggage, but it's been a treat to move about the house without giving her the headache, I must say."

Amaranthe sagged in her chair. "Your mother is gone, the servants abandoned their posts, the house has been robbed—and my brother has noticed nothing of your distress in all this time?"

The young duke lifted his chin, and Amaranthe gleaned that whatever this boy had been raised to be, it was not soft.

"We did not think it the thing to trouble our tutor with our sorry circumstances. And the duchess is *not* our mother."

Amaranthe tried to grasp the situation. These three children had been hiding in their home for days, only a footman for protection, knowing nothing of the world or how to shift for themselves. Derwa, though no older than Camilla, would have lasted for weeks in the same situation, but Derwa knew how to cook, clean, shop, and do laundry. The old duke's children had been raised to know nothing but social etiquette and pride of place.

"Mr. Joseph will be troubled right enough when his wages aren't paid," Ned said glumly. "Leastwise, that's what Nurse said."

Camilla sniffled. "Huey said we couldn't impose upon him, seeing as he's only the tutor, but we didn't know where else to go. Ned asked his address once, when they were studying the history of London."

Ned turned on her with indignation. "How did you know about that?"

Camilla lifted her chin in a gesture much like her brother's. "He said he wasn't supposed to give me lessons, but he never said I couldn't *listen*."

Amaranthe twined her hands together, noticing a stain of gold along her thumb. The three children fell to arguing among themselves about who exactly had proposed they appeal to Mr. Illingworth for aid.

The man they called Grey cleared his throat. "I wonder," he said, "that no one proposed sending for *me*."

Silence fell. Amaranthe glanced at his face and saw that, while he kept his tone neutral with great effort, his towering rage had returned in force. At the children? A hot, protective instinct filled her chest.

She was forever leaping in and taking up unfortunates, and Joseph was forever scolding her for it. He'd get an earful from her, when he returned, about what had been going on at Hunsdon House beneath his very nose. He was very likely to get an earful from this Grey person as well, and lose the position that had finally given him some hope for a future.

For the moment, her greater ire was directed at the man before her. What kind of guardian had no notion that his charges had been left without supervision? Without food, however that happened in a duke's house of all places? No doubt he was too busy sporting around town in pursuit of his own pleasures to take any notice of those who depended upon him. His poor wife must be utterly neglected, were any woman fool enough to fall for that handsome face and the complete lack of soul it concealed.

Eyde slipped into the room, her wool cloak snug around her shoulders, and bobbed a quick curtsey to Grey. "No sign of Mr. Joseph at the Smyrna today, mum," she whispered to Amaranthe. "A man at the Orange said he'd talked of going to a meeting."

Amaranthe hadn't known that. Her ire deflated. She was hardly in a position to chide Grey for neglect when she couldn't attest to the comings and goings of her own brother. Still, at least no one within her household was going hungry. She hoped.

"Thank you for checking, Eyde. It's all right if Joseph can't be located at present. Mr. Grey is here to take the children in hand."

The expression on Grey's face as he turned to her almost made Amaranthe laugh out loud. The man was as helpless as Joseph, who would forget his hat if Amaranthe were not there to hand it to him on his way out the door. But while Joseph was often abstracted due to weighty matters on his mind, he wasn't negligent or cruel. Amaranthe wasn't prepared to make the same allowance for Mr. Grey.

"I cannot take the children to my rooms," the man exclaimed. "I have no accommodations for them."

"I expect you shall return them home, Mr. Grey, and install

a staff capable of proper supervision and care," she said, exasperated.

"But there isn't anyone!" Camilla cried. "Unless you'll come with us?"

"Me?" Amaranthe exclaimed.

"And perhaps your cook?" Ned added hopefully.

Young Hunsdon did not immediately deny this request, the surest sign that he shared his siblings' feelings but was too proud to say so.

Ralph the footman poked his head in the door. "I can get the coach ready in a trice, mum," he said to Amaranthe. "I just sent it 'round to the Blue Posts and set a boy to watch the horses."

Grey, too, looked at her with an expression of distrust, suspicion, and pride warring with helpless appeal. He also was too proud to ask for help, and if it had simply been on his own behalf, Amaranthe would have denied him in an instant. But the children, with crumbs over their smart suits and Lady Camilla's neat apron, gazed at her with desperate longing.

"For heaven's sake," she said. "There must be a housekeeper." A duke's household had to run to a staff of dozens. "Underbutler? Kitchen staff?"

Ralph shrugged. "The housekeeper skipped off right after Cook, and when the rest of the staff learned they weren't to get their wages, they all went back to the agency."

"The agency?" Amaranthe said.

"Aye, mum," Ralph answered. "The duchess turned off all the old duke's staff when his lordship died, so's she could hire her own people. But she has a hard time keeping 'em, you see, and is always sending to the agency for new. The butler came last quarter, and the housekeeper brought on right before him."

"Have you seen Popplewell?" Grey asked, his voice grim.

"Him shot off last month with everything he could carry, and no one's seen the tip of his nose since," Ralph said.

"Or Sybil," said Grey.

Ralph nodded. "No sign of Her Grace in nigh a month, sir, but she took quite a bit with her when she left. Said she needed furnishings for her house in France."

"Leaving no one to look after the children?" Amaranthe asked, incredulous.

"Lady Millie's nurse said she'd stay on for board wages, but then she got word that her pa was poorly." Ralph shrugged.

"And that left you."

Amaranthe poured a cup of tea and passed it and a generous slice of cake to the footman. A clear violation of protocol in a duke's house, but this was her home, and who knew when Ralph had last eaten, considering how gratefully he took the offering.

"My brother does not seem to have been much help," Amaranthe added.

"But you can set everything right, can't you?" Ned said. "I mean, that was a smashing good tea."

"I don't see how I might remedy your situation," Amaranthe said. "Besides being an utter stranger to you, and having no right to interfere."

"But you're a woman," the young duke said. When Amaranthe bent an inquiring gaze on him, he clarified. "You... know how to order such things."

Amaranthe failed to hold back a snort. She was barely domesticated, as such things went. Grey, the dandy who had shattered her peace, must detect that she wore a faded day dress, a tired sack back with a floral print that disguised the occasional spill or ink stain. She never wore a cap indoors, and the efficient chignon in which she dressed her hair had no doubt grown untidy over the course of the day.

"Mr. Grey is your guardian." Amaranthe wasn't about to get her nose bitten off again for sticking it into places that weren't her business.

"Hopeful guardian, if the court rules in my favor," Grey responded. "Popplewell and the duchess have just given the court every reason to support my claim over theirs. But I know nothing about arranging a household."

"Nor does he have a cook," Ned clarified.

Amaranthe rose. "Very well. Let me confer with my staff." She hesitated, torn between protecting her work and protecting her secret. "I pray you will not lean upon that easel, as the ink is drying," she said to Grey.

He rose when she did and stepped away, but regarded the fabric-wrapped easel with great curiosity. "Of course. Ralph, bring the vehicle around. Miss Illingworth, we'll await your pleasure."

Amaranthe slipped belowstairs. Any thought of trying to weasel out of this new demand vanished when she found her staff hard at work. In the kitchen Eyde piled baskets with food at Mrs. Blackthorn's direction, while Derwa whisked back and forth from the tiny room that served as their stillroom and scullery.

"And mind you line the eggs well, Eyde, so they don't break." Mrs. Blackthorn liberated a ham from a hook in the ceiling and deftly encased it in oiled paper. "Derwa, darling, fetch me a handful of onions from the cellar, along with a bundle of sage."

"I had thought we might take the children home tonight and hire a housekeeper tomorrow," Amaranthe said. "Are we to send them *all* our food?"

She watched in dismay as Mrs. Blackthorn wrapped up the oysters Amaranthe had bought at the fish market as a rare and special treat. She could afford oysters but rarely and had bought them while shopping for gold leaf to celebrate nearly being done with her commission.

"I can scrape up a decent supper and send someone to

market tomorrow." Mrs. Blackthorn handed the ham to Eyde. "Now, Eyde can come to do for the children tonight, and Derwa to help me in the kitchen? Davey stepped out to borrow a cart from the pub, so you've a moment to change your gown, Miss Amaranthe."

"They must take me as I am if we're to descend on the duke's household," Amaranthe said testily. "We'll leave some bread and cheese to let Joseph shift for himself? I suppose he's done it before."

"I think I have someone to look after Mr. Joseph." Eyde stuck her head out the door that opened on the narrow alley running behind the neighboring buildings. "Hullo, then! You'd best come in and make your case afore the mistress leaves."

A young woman with long, curly black hair, wide-set dark eyes, and dusky skin stepped inside. She wrung hands chapped raw from laundry soap and lye in an apron that had seen far better days. "*Óla, senhorita,*" she said.

"Hello, Inez," Amaranthe said gently. "Bad times again?"

"I'm not asking alms," Inez said swiftly, her brave tone belied by the sheen of tears in her dark brown eyes. "Looking for work, if ye have it. The house I was at let me go when they found out my father was a lascar, and if no one else'll take me, the only way I can eat is if—well, you know."

Her face hardened, and she cast her eyes down. Inez wasn't eligible for the parish workhouse because she had been born in Portugal, a stopping-over on one of her father's sea routes. And she wasn't able to enter the Magdalen House unless she had already resorted, as so many struggling young women did, to earning coin through the sale of her company.

Desperate to avoid prostitution, Inez was forced to beg for scraps each time an employer turned her off because she was too dark, too foreign, or too distracting to the surrounding young men. Eyde had brought her to the house before, confident that Amaranthe would help.

"I am glad you came to us," Amaranthe assured her. "You're the answer to a prayer, really. We need someone to look after the house and see to Mr. Illingworth when he returns home. He'll only need a cold tray and a candle, and wake him at daybreak tomorrow so he can report to Hunsdon House and give us an account of himself. You may eat what you like and sleep in the usual bed. Only, Inez—"

She hesitated, anticipating Joseph's protest. He always rated her when she took in the destitute, fearing someone she sheltered might open the house to thieves. "Mr. Joseph won't permit you to entertain friends, I'm afraid."

"I understand, *senhorita*," Inez said. "No visitors. I will tend to Mr. Illingworth only. *Obrigada*," she added gratefully, squeezing Amaranthe's hand.

"Who knows but that we might have a better position to offer you tomorrow." Amaranthe regarded the growing pile of provisions. "It appears I will be called upon to staff a ducal household."

Mrs. Blackthorn's eyes glowed. She enjoyed a challenge for her skills.

"We can't leave those poor mites to shift for themselves, Miss Amaranthe. Abandoned in their own house, and the servants nicking whatever they can carry! Have you ever heard of such a scrape?"

"Mr. Grey, whoever he is, certainly seems to have made a mull of things," Amaranthe replied. "To think that he expects me to set things in order, after he crashed into my house accusing me of kidnapping the children!" She sniffed. "He does not seem awake on all suits, as Joseph would say."

"Oh, is that the way of it, then?" Eyde raised a curious brow, then scoffed at the sight of Amaranthe's plain gown. "Will ye nil ye, you'd best spruce yourself up if you're dining in a duke's home, Miss Amaranthe. I can have your hair fixed in a trice."

"I am not sprucing myself up for Mr. Grey or anyone else," Amaranthe said. "To be clear, I am only doing this so that Joseph's position may be secure."

"And as those poor dear cheelin need a hand." Eyde herded Amaranthe upstairs to her tiny bedchamber and pinned her with swift efficiency into her one decent day gown, a striped wool open robe with a dark blue stomacher.

Amaranthe descended the stairs to find that all had been ordered. The ducal coach sat before her door, blocking traffic in George Court from both directions, while Davey perched atop a wagon hired from the Blue Posts to convey the servants and their luggage. Grey leaned glowering against the coach, where the children had already been settled, but he stepped forward readily enough to help Davey stow the baskets of food and Mrs. Blackthorn's other provisions in the wagon. Amaranthe would have guessed he did nothing more strenuous than stroll in splendid attire up and down the walks of the fashionable all day, but he hefted the heaviest basket with ease.

She turned to climb onto the plank seat of the wagon and jumped at the voice at her shoulder.

"You'll ride with us, of course."

She stared into his surprising blue eyes. Yes, there was intelligence there, and arrogance, and a touch of wariness, too. But there was another element in his expression that she couldn't identify.

He was tall and, standing close to her, too large for comfort. There was something sharp and hard about him that she wasn't accustomed to seeing in the gentlemen of her acquaintance.

Joseph was easy tempered and easily pleased, and the businessmen Amaranthe dealt with were congenial if sometimes shrewd. Grey seemed as if he were always on the alert, as if he didn't trust he could let his guard down for a moment.

He stood with his hand extended, waiting to help her into the ducal coach, regarding her as if she were a puzzle he meant to solve.

She stared. His was a large hand, a strong hand. His riding gloves were of fine material, worn, but in good repair. It was the glove of a man who used his hands. Not at all what she had expected.

Why was she involving herself, again, in something that did not concern her? The last time she had done so, she lost her home. Though Joseph was employed in the household, and she felt the compulsion to make up for his oversight, she had no responsibility to these children. It fell to this man, their erstwhile guardian, to look after them.

And she could not afford to let strangers see too deeply into her affairs. At least not until this latest manuscript was completed and the results of her labors achieved. She needed to be on her guard, too.

"You are coming, aren't you?" Grey said softly, and Amaranthe realized what his uneasiness signified. For all his size and self-assurance, he wasn't a man accustomed to command or to having his wishes met. He waited as if he fully expected she would swat his hand aside and walk away.

The realization, perversely, clarified her resolve. He needed her help, and he resented that, but she did not intend to walk away from someone who needed her.

She took his hand.

CHAPTER FIVE

"His Grace is recently thirteen years of age."

Grey began Amaranthe's education in the family over dinner as he carved the glazed ham. Amaranthe feared the meal would prove plain fare to the aristocratic palate, but Mrs. Blackthorn knew her work, and the eager expressions on the faces of the children said to them a hot meal was as good as nectar and ambrosia.

"I'll go to Eton for the fall term, if Grey permits it and Mr. Joseph thinks I am ready," young Hunsdon added.

"Permit? I insist." Grey laid a thick chunk of meat on the boy's plate and passed it to Amaranthe to fill. "It appears we'll have to find a source of funds, but we needn't discuss that in front of Miss Illingworth."

Amaranthe guessed that remark came more from politeness than mistrust. Grey would have to discuss the ducal finances with her, and soon, if he wished her to help equip the household with staff.

They had returned to find Hunsdon House absent of occupants. The Palladian mansion in Hanover Square echoed like an empty tomb, its cavernous entry hall bare of any servants to greet them, the common rooms quiet under a thin sheen of dust. Mrs. Blackthorn set up at once in the kitchen, sending Derwa out with a summons that conjured half a dozen young helping hands from sources only Mrs. Blackthorn knew. Eyde saw the ducal children bathed and changed for dinner. Ralph engaged Davey to wait on them, even locating a suit of livery, and Davey's delight at serving at a duke's table was written all over his face.

They dined at a small table set up in one of the informal parlors, but even the simplest of the house's rooms made Amaranthe feel glaringly plain. No wonder wealthy ladies spent their days changing from one expensive ensemble into another. They needed to match their rich surroundings.

Grey had not donned formal attire either; he still wore the breeches and frock coat in which he'd thundered into her house. But the children were thrilled by the rare treat of dining with adults, as if it were a holiday, and Amaranthe wished she'd made herself more elegant for them.

"And Lord Edward?" She passed his plate to Ned.

Eyde had laid a splendid table, though they dined *en famille*, serving themselves while the footmen brought dishes and poured drinks. Candles gleamed in crystal holders along a table draped in white linen, and the bone china's delicate gilded pattern would have turned Favella green with envy. Something about Hunsdon House brought her cousin the baronet to mind, and Amaranthe pushed the memories away before they could cast an unpleasant shadow.

"Ned is eleven, and I am eight." Camilla eagerly accepted her plate but watched Amaranthe for cues. Lady Camilla had turned herself out in all the finery she had, a white silk frock awash with lace and paste pearls about her throat. Eyde's handiwork showed in the twists of curls tied up with silk ribbons, and Amaranthe smiled.

"Two years older than Derwa, then," she said.

Grey met her eyes as he held out Amaranthe's plate, adorned with two tidy slices of ham. He'd saved her the tenderest pieces, and the recognition flustered her.

So did the sight of him at the head of the table, his unpowdered hair drawn back in a queue and showing here and there a streak of gold among the darker brown. A shadow of stubble covered his jaw, giving him a roguish look, and the candlelight sculpted his features into strong lines and intriguing shadows. She turned to the dish of asparagus spears simmered in cream that Davey slid onto the table beside her.

"Tell us about your household, Miss Illingworth," Grey said. "Your servants seem unusually devoted to you. Almost like friends."

Davey tensed as he withdrew to his post next to the sideboard, and Amaranthe spoke carefully, sensing a trap.

"Eyde and I left Cornwall six years ago." She distributed the asparagus among the children's plates. "We went to stay with Joseph in Oxford until he completed his studies, and then we moved to London. Davey found us shortly thereafter, and Mrs. Blackthorn came to us that first summer as well." She dished a portion of vegetables onto Grey's plate and decided to change the subject. "I understand the passing of the duke was fairly recent? My condolences for your loss."

"It was only a loss for some," Grey said in a biting tone, and the young duke looked up, hurt.

"He was your father too, Grey."

Amaranthe sat back at this. "You are brothers?" She looked from Grey to Hugh, wondering why the younger boy had the title.

"Half-brothers," Grey said. He sank his knife into his ham with a savage motion. "I am not in the line of succession."

Illegitimate. That might account for the hard shell around

him, Amaranthe thought. It did not, however, excuse his poor manners. Plenty of the nobility's illegitimate children were brought up in polite society, if often in a different home.

She peered into a covered dish and discovered her oysters nestled in a buttery sauce. She portioned them onto plates, trying not to feel covetous. Rich people no doubt ate oysters with every meal, but for Amaranthe they were a rare indulgence once she'd left Cornwall and its bordering sea behind.

"Then the duchess—?" She let the question dangle, fearing she was being intrusive, but she wanted to understand. Grey called the duchess Sybil, and the young duke emphasized that she was not their mother. Still, a stepmother ought to feel some sort of compunction, even if child rearing was much different in the highest circles.

Grey snorted. "Sybil lacks even the slightest maternal impulse." His voice softened as he looked across the table. "Christine, their mother, died when Camilla was three, I am sorry to say."

All three children looked at their plates.

Amaranthe slid the oyster around on her tongue. So Sybil was the old duke's second wife, and Christine the first. Who, then, was the Marguerite, Lady Vernay inscribed in the flyleaf of her Book of Hours? Amaranthe still thought of the book as hers, though she was likely never to see it again while Reuben was alive. Searching it out would require confronting him, and she had no desire to be anywhere in his vicinity.

"My condolences on that loss as well," Amaranthe said. She wanted to know more of Grey's mother, but this was not the time to quiz him on his ancestry. "And you, Mr. Grey, are the children's appointed guardian?"

His face hardened, the candlelight catching the flex of a muscle in his jaw.

"I ought to be, as it's what the old duke wished, but Sybil

challenged the terms of the will. She insisted she was the more fit to oversee the estate and the children."

His lips thinned as he pressed them together. He had extraordinarily well-shaped lips for a man. "Given that she has not waited for the court case to be resolved, I can only conclude that her primary interest all along has been in the estate's income."

"You'll win the case now, won't you, Grey?" Ned spoke around the steady progress of transferring food to his mouth. "Or you'll be able to argue it yourself, once you're called to the bar?"

"However do you know anything about the case?" Grey wanted to know. "Sybil ought not have been discussing it with you."

"Why not, if it concerns us?" said Hugh indignantly. "And servants talk, Grey."

"You're a barrister?" Amaranthe asked.

She had once thought the law a respectable profession, until Joseph informed her that the Inns of Court admitted too many young men who had no ambition to study and instead found the Inns a source of entertainment replete with masques, revels, and riotous feasts. She had judged him a dandy when Grey arrived at her door, frivolous and not overly intelligent, but here in the company of his family, dining at home, he seemed composed and serious.

Perhaps he was behaving so for her benefit. After his initial belligerence, followed by his forced plea for aid, he had treated her with scrupulous courtesy, as if he thought Amaranthe one of those dull and humorless ladies who always followed the rules.

Better he think that than know the truth.

"I'll be a barrister if the Benchers ever admit me." Grey skewered the ham as he cut a fresh slide. "But a solicitor is arguing our case in Chancery, Ned. I imagine the court will rule in our favor once the new evidence is admitted."

"Then you hold out no hope that Her Grace and your steward are somehow acting in the children's best interests," Amaranthe said.

Grey regarded her as if she had just stood up and turned a cartwheel. His harsh expression cracked into a smile.

"How I wish I had your optimism, Miss Illingworth," he said. "But I fear the interests that Sybil and Mr. Popplewell serve are entirely their own. As a matter of fact," he added, "I suspect Mr. Popplewell serves Sybil's interests entirely, as he will very likely go to prison or be transported for what he's done."

Amaranthe was about to inquire further about the duchess when Grey passed her the oysters from his plate. It was such a domineering move—he had not even inquired if she wanted them—yet she guessed he had noticed her enjoyment.

Her cheeks heated. He was more observant than he seemed.

That made him more dangerous.

"Tell us of your family, Miss Illingworth," Grey prompted as Amaranthe doled out cauliflower pudding. "Your brother has told us little about himself, and nothing about you."

More dangerous ground still, and she did not have a ready answer, for she was not accustomed to people showing interest in her, particularly gentlemen. Amaranthe wondered how much explanation would satisfy his curiosity.

"Our father was a rector in the small parish of St. Cleer in Cornwall, where we grew up. My mother was the daughter of a lens maker, and Joseph was their first child." She opted not to mention that her father was the younger son of a baronet; she did not wish to introduce Reuben into the conversation. "After our parents died, I was sent to live with a cousin while Joseph went up to Oxford."

She gave the young duke a smile that included his siblings.

"My upbringing was quite modest. I have never had occasion to interact with a ducal family."

"My mother was a haberdasher's daughter," Grey said, and Amaranthe wondered if he meant the remark to establish that he, too, had humbler origins. She was intensely curious what a duke's heir had seen in a haberdasher's daughter. That it had ended unhappily for Grey's mother was unfortunately the way of the world, a warning of what awaited if a woman attempted to vault too high above her station.

"I have never met a woman who knows Latin," young Hugh said, "so we have both had a novel experience today, Miss Illingworth."

Grey raised his brows. "Latin?"

"Miss Illingworth is a copyist," Ned said, "but she actually reads the old books. Can you fancy!"

"Ah." Grey helped himself to the chicken fricassee. "I wondered what that setup in your parlor entailed."

"My workroom." For some reasons Amaranthe did not want him to think her a mere dabbler, one of those leisured women who had obscure hobbies. She supported their household with her work while Joseph saved his earnings for his eventual marriage, and she took pride in her self-sufficiency.

"But I only reproduce the script, and some of the marginalia," she added. "My pages go to another artist for the truly intricate illuminations, and then a bookbinder to be sewn together."

"I see," said Grey. "And what is the market for such things, might I ask? Reproductions of medieval manuscripts."

"Of benefit, first, to scholars and antiquarians, who value such artifacts." And for people like her, who could trade on the value of priceless originals with skillfully made copies. Amaranthe kept her eyes on her ham so guilt would not show on her face.

The secret copies she made of her commissions were meant

to begin her own collection, for the purposes of historical preservation and literary enjoyment, but she wasn't prepared to
explain to him what would very well look like stealing to the
untrained eye.

"And of value," she added, "to owners, who may wish to
have a duplicate of an original manuscript in the event of
unforeseen disasters. Do you know how many priceless books
were lost in the fire in Sir Robert Cotton's library?"

The looks of respectful blankness around the table told her
they did not.

"Sir Robert Cotton gathered the collection that became the
cornerstone of our National Library," Amaranthe explained.
"He had innumerable treasures. The Lindisfarne Gospels. The
Vespasian Psalter. But in 1731, when a fire broke out at
Ashburnham House, where the collection was stored, the loss
was devastating. One of the original manuscripts of the *Magna
Carta* was so damaged as to be illegible. Asser's biography of
King Alfred, gone. And the manuscript holding some of the
greatest Old English poems, including that of the hero Beowulf
and the Anglo-Saxon Judith—huge portions were lost."

Her eyes stung, and she blinked quickly. The destruction of
manuscripts of inestimable value, a tragedy to her, did not
compare to the well-being of children abandoned by their stepmother and left to starve in their own home.

She cleared her throat. "At any rate, I like to think my work
helps preserve future knowledge and understanding about our
nation's history and peoples. Joseph ought to have you read
Beowulf, if he hasn't. It's a ripping good story, though the Old
English takes some study."

"Miss Illingworth." Ned's eyes grew wide. "Are you a Blue
Stocking?"

Amaranthe laughed. "No, I am not part of Mrs. Montagu's
circle. Though, like her and her friends, I value literature,

history, and useful conversation. And, like her, I believe that the female mind can be cultivated to a strength and capacity equal to that of a man's." She gave Grey a challenging look.

"As do I!" Camilla exclaimed. "Miss Illingworth, perhaps *you* can be my tutor!"

"Hmm." Grey passed about the dish of brandied cherries that Davey delivered to the table with an exaggerated flourish. She was afraid he was going to dismiss her claim about the strength of the female mind, and she was already assembling her rebuttal when he said, in a teasing tone, "I might need her, Millie, to help me with my readings for the bar, if her Latin is good enough."

"I'm afraid the law is not my forte," Amaranthe said, rather stunned that he would make such a cordial suggestion. Educated men were usually the ones who objected most strenuously that a woman could not be their equal. Even Joseph expressed polite skepticism as to Amaranthe's intelligence, though she read twice as many languages as he did.

And the thought that she would work together with Grey on anything was laughable. The last person she ought to make friends with was someone conversant with the law. Odd circumstances had thrown them together to see to the care of the ducal children, but once she had discharged her duties to help him hire staff and set the household in order, Amaranthe would return to her usual routine.

Moreover, she had agreed to deliver the breviary soon, so she had to finish her copies quickly. The admixture of gold leaf she had made that day would harden the longer it was exposed to air.

Grey raised his glass in a toast. "To medieval manuscripts."

Amaranthe joined him in drinking, restricting herself to a small, ladylike sip. The wine, which he called a Madeira, was delicious. Wine had been served with dinner at the baronet's table, but at home she and Joseph never had such a treat; they drank small beer, such as the children enjoyed.

"To the preservation of history," Amaranthe replied.

"To fine meals!" Ned said heartily.

"The female mind!" Camilla cried.

Everyone looked to Hugh, the young Lord Hunsdon.

He glanced at Ralph and Davey, who stood at attention near the sideboard, Ralph with a self-important look on his face, Davey's back as stiff as if he'd been raised to service in grand homes. Then the young lord's eyes fell on Amaranthe.

"To new friends," he said, lifting his glass, "who have delivered us from unfortunate circumstances."

Amaranthe drank, but the delicious wine turned sour in her mouth.

She did not deserve their trust or their confidences, and most certainly not their regard. She must have as little as possible to do with Grey and his family, and she needed to retire from their notice as quickly as she could.

The knowledge stung. It had been a long, long time since she had made new friends. And now, given her past and what she meant to do with the opportunity that had fallen into her lap, she would make no friends here, either.

CHAPTER SIX

Mal dropped his head into his hands, dislodging his hair from its queue. He was glad he'd not worn a wig for dinner. The periwig he wore for appearances at the Middle Court lay in his chambers off the Strand, and, being obliged to wear the uncomfortable piece during so much of the day, he preferred to dispense with it in the evenings.

Miss Illingworth had not made herself fancy, either. Her gown was plain and well-kept, with nothing to remark it save for a fanciful brooch she wore, the design of which he had not drawn close enough to see. She was in all respects one of those tidy, efficient women whom he had never in his life taken note of.

The women he knew from his days growing up in Little-john's coaching inn had been generally of a more forceful sort, inclined to make their presence known, and the women he met as a bachelor about town were likewise as colorful and memorable, for different reasons. Had he passed Miss Illingworth in the course of his daily business, he wouldn't have had the least cause to take an interest in her.

Now that he depended on her efficiency and her knowledge

of the secret domains of women to extricate him and his wards from a muddle, Mal found himself intensely curious about the woman. Where had she come from? What kind of woman took up a trade as a copyist of ancient manuscripts?

He marveled at how easily she had managed to calm all of them—the children showing up desperate and begging at her door, completely unexpected, and he himself storming in, regrettably under the influence of his temper, which tended to get the better of him at times. He'd been in a near frenzy about what had happened to the children—and what had happened to their income, thanks to that conniving she-demon Sybil—and Miss Illingworth sat them all down for tea.

Then, without a moment's notice and with the help of a handful of servants who seemed to regard her more as a maiden aunt than their employer, she laid out a dinner on the ducal table that was better than anything he was served in the dining hall at Middle Court, and in a warm, comfortable atmosphere that he had never before encountered at Hunsdon House. How had she done it?

The Delaval children were, by nature of the early loss of their mother and the acquisition of a stepmother none of them liked, prone to be distrustful, haughty, and very often disobedient. Yet Camilla had insisted that Amaranthe come up to the nursery and tell her the story of Beowulf before bed. The lure of a story about monsters had drawn Ned immediately, and Hugh, who considered himself far too old for the nursery or for fairy tales, had gone with them.

Leaving Mal to sit in the old duke's study with the household account books and wonder what the hell to do next.

A knock sounded on the door, and Ralph opened it. "Miss Illingworth, sir."

Behind him, Miss Illingworth smiled to herself at Ralph's

dignified manner, a small, amused, smile, and Mal stared. Had he thought she was plain?

"Ralph, have you any experience as a butler?" she asked as she entered.

"None at all, miss, I regret to say."

"Perhaps you might be underbutler, then, and train up when we find a new butler," Mal said.

Ralph, with a dazed expression, inclined his head and closed the door. Miss Amaranthe stared at the portal as if debating whether to open it again.

"Children abed?" Mal asked.

"So it would seem." She glanced at the desk. "Ralph said he brought you the butler's account books." She showed him the leather-bound volume in her arms. "I found the housekeeper's."

Mal continued to stare. Her hair had loosened from its stern arrangement, forming a dark, soft halo about her face. The tresses, dark brown instead of true black, gleamed like silk. Her features were delicately drawn yet at the same time strong, her nose a pronounced slope, her chin pointed, her eyes large and wide set. Her skin was as smooth as porcelain, with a warm sepia tint, and her eyes held a dark gleam offset by thick lashes.

He would be a profound idiot not to notice this woman, on the street or anywhere else.

Hiding his temporary loss of intellect, Mal turned to the inset shelves behind the desk. True to his father's taste, the shelves in his personal space, a combination refuge and work-room, were lined not with books but with oddments obtained from his various travels, arranged next to his assortment of pipes and his selection of spirits. Mal noticed belatedly that many of the small figurines that he had hitherto ignored were of a lewd quality, most lacking clothing, many in suggestive positions. He hoped Miss Illingworth would not notice.

"Spirits?" He held up a bottle filled with a glimmering liquid.

"Perhaps a spot of Canary wine, if you have it. But only a splash. I haven't drunk this much wine since..." She stopped abruptly.

"Since?" he prompted.

"In quite a while." She laid her volume on the corner of the long table that served as a desk and pulled one of the crimson upholstered chairs close. Her gaze flickered over the figurines, then to her task. He should have known that Miss Illingworth would notice. She seemed one of those women who noticed everything. But she merely smiled again, a small tug at the side of her prim, plum-colored mouth.

Miss Illingworth had a delicious mouth. Mal poured wine for her and a liberal splash of brandy for himself.

"Shall we do this tonight, then?" At her inquiring look, he indicated the volumes laid side by side on the leather tabletop. "Go over the account books, I mean."

"We needn't go into detail, if you don't wish, but you must have a notion of what you can offer to pay if you are hoping to engage servants. And I should think this the first task, given what's happened."

She sat, and as Mal seated himself also, he realized she had brought her chair too close. It was not an unseemly distance, by any means—he sat at the long side of the table, she the short—yet he could smell her scent, the warm, rich scent of an English garden in high summer. Good Lord. How was supposed to focus on numbers and not her polished skin, the fine hairs waving about her very intelligent head, the shape of that very intriguing mouth?

His brain had been disordered by the rude surprises of the day. Mal swallowed the brandy in his glass and stood for more.

"That bad?" She watched him pour.

He sat again, the words jolting out of him. "There's no money."

She lifted her eyebrows. They were dark brows, delicately arched, prim yet enchanting as the rest of her, hinting at secrets buried below the surface. Everything about Miss Illingworth called for a closer investigation.

"No money," she repeated, "or no income?"

He set his glass on the table with a thunk. "Sybil cut sticks with everything due us for the second quarter. The income from the estates, the income set aside for the household, the trust money for the children. My allowance," he added. "Gone."

She folded her hands on the table and tapped a knuckle with an index finger. "Can you borrow against the third quarter income?"

"I can talk to Mr. Coutts, the banker. I don't see any other option. Unless we try to sell movables from the house, but it appears that Sybil and Popplewell already took their pick of those as well."

"How much debt is the estate in already?"

How very rational and calm she was being. Then again, it was not her livelihood stolen. She would return to her snug house and her inks and parchment and her servants who looked after her with capable ease.

And her brother, whom Mal knew next to nothing about.

According to Hugh, their tutor arrived at the appointed times and discharged his duties in unobjectionable fashion, but he had seemed distracted of late and in haste to leave when their tasks were complete. Was Joseph Illingworth complicit in the robbery that had befallen the estate? And if so, how much did his sister know about it?

An absurd conclusion. She would not be sitting here asking probing questions about the state of the ducal finances if her brother had abetted a scheme to abscond with Hunsdon's liquid assets.

Unless she were attempting to cover his tracks. Or looking for access to other assets as well.

More than absurd, Mal scolded himself. She was merely the sister of the tutor. She had stepped in to help them out of the goodness of her heart and a womanly instinct of pity for the children who had turned up at her door.

And she told him very little about her past when he questioned her.

How intriguing to meet a woman of reserve. The females of his acquaintance tended to be extremely forthcoming.

"It is good of you to help us." He set aside his glass.

The candles flickering on the side table needed trimming, but Mal was reluctant to call Ralph. He liked having her alone with him in the warm, dim study, hushed in shadows. He might better discover her secrets this way.

"I like solving problems." She opened the housekeeper's account book and turned her attention to it. "This isn't the worst I've faced."

"What was the worst?"

He was being forward, but he'd been worse than rude with her earlier, and her female sensibilities had recovered from the shock. Besides, he needed to know something about her if he were trusting the welfare of his would-be wards to her hands.

She stared at the tidy page of entries, but he had the sense she was not reading. Finally she said, in a light tone that sounded forced, "I was commissioned once to copy a set of Gospels that the owner thought was in early Latin. Turns out it was Flemish." She tapped a finger against the open page. "I do not read Flemish."

Mal stared, stupefied, at the small, wry smile that accompanied these words. A bell rang in his ears, as if he'd taken a blow to the head.

"Somehow I believe you could master anything you set your mind to, Miss Illingworth. Including Flemish."

"It is close enough to Dutch that I was able to make it out, once I found someone who speaks Flemish," she said. "Either your chandler has been overcharging your housekeeper obscenely, or your housekeeper has been pocketing a profit margin on the household's purchase of candles. I've noted an absurdly high price for several other items as well. Also recent entries for mourning clothes, yet I notice you and the children have put off mourning."

He stiffened. Was that a reprimand? He was not here to take reprimands from Miss Illingworth, as much as he might require her help.

"I noticed a similar inflation of prices in the butler's books. Wine seems to have been extortionately expensive of late."

She put down the small glass of Canary wine that she had just raised to her mouth. Mal noted the shimmer of liquid on her lips and tore his mind away. He was not here to catalogue Miss Illingworth's anatomy, though he was noting new points of interest with every glance.

"I'm told it is common in wealthy households for the servants to line their pockets," she said. "A housekeeper selling the candle stubs or cast-off rags as a perk, for example. But I wonder if your steward was aware of the extent of the skimming."

"He was in no position to scold, given he was robbing from the estate, or planning to."

"And Her Grace?" She turned to the last page of entries.

"Don't Grace her," Mal snapped. "She's Sybil. A name synonymous with witch."

She gave him a level look. "The Sybils were oracles of the

Greco-Roman world. Their prophecies were considered divine revelation."

"My father thought Sybil a divine revelation when he found comfort in her arms, though she was but a viscount's widow, and he was not done mourning his first wife," Mal said. "Turns out the comfort Sybil took was in having a high title, a country seat, and a townhouse in London, as well as a great increase in her pin money. I expect she and Popplewell have been pocketing the estate's profits for some time, though our solicitor can tell us for sure. I'll meet with him tomorrow."

"And I shall give you the direction of the Sisters of Benevolence Hospital for the Relief of Orphans and Distressed Women," Miss Illingworth said, closing the book as if the conversation were finished. "They are not a regular agency, but they engage frequently in the placement of servants. Anyone they recommend will be trustworthy and grateful for the work. The matron will recognize my name."

"Surely, if that is the case, you are in the best position to discuss orphans and distressed women with her?" Mal said with alarm. He could only imagine how he, with his disastrous luck, would be met in such an endeavor. The care of his wards, or soon-to-be wards, was at stake. "More to the point, I don't have the least notion how to go about staffing a house like this one. I don't even employ a valet."

"A chambermaid to tidy?"

"Arranged by my landlady, and I pay for the service with my rent."

Again those brows raised. Miss Illingworth managed to convey much with just a few twitches of a facial muscle. This one said she found him a useless dandy, which he preferred to admitting that, due to his rebelliousness as a youth and the position of entrenched resentment he had maintained toward his father as an adult, he knew as much or less than she did about running a ducal house.

"I can inquire at the Hospital, but I should think you would rather see the back of me," she said finally.

If he longed to see the back of her, it was so he might examine her from that angle as well. The brandy had left a pleasant burn in his belly, the warmth spreading to regions lower the longer he sat with her. He had the unadvisable urge to touch her, to settle once and for all whether her hair was comprised of clouds or fairy dust, and whether her skin was silk or velvet.

Whether, if he dipped his finger in the brandy and drew it across those plum-colored lips, she would rear from his touch like a frightened horse. Or if she would bite his finger and suck it inside her clever mouth, warm and wet and—

Mal wrenched his mind from the tightness that suddenly filled his groin.

"You cannot abandon us now," Miss Illingworth," he rasped. "The children have thrown themselves upon your mercy, and I do as well."

She drew back as if she feared he meant to literally launch himself. He reined himself in. The set of her eyes, that canny way she looked at the world, suggested she was not entirely an innocent, but that didn't mean she was open to an interlude with a duke's bastard son. Or anyone.

What he would give, though, to have her look upon him with longing. To see desire in those deep, veiled eyes, a pout of want on her prim lips, to have her turn to him with a sultry invitation and—

"My brother, Joseph, could make the necessary arrangements. I cannot think you welcome me poking my nose in your business."

He wanted her nose and every other part of her in his business. No. Mal struggled to cut through the haze clouding his thoughts. No, he did not want her prying into his affairs, as attractive as her nose was.

"Your brother does not seem to have been aware of what was going on here any more than I was," Mal managed to point out.

A small line appeared between her deep-set, altogether too perceptive eyes. She pressed her hands together as if she were a medieval nun at prayer.

"Things have been deteriorating for some time, from what Ralph could tell me. I cannot say how long it's been since the children had a proper meal. Their nurse left days ago. Yet my brother noticed nothing."

"The boys would have too much pride to tell him anything was wrong," Mal said. A new, heavy weight on his chest pressed those snaking tendrils of desire into their proper place. "Ever since their father died..."

He studied the amber liquid in his glass, avoiding her gaze. "I suspect things have been deteriorating at least since then. Sybil would have had nothing but contempt or neglect for them until she saw Hugh's inheritance as a way to enrich herself. And when she set herself against me, she restricted my access to the house and to them, which is why I had no notion she'd abandoned them to the servants, and the servants had abandoned them as well."

Mal looked at her in appeal. She couldn't blame him any more than he blamed himself. He'd gotten so caught up in his own concerns that he neglected to look in on the children he meant to make his wards. Children who shared his blood.

He saw no contempt in her expression, only a look of puzzlement as she studied his features.

"He was your father too," she observed. "You must feel his loss in some way."

Mal upended the last of his brandy. "I feel the loss of his attempting to make up for the circumstances of my birth with his money," he said shortly. "His passing brought a period to a bitter life that in the end descended to madness. It was a relief, if you must know. He was never a happy man. He told me once, in a maudlin fit, that my mother was the only person he ever loved, and when his father forced them apart, his life held no real satisfaction for him thereafter."

"That is a heavy burden for him to lay upon you," she said quietly.

Mal stared at the leather surface of the table, marked with small cuts and tobacco stains. Miss Illingworth was alarmingly easy to confide in. No wonder the children had unburdened themselves to her at once, when they came to enlist the aid of her brother and found him not at home.

And why had they not come to Mal? That omission stung more than being left without the funds to support them. Or himself.

She picked up a small portrait that sat on a delicate table placed between two chairs. The face of a hauntingly lovely woman with delicate features and clouds of hair stared distantly from the frame.

Mal stared back. His mother had always been half-angel to him, fragile and luminous from the illness that eventually claimed her life. All the times his father had called him into this study for a raking over about his wild ways and unknown future, Mal had never seen this sketch. He wondered who had done it, and when.

"Was this her?" Amaranthe questioned. "I see a resemblance."

"Yes, that was my mother. Marguerite."

She startled and nearly dropped the silver frame. Her

fingers were graceful but strong like the rest of her, with ink staining the tips and a streak of gold along her thumb.

"Would she have styled herself Lady Vernay, by any chance?" A light blush touched her cheek as he stared at her. "I came across a book once with the name Marguerite, Lady Vernay inscribed in it, and I was curious about her. I am sorry to pry."

"Where did you find this book?" His voice abraded his ears.

"It was an old manuscript in my—a place I lived for a time. In Cornwall. I don't know where it is now." Her eyes fell, but not before he glimpsed the shadow that crossed her expression.

So many things she was hiding from him, but he was caught in the sweep of her eyelashes as she studied the table. Miss Illingworth had the same subtle, ethereal beauty that his mother had possessed. Not the kind of assertive handsomeness that announced itself, or the kind of astonishing beauty that smacked a man across the face. Rather, she was a small, willowy shadow that stepped into a man's fractured world and, by the time she came into focus, she had somehow, magically, made everything right and calm and beautiful.

"It's possible your book was hers. She was mad about old things." Mal took a bracing swig that emptied his glass again. "I suppose my mother might have used the title. She always insisted my father had wed her properly, but of course he would have said anything to win her. No record of a legal marriage, though. My grandfather claimed that my father deceived her, and I've never doubted he did."

Mal debated whether to refresh his glass. The brandy was fuzzing his perceptions, making him think imprudent things about Miss Illingworth. Enchanting, indeed! When she sat across from him as prim and proper as a governess.

He'd best get a grip on these galloping fancies. There was no sylph hidden beneath that drab, worn gown, no passionate heart subdued by the constraints of her station just waiting to be awakened by a kiss.

And if there were, he had no business knowing such things about her. Not when he had so little to offer her in return.

"When my father married Christine, she became Lady Vernay for a short time." Mal moved his mind back to the matter at hand. "My grandfather didn't live long after the wedding, from what I understand. It was the aim of his life to ensure his heir married into a family of suitable wealth and station, and he achieved it."

She set the portrait gently in its place. Mal battled the impulse to take those cool, capable fingers and press them against his aching head.

"And where is your mother now?" Her steady, fathomless gaze rested on him.

"She died when I was young." Dear Lord, he was becoming sentimental. He pushed the weakness aside. "You are coming to know a great deal about us, Miss Illingworth, and I know very little about you."

Her eyes crinkled as she smiled widely, and Mal cast about for breath. "We have not even been properly introduced."

"Malden Grey of Bristol, aspiring to the bar." He held out his hand.

"Malden," she said, and a silken quality in her voice made him shudder, as did the slide of her fingers as she placed them in his. "There is an Anglo-Saxon poem about a battle at an English ford called Maldon. One of those manuscripts sadly lost in the Cotton fire, actually."

"You haven't told me your name." His voice roughed his chest.

"Miss Amaranthe Illingworth of St. Cleer, Cornwall. My father was very fond of classical antiquity, so he chose a Greek name for me. He gave my mother the honor of naming my brother."

"Joseph," Mal said. "A Hebrew name. Very different tradition."

"My mother's family were Portuguese conversos." She withdrew her hand. "Jews who converted to Christianity so they might escape the Inquisition with their businesses and their lives. They practiced in secret for centuries, or so I've been told, but in the end my mother converted in truth and married a man bound for the Anglican church." She held the housekeeper's volume close to her chest, like a shield.

He sat back. The confidence stunned him. She'd learned he was a bastard, the status he wore like a brand on his forehead, marking him as deficient. But if her family had been Jewish, then she knew something as well about being set apart.

She rose, and he scrambled to his feet. Very neatly she placed her glass on the shelf beneath the decanter. Her eyes traced the figurines above, all of them representing mythological half-women with breasts prominently displayed.

"They're not mine," Mal said.

That small, maddening smile quirked her lips again. "No, they are young Hunsdon's now, I imagine. I've seen this and worse among some of the medieval marginalia I've copied, Mr. Grey. You wouldn't believe some of the grotesques those monks could dream up. I suppose it comes from being locked away day after day with no company but other men."

That was his problem as well, Mal decided. Too much time in the company of other men. That was why she'd riled his senses so potently. He needed a woman now and again to relieve the pressure.

Mal moved around the table toward her as she stepped away. "I can drive you tomorrow. To the orphan place with the distressed women."

Again the dance of those interesting brows. "You sound terrified at the very thought of confronting those in distress. Yet as a barrister, I imagine you frequently encounter persons in unfortunate circumstances."

"Prospective barrister. I am waiting to be called to the bar." He hated appearing so helpless, so insufficient around her. A woman could not desire a man she pitied. "What time shall I bring the carriage round?"

She hesitated, and her face went studiously blank. A slither across the back of his neck told him this was the expression she assumed when she was withholding something. He was beginning to recognize it.

"Eyde made up a room for me here," she said. "Do you mind?"

"Of course not. There are dozens of rooms." Or so he thought. Hunsdon House was not his, as nothing about the Hunsdon estate was to be his—not even the family name—and so he'd never let much of it occupy his attention.

He wondered which room Miss Amaranthe Illingworth would select for her own. Did she see her silk-smooth skin as best set off by the draperies in the Blue Room? Would she choose the Oriental patterns of the Jade Room? Or would she, like an empress of old, demand the royal purple? He imagined her nearby in the house going about her nightly routine, taking down her hair, drawing off her prim robe, perhaps splashing water onto her face that would run down that softly stern neck to the collarbones hidden beneath her gown and—

He'd best stop imagining Miss Illingworth at her ablutions. He was about to embarrass himself.

"Till tomorrow then, Miss Illingworth." Had she said he could call her Amaranthe? He wanted to roll the name over his tongue. It was exotic, yet robust. A name with command and presence, much like the woman.

Good Lord! That brandy had turned his wits. He was behaving like a moonstruck calf. No, worse.

"Till tomorrow," she said softly, and her gaze held his. The flickering candlelight brought out violet shadows in her eyes, and all the air left Mal's body. He wanted to be found worthy of that calm, assessing gaze.

There was no way she would ever find him worthy.

The door shut behind her, and Mal smacked a hand to his head to clear it. He'd best bring himself in order. They had business to conduct. Problems to solve.

She had secrets he wanted very much to discover.

He had gotten his first good look at Miss Amaranthe Illingworth. He wanted a second. And a third.

In fact, he wanted her in his bed, without a stitch of clothing, where he could study her at leisure and finally form a full picture of this alluring but very mysterious woman.

CHAPTER SEVEN

Holding her chamber candlestick steady in one hand, Amaranthe pressed lightly on the paneled door to the library. The polished wood swung inward, revealing a long, narrow room that appeared much more frequently inhabited than the rather bare study in which she'd found Malden Grey. She guessed the study had been the duke's private retreat, while the library was considered a more social space. The halo of light, as she moved it about, glanced on books heaped about chairs, piled on side tables, and lying open upon the great table that dominated the room.

This would be where Joseph spent his time with his charges, or so she guessed from the hastily erased slates, stacks of parchment, and tightly stoppered jars of ink that entered the soft circle of light as she approached.

Joseph tended to forget everything else when he was working. Mrs. Blackthorn made it a point of pride to concoct treats that could lure him to raise his head from a book when he was lost in thought. It was not beyond the realm of belief that he would simply fail to notice that his charges were not being supplied with luncheon, he being more accustomed to a hearty breakfast and substantial early dinner to tide him through the day. But he dismissed them for a reprieve and a light meal at some point, didn't he? How had he not seen that they returned to him as hungry as before?

Scouting out Joseph's error was not her purpose here; she would take the matter up with him tomorrow. Rather, the silent house, with everyone else abed, gave Amaranthe the perfect opportunity to walk through the library at her leisure and see what she could find.

Her own servants wouldn't question her curiosity, and there were no Hunsdon servants about save Ralph, whom she had already sent to bed. Dear, stout Ralph, the one soul who had seen the children had no one and stayed to look after them. She must see that he was duly rewarded. Grey's suggestion that he be promoted had so naturally followed her own thought that she'd gone silent with surprise. She had not expected she and the blustering, menacingly tall Malden Grey would be of like mind on anything.

The exchange in the study had unsettled her. He'd not at all been the rude, demanding man who swept into her house and accused her of kidnapping. At dinner, he'd been an excellent host, the gentlemanly *bon vivant* keeping the conversation afloat.

He'd heaped her plate with oysters as if he'd discerned her fondness for them.

And in their conference in the library, he had looked at her, more than once, as if he were trying to see below the surface. Past the Amaranthe Illingworth who made it a point to be unprepossessing and close-lipped, so she did not intimidate gentleman who might commissions copies from her.

Gentlemen did not approach her for other reasons, and men not gentlemen did not approach her at all, as she gave them no opportunity. Yet sitting so long near Malden Grey made

Amaranthe feel she'd swallowed ink and it sat in her belly, heavy and thick.

Slightly galling, as if her stomach hadn't settled for the food she'd introduced. As if she wanted a taste of something different, but knew not what.

A shiver of guilt edged her shoulders, and Amaranthe shrugged it off. She was not lurking about uninvited. He'd allowed her to stay. She had an excuse ready if Mr. Malden Grey came upon her and demanded to know why she was making free of the house. She was in search of something to read. The day being somewhat stimulating, she wished to soothe her nerves before bed. A perfectly reasonable request.

The ducal library had been built for a larger collection than the family had thus far acquired. The sturdy shelves reached to the ceiling, but the books did not. Several shelves showed large gaps filled with plaster busts or covered by watercolor landscapes not of the best execution. Nor were the rows tidy, with books leaning upon one another or piled in haphazard stacks. She doubted any of them were organized or catalogued.

She moved the small pewter saucer that held her candle before a range of calf leather-bound books, and the motley assortment of titles proved her suspicions correct. *Don Quixote* next to Ovid next to Hume's *Philosophical Essays Concerning Human Understanding*, followed by a treatise on botany and assorted, non-sequential volumes of *The Tatler*. Half sideways leaned a Latin edition of the *Thirty-nine Articles of the Church of England*, beside a Latin-English dictionary, like a disliked project abandoned and shelved.

Beneath this was every issue to date of *The Lady's Magazine*. Her Grace must be a subscriber. Her instinct for order made Amaranthe long to put the volumes in sequence, but she squelched the urge. She was not here to sort and catalogue, nor to do Sybil any favors.

Her candle teased the deep pockets of shadow in the corners of the room. Here and there on a chair back and on the standing globe she detected traces of dust. Joseph wouldn't have noticed that, either. She inspected the books heaped upon the table for an insight into the kind of lessons he held, hoping in that, at least, her brother was performing as well as could be wished.

If Malden Grey released him from this position, Amaranthe could support her brother in modest style. But if he left without a good reference, he would have difficulty finding a new post, and without a post, he would not be able to marry and support a wife, which Amaranthe knew was Joseph's most cherished goal.

The heavy worktable held the account of the travels of the Honourable John Byron, the open pages illustrating the commodore's travels through Patagonia and his encounters with its natives. Near it lay a copy of Artidemorus' book on the inter- pretation of dreams, in Greek, with a painstaking translation in English tucked between the pages. She spied a slender volume on *The Pythagorean Diet of Vegetables Only* tucked under Benjamin Franklin's observations on electricity. One side of the table was predominated by several volumes of Blackstone's commentaries on the laws of England—someone, it seemed, was doing legal research. Grey? But he had said Sybil barred him access to the house.

The shelves yielded only one interesting find: George Bick- ham's *The Universal Penman*. Bickham was considered Britain's greatest calligrapher and engraver, and this volume laid out the scripts Bickham had himself designed along with every other script currently in use among printers. It would be extraordi- narily useful to her, but given its folio size, she could hardly slip it in her pocket. Perhaps there was a way she could ask Joseph to borrow and bring it home on some pretext.

Aside from the fashion magazines, the library's tomes

offered an assortment of classics and instructional nonfiction, exactly what an upper-class gentleman would be expected to display on his shelves. Tucked away in one corner she found a few novels, among them Sarah Fielding's *The Adventures of David Simple*. Amaranthe's good reverend father had frowned upon novels, but her mother had managed to hide her copy of *David Simple* beneath a pile of quilts in an old cedar chest, and Amaranthe had snuck it out to read several times during her youth. She had been particularly struck by the heroine's arguments about the strength of women's intellect and the benefit of gentlewomen earning their own living.

Her mother's book, like everything else Amaranthe had brought with her from the first home she'd ever known, was at Penwellen, lost in Reuben's clutches. With a pang of longing and grief she slipped the novel into the pocket of her bedgown. She'd return it, of course; she wasn't a thief. But the book made her mother feel close. How she missed her guidance, her warmth, her calm.

What would her mother think of the means Amaranthe had hit upon to support herself, Joseph, Eyde, and Derwa? She knew what her father would say. His moral code was strict and without grey areas. Her father had been an intelligent and gifted man, Scripture his guide for human relations, and its requirements were very clear.

Amaranthe lingered before the fullest set of shelves, heavy with books on medical lore, cures, and treatments, as well as witchcraft, mysticism, and several slim volumes on the beneficial uses of opium. One of the dukes had had rather arcane tastes—or a desperate interest in curatives? She had not thought to ask what the late Duke of Hunsdon had died of. She combed this section carefully, but all the books were cheap and recent, with half-calf bindings and fading ink, paper already browning at the edges.

The tome Joseph had mentioned wasn't here, and neither was anything else that could be called valuable or rare, at least not upon first perusal. She would have to return during the light of day to inspect the drawers and cabinets, and to do so she would need to find some pretext that did not strain credulity. Malden Grey had already proven suspicious of her.

With good reason, she had to admit.

Malden. She said the name to herself as she quietly pulled the door closed and stole down the darkened hallways of Hunsdon House in what she hoped was the direction of her chamber. Now here was a puzzle as well.

The duke's illegitimate eldest son spent his days in the dissolute pursuits of a gentleman. From what Amaranthe gathered, studying law was for most young men a thin veil of respectability pulled over a generally riotous lifestyle of funded leisure. Most would be called to the bar as it suited their relatives and patrons, the ancient ritual of British preferment at work.

Once gowned and wigged as a proper barrister they were at liberty to hire out their work to clerks as much as they wished. Seated as judges, they became the guardians of English law and precedent, holding intact the ages-old class structures and customs that kept people carefully slotted into their station and obedient to the rules governing their class and sex.

Yet Malden Grey was a bastard, his illegitimate birth barring him from what otherwise would have been an impressive inheritance and unchecked influence. He lived among the highest, yet he had to survive by his wits. Just as she did.

He had seemed genuinely distressed when he discovered the predicament the children were in. It was more than outrage that Sybil had robbed him of his means of financial support. For a dissolute gentleman, he seemed devoted to his half-siblings, making a bid to be their legal guardian. Nothing obliged him to do so, and few men in his situation would. Yet he had accepted without question his responsibility for them, and she had seen his guilt that he had not noticed their predicament. That was not the gesture of the callous, self-interested dandy she had taken him for.

Amaranthe undressed and dispensed with her evening routine with efficiency, then nearly groaned as she climbed into the large bed. The feather mattress had been plumped and Eyde had slipped a warm brick between the sheets, a greedy comfort. She blew out the candle and watched the shadows of tossing tree limbs twist across the papered walls of her luxurious room.

Favella would eat her heart out to see the luxury of this place. Amaranthe almost wished she could invite her cousin's wife to visit, just to see the pleasure that vain Favella would take in everything. But of course that was impossible, because Reuben could not know where she was.

Someday, Amaranthe would return to Penwellen—someday when she was in a position to demand that Reuben return her things. She would find that manuscript, her Book of Hours, the keystone of her collection. She would demand the return of everything her cousin had taken from her. Someday her whole body would not go over cold and sick at the memory of him touching her—of what he had threatened before she left—and she would have the courage to face him.

Tomorrow she had a problem to solve, and she was stimulated by the challenge. She was stimulated, also, by the conundrum of Malden Grey. His presence called her nerves to alertness, sharpening her wits and making her blood hum. His power, from his position and the fact of his large, very male presence, put her on her toes. She would relish resolving his difficulties and putting him in her debt. He was the man the likes of which she did not encounter in her day-to-day life; he was more like the hero of a stage play, debonair, destructively handsome, bigger than life.

He had stared at her in such an unsettling way over dinner, and then again in his study. His intense focus raised nervous sensations in her belly and across her skin, like the lifting of hair when one sensed danger. It was well he did not know why she had agreed without argument to accompany him to Hunsdon House. His look of curious fascination would turn to scorn and rejection. It might be base and an indication of feminine vanity, but she wanted to enjoy his interest as long as she could.

CHAPTER EIGHT

"This can't be proper," Amaranthe said to the eager faces ranged before her in the borrowed chamber. "Wearing the duchess's clothes?"

"She's not about ta wear 'em, is 'er?" Eyde shrugged. "Ye ought to see how many they are, miss. Heaps, and all boughten, not a whit handmade."

Amaranthe slid a hand over the fine printed muslin robe that Eyde held. "You shouldn't have gone through the duchess's wardrobe. Either of you."

"We just took a peep now, didnus?" Eyde said to Mrs. Blackthorn, who brandished a saffron open robe with a green front. Derwa draped herself in a soft Paisley shawl and twirled before the cheval glass in admiration.

A knock sounded at the door, and Amaranthe clutched at the loose neckline of her bedgown. Letting Eyde borrow a night shift from Sybil's chambers for Amaranthe to sleep in was one thing. Wearing the duchess's luxurious gowns was far and away a different matter.

Ralph entered with a pile of indigo silk in his arms. "Mr. Grey said as I ought to bring this to you, miss, seeing as you came yesterday without a bag or luggage." He smiled shyly. "Picked it out himself, he did."

Amaranthe couldn't stop her hand sliding over the expensive silk. The other women joined her, cooing in pleasure at the smooth, luscious fabric. Amaranthe's resolve weakened. If Grey thought it all right to wear borrowed finery—

"Ooh, miss, you must have un," Eyde insisted, and Amaranthe caved.

She didn't have the proper foundational garments for such a gown, but once Eyde had tied up the skirts and pinned on the stomacher, Amaranthe had no will left to argue. Derwa clapped her hands in approval, and Mrs. Blackthorn held out an elaborate wig. The powder was old and Amaranthe feared the false hair was crawling with vermin, but it was too fashionable to resist. Great ladies dressed like this, Amaranthe thought as she stared at herself in the glass.

"Here's a reticule to go with, since your other won't do." Derwa held out her find.

"I am transformed," Amaranthe said in surprise.

"Quite stripped up," Eyde confirmed, plumping pillows on the bed. "Now, miss, flutter your eyelashes at Mr. Grey once or twice, and say us two needs a day more here. We needs be sure any maids you bring on can do the place proper."

Mrs. Blackthorn, hanging the other gowns in the small wardrobe, agreed. "I want a day or more to learn the new cook and be certain the kitchen maids know their work. That scullery needs a scrub like Heaven's never seen."

Derwa draped her shawl over Amaranthe's shoulders, arranging it to her satisfaction. "And Miss Millie wants a governess. You're best to find her one."

"Lady Camilla," Amaranthe said automatically, glancing at the other women. "You don't wish to return home directly?"

"And leave a duke's house?" Edye exclaimed. "Is ee daft?"

Amaranthe tamped down a smile. "We'd best not get comfortable with the duke's things. Mr. Grey means to turn us out as soon as he can, I don't doubt."

"Then Mr. Grey can make sure his new cook knows the difference twixt a swede and a potato," Mrs. Blackthorn answered. "Didn't you hear Eyde? Use them eyelashes, Miss Amaranthe."

"And these." Eyde rearranged the scarf Amaranthe had tucked into her neckline, folding it down an inch so that a slight rise of breast peeked above the stomacher.

"I prefer to use intelligence as my weapon," Amaranthe called as Eyde gathered up her bedgown and skipped out the door, Derwa giggling in her wake.

"Always best to have a full arsenal." Mrs. Blackthorn whisked away the breakfast tray with a wink. "Luck be upon you today, Miss Amaranthe!"

Grey went completely still when Amaranthe joined him in one of the smaller parlors, different from that they had dined in the night before. For once Amaranthe didn't feel overshadowed by the expensive elegance of her new surroundings. The rustle and gleam of French silk was as good as plate armor.

The gown held its own against the velvet upholstery and damask draperies, the mirrors and portraits in their heavy gilt frames and the dizzying pattern of the carpet. She was more a match today for Grey's smart suit of brown silk with heavy bronze buttons and gold embroidery. He looked considerably more expensive, and she wondered if he considered his attire a sort of armor also.

"I felt obliged to wear the gown, since Ralph said you recommended it," Amaranthe said, suddenly shy. "But are you sure it is wise? Any servants we hire will expect a higher wage, with me looking so fine."

Grey leaned close and peered into her eyes. She reared back, startled.

"Violet," he exclaimed.

"I have brown eyes," she said, feeling strangely overset by his nearness. Had donning a fine dress vanquished her wits?

"Light brown," he agreed, "but with a ring of violet around the iris. Most unusual. The color of your gown brings it out." He did not take his eyes from her face.

Amaranthe stepped back, flustered. No one in her life, not since her mother died, had been close enough to note such an intimate detail about her person. No man, not even her brother, had ever showed interest in the composition of her eyes.

Eyde sailed in cradling an exquisite ribboned cap along with a set of cream-colored kid gloves. "Flam-new!" she exclaimed. "It be a shame not to sport un, miss."

She perched the cap atop Amaranthe's high wig, fixing it in place with a firm shove of a hatpin. Then she stepped back and blinked her eyelashes rapidly, reminding Amaranthe of her task.

"Shoo," Amaranthe said. "You may trust I'll broach the subject with Mr. Grey in due time."

Eyde bobbed the briefest curtsy and left. Grey raised his eyebrows.

"My staff want an opportunity to review any servants we hire and ensure they will properly execute their duties," she explained. "They have taken a proprietary interest in the house, as well as a personal interest in the welfare of your wards."

"And in finding a governess!" sang a voice from outside the room that sounded very like Lady Camilla. "Who knows Latin *and* Greek!"

Grey's lips twitched with humor, and Amaranthe smiled in helpless response. Oh, but the fascination was stronger, here in the light of day. Spending time with this man, in this gown, was dangerous to her good sense. With his walking stick and hat, his easy assurance and good humor, he was another step yet from the arrogant cad who'd barreled into her house yesterday. Now he was making headway into her approval, and that simply would not do.

He held out his arm to escort her from the room, and Amaranthe hesitated. She had never had an escort. As a girl she'd had playmates and tagged along after Joseph. Under Reuben's roof, whether due to her state of dependence or Reuben's forbidding nature, she had never been courted. She and Joseph rubbed along fairly well as long as she was allowed her pursuits and he his. But she did not circulate among social circles, and for a gentleman to hold out his arm to her—that was new.

She slid her hand about his elbow, and something slipped into place. She felt the same eager anticipation as when she opened a new manuscript, knowing the beauties and the oddities and the discoveries that awaited.

She pushed the feeling away. She had a series of tasks before her, and only one of them was to equip the ducal house with servants. The other was, somehow, to keep Malden Grey from learning too much about her work. The closer he drew, the greater the risk. She could not afford to lose her head simply because she was wearing a gorgeous gown.

THE MATRON of the Sisters of Benevolence Hospital for Orphans and Women in Distressed Circumstances supplied almost all of Amaranthe's needs in a short span of time. The Hospital prided itself on training its residents for careers, and many of them entered service. The name of Miss Gregoire served better than guineas to smooth Amaranthe's way; Miss Gregoire was a founder and patroness, and Amaranthe needed only to mention she had attended her academy for young ladies to be welcomed with the utmost warmth.

Before she left she had a complete roster of parlormaids, chambermaids, kitchen maids, a scullery maid, a tweenie, and a nursemaid. She lacked only a housekeeper—a position that usually required some experience—and a butler and footmen, since the Sisters of Benevolence served women and young orphans. But the matron gave her the name of a hiring agency where several previous beneficiaries of the Sisters' benevolence had found positions, and Amaranthe suspected she would be just as well supplied if she mentioned the magical name of Miss Gregoire there, too.

"I don't know how to begin to thank you," Amaranthe said in gratitude as the matron blew on her list of names to dry the ink, then handed the paper to Amaranthe. They sat in a cozy parlor set back from the street, off a small garden that ran alongside the main entrance. Herbs grew in tidy beds framed by ornamental flowers, and now and again a girl walked by alone or with a set of children, all of them in crisp undyed linen, clean and shod. It was Amaranthe's first glimpse of the Benevolence Hospital, and she could see Miss Gregoire's quiet influence on the place.

"Only tell us how the girls get on, and let us know if there are any problems," the matron said. She replaced her pen in its stand and rose, shaking out her apron. Amaranthe thought her young to have a position of responsibility over at least a hundred residents and staff, but her demeanor was one of unassailable calm.

"Of course," Amaranthe answered. "But do you ask no placement fee, or otherwise?" Perhaps she would have to ask Miss Gregoire what was necessary.

The matron's smile held boundless compassion, humor, wisdom, and a steel backbone beneath it all. "If a donation comes our way that supports the work of the Hospital, we would of course be grateful, Miss Illingworth," she said. "Each according to his need, and each according to his means."

Amaranthe nodded. She didn't know how they were to negotiate wages for the new staff, but Grey had promised to work that out in his visit to the solicitor. Hopefully he would meet her with good news, and they could spend the day preparing Hunsdon House, and the children, to welcome their new servants.

That left her one more day to finish her quest through the ducal library. She hoped Joseph, who was due to present himself that morning to tutor the duke and his brother, would prove of use in this. And that the watchful and, she feared, all too intelligent Malden Grey would not guess how she had set out to deceive him.

MAL HAD A FRUSTRATING MORNING. He had hoped setting Hunsdon House in order was a task he could make short work of. But Mr. Coutts, the banker, proved less than illuminating on the subject of returning to financial solvency. With the income from the second quarter having evaporated, the only means of finding funds was sale of property, which Grey did not have the authority to do.

With an apologetic cough, Mr. Coutts suggested the possibility of a small, discreet loan, but that line of inquiry ended with the subject of collateral. Mal had nothing of his own to forfeit. He let his rooms, lived as modestly as he could in order to invest in his appearance as a gentleman, and had no savings. He had spent everything in preparing for the bar, and with his father the old duke dead, there was no one left to pull the strings of preferment on Mal's behalf. He could languish for years in the Middle Temple before the Benchers called him.

"Are there other professions you might consider?" Mr. Coutts inquired.

"The Household Cavalry," Mal said gloomily, getting to his feet. "The Grenadier Guards. The King at least pays a decent salary."

"You would cut a fine figure in the uniform," Mr. Coutts agreed.

Mal jammed his hat on his head as he strode into the street, looking for the curricle. It had seemed wise to take the lighter, two-wheeled carriage for his errands with Miss Illingworth that day. But the lack of space obliged Miss Illingworth to sit quite close to him, her silk skirts spilling over his leg, his elbow occasionally brushing hers when he pulled back on the reins, and that had proved a very distracting prospect.

A trio of women emerged from a shop across the street, pausing to watch as Mal leapt into his vehicle, and they giggled when he glanced their way. He tipped his hat out of habit, but today the female attention annoyed him. All anyone seemed to think he was good for was lounging about well-dressed and occasionally saying something droll.

He was stuck without hope of professional advancement. He was such a terrible half-brother that his siblings had been abandoned in their own home and he hadn't known it. And now he didn't have the first clue how to resolve the situation Sybil had left them in. Were he anything more than a bastard—if he had a title to throw around, itself collateral for any loan; if he had property, savings, anything of his own—they wouldn't be in this quandary. He'd never felt so useless in his life.

He wondered if Miss Illingworth was one of those women who went soft-headed over a man in uniform, but that line of thought was unproductive, and he pushed it aside. He would rather be appreciated for his intellect and his accomplishments, rather than his looks.

And while he'd glimpsed a glimmer of appreciation in her eyes when they met in the parlor at Hunsdon House that morning, Miss Illingworth didn't seem the type to be impressed by appearances. She had far too exacting a mind.

Mal fell into a brown study as the carriage bumped along the crowded, noisy Strand back to Middle Temple, where he entered the Hall to find the barrister and friend who had taken on his guardianship case. Rosenfeld was engaged with other pleaders and students in a lively debate taking place over several pints of ale, but he allowed Mal to draw him off for a stroll through the gardens and a consultation.

Discussion of his court case made no improvement in his mood. Rosenfeld agreed that Sybil's absconding to the Continent with the duke's steward, income, and several household items should have the effect of dismissing her case obstructing his efforts to gain guardianship. But he didn't have to remind Mal that the Courts of Chancery moved at a pace best called glacial. Rosenfeld could enter a bill for a provisional appointment of Mal as the children's guardian, but the Lord Chancellor was likely to impose restrictions on Mal's access to the estate's income and other assets, given the estate in question belonged to a duke.

"Rosenfeld," Mal said as they strolled out of the lush, tranquil gardens, a haven of peace inside busy London, and came to the broad square before the Hall. "That's a Jewish name, isn't it?"

His friend's face assumed a bland expression. "I suppose it is, in some families," he said, his tone neutral. "But, of course, to graduate Oxford with my civil law degree, I took the Oath of Communion as a member of the Anglican Church."

"Yes, naturally," Mal murmured. He'd taken the same oath, though he couldn't say he was a church member in good standing. Such a thing would require church attendance, possibly tithes, and most certainly a subscription to the doctrines and dogma of belief. Mal had his doubts.

But all students of England's greatest colleges were required to be Church of England. No Dissenters, Protestants, Quakers, Methodists, or Jews.

"It's recently occurred to me," Mal remarked, "how long, and how often, Jews have had to hide their culture and their religion to survive." He supposed many, like Amaranthe's mother's family, had chosen to conform as a means of survival when to cling to their faith would mean penury, exile, or death at the stake.

"Prickly history, that," Rosenfeld said dryly, and there the matter rested.

Mal wondered about Rosenfeld's private beliefs, but a man ought to have some things he could keep to himself. For his own part, Mal didn't advertise that he was a bastard any more than he needed to. He liked the way he was treated when he was accepted as just another young man about town, erstwhile gentleman, aspiring barrister. He could usually tell when his parentage had reached a new acquaintance's ears. Invitations from their mothers and requests to escort their sisters stopped, but he was invited just as often, if not more frequently, to less savory entertainments like gambling clubs, cock fights, and drunken rambles.

Mal's mood turned decidedly glum as he fought his way down the narrow, twisting lanes of the City to the office of his solicitor and the estate's man of business. It seemed his traditional bad luck was holding true. He wondered if Miss Illingworth were having better luck than he with her errands of the morning.

With that serene face and that clever, wry twist of her lips, she could wring anything from anyone, he had no doubt. When she drifted into the parlor in a cloud of indigo silk, he'd been struck dumb. He had expected to find his fancies of the evening before and the strange, erotic dreams that had followed him into sleep would be banished in the morning, and in the light of day he would find her again prim and plain, a steely-eyed spinster bluestocking.

Instead he found a ravishing beauty. Against a backdrop of expensive silk, the severe lines of her face looked elegant, her coloring became vivid and arresting, and that all-too-expressive mouth looked decidedly alluring. Wondering about the shape of her beneath the stylish gown fired his blood in the light of day every bit as much as it had in the candlelit shadows of his father's study the night before.

But her transformation posed a sobering reminder that in the world of the *haut ton,* it was easy to confuse worth with how much money someone possessed. The right trimmings could make any woman appealing, elegant, well-bred. He had to teach Hugh how to discern a woman's character beneath the plumage.

Amaranthe Illingworth had character in spades. It was written in the high curve of her cheek, the way her mouth pinched when she was angry, the brows that rose up and down with curiosity, and the eyes that gleamed with intelligence. In the violet glow that stunned him when he got close enough to look.

Mal shook his head to clear it of fanciful images. Money. The subject at hand was money. Where was he to get it? He couldn't ask Viktor for a loan. Like most of their friends, Viktor spent coin as freely as it came to him, not letting a guinea grow warm in his pocket before it was gone in the pursuit of some pleasure.

Neither could he write home and ask Aunt Beatrice for money. She and Littlejohn were getting on in life and needed every penny of their tiny, well-earned savings to serve as a pension for when they were too old to finally work. It had always been vaguely in Mal's mind that, when he became a sergeant at law, he would be able to send money home, not ask for it.

Not for the first time, he cursed the slippery Popplewell and the bewitching, heartless Sybil who had seduced him to her evil cause. He wished he could hire men to go abroad, find them both, and haul them back to England to account for their crimes. But he didn't have the money to hire a hack, much less offer a bounty on the duchess's head.

"I really cannot advise returning Her Grace to England, if that is your intent," his solicitor answered when Mal shared what was on his mind. "I feel it will support your case if she is absent and cannot account for herself. The Lord Chancellor cannot choose but to award guardianship to you."

"True," Mal said heavily. "If the case comes before him before they are all grown and married and out of the house, and my guardianship is rendered irrelevant."

"Indeed, the wheels of justice can move all too slowly at times."

Mr. Thorkelson, of Mssrs. Thorkelson and Sons, sat across from Mal in an office shadowed by a set of heavy, dark oak furniture large enough to kill a man if they happened to topple over on him. Ensconced behind a desk so massive that a fully grown person could take refuge beneath it, Thorkelson slid open a drawer and drew forth a file, two inches thick, which he placed upon his blotter.

"Now, then. Joseph Alexander Illingworth. What is it you would like to know, Mr. Grey?"

"May I?" Mal gestured toward the bulging file.

"I'm afraid not." Thorkelson managed to sound regretful without looking it. Behind a set of thick spectacles, he had the look of a Viking warrior of old who had found a settled life agreed with him. Beneath a heavy brow his cheeks were rather doughy, and his hands were soft and full and smooth. "Some of the information is quite sensitive, you see."

"But I am his employer."

Thorkelson gave a discreet cough. "Or will be, as soon as we are authorized to draw up the proper papers. Naturally we remain willing to expedite your guardianship case however we may." He smiled, or made an expression which Mal assumed was a smile. "Now, what is it you wish to know?"

"Is he a proper influence? My brothers are in his charge for much of the day."

It was humiliating to admit that he had not made proper inquiries before, but Thorkelson had tendered Illingworth's name as a tutor when Mal was in the middle of a heavy spate of reading for the bar while wallowing through a towering stack of decisions about the household following the duke's death, decisions Sybil was useless at making. He'd been glad to let Thorkelson have his way in the matter of selecting a tutor.

"Is he dependable," Mr. Thorkelson murmured. He opened the file and consulted a scrawled set of notes. "Let us see. Twenty-six years of age. Born in Cornwall, in the village of St. Cleer, only son of the vicar Jonas Illingworth and his wife, Bracha Crosby. Educated at home, sent to Oxford, where he took a second in classics and a negligible place in mathematics. Exemplary disciplinary record. Not a single infraction."

"Not one?" Mal echoed.

Not a single riotous act, not a lark, not even a momentary rebellion? That seemed a bit spiritless. Mal had had his share of scrapes at Winchester and then Cambridge, most of them the result of being a bastard. His tutors had often made an example of him, and the boys assured of their stations made him a frequent target.

Then he grew into his inches, and filled out those inches with a larger than average frame, which meant his fists had a longer reach and his legs could cover more ground. The harassment waned considerably once Mal grew bigger than his aggressors. And learned not to care that his birth meant he would always be last in line, an afterthought, not assured of full standing in anything.

"Do you find his spotless record a problem?" Mr. Thorkelson observed Mal over the top of his glasses. "His references were all in order. I can go over them again if you wish."

Mal cleared his throat. "I am curious about the family. As—you know. Added security."

Thorkelson turned over a few pages. "Jonas Illingworth was younger brother to Josiah Illingworth, the 4th Baronet Illingworth. The estate of Penwellen is now held by the 5th baronet, Sir Reuben Illingworth, who has a wife, Favella. There does not seem to be correspondence between the two households."

Her cousin, a baronet? She had not mentioned that. Her birth put her in the class of gentry, even if she practiced a trade. How curious that she had not trotted out her status early in the conversation. But his interest was not in the baronet.

"And what of Mr. Joseph Illingworth's sister?"

"Ah." Mr. Thorkelson dipped into the drawer again and withdrew another file, this one thicker. "This is the rather sensitive portion," he said blandly. "What would you like to know?"

"Good Gad, you're thorough," Mal said, eying the volume of the file.

"We took some initiative in this case," the solicitor answered, "as it concerned the estate of Hunsdon, and we at Thorkelson, Thorkelson, and Son are naturally protective of our clients. Unfortunately, none of our thorough investigations suggested that Mr. Popplewell would violate our collective trust in him in such an egregious fashion."

Mr. Thorkelson's severe expression had something of satisfaction in it. As the old duke's solicitor and man of business in

London, Mr. Thorkelson had a long rivalry with Mr. Popplewell, the estate's land steward. But Mal had no time for that petty history, nor was he inclined to let Mr. Thorkelson bask in his triumph at having proved the superior agent.

"Sensitive in what way?" Mal itched to get his hand on that file. Thorkelson looked disinclined to surrender it.

The solicitor coughed into his hand. "This information, I'm sure you can agree, is not to leave this room. But we understand —the other Mr. Thorkelsons and I—that Miss Amaranthe Illingworth is in the business of making—er, copies. Of rare, and in some cases quite valuable works."

"Copies." Mal raised his eyebrows. "Yes, I knew that."

She seemed quite proud of herself for it. Ladies often cultivated artistic pursuits to show off their accomplishments. But Amaranthe Illingworth took pride in her work and evidenced no shame that she had turned her skills to the pursuit of a trade.

"Surely there is no harm in making copies," Mal said.

"There is when it is forgery," Mr. Thorkelson replied.

CHAPTER NINE

Amaranthe emerged from a side garden when Mal pulled up before the medieval guild hall that had been transformed into the Benevolence Hospital. She looked grand in the expensive silk; he'd been right that the fabric would flatter her dark coloring. As he'd never had occasion to choose a lady's attire before, it pleased him that his instincts had been correct about this one.

To avert a repeat of the thump-over-the-head, thought-clearing reaction he'd had to her earlier, he tried to look about him at the environs of the place. The grounds and buildings of the Benevolence Hospital appeared well-supplied and well-kept, in good repair. It would take money to maintain such an enterprise, and he wondered who the donors were. Miss Illingworth had said little about it other than that it was a charity with some connection to the girls' school she had attended, and he wondered now if he ought to be asking more questions. Apparently he had not been asking close enough questions about a great many things.

As he handed her up into the vehicle, Mal studied her face closely, looking for signs of venality, slyness, or duplicity. But she looked the same as before: well-shaped lips of a natural plum color, high cheekbones, skin smooth and luscious as creamed tea. She didn't look like a liar, a forger, or a thief.

He wondered how on earth he was supposed to bring up the subject. But there were any number of things he needed to know about Amaranthe Illingworth.

"You had some success, then?" He leapt easily into the carriage beside her. "You look pleased."

She scooted to the side when his leg brushed hers, and he took satisfaction in the color that appeared in her cheeks. But her voice was composed as she withdrew a small slip of paper from her reticule.

"The matron supplied me with a list of names. They'll be sent over tomorrow at seven with their things. I've everyone but a butler, a housekeeper, and perhaps you might wish a second footman, to help Ralph."

"We can't keep your man?" Mal said without thinking. When she turned surprised eyes on him, he tried not to stare.

First he had noticed the unusual violet ring around the iris of her eyes, and now he saw that the brown was in fact shot with rays of gold. Miss Amaranthe Illingworth was a deep treasure whose beauties revealed themselves subtly, quietly, with each new observation.

"No, you cannot have Davey. My servants will return home with me. They asked a day or two to help settle in your new staff, and I can't deny that they all love being inside a ducal mansion. They've already raided the duchess's chambers, and I don't doubt that between them they've combed every room in the house. But we'll all go home in short order, and you'll be free of us."

"The children will be sorry." Mal would be sorry, too. He wondered what excuses he could contrive to call on Miss Illingworth once she had removed herself from Hunsdon House back to her own tidy house in George Court.

He was thinking of calling on her. He was already looking for ways to keep her involved in his life. That came as something as a surprise.

And his reasons, if he were being entirely honest with himself, weren't simply to ensure that he wasn't exposing his half-siblings to an inimical influence or a criminal mastermind.

"I need a bracing drink before we visit any hiring agencies. Do you mind?"

When she didn't, Mal navigated them back to the Strand to Tom's Coffee House, which was one of the few premises in town that admitted women. He watched Amaranthe's face suffuse with pleasure at the rich smells that met them at the door, and her gaze followed the busy movement of patrons as they swapped news and gossip. Other gazes followed them, too, or more precisely Amaranthe as she moved to a space at one of the high tables and lay her reticule upon it. There was no denying that in Sybil's things, she looked a duchess in truth. She possessed an air of self-command and a quick, droll wit that did not suffer fools.

"Tea? Coffee? Chocolate?" Mal winked. "They've stronger drinks as well, if you'd like a nip of wine."

"Wine, at this hour." That enchanting twitch to her lips. "Tea, please."

"I would have taken you for a chocolate drinker."

"Indeed I adore it, but only on very special occasions. We do not often have tea."

"You served it yesterday to the children."

"Yes, because they were guests. The tax makes it dear for our household."

The server drew the liquid tea from its cask and heated it, and Amaranthe closed her eyes in bliss as she sipped. Mal tried not to stare like a fool. Or try to imagine other ways he might bring that look to her face.

"Grey, I thought I spotted you down the street. And with a companion of the female persuasion. I simply had to come see for myself."

"Vierling." Mal greeted his friend, though Viktor was not as welcome a sight as usual. He was in uniform, and the scarlet coat with its gold sash made his chest look impressively broad, while the tall black jack boots and golden breeches showed the shape of his muscular legs. He carried his red and gold head-dress under one arm and stood easily before Amaranthe, looking down at her with a smile.

"You look like you ought to be to horse," Mal added. "Drill today?"

"We're seeing off the next shipment of troops to the American colonies. Surprised you aren't with them, old boy. When I didn't see the tip of your nose all last night, I thought you'd made good on your promise to enlist."

"I had other matters to preoccupy me," Mal answered.

"I see that." Viktor's grin widened as he studied Amaranthe.

"Miss Illingworth," Mal said shortly. "Viktor Vierling, the wastrel son of an obscure German count, presently of the 2d Horse Grenadier Guards, where he has made no good account of himself. Viktor, this is Miss Amaranthe Illingworth, sister to the tutor who looks after Hugh and Ned."

Viktor bowed over the hand Amaranthe extended. Mal was glad she was wearing the kid glove and Viktor didn't get to touch her skin. "I would have been a much better student if my tutors had a sister so pretty," Viktor said.

"Yes, I imagine you would have suddenly been inspired to pay keen attention to your Latin conjugations and historical studies," Amaranthe said with cool calm. "Whereas my brother relies on the authority of his knowledge to make his students behave. As Cicero says, *si hortum et bibliotheca habes, nihil deerit.*"

Mal smothered a laugh as Viktor mastered his look of dismay. He had no doubt Amaranthe intended to flourish her Latin as a weapon. Viktor recovered his customary aplomb. "I'll agree with anything Cicero spouts if you support it, Miss Illingworth."

Amaranthe cast an exasperated look at Mal, who suddenly felt buoyant. So she was not the type of woman to go soft over a man in uniform. Mal was glad to see it. He wasn't certain the uniform would suit him, come to that, and the headgear bordered on the ridiculous.

"So Cicero is what intelligent young ladies use to drive away unwanted gentlemen," Mal said after Viktor moved away to hail another friend. "I think you meant it. 'He who possesses a garden and a library lacks nothing.'"

Her pleased, slightly abashed smile warmed him to a far greater extent than his coffee. "I couldn't think of anything more appropriate in the moment," she said. "But it's my favorite of his sayings, nevertheless."

"'Faithfulness and truth are the most sacred excellences and endowments of the human mind,'" Mal quoted. "One of my favorites."

She turned her face away. "Quite."

Now why had he taunted her thus? It was no way to find answers. "You like tea," he said stupidly, trying to draw her attention back to himself.

"Brought to England by Catherine de Braganza, the wife of King Charles II, so they say," she murmured, still not meeting his eyes.

"Who was Portuguese," Mal said. "As, I believe you mentioned, was your mother's family?"

"We always hoped to travel there," Amaranthe answered.

"My mother taught me a bit of the language, what bits had been handed down to her. I use it now and again with a girl we met, a young woman named Inez. Her father was an Indian sailor and her mother his Portuguese wife, left stranded in England when his employer went bankrupt and the crew was relieved of their duties. Inez is looking after my house while we are gone."

"You seem inclined to take in people in distress," Mal noted. "You mentioned you brought your maid from Cornwall with you."

Her eyes met his, wide with surprise. "Why would you think Inez is in distress? Or Eyde?"

"You leapt in to help my brothers and sister on the basis of no prior acquaintance," Mal said. "At the notion of hiring staff, you went immediately to a charitable institution that places orphans into service. And you mentioned you left Cornwall around six years ago, which I am guessing is the age of your maid's daughter. Very few employers keep a servant who comes burdened with a child."

Her gaze fell to the liquid in her cup, lips pursed as she blew on the warm liquid. "It is not a remarkable inclination," she observed. "To help people in need."

"It's why I chose the law," Mal blurted. There it was: her eyes on him again, quizzical, interested. He wanted to hold her attention.

"Parliament makes the laws, but it comes to justices and magistrates to find remedies for errors in the application of them. The decisions of judges can have great power for justice. Look at the Somerset ruling and the profound effect it has had. If Parliament cannot bring itself to pass legislation, then it falls to judges to ensure only just laws are upheld." He faltered as her look grew sharp, interested. "I only mean to say—"

"You have a real interest in the law after all," she said quietly. "I misjudged you, Mr. Grey."

"Call me Mal. Please."

"Far too forward." Her gaze fell again. He watched the sweep of her long, dark eyelashes on that soft cheek and his fingers itched to follow. He curled both hands around his coffee cup to keep them in place.

He was already using her Christian name in his head. He'd known her less than a day, but the hours they'd spent together made her feel familiar. He had more insight into her history and character than with many casual acquaintances he'd known for years.

And nothing he'd seen so far suggested she might engage in illicit activities.

He swallowed the rest of his coffee, letting the hot liquid refresh his brain. "So it remains to hire the most expensive servants. But without any ready source of income to cover their salary."

Briefly he related the gist of his conversation with Rosenfeld, who had suggested it might take some time to grant Mal provisional guardianship of the children, and with Mr. Coutts, who was prepared to stand a loan provided Mal had some guarantee he would ever be in a position to repay it.

She remained silent for a moment, those lovely eyes veiled. "I may be able to propose something," she said at last.

"We can't sell off things from the house." Most of the valuable ornaments were gone already, and the furnishings and fixtures belonged to Hunsdon.

Her eyes narrowed. "The children need to eat, Mr. Grey."

He wrestled down his pride, which took an effort. "What do you propose?"

"I suggest you visit the hiring agency the matron told me about and arrange for a handful of prospects to come interview at the house. In the meantime, if you drop me at my house, I will look into—a matter there. You may meet me at Mr. Karim's bookshop when you are free. It is in Queen's Head Passage, just off Paternoster Row."

"The Moor's bookshop?" He startled at the name, with which he had but recently become acquainted.

Her eyes flashed with anger, and color rose in her cheek. "If you are reluctant to patronize the premises of a Moor, as you call him, you may of course wait for me outside."

She was beautiful in her wrath, like an avenging goddess of old. Mal decided it was not time to bring up Mr. Thorkelson, his weighty file, his interesting intelligence.

In the course of appraising the estate of a recently deceased scholar, Thorkelsons & Son had been assured that a certain very old and very valuable manuscript, the pride of the scholar's collection, was the only such copy in existence. Mr. Thorkelson asked Mal to consider his surprise, then, when another client of theirs boasted shortly thereafter of having procured the single existing copy of the same work. Tracing this second manuscript had led Mr. Thorkelson to the bookshop of one Mr. Karim, commonly known as the Moor, who revealed that he had been furnished this valuable and unique manuscript by one Miss Amaranthe Illingworth.

Mr. Thorkelson had seen no reason to bring this troubling coincidence to light, since, he said blandly, the only possible consequence could be discomfiture for all parties involved. Mal promised to look into the matter himself.

Which, as someone who interested himself in the law, he was rather obliged to do. At some point, the rare book world being small and the supply of medieval manuscripts even smaller, the duplicate was bound to be discovered by others, and inquiries would be made. Mal wanted to know Amaranthe's role in all this before it came to such a point, so he could protect her.

That realization shocked him so profoundly that, having pulled the curricle into the narrow alley of George Court—

much to the chagrin of the pedestrians using the corridor, many of whom shouted or threw him looks of umbrage—Mal sat frozen for a moment instead of helping Amaranthe down. He'd gone from thinking her a forger to wanting to protect her, all in the matter of an hour or two?

No, he suspected she *was* a forger, but he wanted to protect her nonetheless.

She untied the ribbons of her bonnet, preparing to go inside, and Mal watched greedily as she uncovered her thick, lustrous coils of hair. It had been so long since he'd been fascinated by a woman that he'd forgotten to guard himself against the thought-scattering power of flashing eyes, garden scents rising from silken skin, and bewitching masses of gleaming hair. He speculated on the length of it, guessing that once unpinned that gorgeous hair reached all the way to her—

"Queen's Head Passage," she reminded him as if he were daft, which he was well on his way to becoming.

"How will you get there?" It was a good two miles from her home back to the middle of the City.

"Walk, or take a chair." Her wariness changed to concern. "You do feel confident in hiring servants, yes?"

"I feel confident in having them come to the house so you might interview them," he admitted.

He'd never in his life had servants. The coaching inn where he grew up had employed plenty of boys, all of whom would have beaten Mal to a pulp if he tried to lord it over them. At school he was expected to turn himself out to the satisfaction of the schoolmaster or there was hell to pay in the form of rapped knuckles, a caned backside, or the task of cleaning the privies. Even in his own apartments he saw no need for a valet, though several of his friends, like Viktor, swore they could not live without a manservant.

Mal was an independent creature and had been so from the

awful night his mother died. He looked after himself. But he had no notion how to look after another being.

Witness his carelessness with his own siblings.

"Don't forget to have a bite," she scolded in exasperation. "You haven't eaten a thing since breakfast."

And now Miss Illingworth was looking after him as well. Mal felt an unaccountable glow as he clucked at the horses to walk on, ignoring the porter from the Blue Posts who was once again waving his fist over nobs and their fancy rigs blocking the conduct of honest business.

He hoped she would not turn up a criminal after all. He wouldn't be able to like her half so well as he did.

HER HOUSE WAS QUIET. Amaranthe paused on her threshold to savor the calm. Her small front parlor caught the light, as designed, and she looked with longing at the fabric-draped easel and the covered bowls of paint. Her gold leaf paint would grow crusty and cracked if not applied soon. She would have to settle matters at Hunsdon House as quickly as she could, no matter what Edye and Mrs. Blackthorn had to say. The commission was not large, not for the few touch-ups the owner had requested from this Book of Hours, but she could not afford to lose it.

Amaranthe rested her fingers on the aged vellum of the original book, enjoying the texture of it. She hadn't aged the vellum she was using for her copy, and wouldn't attempt to. It would sell better if it were new and readable. But she had several pages left to copy, and some final color to add to the marginalia after the gilding was done. It couldn't be done in time, nor arranged to be sold soon enough to suit her purpose today.

No, she would have to sell something else. One of the books she had been keeping for her own collection, to display in her bookshop as a sample of her work when the time came. It tore at her heart to part with any of the volumes she had so painstakingly copied and hoarded over the past years. It was like handing over a child.

But she had sold off her treasures before, when she needed the money for the lease on a home for her and Joseph and their household, and she could sell one again if it meant the ducal children would be cared for properly and Joseph could not be accused of gross negligence.

"Óla, senhorita. I did not expect anyone this morning."

Inez appeared in the doorway. Quite a departure from the bedraggled waif who had shown up at her kitchen door the day before, the young woman was washed and tidy in one of Eyde's old gowns, with a neat white apron tied about her waist and a white mob cap covering her wild black curls. A good meal and rest under a safe, solid roof had done her good; her eyes were bright and her smile quick and wide.

"Óla, Inez. Is everything well? Did Joseph leave for Hunsdon House this morning?"

"All's well as can be, though Mr. Illingworth didn't like the broa I baked for him." Inez wrinkled her nose. "A finicky eater, is he?"

"I thought I smelled cornmeal. I'll take a piece or two with me, if there's extra. I think your bread is delicious, and I appreciate you cooking for him on top of everything else."

"If only he appreciated it." Inez sniffed. "I mean to earn my keep, senhorita. You've given me charity enough."

"I'll ask you to stay a few more days, then. It looks like we need some time to set things in order at Hunsdon House."

Inez's dark brown eyes widened. "Is it very grand? Mr. Illingworth wouldn't tell me a word about it."

"It's—" Amaranthe hesitated.

Nothing about Hunsdon House appealed to her as a place

people could feel at home in. The front state rooms, meant for public entertainment, were built and furnished on a grand scale, compounded of so many rich beauties that the eyes could hardly take them all in. The rest of the place, like her bedchamber, struck her as stiff and empty. Only the small parlor where the family had dined together had felt anything close to comfortable.

Being in Hunsdon House was like being on a stage. One was aware every moment of what the station and the grandeur demanded. She was glad she did not have to live there.

"It is grand," Amaranthe allowed. "Are there any apples left in the barrel? I might take one or two with me as well. I have more errands to run, and then I must return to Hunsdon House and speak with Joseph."

"I can have dinner here for him, if he wants it," Inez said. "He needn't go by the cookshop, as he threatened to do."

"I think you needn't take the trouble tonight, as I shall ask him to dinner at Hunsdon House. Take the evening to rest and enjoy yourself."

"I will, at that, and perhaps he'll settle his feathers as well."

Amaranthe watched as Inez flounced from the room, her curiosity stirred. Joseph was customarily the most sweet-tempered of men, so why was he being contrary with Inez?

She had larger concerns at the moment. Her manuscripts were locked in a small cedar cabinet beneath the window seat, beside the cabinet where she locked her tools and paints. Amaranthe drew her fingers over the tight folds of vellum and paper, pressed with heavy boards to keep the pages flat and the edges crisp. It took a moment to decide which volume would be the most ready source of funds, and of most immediate interest to Mr. Karim. She withdrew a stack of folio-sized pages and tucked them carefully into a leather valise.

She was relocking the cabinet, concealing its precious

contents, when Inez reappeared with a small bundle of bread wrapped in a napkin.

"Will you return here tonight to sleep, *senhorita*?"

Amaranthe's mind flitted to the candlelight glowing on the faces of the children last night as they enjoyed a warm, filling dinner, their first in days. She lingered overlong on the memory of Grey's face sculpted by candlelight, the casual queue in his unpowdered hair. The look of amused dismay on his face when she noticed the old duke's collection of bosomy mermaids and other half-clad female figures on the shelves of the study.

The quiet, dark library and its many secrets, including, somewhere, the book she sought.

"I think to be gone at least one more night, but not longer," Amaranthe said.

The other woman smiled shyly. "You look very fine. They dress you there, then?"

"This was left by the duchess, who seems to have departed the country. I am only borrowing it to—ah..."

She had no good reason to be wearing this gown, and Amaranthe glanced self-consciously at the indigo silk. It had begun to feel natural to be dressed so grandly. That would never do, since in a day she'd be back to plain Amaranthe Illingworth, a pigeon, no longer a dove.

And she would no longer attract the attention of men like Grey's friend from the coffeehouse, or see heads turning in the street to regard them as they passed in the curricle. Or the look Grey himself wore when she pranced into the parlor that morning to meet him. She didn't know why that look, or the strange, awakened feeling it gave her, would not leave her mind.

"I find it quite dismaying how much better one is treated when one wears a gown like this," Amaranthe said.

Inez's face darkened with a scowl. "Don't I know that," she muttered, and on that note, Amaranthe left.

CHAPTER TEN

A maranthe hired a chair to take her back through The Strand and Fleet Street, having no desire to cover the duchess's silk skirts with the muck and dirt of London traffic. But she disembarked in Ludgate Street, within sight of the great edifice of St. Paul's, so she might stroll through Ave Marie Lane and admire the imposing Stationer's Hall, home of the Worshipful Company of Stationers, who controlled most of the publishing trade in London.

She was not a member, and not likely to become one, which was just as well. The Stationers controlled copyright for all works registered with them, and while their concern was more for preserving the property and income of modern authors and publishers, her work in reproducing ancient manuscripts fell into an undefined grey area.

Was it not a public service to preserve ancient works of historic value? Look what else might be known, for instance, about the world of her father's Anglo-Saxon forebears if half of their poetry had not burned in the fire at Ashburnham House. She made reproductions so she might have samples of her art to display when it came time to open her antiquarian bookshop, specializing in old and rare volumes. But one could not live on books by eating them. She wondered what Mal and his compatriots in the Middle Temple would have to say about the very, very grey areas into which she was venturing. She hugged her valise close, not entirely out of concern for pickpockets.

Traffic was light on Paternoster Row, as it customarily was save for Magazine Day, when the periodicals were published, or the release of a highly anticipated work. The street had of old belonged to stationers and booksellers, with most of the printers, book binders, and booksellers in London clustered here or nearby.

Amaranthe attracted much attention as the sole woman in evidence, and in such gorgeous dress. She took care to step carefully over the old, uneven cobbles, generally kept clean by the sweep boys. Women were a rarity in the publishing field, though she had heard a Mary Cooper had kept a shop here until recently and had made a success of the business, buying several copyrights in her own name.

She looked fondly into the tall windows letting light into Longman and Rees, one of the most venerable publishing houses in Britain, then picked her way past Dolly's, famous for its beefsteak, and the Chapter Coffee House, frequented by hopeful authors and booksellers taking a break. The many bookshops beckoned her like siren calls, but one was not welcome to amble and browse through the more traditional establishments. Most booksellers still operated as combined printers and publishers, like Mr. Karim, and one was expected to discharge their business and depart, not linger.

A musical chime rang out as she entered under the Sign of the Scroll, and for a moment the quiet, crowded stacks of the bookshop, with dust motes glimmering in the air, called her back to Mr. Finney's in Callington and the treasure Amaranthe had labored long for. Now she was parting with another treasure, one she had labored less over, but which she had considered a stepping stone to her own future. Was Malden Grey worth parting with it?

She thought of young Camilla in her fancy white dress, her exasperation that she was not allowed a tutor, and it was easy to push her doubts away.

"Miss Illingworth. *Salaam alaykum*," Mr. Karim greeted her, emerging from the back room and wiping his hands on a cloth dark with ink.

"*Wa 'alaykum as-salaam*," she replied, and he smiled broadly.

"Your Arabic is improving." His dark eyes flared as he noted the leather bag beneath her arm. "You have something for me?"

She looked around to ensure they were alone, save for his apprentice in the back room. She didn't wish witnesses to this discussion.

She withdrew the vellum pages from the valise carefully, so as not to put them out of order. With reverent hands Mr. Karim spread the first few over the wooden counter, pushing aside a stack of books to make room.

"The *Kitāb Sirr-al-asrâr*," he breathed. "Where did you find this?" He lifted the pages one by one. "Parchment, in fine condition. Gothic script, Latin—twelfth century?" He gave her a quick, sharp look from beneath knitted brows.

"Thirteenth," Amaranthe replied.

"This is astonishing," he muttered, lost in the pages.

Masoud Karim, who had been born in Morocco, had never adopted the dress of his new home but still wore his culture's traditional tunic and pantaloons underneath a caftan. The colorful turban wrapped around his head and the slippers that curled ever so slightly at the toes attracted attention whenever he set foot outside his shop, but he appeared content to be singled out as the Moor, as long as it brought recognition to his bookshop. Quite unusual for the traditions of his birth country and hers, Karim didn't mind doing business with a woman, and Amaranthe had come to rely on him for many of her commissions.

"It is complete. Not just the sections of advice on kingship, which are so often redacted into a mirror for princes. This contains the sections on medicine, astrology, alchemy, magic." His face held the wonder Amaranthe had felt when she first held the parent of this copy in her hands. "The *Book of the Secret of Secrets*. It is all here."

"Aristotle's advice to his young protégé, Alexander, who would go on to establish a great kingdom," Amaranthe confirmed. "An extremely popular medieval work."

She'd chosen it for that purpose. It was marvelous, but not impossible for a well-known ancient work to surface. She'd made a mistake early on in her career, one she didn't mean to replicate. An Oxford don and a mentor of Joseph's, in learning of Amaranthe's skill, had asked her to restore a valuable and unique manuscript he held in his personal collection. She'd made a practice copy first to ensure her restoration was perfect, and he'd been pleased with the result.

Later, when they'd come to London and the existence of Derwa meant they were unwelcome in most lodgings, Amaranthe in desperation had brought the copy to Mr. Karim to see if he could sell it for her. Her reproduction had been so exact he'd thought it dated to the Conquest—a result of the skill she'd acquired from working with Mr. Finney on his replications of the Domesday Book. As the supposed age and uniqueness of the manuscript fetched a much higher selling price, one that made the difference between a small flat above a shop or a shop and rooms of their own, Amaranthe hadn't disabused Mr. Karim of his conclusions.

Tracing the provenance of valuable manuscripts was a

matter of hearsay and luck, but Amaranthe hadn't dared thereafter to peddle a manuscript she knew was unique. If the buyer
of that first manuscript ever discovered he'd paid for a clever
copy, a long explanation would be due, and the result was sure
to require a fine or time in prison.

Or worse.

"The earliest surviving manuscript of the *Kitāb* is a tenth-
century Arabic text," Karim mused. "I have seen many transla-
tions into vernacular tongues, but not many of the Latin manuscripts survive. This is truly remarkable, Miss Illingworth. You
happened upon it combing the bookshops, as you love to do?"

"Mmm." She had found a copy of the revered Latin work
called the *Secretum Secretorum* in one of the Oxford libraries,
managed through Joseph to obtain access, and made a copy
working at night while he was away or asleep, burning their
precious candles and using her own recipe for ink to save coin.
"I acquired this manuscript through—a distant family member.
In Cornwall."

His eyes narrowed, his exuberance faltering. "Ah. That is, I
recall, how you came upon the impeccable *Physiologus* you
brought me some time ago, is it not?"

"Indeed. The same—er, family member. He is a prodigious
collector."

Who thought Reuben would ever prove useful? If Karim
inquired, he would learn Amaranthe did indeed have relations
in Cornwall. Never mind that she wanted nothing to do with
them.

The *Physiologus* had been copied from one of the Oxford
college libraries too. Once one had obtained suitable premises, a
household required candles and fuel and food. The ancient
Christian text had supported them until Mr. Karim, impressed
with her skill, had begun to connect Amaranthe with commissions for work.

"Such a pristine copy," Mr. Karim said. "The parchment looks almost new."

It was new, because she had found a bookmaker in Cheapside who prepared the vellum for her. But Mr. Karim could sell the manuscript for more if he identified it as a thirteenth-century translation, and they both knew that.

"Text is intact," she couldn't help adding.

Mr. Karim studied the manuscript, and Amaranthe quaked in anticipation of further questions. He was an honest businessman; he had to be, for prejudice would turn all too quickly against him for his dark skin and foreign birth. The reign of their good King George III was a more tolerant age than some had been—and a more licentious age, too—but it was not a realm where all men were considered equal. And women were well below men in the hierarchy of being.

"I have a patron who would pay five hundred for this, sight unseen," Karim said. "I shall have to bind it, of course, but I see no reason we could not share the profit. Or I could give you two hundred now?"

Amaranthe's chest compressed. "Pounds?" she choked.

He raised his dark eyebrows. "Guineas."

Slightly more than pounds. Two hundred guineas—that ought to be enough to support the Hunsdon household until the next quarter's income came through. Two hundred guineas could buy a fine horse. It was nearly enough to buy a carriage, something well beyond the reach of a simple tradeswoman.

"I think I will take the two hundred now, if you have it," Amaranthe managed to say.

"Very well. How fortunate for us that you have this family member who so carefully preserves these rare manuscripts." Karim regarded her with fresh surprise. "You are very fine today, if it is not rude in me to remark upon it."

"Borrowed finery." She produced a thin smile. Why had it

not occurred to her that they could sell some of the duchess's abandoned gowns for ready coin? Such a wardrobe would fetch a fair price, though Sybil might quarrel at her possessions being parted from her. Too late now. Mr. Karim darted into the back room, and Amaranthe was left to say a quiet goodbye to her manuscript.

She peeked one last time at her signature in the border of the concluding page. A cluster of long, gaudy purplish blooms of the amaranth plant called love-lies-bleeding. The flowers of amaranths kept their color long after they dried, for which the Greeks had named them 'unfading.' Most species of amaranth were considered pigweeds, true, but the oil was nourishing to the skin, and the seeds were delicious if properly cooked.

A hardy and useful plant. *Just like me*, Amaranthe thought.

Karim returned with a small pouch of coins, but he hesitated before he handed them to her. His eyes fell again on the tidy stack of folio pages.

"May I tell this patron of mine that he is buying a unique copy of the *Sirr al-Asrar*?" he asked.

"You may."

It was, in some respects, not a lie. She had learned to give all her copies slight variations. Sometimes she changed the decorations of initial capitals or the border decorations to more pleasing designs. And it went against the grain to preserve the scribal errors she so often found in medieval copies, when monks or clerics predictably skipped or confused lines after staring too long at marching grids of tiny script. It wasn't in her to duplicate an error when she could correct it.

All her works, equally, bore her signature of the amaranth flowers. They would mark the sign above her door when she was finally able to open her bookshop. All her manuscripts were, in this respect, unique.

The weight of the enormous sum in her palm felt heavy on

her heart. How far these guineas might go toward her dream of opening her own bookshop. How much further she might be along the path to that dream if she had never lost her Book of Hours. The study she could have made from it, the copies, the sales—

Amaranthe forced her mind away. Eyde's safety, and Derwa's, and her own, were more important than a book. The welfare of the Hunsdon children was more important than a book, too.

Karim checked that the folio pages were in their correct order, using the small Roman numeral she'd marked at the top of each page, verso and recto.

"Just think if we came across another surviving copy of the tenth-century Arabic text of the *Sirr al-Asrar*," he said, a new gleam in his eye. "What a find that would be!"

"A find indeed." Amaranthe stowed the money in her inside pocket and wondered how much Mr. Karim suspected of her antics. Copies of French, German, Latin, and Flemish manuscripts were all well and good, but mundane fare for antiquarians. Ancient Arabic manuscripts, now—there would be quite a rage for those, were any to be discovered in secret caches and corners of old crumbling homes, where rare treasures might sometimes be found. Karim had begun teaching her Arabic, after she expressed interest, but she wondered now if he were suggesting she apply these skills for their mutual benefit?

"And I have told you already of a different work also known as the Book of Secrets, the *Kitab al-Asrar* by Muhammad al-Razi," Karim continued. "This one is on the practice *al-kimiya,* what I believe you English call alchemy. But the book is much rarer and harder to find. I was told once that the Duke of Hunsdon had something like it in his library. Your brother is tutor to the young duke, I understand."

Amaranthe nodded, holding his gaze. Joseph had come

across such a book, in passing, and mentioned it to her. If Karim knew about it as well, then the manuscript must indeed be a legend among antiquarians. The one to find it would possess a treasure indeed.

Was the bookseller dropping a broad hint? Or had Amaranthe become so sly that she detected subtle meanings now in everything?

There was no slyness in Malden Grey. He was an open book, as such things went.

"I shall keep a lookout for such a volume," Amaranthe said. "I imagine you'd be delighted to negotiate the sale of it, should the young duke be willing."

Depending on how much damage the duchess and her steward had done to the Hunsdon estates, the young duke might well be reduced to selling off his library to feed himself and his siblings. Amaranthe only had so many manuscripts locked in her cedar chest.

Again that needle pierced her chest. If she had found the Hunsdon book last night, she might be making a very different negotiation today. An honest, aboveboard negotiation. But Grey needed money, and she had arranged for two dozen servants to descend on the house tomorrow, servants who must be paid wages, fed, and supplied with uniforms. She pressed her hand to her pocket. Would she return the two hundred guineas to have her *Book of Secrets* back?

No, because she had a second copy, the first and highly inferior one she'd made as practice, attempting such a large work untutored and all on her own. She could use that in her shop display. Joseph had contributed to the terrible state of things at Hunsdon House, and she felt obliged to exonerate him. Sacrificing her *Secretorum* was not too high a price, just as she had been willing to sacrifice her *Physiologus* to keep a roof over their heads.

Sacrificing her Book of Hours had been a steeper price, but necessary to extract herself from Reuben's clutches. She hoped nightmares dogged his sleep and followed him into everlasting torment.

She was not stealing, Amaranthe told herself as she patted her purse. Oxford was an institution designed for education. And if she made a second copy of books she was commissioned to restore or reproduce, they were intended for her private use, as displays for her eventual bookshop and demonstrations of her skill. If she had now and again been obliged to sell those copies to support her household—well, she could justify the necessity, at least to herself.

The chime above the door jangled, and Mr. Karim stepped away, ending their conversation. Amaranthe turned to see Malden Grey enter the shop. Tall, stern, handsome as a devil, he filled the room.

Her heart fluttered with pleasure. He was an imposing man, not to be overlooked. He was also a dangerous man, though his strength lay leashed and civilized under a gentleman's coat. He looked displeased about something, his jaw set in that way she'd noted when he burst into her house, and the little thrill shifted to alarm.

"Buying books, Miss Illingworth?" he inquired.

Malden Grey, man of the law, would have a very firm opinion of the activities she engaged in with her commissions and her copies. Like her father, he would see black and white, wrong and more wrong.

"In truth, I am buying from her," Mr. Karim answered in a pleasant tone. "Miss Illingworth had the good fortune to come across a Latin version of the *Secretum Secretorum*, what we call in Arabic the *Kitāb Sirr-al-asrâr*, the *Book of the Secret of Secrets*. She has done me the very great honor of transferring it to my hands. Look you, sir, do you not find the workmanship astonishing?"

"Aristotle's advice to young Alexander the Great? And Miss Illingworth in possession of a copy? I am astonished indeed," Mal said.

Amaranthe's belly splashed into her heeled slippers. *He knew.*

They exchanged a long look, and the hair on her arms lifted in warning. He was about to expose her. But he mustn't do it here, in front of the bookseller who provided the larger portion of her income. She stepped forward to urge him toward the door when the chimes rang again and another man entered.

Mal's posture grew taut and alert.

"Grey." The new entrant regarded Mal with surprise. "Didn't expect to see you here."

"Oliver." Mal inclined his head, acknowledging a superior. "My first visit."

The newcomer looked at Mr. Karim. "I've come for my set of lectures, if you have them bound."

"Of course. Only a moment." The bookseller whisked into the backroom.

Amaranthe straightened her elaborate skirts, wondering if she could edge out the door while the newcomer distracted Mal. Except that the two men blocked her exit, the shop made narrow by the closely set shelves of books and book-binding supplies. In the awkward silence the noises from the street outside penetrated: the clop of hooves as a wagon rolled past, the calls and conversations of passersby, and, startling in their clarity, the sonorous bells of St. Paul's as they rang the hour.

"Never seen you with a woman, Grey," the newcomer said, regarding Amaranthe with interest.

She lifted her chin. She'd never been looked at so much in her life as she had this day. Next time Eyde and Mrs. Blackthorn tried to coax her into the duchess's clothes, she'd put a flea in their ear.

"Forgive me," Mal said. "Amaranthe, this is Mr. Stephen Oliver, one of the Benchers of the Middle Temple and by far our favorite reader. Mr. Oliver, this is Miss Amaranthe Illingworth, a—friend to the Duke of Hunsdon."

She wished he hadn't put it that way. It sounded like she was a courtesan. She might as well be, plumed in a duchess's gown without the rank or birth to deserve it.

Oliver flicked a gloved hand in the air. "Favorite reader, my foot. No one comes to the lectures. Having them bound to force something between the students' ears. Nothing but a meal requirement to be called to the bar! And thumb a few books!" He shook his bewigged head. "Law was a serious business in my day." He fixed a stern look upon Mal.

"What topics do your readings specialize in, Mr. Oliver?" Amaranthe asked, since Mal looked at a loss for words.

"Commentary on Blackstone," Mr. Oliver growled. "His compendium's all right, now that it's finally issued, but needs some clarification here and there."

"Yes, I'm familiar with the work." She wasn't lying; she'd seen the volumes spread out on the table in the library of Hunsdon House. "What an excellent ambition, to preserve your knowledge for your students. I find Mr. Karim's work of the highest standard."

The man's gimlet eye focused on her. "Shopping with the Moor, are you? A literary lady?"

No lady at all, Amaranthe thought but did not say. Mr. Karim, bustling through from the back room, saved her from reply. "Here it is, Mr. Oliver! Half calf over paper boards, with gilt stamping. I used the basic Coptic stitch for the binding, though you'll see that—"

"Yes, yes, all in order." Oliver reached for the hefty volume. "Send the invoice to my lodgings, of course."

Mr. Karim's face fell. Clearly he would much rather have coin in hand than send a bill that could be ignored. "Can I interest you in something else? I have copies of Mr. Macpherson's history of Great Britain, the Comte de Mirabeau's essay on despotism, in French, of course, Mr. John Wesley's address to the American colonies—"

"And the *Secretum Secretorum*," Mr. Oliver said in surprise, his gaze falling on the sheets of parchment stacked neatly on the counter. "A fine copy, and a neat hand."

"Miss Illingworth is responsible for that fine hand." Mr. Karim's expression grew animated. "I have promised another patron the right of first refusal, but if you are interested, sir—"

"A copyist?" Mr. Oliver glared at her again, and Amaranthe guessed why students avoided his lectures. "I suppose it don't take much to follow the lines."

"No, it does not." She gave him a bland smile.

"That reminds me." Mr. Karim cleared his throat. "Miss Illingworth, here is that Arabic grammar I promised to loan to you, to go along with the dictionary. Perhaps it will aid in recognizing the *Kitab al-Asrar*, should you happen to come across it."

"*Ashkuraka*," Amaranthe murmured as she took the small book, thanking Mr. Karim in Arabic just to see the look on Oliver's face.

It was, to her surprise, a calculating look, and he turned it quickly on Mal. "A learned lady! Grey, I didn't think you had the wits to attract a woman of intellect."

"Er," Mal said, breaking his uncharacteristic silence. "Indeed?"

"Indeed not. We all had you pegged as a worthless lie-about, living off the duke, and made bets on how soon you'd hare off if a better opportunity presented. Kicking up larks with that Vierling, for instance—it don't look well on you, hanging about with the likes of him."

Oliver scrutinized Amaranthe once more. She hoped her bonnet was not askew and she did not have the dust of the street on her hem.

"But if you were, say, to have a wife to support—you'd look a deal more serious to the Benchers," Oliver said. "A clever woman settles a man, teaches him how to go on. A good wife keeps a man's head clear, if you understand me."

Amaranthe stared at the barrister, keeping her expression neutral. She caught his meaning, all too well, and from the look of gathering thunder on Mal's face, he understood, too.

"I appreciate the hint, Mr. Oliver," Mal said through gritted teeth. "I shall take your remarks under careful consideration."

"See that you do." Oliver adjusted his wig and tucked his book under his arm. "I told the Benchers you were smarter than Froggart, but that one just announced his betrothal, and a man needs an income if he's to support his wife." Oliver glared at Mal once more. "Show us you're serious, and I'll have a good word for you when the next call comes, Grey. Duke's throw or not," he added for good measure, and Mal's face shuttered completely.

"You can't begin to comprehend my gratitude," he ground out.

Oliver tipped his hat to Amaranthe and strolled out the door.

Amaranthe tucked the small Arabic grammar into her valise. If she was not mistaken, Mr. Karim was encouraging her to produce a fake original of the much-coveted advice of Aristotle to Alexander; to her knowledge, Arabic copies of the manuscript had never reached Britain. And he had all but begged her to locate Hunsdon's copy of the even more esoteric chemical treatise likewise known as the *Book of Secrets*.

She would have sworn Mr. Karin was both innocent and above her machinations, but perhaps he was in a position similar to hers. She would sort it out in her mind later. Her more immediate concern was that Mal looked consumed by wrath.

"Married!" he muttered under his breath as he conducted her out the door. A street boy held the reins of the pair hitched to the curricle, and when Mal tossed him a coin, he caught it deftly, bit it to test the metal, and shoved it deep into a dirty pocket.

"Married!" Mal seethed again as he steered them through the noisy, crowded intersection with Cheapside and into the quieter environs of St. Paul's Churchyard.

"Stop, please," Amaranthe murmured as she saw the trio of young girls standing in the shadow of the great church, delivering their singing patter to passersby. "Grey, pause here." She put a hand on his sleeve to get his attention, and the firm warmth of his arm sent a shock from her fingers to her head.

"Oranges! Get yer oranges 'ere!" a young girl bawled near them as Mal slowed the horses. She tilted her basket in their direction and caught Amaranthe's eye. "One for thruppence, two for a kick!"

Amaranthe smiled at her accent. "How many for a dozen?" she leaned over to ask.

The girl's eyes flared wide. She was scarcely older than Derwa, her round, childish cheeks blooming pink under the ties of a loose white cap, her apron thrown over one arm as she balanced the heavy basket against her hips. Costermongers started young and typically began with watercress, herbs, and flowers. This girl was already a seasoned hawker if she were selling fruit.

"Three bob, miss! Lovely, are'em?"

"They look delicious," Amaranthe agreed, probing her pocket. She didn't dare give the girl as much as guinea for fear of exposing her to thieves, but she did have some smaller coins. "What's a Cornish party like yourself doing upcountry, I ask?"

"*Aree fah!*" the girl cried, smiling widely. "Where you to, then?"

"Callington," Amaranthe said, and laid two crowns in the girl's upturned palm. "For you and your family, mind."

"Right proper, miss," the girl breathed, handing over a dozen oranges. Her gaze lit on Grey.

"All right, me 'andsome! Violets for your trouble? Lavender for your strife? You've a maid worth the wooing, I might say." She whistled to two other girls, even younger in age, being spurned by the impatient passersby they tried to interest in their own baskets.

"I'm not his wife." Amaranthe laughed, dispensing pennies to the two younger girls in return for a small, fresh bouquet of violets and lavender and a set of shy thanks. Their sweet, canny faces pinched her heart. She'd been a pampered darling at their age, and only later learned what a woman must do to survive in a trade.

"Hear me now. You're a long way from our fair land, and if you ever need a friend, look you for Miss Illingworth in George Court, just off Rupert Street."

"Get on, you!" The orange girl waved with admiration as Mal urged the horses to walk on. "We won't forget that, miss."

"Your accent comes out when you speak with them," Mal observed as the costermongers returned to their work. "As it does with your servants."

"You can take the cheel from Kernow, but not the Kernowak from the cheel," Amaranthe said, tucking her oranges into her bag. At his puzzled look, she smiled slightly. "Cornish. It's a dying language, I fear."

Mal set their course for Hanover Square. "If I were to marry, and be called to the Bench, I would be able to support a wife to pursue whatever scholarly inclinations she wished." He cast her a sidewise look.

"Don't be daft," Amaranthe said. "Though you'll think I am, when I tell you how much Mr. Karim paid for my *Secretorum*."

"How much?" he asked.

She told him.

"And how did you come by a copy of the Secret of Secrets?"

His profile was as hard as the marbled façade of St. Paul's, and Amaranthe's stomach twisted. He was a man who had chosen the law for his profession. He would not lightly dismiss the skirting of it.

"A previous employer of Joseph's." That was more or less true. "They permitted me to make a copy for my own reference." That was patently untrue. The library would never have allowed the borrowing if they'd known what she was about, and Joseph would have frowned upon her thievery, too.

"And you sold it for our benefit. That is indeed very kind in you." A muscle jumped in his jaw, as if he were grinding his teeth together. "I will, of course, repair your loss at the earliest opportunity. I ought to have bought your produce from the costermongers as well."

"Those were purchases of my own," Amaranthe said coolly. "Derwa adores oranges, and I might use the rinds for any number of things."

"Of course," he said. "But you paid those girls enough to feed themselves and their families for a fortnight. Largesse seems to be a habit of yours."

He was sunk in bitterness, she could see. Perhaps his male pride was offended that she had succeeded in raising money where he had not. Well, it was a very stupid male who didn't acknowledge that his life ran on and because of female labor, beginning with the one who had birthed him.

They rode in silence back to Hunsdon House, with Mal

muttering only under his breath now and again, "Married!" as if the condition were a curse. The bumpy road jostled them together often, his firm leg pressing against her skirts, his hard shoulder and arm occasionally pressing against her side. Amaranthe allowed that she was only human and couldn't help the warmth that shot through her every time their bodies touched.

But she was not the type to take fancies into her head. Malden Grey was not for her, and the sooner she could escape his company, the better for her peace of mind and heart.

CHAPTER ELEVEN

Amaranthe was welcomed back to Hunsdon House as if she were the mistress of it. Mal stopped the carriage before the broad white portico and growled, "Wait!" while he gave the reins to a street boy, circled the vehicle, and held out an arm to help her down. Ralph opened the front door as she reached it.

"Miss Illingworth," he greeted her, his expression eager. Ralph would have to work hard to cultivate the classic sneer of the English butler.

"Is Mr. Illingworth here?" she asked, untying her bonnet.

"The library. Mrs. Blackthorn is preparing a tea tray for the young gentlemen. I can arrange for her to make you up one as well."

Amaranthe handed Ralph her produce and proceeded first to her room, where she would set aside her bonnet and gloves and change into her house slippers. She wanted comfortable shoes while she gave her brother the dressing down he deserved.

Her room. She hauled herself up short. She was already imagining herself conducting staff interviews with Grey. Settling in the girls who would arrive tomorrow from the Benevolence Hospital. Part of her brain was thinking about dinner, and who had the key to the house safe where she might store her guineas, and how much to add to Ralph's wages. As if she were the lady of the house indeed, when none of this was hers and never would be.

Joseph sat at the large table in the library, explaining a passage in Latin to Hugh. He scrambled to his feet as she pushed open the door. The young duke rose with more dignity and delivered a whack on the shoulder to rouse his brother.

Ned looked up with a cheerful, "Hullo, Miss Amaranthe!" Hugh smacked him again, reminding his brother that a gentleman stood in a lady's presence.

"Anth?" Joseph's voice was full of surprise. "What are you doing so splendid? I didn't recognize you! Wasn't sure you'd come back here or go home."

"You and I must have a chat. Can your charges give us a moment?"

"Of course. Lord Edward, continue your translation of Cicero, and show me a clean copy if you please. Hunsdon, finish this chapter and give me an account of the history of Patagonia, the customs of the natives, and Bryon's experience—oh, never mind, here's tea."

Davey set the tray on a delicate cherrywood table while Derwa scampered over to show Amaranthe the violets she'd tucked into her hair. "Millie's desperately bored," she confided. "She's been teasing all day about when you'd return." Derwa rolled her eyes as if she were the other girl's senior and had the charge of her.

"We must call her Lady Camilla," Amaranthe said. "Did you arrange the flowers? They're lovely."

A posy of the costermongers' violets and lavender graced the tea tray, along with orange slices. Joseph snatched a handful and ate them while Amaranthe poured tea, dispensed seed cakes, and sent the boys off to a corner of the room. Then she turned to her brother with a stern expression, and his look of enjoyment changed to chagrin.

"What did I do?"

"That." She pointed to Hugh and Ned relaxed near the standing globe, eating their cakes with the speed and intensity of growing boys. "Them." Her throat closed, and she swallowed hard to clear it. "Joseph, those boys were going hungry beneath your very nose. When they came to our house, they hadn't had a proper meal in *days*. How could you not notice?"

She put her hands over her face and sank into a chair at the side of the room, one of the few not mounded with books. Goodness, she was teasy today. Her emotions were in a lather, and her brother's earnest, abashed face made every raw nerve rise to the surface.

"Gor, old girl, don't cry! I'm sorry, truly I am. I don't know how I managed to be so bacon-brained. Days, you say?" Joseph looked appalled.

Amaranthe pressed her fingers to her cheekbones to stop the tears. "A week at least. Ralph was buying them meals from the cookshop, but he ran out of money. He needs to be paid." She sniffled and looked up at her brother with watery surprise. "Didn't you notice you weren't receiving your stipend? Didn't you notice the duchess had disappeared? Along with many of the things in the hall and front rooms, and most of the servants?"

"Er." He fidgeted with the pile of books on the small table. "You know I'm not very good with those sorts of things. When I'm here, my mind's on the boys, and when I'm not...well, I've had other things to think of, you see."

Amaranthe shook her head with a sigh. "What's her name this time?"

Joseph sat in a chair across from her and placed a hand over his heart. "Susannah. Susannah Pettigrew."

His face softened with wonder, and Amaranthe's heart thumped. She was not jealous of her brother's affections. She was not one of those deprived women who put all her stock in the male nearest her and doted on him beyond reason. She adored her brother, but he had his flaws, like any human. Only there was something in his face this time that made her feel a touch sad and wistful.

She had never inspired that look of wondrous rapture in a man, and never would. Her one proposition had come from Reuben, who made his horrible suggestion about an *arrangement* if she continued to live under his roof.

She was too dedicated to her work to be available for courting, even if a man wanted to court her. She was self-sufficient and liked being so, even if, once in a while, she saw a couple pass in the street or heard banns announced in church and thought how nice it must be to have a companion. An object for one's affections, and a steady anchor in an unsteady world.

But she had Eyde and Mrs. Blackthorn to talk to, and the girls they sheltered now and again to save them from begging in the streets. In time she expected Joseph would find a proper young girl to marry and she would have a sister. Only he seemed to be going about it in just the opposite way he ought, and choosing girls who were outrageously inappropriate and unattainable, wringing his heart, and Amaranthe's, in the process.

"Joseph," she said. "Not again."

"No, it's different this time." He munched on a slice of cake. "*She's* different."

Amaranthe sipped the tea she'd poured herself. Tea, with an abundance of sugar, a guilty pleasure. And twice in one day. It was seductive to live so grandly, and the luxury undermined her ire. "Tell me about her, then."

Joseph raised his eyes to the heavens with a look of rapture on his face. The ceiling of the library, fortunately, had not given in to the kinds of murals that decorated the ceilings of the state rooms with the doings of lumpy-looking mythical beings awash in clouds. "The face of a flower."

"Of course," Amaranthe murmured.

"The voice of an angel."

"Naturally."

"Her grace—her form—she is the essence of sweetness. Pure grace."

Amaranthe nodded. "They always are."

"Anth! Attend! She is *different*."

"Oh? She is not dainty, like a little porcelain figure you can move about?"

He frowned. "No, she's quite dainty, very small."

"Not blonde, then."

"Hair as golden as ripe wheat under the sun."

"Then her eyes are not blue."

He shook his head. "Blue as cornflower. As a summer sky."

"So her family is rich this time."

"Not in the least, but—"

"And her family doesn't have high hopes for her, and aren't holding out for a title, or at least a gentleman with a fortune, who doesn't have to work for a living?"

Joseph looked down at his boots. "I could support a wife on what our parents left us. If we lived very modestly. In the country. And if I took in teaching, here and there."

Amaranthe's exasperation ebbed as she looked at him. She glanced toward the boys across the room, slowing down on the cake to enjoy their tea while talking earnestly to each other, and her heart turned over again. She and Joseph had felt nothing lacking in their childhood. Raised by the kindest of parents, they had never known excess, but there had always been enough.

She knew now that was because her parents had carefully conserved her father's inheritance from his father the baronet, money he had been granted from the estate before it went to her uncle, Reuben's father. That was the reason Reuben had felt comfortable stealing Amaranthe's allowance from her when she came to live with him; he'd felt it was due him anyway.

Joseph had managed his way through university on his small allowance and had worked every day since to support himself. He'd never known, never would know, the kind of luxury and security that surrounded the great. He worked hard for everything he gained, and all he wanted was someone to share it and his life with.

Though the Delaval boys hadn't known security, either, Amaranthe had to admit. Neither their name nor their great house had kept them from staring hunger in the face. Perhaps her brother could be forgiven his absent-mindedness. She hoped Malden Grey would turn up the forgiving sort.

"She'll have to take you in the boots you stand in, do you get turned off here," Amaranthe said in a quiet voice. "It will be hard to find another position if Mr. Grey doesn't give you a character."

Joseph looked stunned. "Has he talked of turning me off? I haven't approached Susannah's parents yet. They're Quakers, and they live in Gloucestershire. I'd like to present myself in person and ask for her hand."

"Is that what Susannah wants? Miss Pettigrew, I mean."

Amaranthe shook off another twinge to her heart. Joseph hadn't told her before now about the woman he'd decided to marry. He'd not even brought her to the house so Amaranthe could meet her. How had she managed to make herself so unavailable to her own brother—who lived with her—about a decision that would impact his entire life?

"I only asked her yesterday, and she said yes." He leaned forward, placing a hand on the arm of her chair. Joseph wasn't affectionate; their parents hadn't been, either. Amaranthe still startled when anyone touched her.

Like the several times Malden Grey had taken her hand to help her in and out of the high carriage. The way his thigh brushed her skirts when the vehicle turned a sharp corner.

The way he'd taken her arm to escort her out of Mr. Karim's bookshop. She still felt the imprint of his heat, as if he'd branded her.

She was being a wet goose, and none of this had to do with the current situation. She focused on what her brother was saying.

"—since I only decided last night, and I didn't want to bring her to see you until I was certain. I..." He trailed off and patted the arm of the chair awkwardly, as if attempting to console her.

She stiffened. "You feared I'd disapprove?"

"Er, well, I shouldn't have liked for you to grow attached to someone who meant to throw me over, like all the other times." He gave her the crooked smile that never failed to melt her heart. "I can stand my own heart cast on a thorn bush, but not yours. I know you've steel in your backbone, old girl, but I wanted to have firm plans before I uproot you."

Amaranthe fumbled for her handkerchief and had it in hand before his meaning dawned. "Uproot me?"

"Of course, you'll make your home with us and show Susannah how to go on. And when the children come, we'll need all hands on deck. Susannah wants a rather large brood." For a moment he looked nonplussed, and Amaranthe took the opportunity to tamp down her irritation.

"I might decide to keep my own premises, you know."

"Live alone? Without a companion or chaperone? Not to be thought of."

"Lots of women do, Joseph."

"Not gentlewomen, and not my sister," he said, frowning.

"Besides, you'll love Susannah as much as I do. We'll find a nice little cottage somewhere, and I'll—" His face went wooden, and he bolted to his feet. "Grey."

Amaranthe sensed when he entered the room, though her back was to the library door. Strange how another person could change the very atmosphere; she'd never noticed that before. Perhaps it was his scent she'd picked up on, something dark and smoky, like old papers that had acquired the odor of tobacco. And beneath that something sharp and darker yet, as pungent and striking as the oak gall in her ink, a scent she associated with absolute pleasure and freedom.

She rose and faced him. The most ridiculous sensation suffused her at the sight of him, tall, big, Malden. "You're in time for tea."

"I'd say I'm too late. The boys haven't left a crumb." His gaze raked her, the gleam in his pale blue eyes turning sharp. "What's upset you?"

"Nothing of import. Joseph and I were simply discussing his —situation. And how we might help you."

She was surprised he'd noticed her distress. Joseph only noticed her emotions when they smacked him across the face. Malden Grey seemed unusually attuned to the feelings of those around him, understanding more than their words. It was disconcerting, to say the least.

Or perhaps he was watching her for signs of wrongdoing. She couldn't shake the fear that struck her in the bookshop, that he knew she was a liar and a thief. She *felt* his awareness of her, if such a thing were possible.

"Mr. Grey." Joseph's tone was cool. Her brother didn't like the other man, and Amaranthe wondered why. "I have no excuse and no explanation for the appalling situation that was unfolding, it seems, beneath my very nose. If you demand my resignation, I'm willing to give it."

"Resignation? By no means." Grey's eyes widened in alarm. "You'd put me to the fuss of having to hire another tutor, on top of everything else. I think not."

Joseph exhaled in relief. "Thank you—sir."

Ah. Amaranthe guessed the rub. Joseph knew of Grey's parentage. He would show superficial courtesy to Malden Grey, as the children's guardian and now the employer in charge of his salary. But he didn't see the other man as worthy of his respect.

She couldn't account for that attitude. Their father the rector had been the most tolerant of Christians, a man who felt God's love embraced everyone, sinners and non-believers alike. But Joseph borrowed more from Reuben's hierarchy of social caste and worth, which deemed a man of irregular birth inferior, no matter how high-born his sire.

Amaranthe felt indignant on Grey's behalf. It wasn't his fault he was born on the wrong side of the blanket, and it wasn't fair to punish natural children for their circumstances. Grey was already denied the inheritance that would have otherwise gone to him, and who knows what other obstacles his bastardy had put in his path.

Recalling the dismissive words of the Bencher they'd met in the bookshop, and Grey's stunned reaction to the man, she could guess why the dilemma of the Delaval children had escaped his notice for so long. Grey had been pouring everything he had into his studies and his ambitions to become a barrister, only to find out that what barred his advancement— again—had nothing to do with his efforts and everything to do with his circumstances.

"You can't sack Mr. Joseph!" Ned brought the last of his slice of cake with him as he barreled across the room. "He lets us read travel stories as part of our geography lessons."

"Indeed, Grey, we must retain him," the young duke chimed

in. "His grasp of Latin declensions is so much better than our last tutor's."

Amaranthe smiled to herself. So that was why Joseph asked her to drill him on Latin cases and had been heard muttering word endings to himself as he exited the house on his way to lessons. Would Susannah Pettigrew be able to help him in his work?

Oh, unfair. Miss Pettigrew's appeal was obviously based on factors which had nothing to do with her grasp of Latin. Whereas Amaranthe, who could not politely be called anything but plain, had learned to rely on her intellect. But men like Joseph—men like Grey—noticed women for their more outward charms. Prized them for it, in fact.

She picked uneasily at a ruffle on her billowing skirt. When had she decided she wished to interest Malden Grey? That way lay thorny paths and dragons.

Keep to the straight and narrow, old girl.

"I've no intentions of sacking Mr. Illingworth," Grey told the boys. "Unless he doesn't set you directly back to lessons and give you something useful to do. Did you devour *all* the cakes, you ravening beasts?"

"Miss Illingworth!" Camilla charged in the door and ran straight to Amaranthe, slipping her tiny hand in hers. The contact surprised Amaranthe, and she cautiously curled her fingers around the girl's.

"Mr. Illingworth." Camilla gave Joseph a polite curtsy and regarded him with wide eyes. "How was the Quaker meeting? Did you bring me any more pamphlets?"

Joseph coughed. "I've no literature, I'm afraid, Lady Camilla, and perhaps we might discuss the Quaker meeting at some other time. It was quite, quite different from our Anglican tradition."

Camilla gave Amaranthe an adoring look. "I'm ready to begin our lessons. Oh, hullo, Grey."

"Thank you for acknowledging me, Millie," Grey said. "It appears we all want Miss Illingworth. I've a letter for her that was brought to our door." He met her eyes as he handed her a folded sheet with an address scribbled across the front. "A boy brought it just now. The woman at your house sent him over with it."

Amaranthe stared at the address, too stunned to speak. Joseph looked over her shoulder and read the name that froze her, his astonishment equal to her own.

"Penwellen! We've not heard from Cousin Reuben in an eon. I wonder what he wants?"

"How did he find us?" Amaranthe whispered, her lips as numb as her fingers.

"I imagine our solicitor would have told him anytime he asked," Joseph said, puzzled. "He had to handle the transfer of my funds when I came of age, you know, and he'll have to do the same for you again next year when you turn five and twenty."

That had never occurred to her, that the solicitor who handled the trust from their parents would have contact with Reuben and could tell him where they were. She wasn't safe, and never had been.

Reuben knew where she lived. He could find her at any moment. He could show up at her house, at her sweet and quiet home, and make his obscene demands, insist that—

No. She reached for sense. She had Joseph to protect her, and servants about. Reuben couldn't hurt her, not anymore. He had already done the worst thing, which was steal her manuscript. But her flesh crawled nonetheless at the thought of his heavy hand upon her in the stables of Penwellen, and despite the application of common sense, her heart darted in her chest like a frightened hare bolting for its den.

"Miss Illingworth. I gather you do not anticipate good news in that letter." Grey stood before her, holding out a steaming cup of tea. His gaze moved over her face, reading her again.

She stuffed the letter into her pocket and took the tea. Her hands trembled.

"It's from our cousin, the baronet," Joseph said. "He has little to do with us."

"Sir Reuben Illingworth. I've not heard of him." Grey regarded Joseph with the same perceptive look that made Amaranthe shy from him.

"A baronet," the young duke said. "How did he gain his title, if I might ask?"

"An Illingworth stood for the Royalists during the Civil War and was granted the baronetcy by Charles II for his service," Joseph said. "Cornwall was the scene of much fighting between the Royalists and the Roundheads. We ought to study the history. I'm afraid that since then the Illingworths have done little to distinguish themselves."

"The Hunsdon title goes back to the time of Queen Elizabeth," the young duke said. "Hugh Delaval was one of her favorites, they say, so she made him a lord."

"He was one of Henry VIII's bastards, and the queen made him a baron so he had to come to court where she could keep an eye on him," Grey said, his tone deceptively mild. "It was the first George who made your great-grandfather a duke."

"I know that." Young Hugh's cheeks turned faintly red.

A brief silence followed this. The dukes of Hunsdon did not seem very long-lived nor prolific, Amaranthe thought. And the knowledge had to grate on Grey that, while a royal bastard could be granted titles, men like him could elevate themselves only through great virtue or great luck.

"If his cousin is a baronet, then Mr. Joseph is not so far below us as you said, Hugh," Camilla remarked.

"Yes, you'll need to take back a few of your petty remarks, won't you, Huey?" Ned grinned.

His elder brother flushed a bright red. "I am sure I could have said nothing derogatory about Mr. Illingworth. You must have mistaken me."

"Yes, mistaken you for someone who isn't a complete prat," Ned exclaimed. "Miss Illingworth, while you're here, I want your help deciphering a curious manuscript I found."

"I want her!" Camilla demanded. She darted to the table and withdrew *The Pythagorean Diet of Vegetables Only*. "The translator keeps popping off Greek phrases, and I'm sorry, Mr. Illingworth, but you admitted you're rubbish at Greek."

"I don't read it near as well as my sister does, very true," Joseph said.

"Children, far be it from me to pull rank on you," Grey interposed, "but I need to speak with Miss Amaranthe about the household accounts, and—"

The rest of his words were lost to Amaranthe's ears as Ned moved to one of the built-in bookshelves and bent to rummage through a drawer at its base. He hauled out a quarto-sized volume upon which Amaranthe recognized at once the worm-eaten edges of sheep leather. A strange gilt stamp looked up at her from the cover when Ned thunked it on the table. There had to be hundreds of pages crammed inside the bulging volume, and from the look of the spine, it had been torn apart and rebound, not carefully and not well.

Blood pounded in her ears, and she heard nothing of the conversation around her as she moved to the table, drawn by instinct. What Ned had discovered among the old duke's cache of medically inclined and medically adjacent texts was either worthless or very, very valuable. Of incalculable worth, she guessed.

She wiped her fingertips on her gown before gingerly lifting the cover to look at the title page, plain and unadorned, covered in faded brown scrawls.

It wasn't the *Book of Secrets* Mr. Karim had heard rumors that the old duke held. It was something incomparably better.

It was the ticket, potentially, into the future she had dreamed of and worked toward for years.

She looked up, her ears still clogged with the rush of thoughts, to find everyone watching her. The children were curious, Joseph surprised, and Grey stood transfixed. He watched her closely, and Amaranthe felt as she had when she was small and Joseph dared her to walk out onto the surface of the small pond behind the village church that froze perhaps once a winter. The smooth cold ice, laced with crystals, only looked solid, and at any moment the fragile surface might splinter and a trespasser find herself tumbling into the freezing cold below.

Incomprehensibly, unlooked-for, the thing she most desired had just been handed to her. And in plain sight of Malden Grey. This book held the key to her livelihood, and now, with those cool blue eyes watching her far too closely, she couldn't do a thing about it.

CHAPTER TWELVE

By the end of the week, Amaranthe had a far deeper understanding of how the grand lived than she'd ever thought to have. She had also, once or twice, spared a forgiving thought for Sybil, the Duchess of Hunsdon, for running away to France instead of staying to rule her tiny empire in Britain.

Hunsdon House was a headache in itself, but it was only one part of the ducal holdings. There were estates in Hertfordshire and Kent, a small farm in the Scottish Lowlands, and a crumbling castle in Wales, as well as a manor in Ireland that was leased to tenants. In addition to the land holdings, which were the steward's domain, there were assorted financial investments and other interests which Grey had said were handled by the firm of Thorkelson, Thorkelson, and Son. He'd had dealings with the Thorkelsons once or twice over the week, and unless she was imagining it, he always seemed to spend long periods staring at her after he returned from these ventures.

She hadn't had an opportunity to ask him why. Her days were taken up with hiring and training staff and answering a thousand questions that were brought to her as the de facto lady of the house. She was fortunate there had only been a few bumps. The girls from the Benevolence Hospital had turned out to be gems, ready to work and quick to learn, and many of them already had a good rapport. Giggles, bright chatter, and snatches of song filled the house as they went about their tasks.

Grey's efforts with the hiring agency had proved a complete disaster, and Amaranthe had stepped in to bail him out when one after another the most unfit applicants were sent to them. Either the operator of the agency did not think the Duke of Hunsdon was a worthy enough client, or there was some malice afoot toward Grey.

The butler applicant had been an aged sot who attempted to pilfer a silver serving set when given a tour of the premises. The housekeeper applicants had both looked down their nose at Amaranthe for being no higher than a rector's daughter, and after the third applicant spoke sternly to Lady Camilla when she caught her in the library with the boys, Amaranthe had informed the agency that they might stop sending candidates for that position.

The row Mrs. Blackthorn had with the French cook had been heard to the rafters of the nursery at the top of the house, and Mrs. Blackthorn was the most forbearing of souls. Amaranthe, descending to the kitchen to intervene, heard the Frenchman suggesting the color of Mrs. Blackthorn's skin made it impossible that she could possess any real culinary knowledge beyond folk remedies and plain fare. Amaranthe couldn't eject him from the house fast enough. She sent a few stern words to the agency operator informing them they no longer required the agency's services and would not be recommending them to any of their acquaintances.

Which left them having to make do as they could. Ralph stepped in as butler, with Davey training as footman, his pride straining the buttons on his liveried chest. Eyde was serving as housekeeper until someone could be found, but she also insisted on acting as Amaranthe's personal maid, a confusion Amaranthe knew would never hold in a properly run household.

As for a cook, Mrs. Blackthorn went to market one day and came back with a friend, a formerly enslaved woman made free but also homeless by the death of the man who presumed to own her. Amaranthe had never heard so much laughter drifting up from the kitchens and other offices below, and while at least once a day reports of some culinary disaster reached her ears, the food that reached the table was as fine as Amaranthe had ever tasted. If only the new cook could learn a few French dishes, the young Duke of Hunsdon need have no fear of displeasing any who dined at his table.

Amaranthe finished her entries in the housekeeper's ledger and gave the ink an extra moment to dry. As she set the account book aside, her eyes drifted, as they did dozens of times a day, to the leather-bound volume on a delicate occasional table beside her. Hunsdon House had provided her a study of sorts in the small parlor that had clearly been the duchess's domain, as evidenced by the full-scale indulgence in *chinoserie*. Red dragons crawled down the hand-painted wallpaper, a lacquered screen painted with Chinese landscapes decorated one corner, and everything from the carvings on the furniture to the ormulu clock showed motifs inspired by the Far East. The profusion put Amaranthe in mind of the illuminations in the most priceless medieval manuscripts, and she took a bit of comfort in it.

The problem was the time spent in the duchess's study was time not spent in her own workroom. Her client expected his manuscript soon, and she needed to hurry if she planned to complete her personal copy along with the refurbishing she'd been hired to do. By this time the gold leaf paint she'd mixed a week earlier would be nothing but a hard cake, and she still had red headings to ink in several places. But every time she thought to sneak away from Hunsdon House to her own abode, some new problem cropped up that needed her attention.

In addition, Grey had come to expect that she would take dinner with him and the children. He had extended the invitation to Joseph as well, with the result that the daughter and son of an obscure Cornish rector mingled freely at the table of a British duke. Her father would have been tickled by the idea and would have behaved his same self whether in a tin miner's cottage or a nobleman's manor, but her sweet mother would have been overjoyed by the luxury.

Her fingers tingled at the prospect of a moment alone, and Amaranthe abandoned the urge to resist. She pulled the fat miscellany onto her desk and opened it to the silk ribbon used as a bookmark. What Ned had produced for her from the duke's collection was no less than astonishing.

Decades, if not a century old, the manuscript was the repository of years of research that some unknown scholar had done on the most obscure and arcane reaches of medicine, alchemy, astrology, and herbal remedies. Al-Razi's *Book of Secrets* was quoted at length, as was the *Secretum Secretorum* with which she was already familiar. But there was more buried in these depths, dug from traditions spanning the Arabic sages and classical antiquity to the most bizarre folk remedies from the fringes of Europe and the secret, arcane lore of Renaissance alchemists like Paracelsus.

She knew nothing of the note-taker save that he referred to himself as Theocratus. She'd asked Mr. Karim in passing what such a volume might be worth, and while such things were always dependent on the buyer, he'd thought such a find could fetch up to a thousand guineas.

A thousand guineas. Amaranthe sat back in her chair at the very thought of it. With a thousand guineas she could set out her own sign and advertise as a copyist and a respectable maker and seller of antiquarian books. She could turn her parlor into the bookshop she'd dreamed of when she leased the place. She could be known as a reputable collector and scholar. She could build a library to rival Sir Robert Cotton's, to her everlasting fame.

She could stop duplicating ancient manuscripts. She would descend to no wrongdoing or legerdemain as Amaranthe Illingworth, Antiquarian. She would make copies purely for her own private enjoyment. She would be dedicated to the preservation of knowledge and ancient culture as a public good.

And she would pray her past dealings never came to light.

A swish of fabric made her look up, and Amaranthe was astonished to find she was not alone. On the Chinese ottoman near the fireplace—the study, in an unheard-of luxury, had its own fireplace—Camilla and Derwa sat side by side, completely absorbed in their books.

Camilla, sitting tailor-style with her knees folded, held a Greek-English dictionary while the Pythagoreans lay open on her lap. Her eyes darted back and forth from book to book as she read. Derwa, her wild hair stuffed under a cap, her legs swinging, paged through the copy of *The Universal Penman* that Amaranthe had borrowed from the ducal library, whispering the letters to herself.

Amaranthe let loose a gurgle of laughter. "How long have you two been here?"

"Oh, good, you're done." Camilla squirmed out of her seat and ran to Amaranthe's side. "I don't understand this word." She pointed to the Greek letters. "*Mathēme*."

"It means learning or study, exactly what you are doing," Amaranthe answered. "And what have you learned?"

Camilla shut her book with a delicate snap. "The Pythagoreans believed that the soul was enclosed in the body of a living thing as punishment for doings in a former life, and only by purity and austerity in this life could the soul be freed to rejoin its essence," she said. "Which, and I'm not sure of the translation, is either the stars, or the gods."

"You're making remarkable progress," Amaranthe marveled, and the girl gave her a reproachful look.

"I wish you didn't have to leave us, Miss Amaranthe. Who else in this house can translate ancient Greek?"

Amaranthe decided the best response to this remark was avoidance. "Derwa? What have you got there?"

Derwa thumped her book shut with a guilty look, and jumped when her mother stuck her head around the half-open door.

"*Areah!*" Eyde cried. "It's here ee be! They're never fussing you, miss?"

"They were as quiet as mice," Amaranthe said. "Quieter, in fact." She looked encouragingly at the youngest girl. "Derwa was just telling us what she is reading."

Taking a deep breath, holding her hands behind her exactly like a pupil in dame school, Derwa stood and recited her ABCs in a swift, jumbled rush.

This performance was met by a look of horror from her mother. "A waste of time, that!" Eyde cried. "When will you ever need your letters, cheel?"

"Nay, I think it past time she learned her letters and her figures, too," Amaranthe protested. "In truth it's far past time I taught you as well, Eyde. We ought to set aside time each day to learn together." She felt a stab of guilt that she'd not done so earlier. She'd let her own concerns and her own work take precedence.

"I've never needed all it afore," Eyde said, astonished.

"But think what you could do," Amaranthe answered. "Be a housekeeper in truth in a house like this. Start your own shop.

Be dresser to a great lady," she hinted, for she knew well of Eyde's greatest, if secret ambition.

With regret, Amaranthe laid the leather book aside. She'd scarce had time to read parts of it, much less imagine what she might do with the contents. Soon. Soon Hunsdon House would be running smoothly, and she would withdraw to her own small house.

Leaving the children. And Grey.

Eyde stood dazzled a moment as if dreams danced before her eyes, but then shook her head to clear it. "It's past time to dress you, mum, and Lady Camilla be needed above. You, me pisky," she addressed her daughter, "down you go to help Mrs. Blackthorn and Mrs. Wheatley with the denner."

"Dreckly," Derwa drawled, and dropped a quick curtsey before she scooted out the door, leaping ahead of the playful swat aimed at her bottom and taking the *Penman* with her.

"Now to get you stripped up fitty," Eyde pronounced, shooing Amaranthe out the door and toward the duchess's chamber, which had been taken over as Amaranthe's dressing room.

Her compunction had lessened only slightly at rifling through Sybil's belongings for purposes of her own adornment. The week had been a valuable lesson in how much differently a woman was perceived, and respected, when she turned herself out fine. Plain Amaranthe Illingworth would be run down by a horse in the street, but Amaranthe Illingworth in a sack gown of figured silk or a robe of embroidered brocade could stop traffic.

More rewarding yet was the momentary stupefaction on Malden Grey's face each time he saw her turned out in a new ensemble. Tonight was possibly her last at Hunsdon House, now that she had the household accounts straightened and the staff in place. Tonight was the last opportunity to make the request she'd been trying for days to frame, and she would add every weapon to her arsenal that she could.

Thus she didn't protest when Eyde laid out the most elegant gown yet, a *robe d'anglaise* of ice-blue silk the color of Malden Grey's eyes. The open skirt, folded back by golden tassels, revealed a front panel of goldenrod silk that matched the yellow cuffs on the three-quarter length sleeves. The *decolletage* of the gown dropped nearly to her nipples, but Eyde plucked out every scarf and neckerchief Amaranthe tried to place over her bosom.

A golden tassel wrapped around her waist accentuated the enormous false rump that plumped the skirt and train behind her, creating the *retroussé* effect that was the peak of current fashion. Elbow-length white gloves and a circlet of the duchess's pearls at her throat were all the embellishments needed to make the costume complete.

Amaranthe didn't have the leisure or patience to submit to the kind of hair dressing such a gown required, which would include hours of brushing to arrange her own hair over the pads and frames, then another hour to powder the whole. Instead she let Eyde affix one of the duchess's old wigs, a cloud of delicate white that soared around her face and left a fringe of curls over her neck. Eyde plumped up a discarded ostrich feather for a headdress, and when she turned to face the mirror, Amaranthe didn't recognize herself.

She looked grand. She looked alluring.

She looked like a woman a man would not forget nor easily let go of when she tried to bow out of his life.

The notion surprised her, and she fussed with the buttons on her gloves to hide a sudden blush as Eyde rifled through the duchess's dressing table. Did she want Malden Grey to pursue her? The idea was absurd. She wanted him to let her take the book of Theocratus home with her, and she wanted him to ask no further questions about her use of it.

She wanted him to invite her to dine with him and the children, now and again. She wanted a chance, just one more, to ride in a carriage with him and have his leg press alongside hers.

She wanted him to wish to kiss her. And she wished to kiss him back.

The idea made her blush so fiercely that Eyde put the small pot of rouge back where she found it. "No color needed on your cheeks, mum!" she exclaimed. "But perhaps a bit of paint for your lips?"

"No paint, Eyde, it will feel too strange. I already seem very unlike myself."

Eyde stood next to her, admiring her creation in the long cheval glass. "A duchess dresses like this every day," she noted.

"The odds of me becoming a duchess are the same as me stumbling across the lost books of the Sibylline oracle," Amaranthe said. "Shall I go down?"

"You may go down, but I daresay that Mr. Grey will be up at the very sight of you," Eyde remarked.

"Whist!" Amaranthe hissed at her, and Eyde laughed as Amaranthe flounced from the room, ears burning.

"Gor, look at you, old girl!" Joseph exclaimed when Amaranthe entered the parlor where the family was assembling. It was one of the formal state rooms, an elegant and, to Amaranthe's eyes, rather forbidding display of wealth and taste.

The prevailing colors of blue and gold, an exact match of her dress, confirmed her suspicion that these were Sybil's favorite hues. In pride of place above the mantel hung an enormous oil painting of the duchess, and the expression that the artist had captured on the face of his subject, who met every requirement of classic English beauty, confirmed Amaranthe's suspicions that the previous lady of the house cared for nothing but her own comfort.

"Could get used to this," Joseph remarked, sprawling on a settee which did not look sturdy enough to support him. "The fine rooms. The fine food. Someone to tidy up and do for you in everything."

"You've never tidied a thing at home." Amaranthe spoke freely, since they were alone in the room. "And Inez is there to see to you while I'm here."

Joseph scowled. "That harpy? She's rather a punishment than a help. I thought you installed her to badger me, to be truthful."

"Inez is the sweetest of women. I can't imagine what you did to make her so cross with you," Amaranthe answered. Her head itched beneath the enormous wig, and she now understood why ladies carried a head scratcher about with the rest of their accessories. It was a requirement when wearing these things.

"You'll give her the boot when you go home tomorrow, won't you?" Joseph asked. "After our fête tonight to celebrate Amaranthe rescuing souls and setting all things in order, per the usual."

"Inez will need to stay on at the house should I decide to visit Favella," Amaranthe said. She turned away to admire a porcelain vase, not sure she could control her expression.

Joseph had heard a very scrubbed story, long ago, to explain why she and Eyde showed up on his doorstep at Oxford six years before, begging his help to find lodgings for a homeless sister and her pregnant maid. Once he had seen the benefit of having women to put food on the table and see to his clothes and housekeeping, Joseph adjusted easily to the arrangement, as he had settled readily into London after graduation. Very often Amaranthe wondered why she, the younger and the female, so often felt in charge of her brother.

"So you've decided to run do her bidding, have you? She sends a letter, and you go?"

"This will be her first child, long-awaited," Amaranthe answered. "She asked quite prettily that I be there with her, though I don't know why she would want me."

Perhaps it was a trick of Reuben's to lure Amaranthe back under his roof. Did he have something revolting in mind? While she felt a certain polite fondness for Favella, the only real reason to return to Penwellen would be to find her manuscript. Demand that Reuben return her Book of Hours, and then never trouble her again.

"A free nursemaid and housekeeper," Joseph remarked. "Of course she wants you."

"I don't intend to stay long, but it seems unkind to leave her all on her own. After all, this child will be a relation of ours. We have some duty to look after it and her." Amaranthe moved to examine a display of intricate music boxes on a lacquered table. "Though I have a manuscript to deliver by next week, and I'll need to secure a new commission if we're to continue with a roof over our heads."

"Won't miss this roof?" Her brother pointed to the fresco on the ceiling, grinning. The scene of frolicking gods and cupids exposed a great deal of shapely human forms, both male and female.

"In truth? No," Amaranthe answered. "It's far too much for the likes of us. Please tell me Miss Pettigrew's expectations are more modest."

His face fell. "I won't be able to offer Susannah a hut under a hedge. Thought I was plump in the pocket when you managed to make Grey pay my salary at last, but a new coat will set me back three times that, and I daren't call on Susannah in the same old plowman's jacket I've been wearing for years now." Joseph looked moodily down at his dinner coat, which while tidy and smart enough to sport a small row of bronze buttons was in no way a rival to the beautifully embroidered coats and bright buttons that adorned Malden Grey.

As if conjured by her thoughts Grey walked through the door, and Amaranthe forgot everything in her head, including that she was the source of funds for her brother's stipend. Grey was the most splendid she'd ever seen him in a dinner coat of dark plum with an eye-popping diamond pattern and intricate embroidery at the sides and hem. A cream waistcoat displayed the same embroidery in contrasting colors, and the matching breeches buckled just below the knee led to white stockings showing an excellently shaped male leg. She stared at his shoes, heeled with gold buckles, and then dragged her gaze upward to his face.

Grey stared, his gaze moving from her hair to her waist to the exaggerated rump, then to the expanse of skin bared by her bodice and the little ruffle that flirted with the tops of her breasts. There his eyes lingered for long moments until, at last aware of her staring back, he looked in her face.

"You," he began in a strangled voice, and went no further.

Amaranthe experienced a sensation she had never felt in her life: the satisfaction of vanity. The modesty of her upbringing had taught her to value character above all. But the opportunity to strike an intelligent and normally self-possessed man witless by a mere glimpse of her bosom was an opportunity that a modest life had denied her, and she found she quite enjoyed the power, so long as the man was Malden Grey.

"You," he tried again. "You, ah, have finished with the household accounts?"

"Yes, all up to date," Amaranthe answered, suppressing a flash of irritation that he could look upon her in this exquisite gown and ask for a progress report. But then she realized he was groping for his scattered wits, poor man, and she decided to forgive him. She opened her fan and swished it beneath her chin. Grey's eyes tracked the movement like the pendulum of a clock, and she felt a surge of feminine triumph mingled with exasperation. Honestly, how had men contrived to rule the world when exposure to the mere shape of a female made them useless nodcocks?

Medieval monks had railed at length about the dangers posed by women; she'd copied many a tedious text instructing godly men to beware of female snares. Now she understood the frantic warnings. Unable to control their own responses, they chose instead to throttle and control women.

She quite liked stirring this reaction in him. Wise of the medieval clerics to put frail men on their guard. What woman, having such power, wouldn't use it?

"And you mean to leave us tomorrow." Faint desperation laced Grey's tone.

"All is in order here. I'll leave Mrs. Blackthorn to supervise the new cook, and Eyde can stay until Lady Camilla's nursemaid returns in the next few days. The matron from the Benevolence Hospital found us a housekeeper who can begin next week, and so..."

She had run out of excuses to stay, to be near him. And now was not the moment to ask if she could take the manuscript Ned had found with her. It wasn't for Grey to give permission, anyway; it was the property of the young duke.

"We don't want you to leave." Camilla's plaintive voice floated from the doorway. Amaranthe dragged her gaze away from Grey to see that all three of the ducal children stood in their finery, wearing the same expressions of appeal as they had when they'd turned up on her doorstep a week prior.

"Shush, Millie!" Ned hissed. "Let Hugh say what he planned."

Young Hunsdon bowed to Amaranthe, then held out his

arm. He was a few inches shorter than she, but as the ranking male, it was his privilege to lead the first female into dinner. Amaranthe smiled at the observance of protocol. The boys had turned themselves out in formal suits, hair tucked beneath small white wigs.

"I would be loath to cast away my speech, for besides that it is excellently well penned, I have taken great pains to con it," Hugh said with a mischievous smile.

Amaranthe laughed as she laid her hand lightly on his forearm. "Viola's speech to Olivia. *Twelfth Night,* Act I."

"Ah, I knew it was Shakespeare!" Joseph exclaimed, rising from his couch. "The scene where Viola is dressed as the page Cesario."

"And the speech is to court Olivia on behalf of the Duke Orsino," Grey said.

"Which goes horribly awry, since Olivia falls in love with Cesario, never guessing that another woman so well knows the way to a woman's heart," Amaranthe answered.

"Miss Illingworth, sometimes I think *you* should be teaching us, instead of your brother," Ned exclaimed, clamping Camilla's arm in a poor copy of his brother's courtesy. "Mr. Illingworth, beg your pardon. I meant no offense."

"Joseph knows all the tragedies and can recite every soliloquy from *Hamlet* and *Macbeth*," Amaranthe said. "Besides which he can endure the history plays, which drive me to despair."

She cast a teasing look over her shoulder, meant for her brother, but her eyes landed on Grey, taking his place in the procession behind Ned. The smolder in his eyes made her lose her thought completely.

"We have discussed the issue at length, and this is the conclusion we have come to." Hugh began his recital as they processed to the formal dining room, which had been laid for six. Amaranthe blinked at the dazzle of light on shimmering porcelain and polished silver. The sight of a dozen candles dancing in tall branched candelabras standing against the walls made her recall the figure she'd entered into the household accounts that day, an extravagance when a few candlesticks on the table would do just as well.

But that was the thrift of a tradeswoman dining at a nobleman's table, she reminded herself. Her eyes sought Grey, taking his place at the head. Which was he, really? The sober would-be barrister whiling away his days in study, or the duke's profligate bastard son?

"...and the only solution we can see..." Hugh paused for the culmination of his speech, and Amaranthe realized she hadn't been listening to a word he'd rehearsed with such care.

"Marriage!" Ned exclaimed, rushing in over his brother's weighty pause.

"Marriage," Hugh confirmed.

"I beg your pardon," Amaranthe said. "Who is getting married?"

"You and Grey, of course." Hugh jerked his chin at his elder brother.

Grey stood woodenly behind his chair. His drawn-back hair showed the red tips of his ears. She rather liked seeing these chinks in his armor. But that was not to the point.

Blood roared in her own ears, drowning out her voice. "I beg your pardon, I don't follow."

"But it solves everything!" Camilla burst out. "If you marry Grey, he can make sure Sybil can't steal from us again. And you can live here with us and give me lessons." She beamed with delight.

What surfaced from Amaranthe's riot of thoughts was that Camilla ought not to refer to her stepmother as Sybil. She stared at Joseph, who stood blinking, as caught by surprise as she was.

Grey's expression turned thoughtful.

"You knew this was coming," she accused him. No doubt he had planted the notion in their heads.

"It was their idea," he answered. His hands lay calm on the back of his chair, but she thought she detected a slight tremor in them. "But it has, er, come to my attention recently that I require a wife."

And he'd let the children broach the subject to test her reaction. Rather than approaching her himself on such an intimate matter.

"But *me!*" This was the heart of her astonishment. She and Grey—

The thought sent a thrill of excitement through her. No, alarm at the outrageousness of the suggestion.

"Well, you see." Grey cleared his throat. He made a gesture toward the seat of his chair. She continued staring.

"It would improve my chances of being called to the bench to be married, as you witnessed." His voice sounded far away over the rushing in her ears, and yet at the same time as close as if he spoke in her ear. A shiver moved down her back. "I do not, I'm afraid, have time to court a wife. Neither do I have any fair prospects." He looked faintly abashed, studying his hands on the chair. "So I thought—"

"Since I am available," Amaranthe finished. "I see."

He flung out his hand, and she realized that as she had not seated herself, none of the gentlemen could sit, either. She subsided into her chair, glad she need no longer depend on her wobbly legs.

She didn't see at all. They barely knew each other. They'd spent a week under the same roof. That was hardly enough time to know anything about him, other than that he was tall and ridiculously well-formed, level-headed and for the most part responsible, intelligent and, as far as she could see, not given to overindulgence or vices. Long enough for her to ascertain that she liked his voice, and his style, and his scent, and in fact everything about him.

None of which was a basis for marriage.

You've a tendre for him. Admit it, you goose.

That was not to the point. "Marriage is a serious contract," she said.

The words sounded wooden, not her own. She didn't feel as if she were present in this very surprising moment, but watching a tableau unfold before her. "There are considerations to be made."

"You'd be provided for, Anth." Joseph reached for the nearest dish and lifted the cover. "Oh, Brussels sprouts! Just the way I like them. If you keep Mrs. Blackthorn, I'm moving in with you."

"Yes. Well." Grey was blushing; she discerned the ruddy glow to his face even in the candlelight. "I flatter myself that I would be able to—er, meet your considerations. Once I know what they are."

Oh, the nerve of him. The absolute brass! Arrogant, overweening, dominating man, to assume that she would throw herself gratefully into his arms at the merest suggestion that he required a wife, and—

He looked glumly at the table, seating himself with a deliberate slowness. He was as embarrassed as she was, Amaranthe realized. And in no way confident that she would say yes. His guardedness, that resignation she'd seen him in before, thumped her in the chest. He expected to be denied what he wanted, purely because he was a bastard, not through any other fault.

"I told you this wasn't the way to go about it, Grey," young Hunsdon said, examining Amaranthe's expression.

"I said all along you need to court her." Ned lifted the lid off the dish nearest him, and his eyes closed in rapture as the steam rose to his nostrils.

"But you can't stay here unless you're married, can you, Miss Amaranthe?" Camilla asked. Amaranthe managed a smile, recognizing the logic of a child, that marriage was the only possible relationship between a man and a woman.

The only respectable relationship, true.

If they married, she would see him every day. They would ride about together on their errands and stroll together through parks, her hand tucked under his arm. There would be meals with the children and evenings with wine and conversation.

There would be the marriage bed, of which she knew next to nothing.

He would belong to her. And she would belong to him.

Amaranthe gazed at her plate, helpless against the surge of raw longing that roared through her with that thought.

She looked up to find everyone watching her. Joseph was curious, the children pleading and anxious, and Grey—

He was wary, and a touch desperate, and embarrassed, but there was that smolder in his eyes yet, and it flared as his eyes moved to her chest, then back up.

He wants you to say yes.

The thought forced breath from her body. He was not thinking this through. He saw her as a means to an end, his end. No one had asked her what she wanted.

"You must give me time to consider," she said. She couldn't bear to crush the children's hopes. Not here, on what was possibly her last night with them.

"Yes, of course." Grey exhaled. He was relieved she hadn't rebuffed him before everyone. "As long as you wish."

"Perhaps you ought to go with Miss Illingworth to visit her cousin the baronet," Hugh suggested. He handed his plate over as Grey carved the joint of roast beef. "Then it could all be done properly, with his permission."

"She hasn't decided yet if she's going," Ned huffed.

Joseph looked up. "I'm the one he should ask for permission!"

"I am of age," Amaranthe said sharply. "I shall decide for myself, thank you." She took a long draught of wine, longer than what was prudent. It tasted delicious.

"I imagine the news would delight the baronet," Hugh said. "That his family is to be allied with the Delavals."

"And the Greys," Grey said calmly, making a long, clean cut in the haunch before him.

"Of course." Hugh flushed.

"I wonder that you didn't live with your cousin, if he was a baronet," Camilla piped up. "His house must be grander than the one you have now."

"I did live at Penwellen for a while, after our parents were carried off by the fever." The wine seeped through her, making Amaranthe's blood warm and her limbs feel fluid. The dish beside her held prawns in butter, a delicacy she loved nearly above oysters. Mrs. Blackthorn had outdone herself tonight. She must take care the wine and the fare did not loosen her tongue unduly.

"Typhus," Joseph said, helping himself to a mushroom ragout. "So here I am, starting my third year at Oxford, when all of a sudden who knocks up my door but my sister dragging along a maid with a belly—" He caught Camilla's wide eyes. "That is to say, er, in the family way. And what does she tell me but she is no longer welcome at Penwellen, and has come to Oxford because her old schoolmistress has a connection who might employ her as a copyist. How am I to lodge them, when I've nothing but student chambers? But she's never told me why she left in such a harum-scarum fashion, and we've not had a word from Penwellen before Favella writes to ask her back."

Once again Amaranthe was the cynosure of all eyes. Cool air wafted across the exposed skin of her chest. Grey seemed conscious of her bared skin also.

"Reuben stole a book from me," she blurted.

The wine was making the top of her float away, and the thoughts she normally kept in order spilled out with it.

"I had just acquired a Book of Hours," she said. "Fifteenth-century French translation, Gothic script on vellum parchment, beautiful illuminations." Her throat ached. "It was a girdle book made for Lady Willoughby de Broke. Her husband Sir Nicholas died in Callington and is buried there."

So much for guarding her tongue, but at the quiet attention of her company, Amaranthe let the story pour out. "I worked for Mr. Finney for years making copies of this and that for him, all to earn this book. My first acquisition for my antiquarian book-store. That very day Reuben took a fit into his head and—and cast Eyde and me out of his house. And he took my Book of Hours as well."

Joseph laid down his cutlery, staring in astonishment. "Anth! You never said! Why didn't you demand it from him?"

"I asked you, if you recall, to direct Favella to send my things to you in Oxford," she answered. "I wrote again, through our solicitor, when we took up lodgings in London. Reuben declined to send my possessions."

Her wine glass had mysteriously refilled; she hadn't felt Davey at her elbow, but she took advantage and chased the first glass with half of the second. It did not taste so delicious this time.

"Why didn't you have Mr. Illingworth march down to Cornwall and demand your book, if you valued it?" Ned asked, puzzled.

Amaranthe stared into her wine. She would miss all this when she returned to her quiet house. The wine, the conversation, the glow of dozens of candles warming and softening the elegant room. She would not miss people looking so closely at her all the time, Grey most attentively of all. His eyes seared her skin as if she had splashed hot butter from the prawns.

She had no ready answer for Ned's question. She depended on other people as little as she could. It was her custom to take care of Joseph, not the other way around. And she didn't want her brother knowing what Reuben had done, what he had suggested. He wouldn't know how to address the offense any better than she had, and Reuben's vileness would poison him the way he had poisoned her.

With the wine came the sudden heat of rage. She *wanted* to storm to Cornwall. She wanted to tear Penwellen apart with her bare hands until she found what had been taken from her.

Reuben could never return her innocence, though. She could never take from her mind the memory of his hot thick body pressing against hers, his rotting breath, his damp hands. The memory intruded every time another man drew close to her. Even Grey. She wondered if there would ever be a time when the shadow of Reuben's offense would fade.

How could she marry Grey if his every touch called up the spoiled ghost of Reuben?

"You must go," Camilla said. She looked from Amaranthe to Joseph. "You should take her back to Cornwall now, Mr. Joseph, and get her book back. She worked so hard for it."

"Er." Joseph shifted in his chair. "But I'm engaged to tutor your brothers, you see. I've a whole lesson on classical antiquity planned. And, well, there is a certain young lady who has expectations of me. I fear she wouldn't wait if I went haring off to Cornwall."

Amaranthe tightened her fingers around her glass. Best not

to finish the rest. Davey saw his job as keeping her glass filled to the brim, and the wine was not watered as far as she could tell. If she did not restrain herself, she'd be sliding under the table by the second course.

"Miss Pettigrew wouldn't allow you a fortnight away to visit family?" she asked, trying to keep the brittleness from her tone. "Are there so many other suitors vying for her hand, Joseph?"

"Not suitors, but other matters," he said, shifting in his chair. "She has interested herself in many causes of reform. I must exert myself to stay at the front of her mind, as it were."

Grey made no audible response to this, but Amaranthe glanced sharply his way. He was still at his task of carving the roast, but she sensed by his manner that something in him reacted strongly to Joseph's protestations.

Even Hugh said, "I thought you mentioned Miss Pettigrew's family lived in the West, Mr. Illingworth. You could take Miss Illingworth to meet them, and then proceed to Cornwall."

"I'm not persuaded I have the leisure for such a journey," Amaranthe said. "I'm engaged to deliver a manuscript." She had other commissions to earn. And travel was expensive, besides.

"Miss Pettigrew's family might look kindly on your suit were they to know your family is friendly with the Duke of Hunsdon," Grey remarked.

Amaranthe narrowed her eyes at him. The children took the bait at once.

"Oh, I say," Ned exclaimed. "Cracking good idea, Grey! You marry Miss Amaranthe, and Mr. Joseph might have his pick of Miss Pettigrews."

"And you would get to see the baby if you went to Penwellen," Camilla said.

"Has it escaped everyone that I have not accepted Mr. Grey's suit?" Amaranthe said, her voice overloud.

"Why wouldn't you?" Hugh asked. "Because he is my father's bastard?"

Amaranthe's eyes flew to Grey's face, taut and expressionless.

"That is not the basis of my hesitation," she told him.

"You ought not tease Miss Illingworth, Hugh," Grey said, not meeting her eyes.

He laid the large carving knife aside, and Ralph carried the platter of cuts around the table, serving them all in formal style. Grey took a large draught of his wine. It was courtesy for the men of the table to drink in toast to each other, but Joseph ignored his glass, and Grey was not a man to be constrained by formality in the best of circumstances. Davey leapt forward with the decanter before the bottom of Grey's glass touched the cloth.

"Indeed," Grey went on, "we owe Miss Illingworth a great deal for all she has done for us this week. We ought rather be thinking of ways to reward her, instead of harrying her about her plans."

"By all means," Hugh said, taking the reproof in stride. "Miss Illingworth, please advise us how we may demonstrate our gratitude for the very great service you have done us all."

In for a penny, in for a pound. Amaranthe swilled the last of her wine and cleared her throat.

"I would like to borrow the manuscript that Ned found. For a short time," she said. "I wish the liberty to read it through, and it's rather a weighty tome."

Best make no mention of the plan she was forming to copy out parts of it and sell them separately. Alchemical treatises, astrological tracts, and arcane medical lore fetched very dear prices in certain specialty shops. She could envision the look on Mr. Karim's face when she mentioned she'd found the *Book of Secrets* he coveted. That, and more.

Much as she adored Mr. Karim, it was time to start establishing networks and contacts of her own. This book gave her the power to do so.

But somehow, Grey's ice-blue eyes, riveted to her face, told her he would not approve of her methods.

"You wish to read it!" Ned exclaimed. "*All* of it?"

"It's an unusual book," Amaranthe said. "Someone went to a great deal of trouble to find rare and arcane treatises, some of them now lost or impossible to locate, and then bound the copies into an organized collection. I believe it's of great interest, and possibly great value."

The young duke brightened. "How much value?" he asked.

"I cannot yet say, but I can show it to Mr. Karim and some other antiquarian booksellers I know."

Malden's face grew shadowed and he looked away, avoiding her eyes. Amaranthe's stomach, filled with wine, sloshed uncomfortably. She couldn't shake the certainty that he knew what she planned to do with that book.

Somehow he'd discovered she was a thief and a liar. That she copied manuscripts that weren't hers and sold her copies under the noses of their owners, enriching herself at their expense. If he had found out, he could expose her. There would be fines, possibly time in the bridewell for such subterfuge, if not worse punishment. Even small robberies could be hanging offenses under English law.

"In that case," Hugh said, "I should be happy to let you have a look at it. You can tell us if there is, say, enough of value to—" He glanced at his sister. "Ah, remedy our current financial situation."

"You mean how we're broke because Sybil took all the money," Camilla said matter-of-factly, helping herself to the last of the buttered prawns.

"Yes, that," Hugh muttered, looking at his plate.

Amaranthe didn't take the opportunity to remind Camilla she should address her stepmother by her title, despite her feelings. She had been granted access to this priceless book, but the victory felt hollow.

Grey wouldn't extend an offer of marriage—if offer it was—to a woman he knew to be a thief and a liar. If he suspected her of forgery, the last she'd see of Malden Grey was him hauling her before a magistrate.

The thought of the possible consequences for her crimes ought to terrify her more than the knowledge that Grey wouldn't want to marry her if the truth were known. But the thought of losing his regard hurt Amaranthe more than anything else.

CHAPTER THIRTEEN

M al walked up and down George Court several times before he gathered the courage to rap on Amaranthe's door with his walking stick. After some time the portal opened to reveal a slender young woman. She had the same dark curling hair and wide-set eyes as Amaranthe, but she wasn't the woman he wanted.

"Is Amaranthe at home?"

His voice sounded hoarse. He was as anxious as a schoolboy. He realized he ought to call her Miss Illingworth; she hadn't given him permission to use her given name.

The woman laid a finger against her lips, indicating silence, and led him down the short hallway. The small house was as neat and welcoming as he remembered. Not as grand as Hunsdon House, not nearly, but a far sight more comfortable than the bachelor's quarters he kept above a shop in the Strand. There was a calm, lovely quiet about the place. Much like its mistress.

He paused at the door of the parlor and stared in. Amaranthe sat at her desk, bent toward her easel, completely absorbed in her work. She wore a shapeless, shabby robe and house slippers, and her hair frizzed in a delicate halo about her head. Rich afternoon light gilded the back of her neck and the elegant curve of her cheek. She held a small knife in her left hand and a goose feather quill in her right, which she dipped into a small pot of paint and used to scratch on the parchment. A small exclamation followed, and she employed the knife to scrape away an error, then applied the paint again.

"I am sorry to bother you."

His voice broke the silence and her concentration. He *was* sorry to bother her, but not sorry to be here. He wanted to take a seat and watch her for hours. The mere sight of her soothed the ache that plagued him.

She placed the quill in the inkpot and lifted her eyes to his. Her face made a new ache begin, one stranger and deeper.

"I told Inez I am not at home to visitors."

"I made her admit me." Not true; the girl had let him in readily. He wondered why. "We haven't seen you for four days."

She moved the shawl draped over the back of her chair to the table beside her, covering its surface. He might be mistaken, but he thought he glimpsed the edge-bitten binding of the book that had come from Hunsdon House.

Still hiding things from him, then. How could he ever win her trust?

The light falling through the broad window shifted, softening and warming her face. He longed to trace that bright path with his fingertip.

"I've been quite busy. I'm due to return this manuscript to its owner at the end of the week," she said.

He moved to stand beside her and her easel. She made a small gesture, as if gathering herself to leap like a frightened hare. Why should she be afraid of him?

"I see that you're adding the red."

"Yes, I'm touching up the rubrication now that the gilding is done."

She smelled wonderful, like an English garden in summer. He'd missed her. Mal had never longed for the mere presence of another person like this before.

"But this word stands alone here." He pointed toward the single word hovering in the lower margin. Her script was balanced, even, precise. So characteristic of her. He'd caught himself many times a day, while attending to things at Hunsdon House, listening for her voice in the hall, wondering what she would have to say about an amusing thing the servants or the children did. It was no better when he was able to visit his own apartments. Though she'd never been there, he still found his thoughts occupied with her, wondering where she was, what she was doing.

And if she thought of him nearly as often as he did her, or felt a physical sense of deprivation.

"That single word at the bottom is the catchword. This is the last in a quire of eight pages, and I want to be sure the section is bound to the correct quire that follows. Mr. Karim may send the quires out to separate artists for illuminations, and he must have a way to ensure the pages are bound in proper order when they come back."

Still sitting in that halo of light, she cleaned her knife on the edge of the easel, then tucked it into a small leather case of other tools. He loved this insight into a world he knew nothing of. Her world, filled with light and order and concentrated beauty, so unlike the prosaic, noisy world he knew.

"The writing is so neat and even. It's an art all its own. You're very good at what you do."

"Thank you." As if concluding a play she drew a cloth over the easel and secured it with the bar upon which she rested her wrist. "What did you need?"

To see her. To smell her. To find if the image that had begun to take up space in his head had any relation at all to a real woman.

"To see if you were well. Your brother insists you are merely working, but the children have been disappointed that you've not been able to join us for dinner. They insisted I call upon you." Using the children was a craven excuse, but perhaps it might make her less skittish.

She rubbed her eyebrows as if she were tired. "I am sorry to disappoint them. But I need to get this done."

"Is there no hope of convincing you to take a small break? I don't wish to trouble you." The goal was to see what he could do to help.

And see her.

"I could use a break." She blinked her eyes. He watched the slow, heavy movement of her lashes. The line of violet around her iris was muted, almost brown. She *was* tired. "If I don't rest my eyes, I'll start skipping lines or confusing words, and that won't do."

"Come outside with me for a walk. We can take a turn through Leicester Square."

She rose and reached for her shawl. "I like that idea. Let me dress."

It *was* the Hunsdon manuscript she had covered with her shawl. The volume lay on the table beside her, close to hand. He wondered if she were reading through it as she suggested. He forced his eyes away. He wasn't here to pry.

Yes, he was, but as he prowled around the parlor while she ran upstairs to change, he couldn't see anything out of order. Nothing that roused his suspicions. Nothing that told him he could not trust her.

Nothing that told him how he might win a smile. Her affection.

Her hand.

He was studying one of the paintings on the wall, what appeared to be a reproduction of a picture in an illuminated manuscript, and wondering what about these archaic artifacts appealed to Miss Amaranthe when she descended the stairs. She wore a pair of sturdy half boots and a riding habit that had seen better days and held a small, jaunty hat in her hand.

He was struck anew by her graceful self-possession. She carried herself like a woman of breeding. It made her appealing even in plain garb, but he had to admit he liked to see her splendidly turned out. All those gowns lying untouched in Sybil's dressing room—he should have sent them home with her.

So that she could wear them and interest other men, while he had to beat down her door to see her? That wouldn't do.

"That didn't take long," he observed, setting his own hat on his head.

"Only rich women can afford to spend time dressing. I've one more quire to finish before Saturday, and I must give the ink time to dry before I go back through and look for errors."

"You are very thorough." One of the many things he liked about her. Capable, efficient. Sensible.

No wonder she'd declined to marry him.

"It's said that medieval scribes intentionally introduced at least one error into their manuscripts as a gesture of humility, because only God is perfect." She hesitated as he held out his arm, then took it. The warmth of her small hand around his elbow filled him with a strange triumph.

"I wish I'd known that. I could have used it in defense of my examinations at university."

She laughed, and the warm, low sound filled his chest with delight. He held her arm securely as they stepped from George Court and dodged traffic across bustling Whitcomb Street. He relished the way her body fit beside his, the way their strides matched as they ducked through an alley to come out into the broad expanse of Leicester Square.

Unlike the nearby avenues of commerce, coaches and chairs moved leisurely along the iron fence surrounding the park, over-looked by rows of grand houses. They walked companionably along the fence enclosing the green. Mal felt none of the self-consciousness that he usually felt around women, none of that groping for things to say. Amaranthe was calm and at ease in her demeanor, though he felt alert and full of anticipation, alive to the warmth of her arm entwined with his, the suggestive brush of her skirts against his legs.

She glanced at the neat Palladian expanse of Leicester House, once home to princes and queens. "Have you brought the children to see Sir Ashton Lever's collection?" she asked. "I hear he converted the entire first floor of Leicester House to a gallery, and he has a great many curiosities on display there, including items Captain Cook brought back from his voyages."

"I regret that I haven't had time to take the children to any of the places I should," Mal said. "They deserve a treat, consid-ering they've been mewed up in Hunsdon House since their father died." Was she offering him an opportunity? "Have you been? You can come with and show us your favorite exhibits."

"The entrance fee is five shillings, so I have not yet been inside," she said. "And as for visiting together—I could not presume—that is, I ought not be telling you how to go on with the children. I have no right."

"You'd have the right did you marry me," he blurted, not nearly as casual as he wanted to be.

She paused. "Grey," she said, and the informal address pleased him, though her tone was chiding.

"That isn't what I came to talk to you about." He hadn't meant to show his hand so soon. Why was he so headlong around her? He was known among his fellows for his cool head. His bad luck, and his cool head.

He guided her through the open gate into the enclosed park. The neat green square, quartered by groomed gravel walks, sprouted small shrubs planted with geometric precision. In the center a statue of George I looked down his royal marble nose at them. Mal was surprised that Amaranthe didn't stop to buy something from every flower girl and fruit seller.

"Rather, that is only partially what I came to talk to you about," he said.

He tightened his hold on her as they neared a gentleman who clearly belonged to the Macaroni Club. This marvelous personage shone all over with buttons, and his tricorner cap teetered above a white wig at least two feet high. He raised a glass to his eye to peer at Amaranthe, and Mal glared back.

She paid the man no regard as he pranced by. She didn't care for macaronis, then. Did she think Mal himself too much concerned with dress? It was true he paid attention to his appearance, mostly because in the world of London gentlemen, a man rose or fell by his wit and style. Talent, hard work, and skill had little to do with achievement in that realm, as he'd learned the hard way.

"What did you wish to talk to me about?"

She sounded apprehensive, and he shook off the sense of failure that dogged him. He had to appear relaxed. Inviting. Someone she would confide in.

"Your brother says you have decided to visit your cousin."

She tensed, her brows drawing together. A series of expressions played across her face, and he wondered at the thoughts beneath. He wondered if a time would ever come when she would share them with him.

"I have told Favella I will visit. She sent another letter shortly after the first. She appears greatly worried about childbed, and, since she has no other family, she particularly wants me there."

"I thought I might take you."

She stopped to stare into his face with surprise, and Mal drew them to the side of the gravel walk and the other fashionable strollers on promenade. He hadn't considered chaperones or attendants or the like, and she'd made no mention, either. If anyone recognized her, it was likely they already knew Miss Amaranthe Illingworth was too intelligent to let herself be wooed by a rake to do something completely against common sense and virtue.

Like allow a man who was nearly a stranger accompany her on a journey across southern England.

She sighed. "Are you still clinging to this ridiculous notion that it will solve your problems to marry me?"

"It's not ridiculous," he protested. "You are an excellent candidate for a barrister's wife. Oliver saw you are clever. The children adore you. I'd prove a steady husband, and I won't interfere with your doings."

As long as he could discern her doings were all aboveboard. If he could lay to rest Thorkelson's suspicions that she engaged in forgery, Amaranthe Illingworth offered him a clear path to the future he'd been working for. One better than he'd dreamed, with her in it.

"I think you'd find your life would go on much as before, did you marry me," he said, trying not to sound desperate.

Her laughter this time was a throaty gurgle. "Mr. Grey, no woman in the history of the world has married and found her life going on the same as before."

"But I'm convinced we could find a way to—now where are you going?" He set out after her as she walked briskly toward the gate and the road surrounding the square. Her hat started to slide down her thick curls, and she clapped a hand over it.

"Returning home," she said. "I haven't time to stroll about and be wooed. I've a manuscript to finish."

"But you haven't answered my—will you wait!"

He clasped her arm and hauled her against him as she heedlessly stepped through the gate at the same moment a small, highly decorated carriage wheeled around the corner. Mal's heart slammed against his chest as the driver dragged his cattle to a halt. Amaranthe stood pressed fully against the length of him, her body warm and firm, and her heady scent infused his head, setting his wits swimming.

"Grey, old man! Didn't mean to run your lady down. Apologies." The driver, a dapper gentleman in a smart driving coat and plain black breeches, touched his riding whip to the rim of his hat and gave them an abashed grin.

"Hullo, Algie," Mal replied when he had his voice under command. "No harm done." He felt the fast beat of Amaranthe's heart beneath the arm clamped about her. She was slender and strong. He did not draw his arm away.

"Your Grace." Mal nodded to the matron riding beside the gentleman. She was a commanding figure, wearing a fur stole wrapped about her shoulders and an enormous picture hat blocking out the sun. "May I introduce Miss Amaranthe Illingworth? Miss Illingworth, Her Grace the Duchess of Northumberland and her son, Lord Algernon Percy. Algie, congrats on your new papahood. I hear she's a beauty and wrapping men about her little finger already."

Lord Algernon beamed with pride. "She's fair overset our house, I tell you. Can't hardly tear Mum away. Say, if you bet at Brooks that I'd name her Charlotte, you've a pot waiting for you. Mum was Lady of the Bedchamber to Queen Charlotte for an age, if she hasn't mentioned that a thousand times already." He rolled his eyes.

"Really, Algie." The woman next to him sat forward. She

had penetrating eyes and a handsome, strong-featured face set in the regal lines of age. "Illingworth? I don't know you," she said to Amaranthe, who gaped as if she'd never seen a duchess in the flesh.

"Friend of young Hunsdon," Mal said easily. "Antiquarian. Quite a literary lady, this one."

"Indeed." The duchess sat back and drew her furs around her. "I shall have you to one of my assemblies, then. We need more entertaining women." She lifted an imperious hand. "You'll forgive us, but Sir Ashton is waiting for us, Algie. Good day."

The carriage rolled away, and for a moment Amaranthe simply stood, wrapped in his embrace, her heart beating furiously against his forearm. Then she broke away and was in the alley dividing two polished rows of town houses before he caught up with her angry stride.

"Do you know who that was?" she threw over her shoulder.

"I introduced you," Mal reminded her. "The Duchess of Northumberland, having Algie squire her about since Percy, the heir, is in the Americas fighting the colonists."

Mal had crossed paths with Lord Percy once or twice before he left. The combination of his parents had given the man an overlarge nose, but he was an intelligent commander and the word in the papers was that he had saved British troops more than once from wholesale slaughter by canny patriots who didn't fight like regular men. It was men like Percy who made Mal consider a career in the military, since he was going nowhere in the Middle Temple.

Unless Miss Amaranthe Illingworth consented to smooth his way, as she had ordered things to run seamlessly and with style at Hunsdon House.

"Duchesses!" Amaranthe scoffed. She darted before a wagon crossing Whitcomb Street, and the carter shouted with surprise and hauled on his reins. Mal joined her on the doorstep of her house, catching her muttered stream of words. "Lords! Assemblies!"

"*Senhorita!*" The young woman she'd called Inez appeared at the top of the stairs leading down to the kitchen. "I've a fresh batch of *broa* if your gent would—" She scanned their faces and checked her enthusiasm. "*Oh meu*, is something burning?" She whisked herself away as fast as she'd appeared.

"What are you angry about?" Mal demanded, following Amaranthe into her parlor. She yanked off her hat and tossed it recklessly into a chair, then whirled to face him.

"The Duchess of Northumberland! Did you know she's a baroness in her own right? One of the few in England. She helped elevate her husband from a baronet into a duke. Everyone in town wants invitations to her assemblies. She's... she's...she was a lady in waiting to Queen Charlotte, for heaven's sake!"

He rarely saw Amaranthe at a loss for words. "I know all this," he said warily. "And Algie's a fine chap, too. Likely he'll steady out now that he's a papa."

The roaring rush of envy took Mal by surprise. Algie was only a year or two younger than Mal, but he'd been elected a member of Parliament for Northumberland, married Isabella in great happiness the previous summer, and nine months later could boast of a daughter. He had a respectable career and now a family. And what did Mal have?

He must not be bitter. His best hope for a career and a family of his own stood before him. He had to persuade her to want that, too.

"Duchesses. Dukes. Members of Parliament." She ran a hand through her hair, tousling it beyond repair. "Grey, the people you know live in a world entirely apart from mine. They wait on royalty. Their names are known everywhere. They set the fashion and they make the rules. I am a—" She turned and strode to her easel, throwing back the cover that concealed the pages of parchment. "I am a rector's daughter. I am a tradeswoman. I earn my living by my own hands."

She pointed to the manuscript and its copy. As far as Mal could tell, her replication was identical, a work of art.

"There is no fault in being a tradeswoman, if you are an honest one," he said.

She faced him, crossing her arms over her chest. The movement brought the shape of her bosom into relief. Recalling how her dinner gown the other night had bared a great deal of that bosom put him at a distinct disadvantage.

"What is that supposed to mean?" She narrowed her eyes.

"Do you have anything to hide or be ashamed of?"

He was surprised he'd asked her so boldly. His wits had scattered, or perhaps urgency had pressed him to it. There was no hope of a future for them if she was involved in the shady things Thorkelson suggested. A barrister marry a forger? That certainly wouldn't help his career. No matter how lovely her shape, or how entrancing her eyes as she flashed him a look of scorn.

"Perhaps you ought to have asked me that before you proposed marriage. Not that I can recall your genuinely proposing to me."

"Amaranthe Illingworth." He strode forward and captured one of the slender hands tapping an impatient beat on her elbow. He was shocked by how desperately he wanted to touch her, and what happened to him when he did.

Her index finger bore streaks of red paint and black ink stained her fingertips. He raised those fingers to his lips and kissed them. Her skin was cool and smooth, save for one callus on her finger from holding a quill.

"What would you say," he asked, his voice deep and rough, "did I give you a proper proposal?"

His blood beat in his ears, in his chest. He knew how it looked to her: someone had mentioned to him he would advance if he married, and he had lit on her as the first woman available. What woman would be flattered by such circumstance?

He didn't know how to explain. He had labored for months and years, wondering what held him back in the Middle Temple when all about him men who had entered with and after him were called, one after another. Before Oliver mentioned marriage, he had never considered that the cheerfully careless reputation he cultivated, with his companions, with his habits, with his manner of dress, made him agreeable in fashionable drawing rooms but not a reliable choice for the bar.

And it was equally clear, once marriage entered his mind, that Amaranthe Illingworth was the only woman who would possibly suit him.

He waited, his breath stalled in his lungs. He could read the emotions playing over her face, so attuned was he to her look and manner. Whatever occurred to her first was in his favor; her lips parted and curved softly upward. His chest swelled with air. But then the objections surfaced, and the soft look disappeared. She sucked in a long breath, the lines about her eyes tightening.

He braced himself for the blow, though she dealt it gently. "No."

"There's a bastard in the Percy family," he said, as if that might possibly persuade her.

"What?" Her eyes flared with an ageless human interest in gossip. "I did not know."

Mal nodded. "A lad. I think he's about Ned's age. They smuggled the mother away to give birth in France, as the great ones do. He's at school somewhere. I heard his name is James Louis or something fancy."

"I still—"

"So it's not different," he said. "You're not marrying a duke. You'd marry a duke's bastard. I could do nothing to elevate you. I should have to work to support us, and very likely you might have to work too. It's the same world, Amaranthe. Not as different as you say."

He'd slipped and used her name, but she didn't scold. In fact she didn't say anything for a long while, simply gazed at his face, searching out his every feature, looking long in his eyes. Mal felt his every past peccadillo, lie, and foolish act lay there for her discovery. Amaranthe Illingworth had no foolish acts in her history, but he wished she did. It could bind them together.

"Let me come with you to Cornwall," he said, stepping closer and placing her hand on his chest. Her fingers trembled. "Joseph is taking Miss Pettigrew to Gloucestershire. He told me today she consented. I shall be your escort to Cornwall, and I shall advise your cousin of certain precedents that make it unwise for him to continue in possession of a book that you fairly purchased and paid for. You will ask why I have interested myself in your affairs, and I will answer that I owe you a great boon for the service you did for me. The children approve."

"Who will watch over them while we are away?" She was weakening. The sweep of her long, thick lashes captivated him as she gazed into his eyes, and the violet rim around her iris stood out vividly.

"The excellent staff you have provided. Eyde said she could remain as housekeeper, now that Millie's nursemaid is back. Mrs. Blackthorn says they are training Mrs. Wheatley as both cook and housekeeper until someone can be found. Between them Ralph and Davey have things well in hand, and the children do not object to a short holiday from their lessons."

"You have arranged much without consulting me," she murmured.

"In hopes of making things easier on you." He laid his fingers over hers. The press of her hand against the thick fabric of his coat sent warmth coursing through his body.

"It could be a holiday for you as well. And I shall show you what you stand to gain by marrying me."

Those delectable eyelashes lowered as she frowned. "I won't —I shouldn't—" Her delicate throat pulsed as she swallowed, and he wanted to kiss the blush that rose to her cheeks. "Don't hope for anything," she warned him.

"Lovely Amaranthe. Flower unfading." It wasn't like him to be poetical, but her capitulation left him giddy. "I hope for *everything.*"

He bent his head, but waited. Her eyelashes lowered further still, and that lovely blush lingered on her cheeks, but she didn't move to bring her lips to his. He wouldn't press himself upon her. Instead he brushed his mouth against her cheek, slowly, and a tremor ran through her. His blood heated and he wanted to snake an arm about her and crush her to him. His body was eager to replay that stolen embrace in the square. But it was enough that she trembled, that her blush deepened, that she shivered when his breath drifted over her ear, fanning the tendrils of hair curling there.

She wasn't unmoved. She was resisting, but she wasn't unmoved. He would wait. In fact, he looked forward to it.

With deliberate slowness he dragged his lips across the silken skin of her other cheek and then withdrew, releasing her hand as he stepped away. She swayed toward him, her expression dazed, and he smiled.

"Send word to Hunsdon House as to when we will depart,"

he said. "The children shall expect to give you a farewell dinner. I shall make all the arrangements." He gave her a courteous bow, gentleman to lady. "Goodbye for now, Amaranthe."

"Goodbye," she said faintly, and he was certain her eyes followed him out the door.

Mal placed his hat firmly atop his head and walked George Court with a jaunty step. He hadn't ever set out to seduce a woman before, with calculation and cunning, with measured slowness, and with so much at stake on winning the prize. But his problem-solving mind looked forward to the task.

She might find any number of reasons they would not match, but he would remind her of the ways they did. An important point had already been established. She was as affected by his nearness as he was by hers. He already guessed her to be the type of woman who did not yearn lightly or in fantasy. For her, regard and care were the foundations for passion, and the same was true for him; he only desired where he admired. He needed no other proof that he had made the right decision to choose her, as sudden and unwarranted as the choice might seem.

As long as she wasn't a thief or a forger, Amaranthe Illingworth would make him a splendid wife.

CHAPTER FOURTEEN

"All right, mum, off with you!" Davey said in exasperation as Amaranthe circled the vehicle for the fourth time, watching him cinch the baggage onto the platform at the front of the post chaise. "If I let any of your fribbles tumble into the dirt of the road, I'm no true Welshman."

"I didn't pack any fribbles," she said. "They're too heavy. You marked Joseph's luggage, I hope? I'm sure he forgot. He and Miss Pettigrew will part with us at Bristol, and I don't want to send the wrong bags."

She inspected the wheels and axles of the hired coach, though she had no way of knowing if it was in good condition. Grey had hired the chaise and horses and it turned out Inez knew the post boy, who was another lascar like her father, a sailor of South Indian descent who had stayed in England when his crew was put out of work and had been making a living at odd jobs since. He spoke limited English, but he would perch atop one of the horses to guide them on the road and then return these animals when they changed teams at the next post. Amaranthe offered him a smile and he smiled back, showing several missing teeth.

"Much of Bristol's sea traffic comes from the slave trade." Camilla clutched Amaranthe's hand. Amaranthe was becoming more accustomed to the casual and frequent touch, though Camilla's unhesitant trust still took her aback. Amaranthe couldn't recall as a young child that she had ever held an adult's hand. Though the youngest and from a caring home, she had been a cautious and reserved child, hesitant to rely on anyone.

She was relying on Grey now to make this journey with her, walking backward into the life she'd left long ago. Not for the first time, she wondered what threats and bitter memories lay in store for her.

"There will be ships from all over in Bristol harbor," Amaranthe said. "Europe and the Middle East. Africa. The Americas. Perhaps a ship visiting some remote and undiscovered island will bring back a wonder we've never dreamed."

"Mr. John Wesley set up his first Methodist chapel in Bristol," Camilla said, her expression somber. She had been vocal in her disappointment that Amaranthe and Grey were both leaving, but as attempts to talk them out of their decision had proven unsuccessful, she'd resigned herself to being abandoned for a fortnight or more. As recourse she had contented herself with studying everything about Bristol that the ducal library could yield.

Amaranthe hoped they would not be gone longer than a fortnight. It would take some days to travel to Callington, but she planned only to show her face, say a few encouraging things to Favella, make sure her cousin's wife had reliable help with the babe, and then depart before Reuben could take any evil ideas into his head.

Depart with her Book of Hours in hand, if all went well.

She'd been waiting for this opportunity for years, dreaming of it. She'd accepted Grey's escort because, as he'd suggested, showing up with a man of the law was a wonderful tactic of

THE FORGER AND THE DUKE   193

intimidation. But by now Reuben could have discarded the manuscript in any number of ways: sold it, given it away, or worst of all, let a maid use the aged parchment to light fires. Every antiquarian knew the cautionary tale of John Warburton, who had stored dozens of unique manuscripts in his kitchen and discovered later his cook was using the pages to line pie plates.

"You will give our regards to your Uncle Littlejohn and your Aunt Beatrice, of course." Hugh, the young duke, walked with Grey into the mews that ran behind Hunsdon House and its garden.

"Remember you are to ask him about being trampled by the bull and getting his leg taken off," Ned exclaimed, hurrying behind them. "I want the full tale, Grey. You don't know nearly enough of the details."

"I'll ask him. Where are Joseph and Miss Pettigrew?"

Grey looked around and his gaze fell on Amaranthe and lingered. She had upon persuasion borrowed one of the duchess's riding habits, a smart and well-tailored ensemble of dark green wool that was extremely comfortable. Sybil was considerably more curved than Amaranthe, but Eyde had accounted for the difference in shape with a few quick stitches. There were two other traveling gowns packed in her trunk. She only meant to borrow the gowns, not keep them, and she couldn't see the extravagance of buying traveling attire for herself. The unplanned trip to Cornwall would strain her expenses enough.

She supposed the money for the coach had come, like the staff salaries and the coin for groceries, from the sale of her manuscript to Mr. Karim. She wondered if she would ever learn who bought her copy of the *Secretorum*. She hoped it went to a good home, to someone who would store and care for the book properly, and perhaps on occasion read it.

"These are all your things?" Grey asked. Amaranthe's

middle warmed at his attention, but also with embarrassment. Did the paltriness of her personal possessions dismay him? He already knew she was not a woman of means.

"This is all I need. I am looking forward to meeting your aunt and uncle," she said to distract him. "They sound like very interesting people."

She was also looking forward to spending time with him, though she would never say this aloud. Days together in a traveling coach, nights under the shared roof of a coaching inn. She would come to know a great deal more about Malden Grey.

Not that she intended to marry him. He'd come to his senses in time and realize there were other opportunities about him, women who would make a better barrister's wife. Women who didn't make a living skirting the law, for instance.

But for now, she had him more or less to herself. This large, solid, and very intimidating man, at her side. The thought made her insides glow like live coals.

"At last," Grey said as Joseph emerged from the carriage house. Miss Pettigrew, behind him, clutched her valise and looked about with wide blue eyes.

She was everything Joseph had described, fair and fragile, with a bewildered air that roused Amaranthe's protective instincts. Her translucent, delicate beauty held the viewer captive, and Amaranthe could easily see how Joseph had been ensnared.

She hoped she might learn more about Miss Pettigrew, also. Joseph would not be swayed from his determination to marry. He had decided Miss Susannah Pettigrew was for him, and no other would do.

Much like Malden Grey, who when instructed to marry had simply looked around and lit on the first female in the vicinity, Amaranthe thought. The curl of resentment pricked, and she pushed it aside. He was doing her a service. She must keep that in mind, even if it rankled to be valued only for her usefulness.

"Miss Illingworth, we wish you the best and easiest of travels. Our regards to your family." The young duke bowed to her, and Amaranthe curtsied before she could stop herself. Hugh's formality had a way of intimidating her still.

"Have loads of fun, and don't turn over on the road!" Ned exclaimed, pumping her hand. Amaranthe grinned at him.

Camilla, in a sudden move, threw her arms around Amaranthe's waist. "Don't come back *different*," she said, holding back sobs. Amaranthe wrapped her arms around the girl, for once feeling the effort was not forced.

"Ladies first." Grey placed the step and held out a hand to help Amaranthe climb into the enclosed cab. It had been agreed that the girls would take the interior seats for the first leg of the journey and the men would take the seat behind.

The horses stirred and stamped in their harness, their shod hooves echoing on the cobblestones. Amaranthe took a last look about as the sun broke briefly through the morning fog. She had already said goodbye to the servants indoors, with Mrs. Blackthorn giving brisk advice, Davey looking mournful, Derwa hanging about her waist, and Eyde adding to an ever-growing list of people she remembered about Haye and Callington whom she hoped Amaranthe would look in on and make sure they were getting on.

"Grey, you worthless sot!" The tall soldier from the coffee shop strolled up the cobbled mews, his sword banging lightly against his legs. "Lighting out for the country? What, are you avoiding a duel? Escaping creditors? Ah, I see—carrying away beautiful young ladies. I always knew that buttoned-up demeanor was an act."

"Viktor! What in God's name are you doing here?" Grey

exclaimed. "Aren't you supposed to be on parade or some such, showing off that expensive uniform?"

"Here to send you off, old man." Grey's friend removed the tall cap and became ten times more handsome without it, his eyes alight with mischief, his sharp features thrown into relief. He flipped the black cape over his broad shoulders and his eyes flickered around the group, taking them all in. "Where did you say you were headed?"

"Callington, Cornwall. We're escorting Illingworth and Miss Pettigrew to Bristol. Miss Pettigrew, this is Viktor Vierling of the Horse Guards, the unremarkable son of a—"

"We've met." Miss Pettigrew's voice was high and strained. She held her valise to her middle and watched Vierling as if he were the devil incarnate. Joseph looked up in surprise from his task of triple-checking that Davey had properly secured the luggage.

"Oh?" Grey recovered quickly. "Then I give you Mr. Joseph Illingworth, the boys' tutor. Miss Illingworth you've met. And you'll recall my siblings, the Duke of Hunsdon, Lord Edward, Lady Camilla."

"We've met as well," Camilla said somberly, regarding Vierling with wide eyes and an expression as alarmed and interested as Miss Pettigrew's. Hugh inclined his head while Ned stuck out his hand with an unabashed grin.

"Smashing uniform! Suppose I should go into the Horse Guards, Grey?"

"If you want to do nothing better with your time than polish buttons and march in parade," Grey said. "Study the lessons Illingworth sets you and you might aspire to more, I hope."

"So Bristol is where your people are, Miss Pettigrew?" Viktor drawled, giving the blonde girl a careless smile.

"My parents live nearby." The girl was all nerves. "Mr. Illingworth intends to ask their permission to marry me."

"Thought Friends weren't supposed to marry outside of the clan," Vierling said. "Quakers for Quakers, that sort of thing."

"Mr. Illingworth is willing to convert."

Amaranthe's head snapped up and she nearly fell off the step. Grey steadied her and she leaned against the warm, strong expanse of him. She wasn't against Quakers, by any means, but Joseph had said nothing to her about converting. The news stung like a betrayal. What else did she not know about her brother?

She'd chided Joseph for not seeing what was going on under his nose at Hunsdon House as the servants fled and the children went hungry. But what was going on under her own nose that she'd missed? She dove into the cab, hiding a face burning with shame.

"You might take the children out for some amusement while I'm gone," Grey said to Vierling, holding the door to the carriage. "Miss Illingworth thinks they would fancy Leverton's collection at Leicester House."

"Dusty old artifacts aren't much in my style," Vierling drawled. "Astley's Circus, perhaps, or the menagerie at Exeter 'Change, children?"

"Lions and tigers? Indeed, yes!" Ned's face lit up. "Grey says he can hear the big cats roaring when he walks down the Strand. They scare the horses."

"Run along then and leave the darlings to me," Vierling said. "And if you come back married, do send me a card, Mal. Miss Illingworth." His head appeared in the window of the coach, giving her a rakish smile as he lifted his cap. Amaranthe jumped with surprise.

Married! Is that what Grey had told his friends about his reasons for this journey?

"You've met Captain Vierling before?" Amaranthe inquired when Miss Pettigrew joined her in the carriage.

The girl flashed her a startled, unsettled look. "Yes, Miss Illingworth," she said. "In passing."

Her companion settled herself with a great deal of fuss, smoothing her skirts, patting her hair, and making sure her bonnet was positioned just so. It was rather a large bonnet, and Amaranthe feared she would end up with a hat brim in the eye at some point in their journey.

"You will call me Amaranthe, I hope," she said. "If we're to be sisters."

"Oh." The girl's face still wore that wary look, as if taken back that Amaranthe should make overtures of friendship. "I am Miss Pettigrew."

And that was the most she said to Amaranthe as the chaise rolled out of the mews and set off down Oxford Street toward the Great Western Road to Bristol. Getting acquainted with Miss Pettigrew was going to be much more difficult than Amaranthe had thought.

She'd been looking forward to this trip, her first holiday away from London since they'd moved here—her first holiday since her parents died, in fact. It had seemed full of promise and delight as she packed, thinking about getting to know her brother's future wife, spending more time with Grey.

But now she realized that Joseph was moving away from her, making decisions about his life that did not include her. It did not seem that his future wife liked Amaranthe very much.

And Grey—he had never been hers to begin with. This trip was a stolen interlude, but it would change nothing. She had given him the only answer she possibly could to his proposal, or to any man's. When they returned, Grey would move on to the rest of his life and he would be lost to her, too.

And what would she be left with then?

CHAPTER FIFTEEN

"Oh, the most blessed ill luck the boy had!" Mal's aunt Beatrice unrolled an apronful of root vegetables onto the broad oaken table where Amaranthe stood, knife in hand. She gave Amaranthe an audacious wink. "We used to call him Mal o' Misfortune, didn't we, Littlejohn?"

"Aye, we did," said her husband in his low, pleasant rumble. "Put that 'un there, lad, and th'other above. I've needed a strong back, boy! 'Tis good you've come."

Mal grunted as he moved crates about the storeroom at his uncle's direction. Amaranthe tried not to stare. They'd not been at the Green Man above five minutes when Mal had stripped off his gentleman's frock coat, rolled up his sleeves, and set to the tasks needing done. Unwilling to be left behind, Amaranthe volunteered to help Beatrice in the kitchen, and therefore had a close view of Mal's flexing muscles as he hauled and stacked. The man might live the life of a gentleman, but he had the physique of a laborer, and he moved the largest boxes about as if they were no heavier than her traveling valise.

"Aye, 'tis good to have you." Beatrice beamed at her nephew. "And in the company of a lady, too!" Again she winked at

Amaranthe, who fought the urge to giggle. Beatrice's warm, expansive personality had set her instantly at ease. "Long past time our Mal took up with a respectable lady."

"Did you hear that?" Mal called from the storeroom. "Bea thinks you're respectable."

Amaranthe laughed and pulled a turnip from the tumbled stack. "I am not a lady," she admitted. "No more than a poor rector's daughter from Cornwall."

"Aye, but will ye take on a bastard, then? What?" Littlejohn protested when Bea pinned him with a stern glare. "I'm one meself, ain't I?"

"True, that," Bea said, selecting a pair of onions. "Thrown on the parish as an orphan, my Littlejohn was, and the work-house couldn't afford to feed such a roaring big boy. But Mr. Green as ran the coaching inn took em in, bless his heart, and here you see em before you, grown to a man. Well, most o' one," she added with a giggle. Littlejohn lifted the cane he used to walk and shook it in her direction.

Amaranthe tried not to stare, but Littlejohn's prosthesis was unlike any she'd seen. Attached to his thigh by a leather cuff, the two wooden pieces, covered in leather, connected with an iron clamp that hinged at the knee and ended in a wooden block carved into the shape of a shoe. He used a cane for balance but navigated the small stairs leading to the kitchen with ease, and he'd outpaced Bea when they both poured from the inn to greet the post chaise, hearing Mal's halloo.

"How did you come by the name Littlejohn?" Amaranthe asked. "It puts me in mind of Robin Hood and his Merry Men."

"That's what they called me at the workhouse, seeing my size," Littlejohn said. "Stout heart, that Green. Always taking in strays. All said Bristol had the lowest poor relief rate in the south o' Britain as Green took on the orphans."

"They say the same of you, love." Beatrice buried her knife

in an onion with a thwack. "They look em over at the parish workhouse and say aye, this 'un will do as an ostler for Little-john, and this one for a chambermaid to help Miz Beatrice."

"Amaranthe is the same way," Mal called, hefting a crate of bottles onto a high shelf with ease. "Always taking in strays. You should see her household. And don't try to walk through a market with her. She stops for every girl selling violets and watercress."

Amaranthe protested, but Bea smiled and handed her another turnip. "Then perhaps your luck's changing at last, me lad. To think what our boy's been through, miss! Losing his ma at such a young age, and she such a fine, sweet sister, the dearest gel you could ever meet." She sighed. "You remind me of her, don't you, with that sweet, quiet air about ye."

Amaranthe waited to hear more of Mal's mother, and Mal paused over another crate full of bottles. But Beatrice went on with her subject. "Then when the duke comes for him, ready to take the boy in as his own, what does our Mal do but run off to sea, and find out he don't have his sea legs." She sliced the onion with lightning speed and swept the pieces into a bowl.

"Born in Bristol and can't sail the bay." Littlejohn laughed and shunted aside a trunk of goods.

"Comes back from Winchester as fine a lad you'll ever see," Bea went on, dispatching a second onion with the same effi-ciency as the first. "And what does he do but fall in love with a girl who won't have em, because she's got eyes for this Tew. And wasn't Tew the boy you battled with so, the one as always fretted you for being a bastard?"

"I've more than one scar Tew gave me," Mal said. "Where is he now, I wonder?"

"Took over his father's brewery, and a justice of the peace besides," Bea said. "Shifted quite well for himself, didn't he?"

Mal's response to this was a violent shove of the crate he held, making the bottles within creak and rattle.

"And now look at ye." Bea shook her head and dabbed with a corner of her apron at an onion-induced tear in her eye. "Waiting and waiting to be called to the bar, and those poor bairns of your father's to look after, with no mother to speak of."

"I'll be called do I take a clever wife." Mal moved another crate with an emphatic shove. "More or less guaranteed. But she must be clever, and she must be a wife."

Bea paused, knife in the air, to bend her gaze on Amaranthe. Littlejohn, leaning on his cane, regarded her as well. She fixed her eyes on the turnip, chopping the slices she'd carefully cut.

"Well, that's a right fix then!" Bea exclaimed, as if the matter were settled. "Bad luck's all right long enough if the end turns it all to good. Littlejohn, me love, come fetch me down this joint that I want for the stew, will you now?" And she and her husband moved off to a second storeroom to investigate the hanging meats.

Mal entered the kitchen and moved to the table, stealing a carrot slice from the bowl awaiting the stew pot. Amaranthe smelled his sweat. Delicious. She tried not to look at his bare forearms, lightly dusted with hair, his strong, capable, well-shaped hands.

"What was her name?" she asked despite herself.

He paused in munching. "Who?"

Warmth flushed her face, and she ducked her head. "The girl you fancied."

"Sally." He leaned a hip against the table, crowding her. He'd removed his cravat and from the corner of her eye she could see the dip between his collarbones, the skin of his throat, the sheen of sweat. She drew in a deep breath and his scent surrounded her, filling her head, scattering thought.

"Sweet Sally," he murmured. "I wonder where she is now?"

"Married to Tew, teaching the bairns to brew, and wondering every day if she chose aright," Amaranthe answered.

"Jealous, are you?" Mal bent close, his nose behind her ear. His breath fanned her neck, and she shivered. His lips hovered a hair's breadth above her skin.

"Don't be daft." She pushed her pile of chopped turnip towards the bowl. "And don't take liberties," she added. "Your aunt and uncle will see you."

"They'll approve. Didn't you hear? Bea gave us her blessing." He pressed his nose into her hair. "Mmm. You smell like turnip."

She let her knife hang in the air but found she had no wish to push him away. If she turned her head slightly, his lips would brush her cheek. And if she turned just a bit more, her lips would meet his, and—

She didn't dare find out what would happen after that.

She laid the knife on the table. *Coward.*

He'd been a gentleman the three-day trip to Bristol, looking out for both women, arranging for the best rooms at the coaching inns, ordering dinners in private parlors. Amaranthe found she had nothing to do but make up the bed with the linens she'd brought from home and brush out the duchess's riding habit each night, removing the dust of the road. Mal saw to everything, the changing of horses, inspecting the carriage, and when the weather was fine he and Joseph took turns sharing the open back seat with the women.

She and Mal had spent hours together on the road, and he was a far better companion than either Miss Pettigrew, who was cautiously silent and appeared ever on edge, or Joseph, who was preoccupied with Miss Pettigrew. Mal on the other hand spoke with her long and amusingly of his childhood, his schools and studies, the sights of London that he'd seen. He'd regaled her with tale after tale of Beatrice and Littlejohn and life at the

Green Man, to the point that when the chaise turned into Bristol's Old Market and the pair poured out to meet them, Amaranthe felt she was being welcomed by friends.

But this was the first time since that moment in her parlor that he'd pressed close or tried to touch her. She held still in fear. What if his touch was as revolting as Reuben's had been? What if it wasn't just her cousin but the very touch of a man that she reviled?

"Unless you be wanting to post the banns here and marry from the Green Man, you'll be treating her like the gentle miss she is, me lad," Bea warned as she reappeared in the kitchen. "Littlejohn, me love, find our Mal else more to do, won't you? Idle hands are the devil's work, I be thinking."

Amaranthe sighed as he moved away, claiming that he'd meant nothing untoward and a man couldn't be faulted if he wanted to be near Miss Amaranthe. His playfulness and his potency left her nervous and jumpy long after he left the room. The warmth curling through her middle told her she might feel much differently about Mal's hands on her body than Reuben's unwanted advances, but fear that she might be wrong kept her from moving toward his embrace. Her fear might be safer than the truth.

AMARANTHE BID JOSEPH goodbye the next day with a few admonitions and no tears. He shrugged off her cautions to take care on the road and be wary of robbers, and to write her at Penwellen if he had need. Joseph only had eyes for Miss Pettigrew, who looked peaked and resolved in a plain grey bonnet and cloak. The nearer they drew to the small town in Gloucestershire where she'd been raised, the more Miss Pettigrew reverted to her proper and retiring Quaker roots, setting aside the fashionable bonnet and fur-lined cape she'd worn from

London. She'd had little to say to any of them, even Joseph, and Amaranthe worried at what her lack of warmth signified.

Of course, Amaranthe herself was making a point not to hang too much upon Malden Grey, particularly here where he was among his family. She might feel a great deal of warmth, but she attempted to keep it within reasonable limits of expression. Perhaps Miss Pettigrew was being equally conscious about any show of preference, but inwardly felt all for Joseph that she ought to feel for a man she was inclined to give her hand to.

"But if you do convert. To the Quakers, that is." Amaranthe held to the frame of the hired gig as Joseph leapt up to the driver's seat. "They won't keep you from us, will they? That is, you won't have to repudiate me to join them?"

"Anth, don't be a peagoose." He didn't spare a glance for her. "I won't throw you over when I marry. I've already said you'll have a home with us, didn't I? You'll be able to dandle your nieces and nephews on your knee from their first days. Consider Favella's brat practice."

"Don't marry in haste, mind," Amaranthe retorted. "I want at least to attend your wedding."

Joseph turned to ensure his passenger was settled, and his expression went soft as he watched Miss Pettigrew tuck her skirts around her. Beneath the plain grey bonnet the delicate lines of her face were achingly lovely.

"I'll marry her the moment she'll have me," he said with a foolish, lovestruck grin. "An angel come down to earth, she is."

He chucked the horses to walk on and lifted a hand in farewell as the gig passed from the broad courtyard of the coaching inn to the busy Old Market beyond. Miss Pettigrew did not wave.

"That's trouble, there," Mal said low in her ear. Amaranthe startled to find him standing next to her in a sheltered corner of the yard, apart from the traffic to and from the stables or the flow of passengers seeking relief in the common room, where Bea's hearty stew and Littlejohn's equally hearty laugh awaited them.

"What do you mean?" Amaranthe asked, fearing highwaymen, an accident that overturned them on the road. It happened all too often.

"A man who wears that look for a woman is bound to have his heart broken in two," Mal said.

She glanced up into his face and found his expression serious. His blue eyes, so often sparkling with merriment these past days, were quiet and somber.

"He will?" Her own heart clutched as if she'd taken a blow. Joseph was the closest person in the world to her, the only family she had left. "You don't think she feels the same for him."

"She certainly doesn't look at him in the same way. As if he hung the moon and could make the stars dance if he wanted."

That odd pain rippled through her chest again. No one had ever looked at her as if she hung the moon. But how foolish to wish such a thing. "You can't know it will mean heartbreak," she said. "She may simply be very reserved."

"It's true, I can't know her heart. But I know that's the look I wore for Sally. And it's the look my father wore when he met Sybil, come to that."

"But your father married Sybil." Her heart, ridiculously, sank in her chest. She wished the organ would stay in its proper place. Mal had looked at his sweet Sally with adoration. He had lost his heart to another woman, long ago.

"It's calf love," Mal said. "Sentimental and self-indulgent. 'Tis not how a man looks at the woman he considers his proper mate."

"Oh? And what does that expression resemble, pray tell?" she asked, more sharply than she intended.

She twisted to face him, and his look halted the rest of her accusation. His eyes were still serious but held a deep, warm light. He studied her as if he were probing her mind, weighing the emotions behind her words. His gaze touched every part of her face, not with timid reverence or indulgent fancy but with thoughtful attention. As if he inspected a real woman, cataloging all her perfections and flaws, and understood the person they came to form in whole.

As if he saw her, through and through. And approved what he saw.

Her response to this attention was much more than gentle warmth. A raw rush of vulnerability plummeted through her core, stunning in its intensity. She felt the absurd and very dangerous urge to lean against the tall, broad strength of him and fasten her lips to his. She wanted to twine her arms about him and never let go.

She stepped backwards. Her foot caught in the groove between cobbles, and she righted herself as his hand snaked out to grasp her wrist.

Mal could not see her and like her. He could not know the truth. The real Amaranthe was a liar and a thief. He would never look at her again with that warmth, with that cherishing, if he knew the things she had done.

"I hope Joseph will still have his position at Hunsdon House if he returns to us heartbroken and alone," she said instead. "He is likely to need it."

She turned away as if she had not just read his heart in his eyes, an honest declaration. As if she had not just admitted she had nothing to give him in return.

"TELL ME ABOUT MAL'S MOTHER."

Amaranthe sat in the warm kitchen with the Littlejohns. For two days they'd pitched in with projects around the inn, Mal hammering and hauling, painting shutters and fixing signs, and Amaranthe helping Beatrice air linens and organize the storerooms. The Littlejohns had plenty of assistance in the youths of many ages, boy and girl, who darted around the place, for they had continued the practice of taking children from the workhouse and giving them employment and a home. They had no children of their own making, but Bea had expressed no lament about that. She treated their helpers as part of the family, and she was full of stories about a coaching daughter who had lately married and set up a home of her own, with a baby on the way.

Amaranthe found the delay in reaching Favella, and Reuben, did not bother her very much. She liked Mal's sense of duty toward his family. Besides, the thought of seeing her cousin again filled her with cold dread.

"I'm curious about her. Mal's mother," she said in answer to Bea's surprised look. "I've gathered what his relationship with his father was like, but Mal doesn't speak of his mother very often."

Mal was busy in one of the storerooms that opened off the kitchen, fixing the hooks in the rafters that held cuts of meat for curing and herbs for drying. She watched his back, coatless again, shirtsleeves rolled up, muscles flexing beneath his waistcoat. He had to have heard, but he didn't comment on her interference.

"Marguerite," Beatrice said softly. "Her name was Marguerite. Born two years afore me, she was, and lovely as a flower."

Between them on the table sat wooden bowls overflowing with the cherries the two women had gathered that afternoon from the gardens behind the coaching inn. Beatrice's pile of pits was already much larger than Amaranthe's, but she was making a good show of herself.

"That's the name of a flower in medieval French,"

Amaranthe remarked. "The daisy. Though in Latin sources *marguerite* could also mean pearl, a word that comes from Old Persian. Marguerite, Queen of Navarre wrote a wonderful collection of short stories, the *Heptameron,* sixteenth-century French. I translated a poem of hers, 'The Mirror of the Sinful Soul,' for which she was called a heretic, because—"

She looked up and paused, her small knife halfway through a round ripe cherry, and blinked to see all of them watching her. "Forgive my prattle. I am interested in languages and old literature."

"Marguerite liked old things, too," Beatrice said with a smile, pushing aside a cherry pit with the side of her knife. "Our girl was as quick and lively as you ever saw. It was no surprise to us that she captured a duke."

"He wasn't a duke at the time." Mal's voice drifted to them, subdued. "Just an elder son and heir back from his Grand Tour, with nothing to do but roister around the countryside seducing innocent damsels."

"He was Lord Vernay then?" Amaranthe focused on extracting the pit of the fruit before her, as if the inquiry were entirely casual, but still she felt Mal's eyes upon her.

"Aye." Beatrice sighed. "She always swore they married, but she could never say where she put her copy of the marriage lines that she took from the priest. She had a spell when the lad left her, you see. Quite wild and out of her head with fever for a long while. I was married to Littlejohn by then, but Vernay put her up in a little home of her own overlooking the Avon Gorge. When I moved her here with us I searched all her things and found no trace of a document.

"We all begged him not to trifle with her, we did," Bea went on. "Knowing she was already sick. But young ones in love? When do they ever heed sense?" She shook her head as if she had not been young herself then, and equally in love, though to a steadier man.

"Sick with what?" Amaranthe couldn't help asking.

"Consumption," Beatrice answered. "Caught it as a girl, methinks, and was never free of it. When you live by the water, how do you escape the damp?" She dabbed at her eye with a corner of her apron, her fingers stained red with juice.

"She might have lived if he could have taken her away somewhere," Beatrice went on. "I often think that. Fresh, clean air on a country estate might have saved her. But the duke came looking for his heir, and when he found the lad had set up house with Marguerite, he was livid. He forced the boy to leave her behind, and I brought her here when she started to swell with child."

Bea sniffed and pressed the back of her hand to her nose. "She lingered a long time, with proper care, but when she learned he'd married...I think that broke her heart. After that, she lost strength so quickly."

She glanced toward the storeroom with blurry eyes. "She wanted more than anything to see you a grown man, Mal, but her lungs *and* her heart, broken together—she couldn't bear it."

"My father told me once she was the only woman he'd loved." Mal spoke with his back to them, but Amaranthe heard the stiffness in his voice and guessed he held back strong emotion. "Yet I notice he never came back until well after she'd died."

"Nay, you can't blame him if he couldn't bear to see her so ill," Bea sniffled. "Not many as could. They're not all as hale and brave as your Uncle Littlejohn, are they?" She gave her husband a watery smile, and he responded with a gruff rumble of confirmation.

"And he had to wait till his father the old duke died, didn't he? Methinks he came as soon as he could, Mal. 'Twas you who wouldn't let him be a father to you."

"As if I wanted to learn to shoot and ride to hounds with him, and bow to his duchess when it should have been my mother in her place," Mal said. "Christine could have been the most generous, noble woman in the world, and I still would have hated her. Though she was a paragon compared to Sybil," he added.

Beatrice smiled fondly at his tall, broad back. "Aye, you were a tough nut, our Mal o' Misfortune," she said. "But at the last you let him send you to school, and you're doing all right now, aren't you."

"If you call being robbed of my income and the children abandoned by their stepmother and servants in their own home all right." Mal emerged from the storeroom to join them in the kitchen, swiping a handful of pitted cherries from his aunt's bowl and popping them in his mouth. She swatted at him with her free hand.

"Aye, you'll sort that, I've no doubt. Sounds like our Miss Amaranthe extracted you from a proper scrape. It takes a clever woman, I always say."

"You always say it takes a strong back, when you want me to do something." Littlejohn swung across the room, a bundle of wood beneath his arm, and deposited the fuel next to the hearth.

"You always told me it takes cleverness in a lad, which is why I should let the duke pay me through school." Mal reached across the table and plucked a few pitted cherries from Amaranthe's smaller bowl. She didn't protest, feeling absurdly pleased by the attention. In the comfort of the family, with his coat off and cravat discarded, his state of undress was unbearably intimate. She could see every line of his body, and he was as well-made as a man could be.

"Where is she buried?" Amaranthe asked. "Marguerite."

"Around the corner at Saints Philip and James," Mal replied. "The duke was so kind as to give her a memorial in the church, though she wanted to be buried in St. Mary Redcliffe, which is where she swore Vernay pledged his vows to her, though the priest never could produce a record of the marriage, either."

"We can take her daisies," Amaranthe said, and his smile filled her with a giddy pleasure from head to toe.

After a pleasant evening she headed to bed in the room she'd been given, one of the nicer rooms overlooking the rear gardens and away from the noisy bustle of the yard. She'd shared the room with Miss Pettigrew, and it felt strangely empty though the girl had hardly filled it when she'd been present. She had washed her face, cleaned her teeth, and was braiding her hair for the night when a knock on the door surprised her.

"Come in."

The sight of Mal's face, caressed by the dancing shadows of the candle he held, pulled a chord deep in her belly. Ordinarily it would have shocked her to have a man in her room, even Joseph, but something about working, traveling, thinking out loud side by side with Mal over the past days and weeks made it feel natural for him to be in the room. At her side.

That was a silly thought. She pushed it aside. "Did you need something?"

"I came to see if you wanted a change of linens. Bea says she'll do the washing tomorrow."

Amaranthe made a face. She did not look forward to helping with laundry. "I think these are still fresh enough to take with us to Penwellen. I'll have Favella's staff launder them while we're there."

Traveling with one's own linens was one of the many small bits of advice from Miss Gregoire's Academy that had made a lasting impression on Amaranthe's mind. The Green Man she guessed was subject to far less vermin than many other places, but still, it never hurt to be cautious.

"Very well then. We're still leaving tomorrow?" he asked.

"If the chaise is ready, and you."

She tied a strip of cloth around the end of her braid to hold it, then met his eyes. The breath stopped in her throat. He still lacked a coat, and his powerful body made the room seem small. His hair had come free of its queue—he hadn't worn a wig for days—and she longed to run her fingers through the thick mass to see if his hair could truly be as soft as it looked. In the light of the small candle beside her bed his face looked harsh and hand-some, planed by the stubble covering his jaw. His lips were warm and firm and curved into a smile as she stared.

"I think your mother's name is in my book," Amaranthe blurted, undone by his presence in the small, darkened room where she slept. What fortune that she hadn't stripped down to her shift yet. She'd never have let him in the room if she were undressed.

Would she? Some part of her wanted to tempt Malden Grey. Wanted him to look at her again the way he had in the coaching yard when she saw Joseph off. When he meant to show her, presumably, how a man looked at a woman he truly prized, and she'd shied away, too afraid to hold his gaze.

A curiosity was growing beside her fear. A curiosity to know where such things led.

His eyes were veiled in shadow, their bright blue muted by the dark. The scent of flowering quince drifted through the open window, a welcome change from the ever-present coal smoke of London. Behind it swelled the damp reek of the sea, the scent that suffused her childhood. Something about that smell and its memories made Mal in her room, he undressed and she ready for bed, feel perfectly natural and right.

"In the book your cousin stole from you?" His voice was low

and soft, a caress that curled around her. She lifted her shoulders to her ears.

"Yes. I cannot say why, but I'm sure of it. Her name is in there. Marguerite, Lady Vernay. She would have styled herself such if she thought they were truly married."

How she hated conjuring Reuben in this intimate space. He was a draught of cold, dank air dousing the warmth.

"I'll help you get your book back simply because you want it, Amaranthe," he said softly. He stepped forward and took the end of her braid between his fingers, rubbing the dark curls. She watched, fascinated, warmth spreading through her body. Yet she shivered when his eyes met hers, dark, unfathomable. "I don't need any other reason."

"I do wonder how she came by the book, and how it traveled to Callington. But if I can get it back from him, you'll have a piece of her. Or something that was hers, I mean."

His mother's name in her book was a way to bind him to her. As if his hand in her hair wasn't entanglement enough. She was bound to him already, like it or not.

"I think my mother would have loved you as much as Beatrice does. You've won them over completely." He laid her long braid against her shoulder, the thick mass touching her breast, and let his fingers trail across her cheek as if he were exploring that texture, too. His thumb traced beneath her lower lip and her knees buckled.

He said nothing to suggest that he was won over. He was staring at her mouth, but she couldn't be sure what that meant. Reuben had pressed his body on hers without passion or love or care, only the will to dominate.

The swift pulse of blood in her ears felt different than when Reuben had held her tightly. The tremor in her body was of a different nature. But it shared something with fear, perhaps fear of the unknown, or fear of what she might learn if he kissed her.

As Mal leaned close Amaranthe smelled again Reuben's rank beery breath, felt the fleshy press of his stomach against her belly. Heard Eyde's whimpers of pain as she knelt on the floor, beaten raw.

She stepped back and sucked in a long breath. Mal blinked with surprise and let his hand fall. She saw hurt flash through his eyes before he guarded his expression. He too fell back, putting distance between them.

"I apologize if I've imposed."

"You haven't," she said quickly. "I appreciate your concern. About the linens. I—" She turned away to regard the trunk against the wall, the valise on the single chair. "I suppose I must pack for tomorrow."

Her things were already packed, that was plain. "We should be there in a day or two, I should think," she said. "And then we can talk to Reuben. I very much want to show you my book."

He withdrew into the shadows by the door, and a small ache unfurled in her middle, watching him move away from her. She wanted him close. If only she could master this urge to flinch. She wanted him to touch her. She wanted not to think of Reuben every time he drew near. She wanted her wish to be close to him to overcome her fear that the reality would be a disappointment, nothing at all like the luscious feelings that wove through her thoughts and dreams.

"I wish for you to have what you what, Amaranthe," he said quietly.

Him. She wanted him. There was no doubt now what the response in her body meant, despite the flinching. Perhaps it was always this way to be close to a man, the combination of wariness and desire, the fear that passion would lead to abandonment and hurt. It had for Eyde. It had for Mal's mother. It had for women the world over, for centuries. How could she trust that the gentleness of his touch, the steadiness of his eyes, the promise in his smile meant he would cherish her?

How could she trust that he would understand and forgive what she had done to support herself and the people she loved?

That thought kept her from calling his name as he stepped through the door and left her. She'd not needed to see him among his family to know Malden Grey was a good man, decent and generous and steady to the bone, whatever wild fits he'd shown in his youth. She'd not needed the thrill of his nearness and touch to tell her she longed to reach out for him and never let go.

It would harm him to marry her. But he didn't know that. And one rising, rebellious part of her wanted to explore what might happen between them before he found out.

CHAPTER SIXTEEN

"Well, that's as stuck as it could be," Mal said.
They stood by the side of the posting road, regarding the chaise buried up to its axle in mud. Mal was impressed by how quickly, and securely, they had managed to mire the vehicle in a fairly obvious obstacle, but the worn ruts in the well-used road were hard to avoid.

"There must be a way to get it free," Amaranthe fretted. They were a day's drive from Callington, still in Devonshire but close to the border with Cornwall. "Favella expects her babe any moment."

"Aye, another brace of 'orses could get it out." The post boy they'd gained at the last coaching inn took off his cap and scratched his head, regarding the enormous soup of thick dank mud that had caught their vehicle fast. "But it's a dry night we'll need afore we try it, and they must be a sturdy pair of cattle, and that's that."

"A night before we can get free?" Amaranthe moaned. "But where are we to stay?"

"Hi, now!" The post boy called to a farmer pushing a wheeled barrow in the field across the way. A small stream let out into the hedged ditch lining the road, the source of the mud since it had rained most of the two days since they'd left Bristol. "How far to the next coaching inn, father? And have ye a brace of oxen to pull us free from our puddle, aye?"

"Me oxen you can have for a fair price tomorrow, if they finish plowing the north farthing tonight," the farmer called back. "And you've a mile or two yet to the Queen's Head in Tavistock." He rested his barrow to regard the bright yellow vehicle splashed with smelly mud. "That's a fair right fix you're in!" he marveled. "You'll lose a wheel do you try pulling 'er out now, I reckon."

"And we'll lose our luggage if we leave the coach here overnight," Amaranthe guessed.

But the farmer had a solution for them. The post boy unhitched the horses and followed the farmer away, disappearing down a small lane leading along the edge of the field. Amaranthe paced a stretch of narrow earth verging the road, high enough to be away from the mud. The skirts of her riding habit swirled about her as she walked, and Mal admired the view a while before he took a seat on a fallen tree and patted the log beside him.

"The farmer said he had a cart we can borrow. He'll not abandon us."

She sat beside him, and her subtle, rich scent drifted to his nose, like cherries in vanilla.

"Heliotrope," he said suddenly. "That's what you smell like."

She smiled, and he felt ridiculously pleased at being able to divert her mind. "Not many people can place the scent."

"The flower that turns toward the sun," he said. "There's a myth about some poor nymph wasting away for love of the sun god Helios, I think."

"Her name was Clytie," Amaranthe said. "There's a plant

called turnsole, named for the same reason, that was used as a dye in medieval manuscripts. It made a beautiful blue for colorists who couldn't afford lapis lazuli. Something like the shade of your eyes, in fact," she said, leaning close to peer into his face.

He stared back at her. Going about without her bonnet as she gardened with his aunt in Bristol had subtly darkened her nose and cheeks, deepening her natural color. Stranded at the side of the road in a costly habit, she was the most beautiful creature he'd ever seen. He was very glad he was the one stranded with her.

"You're saying my eyes are the second best blue," he said.

Instead of amusing her, as he'd hoped, her face turned gloomy and she sat back with a sigh. "My book," she said. "It's so close I can practically feel the vellum and the pinpricks the scribe used to rule the pages. I can smell the leather binding."

She inhaled, and her small moan of longing scored straight to Mal's gut. He didn't blame her if the book was rather more on her mind than the condition of her cousin's wife. From what he had gathered in their conversations on the road, the baronet and his lady had treated Amaranthe like an unpaid servant when she'd lived in their household, expecting her to tend to their needs while having no regard for her own.

He couldn't help but resent, however, that he was further from her mind than both her cousin's wife and her manuscript. She confused him to no end. The way she watched him sometimes suggested she liked what she saw. Very often their eyes met in shared understanding or a secret joke, even when other people were about them. But every time he drew near, she stiffened and pulled away.

It was not alone the innocence of a maid; he sensed some caution or fear. It was not dislike, he knew. She sat next to him as easily as she would have one of the children, or her brother.

But if he tried to touch her, even in the smallest fashion, he sensed she would bolt. It was frustrating and bewildering and arousing all at once, and she had him as intent on her as a cat watching a moving string.

Oliver had been highly mistaken to suggest a wife steadied a man. Amaranthe Illingworth was driving him to distraction.

"Hi now," the post boy called cheerily as he rode the team up the road, the farmer's cart fastened behind him and the farmer in it. "I've borrowed us a wagon that gets us to the Queen's Head, and father here will bring it back when we're finished, and all for a fair price, aye?"

Amaranthe reached into the stuck chaise for her small valise, then watched from the side of the road as Mal transferred the luggage. When he turned he caught her appreciative expression as she watched him work, but when he met her eye, questioning, she looked away. The warm imprint of her gaze left him with a different kind of frustration. She wasn't a woman who played games or affected coyness, and he sensed she didn't mean to toy with him, either. He would have to ask an honest answer of her, and soon, because he didn't think he could take much more of her hungry looks. And what would it mean for a marriage if she avoided his touch?

They received glares from the ostlers and drivers in the cobbled yard of the Queen's Head when they rolled beneath the arched entrance in their humble wagon, blocking the way of faster and more important vehicles. A quick consultation with the landlord revealed a different problem.

The rain and mired roads had left several travelers at the inn awaiting a drier day, and the host had only one private room available. They could share accommodations in a common room, men in one bed and women in another, but Mal saw the look of quiet horror on Amaranthe's face at the thought of having to bunk with strangers in linens not her own. He drew her aside to confer in a corner of the noisy office while passengers bustled past to and from the coffee room, the bar, the sitting rooms near the front of the inn that overlooked a quieter street, and the drawing room above.

"We can look for another inn in town," he said as she worried her lip with small white teeth. "I'm sure there are several, and many quieter than a noisy coaching inn."

"But what if they are full as well?" she asked. "We should have to travel further yet to reclaim our coach tomorrow, even granted we can pull it out of the muck."

"We could take the private room together if we say we are married," Mal said slowly.

A tightening around her eyes said she'd already considered it. "I'll be a gentleman, of course," he hastened to assure her.

"I believe you would. But all the same—the impropriety of it. What would Joseph say? Or Mrs. Blackthorn?"

He spared a smile for the notion that a self-sufficient woman like Amaranthe went about in fear of a scolding from her strong-minded servants. "You might stay here while I look elsewhere, and—"

"My word, the hubble-bubble of this place!" A woman's voice carried across the traffic and chatter. "I was told this was one of the finer inns. George, see that there is a private room secured for me, and a private sitting parlor for our dinner. I do not think I can bear more of this common press."

Amaranthe whirled to watch the imposing lady marching down the hall to the office. A tailed Pierrot jacket with military style buttons, an expansive skirt over panniers that nearly touched each wall, and an enormous hat atop a tall, powdered wig proclaimed her wealth and importance. A pale, skinny boy, no doubt her George, trotted ahead of her dutifully.

Before Mal could say a word, or George for that matter, Amaranthe darted to the counter and the red-faced landlord behind it. She pointed over her shoulder at Mal, passed a handful of coins to the landlord, and in return received a metal key.

Mal didn't try to contain his smile as she rejoined him. "Mrs. Illingworth, I presume?" he said at her guilty, triumphant expression.

"Mr. and Mrs. Delaval," she muttered, taking his arm and pulling him out of the way of the great lady still bearing down on them. "I'm sorry. I didn't want to use my name, and to take yours—"

Would seem too much like they were truly married. He understood. "Which room have we, then, Mrs. Delaval?" he asked. Just her pretending to be his wife filled him with a ballooning sense of satisfaction. It made her his, for a time, in the smallest way.

"Well, I never heard of such a preposterous thing!" the great lady sputtered when George made his inquiries and was presumably denied. She turned to glare at Amaranthe and Mal when the landlord gestured in their direction, obviously indicating that they had claimed the last room. "George, we will go to the Duke of Bedford's inn and find rooms there. I hear it's on the grounds of the old abbey. Monastics know how to show better hospitality to weary travelers, I should hope!"

"She does know that Henry VIII dissolved the monasteries, including Tavistock Abbey?" Mal whispered in Amaranthe's ear. Her hair, coming loose from its twist, tickled his cheek. "I thought much of the green stone used around the town came from villagers dismantling the abbey after it closed."

"I lied to that man," Amaranthe said, looking stricken, and holding her valise as if she had the leash of a recalcitrant pet. "But she was about to claim our room, and I'm too weary to continue on today. I want a wash and a cream tea."

"Whatever my lady desires," Mal promised, taking the key with a small bow.

If she detested lies, then she couldn't be a liar, could she? Mal felt considerably lighter in the chest area as they took turns freshening up.

After his own wash and donning a fresh cravat, Mal looked for Amaranthe in one of the small private parlors on the first floor. Their window looked out on the spired tower of St. Eustachius church and, beyond, the green bogs and stony tors of Dartmoor.

Mal paused to appreciate the view. He had grown up around dramatic scenery, climbing the Avon Gorge with friends and hunting for bilberries in Leigh Woods. But there was something lonely and haunted about the bare, wild moors dotted with the occasional longhouse and standing stones. It was a pocket of ancient myth lying, mouth open, beside the modern world, and he relished it.

He savored also the sight of Amaranthe presiding over tea, pouring him a dish and adding the one lump of sugar she knew he liked. He had seen her habit hanging in the room, neatly brushed, when it was his turn to change and freshen. She wore a simple open robe of blue silk with a saffron stomacher, a gown of Sybil's that he had seen her wear for dinner at home, and though her hair was unpowdered and arranged quite simply, her quiet loveliness and the intimate domestic arrangement drew a thread around his heart and pulled it tight.

He'd not been mistaken to choose her. It had been the single truest and most accurate instinct of his unlucky life.

"Feeling better?" she asked as he seated himself. She cut open a scone and passed it to him.

"Much. I like our room. I'm very glad you didn't let Lady Abbey take it. I'm sure she'll be much more comfortable with the accommodations at the Bedford Inn."

"Emmet!" she exclaimed, watching him, and he paused with a spoon in the air.

"What did you call me?"

"Foreigner. You put your cream on your scone first," she scolded.

"I thought that's how it's done."

"Upcountry." She shook her head. "We Cornish put the jam on first, see? It's a dead giveaway where he's from, how a man takes his cream tea." She showed him her own scone, solidly heaped with jam beneath a generous dollop of cream. "The cream, at least, is clotted, not whipped."

"Have mercy," Mal said, and commenced dressing his scone exactly as he wished. "I imagine I'll be putting a foot wrong everywhere at Penwellen. I hear your accent strengthening the closer you get to the Tamar River."

"They say the devil daren't set foot in Cornwall," she answered, her eyes sparkling with humor. "King Arthur was born in Cornwall, don't you remember? The stones of the old giants are scattered all over, and you've to watch for mermaids and selkies on the shore. If you find the selkie's seal skin you can keep her with you in her human form, but a mermaid will lure you to the depths of the sea and drown you."

"Or take me to lost land of Lyonesse," he said, entering into her playful spirit. "Lying beneath the sea between Land's End and the Isles of Scilly. Home of the hero Tristan, of Tristan and Isolde fame."

"We call it Lethowsow," she said solemnly. "A mighty king-dom, prosperous and peaceful, with hundreds of churches and great forests. Sunk beneath the sea in one night of terrible storms. On a calm day you can see the spires of the churches beneath the water and hear the ringing of their bells."

He adored her like this. "I had not taken you for such a fanciful creature, Mrs. Delaval," Mal teased. "You seemed so proper and serious when I came upon you in your home. Hard at work on your medieval manuscripts, preserving centuries-old knowledge."

Her eyes fell and her manner changed, the gleam of mischief fading. He immediately wanted it back. "Tell me how you became so preoccupied with old books and lost languages," he said.

"My father, mostly." She stirred milk into her tea and sniffed it. Her fleeting expression of pleasure tugged at him. "He was fond of classical antiquity, as I mentioned, but he was also a linguist of sorts. He made a study of the Cornish language and was compiling a manuscript of old Cornish myths and legends. One of his colleagues laid claim to it when he died, but I've always thought about finding and finishing it." She sipped her tea and lifted her eyes to his. "Tell me how you became interested in the law."

"Because I haven't the temperament to take orders in the military, and I haven't the proper meekness to be a priest. As a bastard I cannot inherit so must make my own way, and I haven't any skills for a trade." He shrugged. "But I can read, and I can argue for as long as necessary, so the law seemed appropriate, and my father paid my fees."

"Were you close with him?"

"Not in the least. Once a quarter he hauled me into his study to give me a full accounting of my errors and flaws, then handed over the allowance by which I was supposed to amend my ways." Mal shook his head at the memories. "I might have been better off if he'd left me to run a coaching inn in Bristol."

"You seem suited for the law," she said softly. "I think you'll be able to accomplish great things, once you're called."

"Once I am married and therefore called." He met her eyes, and again her gaze fell. Her constant retreat was wearing on him. What was wrong with him that she would not accept him?

That she could enjoy his company, even desire him—for he was sure he read her gaze correctly—but refused to act?

"Is it difficult, being illegitimate?"

"Yes," he said harshly. "So many people judge me on that alone. I know it weighs on how people regard me, even when they claim it doesn't."

She stared at him, her eyes dark but steady. "It doesn't matter to me."

"You say that." The words tumbled from him against his better judgment. "Yet I notice you cannot bear my touch."

She sprang from her seat as if a fire had begun there. "That's not true."

"It isn't?" Ever the gentleman, he stood as well. "You draw back whenever I am near you."

"That is not because of you."

"Indeed?" He hated the bark of laughter that followed. He heard the hurt in it, too many long years of being teased, rejected, and passed over. Mal o' Misfortune. The bastard of a duke. The orphan of a lightskirt and a rogue. "Who else would it be concerning, then?"

All his life when he saw others with advantages and pleasures he'd never have, he told himself he didn't care, that he'd never wanted anything that had been denied him because of his birth. But she denied him, and he regretted that bitterly.

She paced around the small room, twisting her hands together. She must be truly overset to leave her tea growing cold. She paused before him, and her scent filled his nose. Damn her for affecting him the way she did.

"I should have known," she said in a halting fashion. "I should have seen that—" She shook herself and breathed deeply. "I owe you an explanation."

"You owe me nothing," he said woodenly.

"I want you to know." She dragged her gaze up to meet his,

and he felt lost at the look of hopeless longing in her eyes. "I haven't...allowed myself to be—close to anyone. Because of Reuben," she said.

"I see." He steeled himself against the blow of this knowledge. "You have a *tendre* for your cousin. Carrying a torch for him, I take it?"

"No!" The word burst from her. He felt the small rush of air between them. "Good heavens, no." She took his hand, and he reeled at the warmth and desire that shot through him at her touch. "Not that. Quite the opposite."

He struggled to understand, and horror twined with suspicion. "He—?"

"Not me. He forced himself on Eyde and then turned her out of his house when she fell pregnant. When I found out—"

She clutched his hand with both of hers, and as much as he wanted to draw her close, instinct warned him to make no move. To let her be in control of how their bodies touched.

She swallowed. "When I found out, he demanded to have his way with me. Eyde and I left that day. I couldn't stay in the house, and she had nowhere to go. Derwa is my cousin's illegitimate daughter," she said softly.

This was news; he'd assumed Derwa was Davey's child. Mal curled his fingers gently around her palm, still holding his. "You escaped to Oxford then," he said.

"We went to Bath first, to my old schoolmistress, who gave us shelter for a time. She had connections in Oxford who could give me work, since Joseph had no means to support us. I was certain that if I were with Joseph, Reuben could not force me back into his home. He never tried, and we moved to London and were quite happily free of him, until Favella wrote. But every time—"

She halted, then straightened her shoulders and looked him

in the eye. "Each time you came close to me, I feared I would feel not you, but Reuben's slime."

"I see," he said again, trying desperately to shut off the surge of despair. She would have nothing to do with him because of what her cousin had done. He cursed the man silently with the vilest curses he could conjure. "I understand you would want no one to touch you."

"That's not true. I want you to touch me." She gulped, and he watched the delicate movement of her throat, of her lips as they opened to speak again, her voice low and throaty. "I want to touch you. But I'm afraid of what I might *feel*."

"That would be the first time in your life you've been afraid of anything, I'm guessing." He stroked a thumb along the side of her hand, the lightest gesture he could think of to show understanding, support.

"Oh, I fear many things."

He was trapped in her eyes. Dusk descended outside, the room fading into shadow as they had not thought to light candles. But the light in her eyes was clear and strong. "What I fear most, I think, is never finding out how it would feel. To touch you. To have you touch me."

An overpowering hope slammed him, a sudden turnaround of his despair. "Perhaps you ought to lay that fear to rest, then."

A smile tugged at the corner of her mouth. "You are not a dog I am to try patting on the head, to overcome my fear it might bite me."

"I am exactly that." His voice came as a low rumble. He felt her answering laugh inside his chest. "Try me and see."

He stood still, waiting for her decision. He feared he might die if she couldn't conquer her fear. *I want you to touch me.* He'd never heard sweeter words in his life.

Holding his gaze, her eyes dark pools, she raised his hand to her mouth and slowly slid his fingers over her lips. Desire crashed through him. Her lips were cool as cream. She pressed her cheek to his palm, then moved his hand to her throat, pressing the heel of his palm beneath her collarbone. The fabric of the fichu tucked into her neckline fluttered beneath his fingers, and her breath grew fast. His own sounded ragged in his ears.

"All right?" she whispered, as if asking permission.

"Very much so." His voice scratched his throat. Desire had him tight and hard, but he stood riveted as if he were one of the standing stones on the moors. Nothing could induce him to move and frighten her away.

She rose to her tiptoes and brought her cheek close to his, as he had done to her on other occasions. The soft, warm breath against his ear stirred a nearly painful ache. She slid her fingers into his hair beneath the leather strip that held his queue and her touch on his scalp made him groan with pleasure.

She pressed her lips to his cheek, dragging her mouth over the day's stubble, and he squeezed his eyes shut to hold himself at bay. Her scent, her touch, her heat surrounded him. The sight of her hazy eyes and soft skin was too much for mortal man to bear.

The press of her mouth against his obliterated all thought. The sheer joy that shot through him was like nothing he'd ever experienced. As much as he wanted to lock his arms about her, devour her completely, he also wanted to stand here for the next eternity and simply enjoy the sensation of Amaranthe's soft, shy kisses. She tasted of strawberries and when she brought her palms to rest on his cheeks and hold his face still for her exploration, he thought his head might explode.

He moved his lips in return, answering her gentle foray, responding as delicately as he could. Her lips pressed against his more firmly, her mouth shaping to his. She twined her arms about his shoulders, pulling herself firmly against him, and the press of her soft breasts against his chest filled his mind with fog. Thoughtlessly, he lifted a hand to the small of her back, urging her closer, and she snuggled in with a soft sigh that was his undoing. When he opened his mouth against hers, the tip of her tongue ventured against his lips, tasting him, and his heroic restraint snapped.

With a groan of satisfaction, he dipped his arms about her slender back and hauled her onto his chest. Her head fell back, giving him the perfect angle to delve his tongue into her mouth, exploring, possessing. She was every kind of sweetness. She matched his greed with a sweet earnestness that made him press her closer. Her breath came in soft pants, and her hands slid from his face to his hair to his shoulders as if she wanted to touch him everywhere at once. She burrowed against him, as if she couldn't be close enough, and his hands wandered down her back, pressing, squeezing, curving her body into his. He was sure he gripped a rump pad, there to fill out the back of her gown, and she reared back, her eyes flying wide.

He wanted to sip at her mouth for hours, but he wanted to taste her everywhere. He kissed along the line of her jaw, nipping a tender earlobe, and she shivered with delight. Her chest rose and fell in short pants as he nibbled and licked his way down her neck, flicking his tone into the dent between her collarbones. The pulse there beat madly, answering the high tide that pulsed through him.

"*Mal.*" Her whisper of delight spurred him on, a sense of triumph soaring through him as she yielded beneath his mouth, his hands. He pulled the lace tucked into the neckline of her gown, sliding the delicate fabric across her skin, and relished her shudder at the sensation. Her breath hitched as he bent his mouth to the bare skin left exposed, using lips and teeth and tongue to explore the warm, scented expanse. She tasted of cream, richly sweet with a hint of salt, maddeningly delicious.

He canted her hips to slide her up his body, bringing more of that luscious skin within reach. He dragged his mouth over the tops of her breasts, heady with the need to devour her, to discover as much as he could. The stomacher pushed her breasts up firmly and he laved the soft, plump flesh with his tongue, reveling in her gasps. Her fingers dug into his shoulders as she clung to him. He would have to unpin her robe to go further, and Mal growled with frustration. Like a starved man he pulled her hips against him, burrowing his aching arousal into the thick folds of her skirts. At the same time he tugged with his teeth at the fabric of her neckline, growling with satisfaction when he exposed the top of one delicate nipple.

She froze, and her eyes popped open, dazed with passion and alarm. Mal lifted his head. Her arms stayed clasped tightly around him but her body went taut as a bow, and he didn't know if it was from pleasure or shock.

Slowly he lowered her until her feet once again touched the ground, hissing as she slid against his body. He was no better than her rotter of a cousin, mindless to everything but his own passion.

"Too much." With an effort he loosened his arms, forced himself to step away, hoping he didn't fall over. His entire body was a wall of flame. "I'm sorry."

"I'm not." She tugged her bodice into place, and he gritted his teeth at the loss of her warmth. "That was—just right."

He couldn't resist touching her lower lip, plum-colored with his kisses. "All the same, I'd best sleep on the floor tonight."

"Don't be daft." Her voice was breathy, full of laughter and wonder. "We can roll up a blanket and divide the bed. Or put a sword between us, like Lancelot and Guinevere. I trust you."

That confession moved him more than anything else she'd said or done. After he'd invited her to touch him, then lost his head and nearly ravished her on the spot, her simple declaration of trust gutted him completely.

"I didn't ruin it, then."

Her eyes held his, brimming with an expression he couldn't decipher, but he saw the signs of a woman who had discovered passion and was not put off by either her body's response or his.

"I'm not ruined," she said softly.

He cupped his hands about her cheeks, flushed the red she used in her manuscripts. "You must marry me."

That broke the reverie. A shadow fell across her face, and she lowered her eyes and stepped away. "I cannot."

"I thought you didn't care that I'm a bastard." The old bitterness rose like bile in his throat, wiping away every trace of bliss.

"That's not it at all." She reached for her lace, still in his hand.

Like a beast, he held it out of her reach. "Your cousin, then? Or your brother. I thought he would approve." His rage surprised him, frustrated desire making him snap like a fox at bay.

"My reasons are my own." She snatched her lace and turned toward the door.

"So you can kiss me," he said, his voice low but filled with savagery. "You can touch me, hold me, *desire* me...but you won't wed me."

"I'm sorry, Mal," she whispered, and slipped out the door.

Mal felt like smashing his fist into the wall. She'd drawn away from him again, and he had no idea how to lure her back.

CHAPTER SEVENTEEN

C ornwall had changed almost as much as Amaranthe had.
The lush Tamar Valley was green with the growth of spring, but what she remembered was walking away from it. Coming back felt strange. For Mal's enjoyment she pointed out the rugged granite moorlands called Goen Bren, with the peaks known as Rough Tor and Brown Willy, the highest point in Cornwall, carving the sky. The turnpike road was new and smooth, unlike the rutted track she and Eyde had walked on their flight from Penwellen. Her stomach tensed as they neared Hingston Downs and Kit Hill, with its ancient mines and quarries, casting its shadow on the old market town of Callington.

"King Arthur had a court here, they say." She chattered foolishly as she directed the coach through town so she could show him the sights she remembered. Putting off the approach to Reuben as long as possible. "The town is mentioned in the Domesday Book. I made copies of the page for the bookseller to sell to tourists. That is St. Mary's Church with its Celtic cross and the tombs of Lord Assheton and Willoughby de Broke. His wife was the first owner of my Book of Hours. There is Well

Street, where all the water comes from, and down that street, about a mile, is Dupath Well, which has curative powers."

"Is there anyone you wish to see while you are here?" Mal asked. "Anyone you, er, might have left behind. The reams of suitors with broken hearts left scattered in your wake, perhaps."

She looked away, her heart pinching though he said the words in jest. If only he knew. No man had stirred her heart, or caught at her soul, the way he did.

"I would like to visit Mr. Finney's bookshop, if we have an occasion. But no, there were no abandoned suitors left in my wake. I danced with Mr. Treen at an assembly once, but that was..." She shook her head, smiling at the memory. "A brief, passing fancy."

"I detest him already," Mal said in the most cordial tone.

She forced a laugh at his teasing, but steeled herself as the coach rolled out of Callington toward the tiny village of Haye. The shadow of six years past hovered over her. She could almost see the ghost of her old self trudging along this road, a frightened Eyde at her side, fearing with every sound behind them that Reuben was on their heels.

At St. Ann's Chapel they had found space on a mining cart that took them all the way to Devon, and from there they managed a place atop the stagecoach to Bath. Looking back, it was a miracle that two young women traveling alone had not been robbed, beaten, and left for dead. Surely some angel had walked at their weary side.

When the chaise turned down the lane heading to Penwellen, the house was not nearly as imposing as Amaranthe remembered. Coming from the tiny rector's cottage in St. Cleer, the stone manor house with its Palladian windows and small porch had seemed a veritable mansion to a girl of sixteen. Now that she had run tame through Hunsdon House, Penwellen looked tiny. The fountain in front stood empty of water, green moss lining the basin. The formal flower beds lay untended and bare, their edges untrimmed. Grass grew through the gravel in the drive, and panes in several of the windows looked dark as if broken.

A large black wreath hung on the front door.

"The house is in mourning," Mal murmured. "What should we do?"

Her heart crashed against her ribs. Was Reuben dead? If he were, it would mean an end to all her fears and worries. But on the heels of that hope came the more likely realization. Favella had not survived childbirth.

"We'll stop in the stables," Amaranthe said. "The post boy can water and rest the horses before he returns. Thaker, the stable boy, can tell us what happened, if he's still here."

"Thaker?" Mal lifted her down from the chaise, and Amaranthe was not so lost in worry that she did not appreciate the swift, firm squeeze of his hands about her. He communicated reassurance and strength.

She had left Penwellen in the clothes she stood up in, welts on her hands and a deep bruise to her pride and her innocence. She returned with far more confidence. And with Mal at her side. How grateful she was to have him with her, sensible, steady, resourceful Malden Grey.

She'd fallen hard and deeply in love with him on this journey south, and she could never tell him that.

"It's a Cornish word for child, usually a boy," she answered as Mal unloaded their luggage. "He was left on the parish with no note, no name, no known parents, much like your Littlejohn. So they named him 'boy.' You say 'cheel' or 'maid' if you mean girl. You say 'brae' to mean many, you say 'proper' to mean good. And if everyone calls you 'me luv' or 'me andsome,'" and here she gave him a stern look, "you are to think nothing of it. That's just how we be."

He grinned at her. "I do like when your Cornish comes out. It's very charming."

"Giss on, you!" she tossed over her shoulder, then turned and lifted a long pole to thump on the ceiling of the hay mow above them. "Thaker used to relax there in between duties," she explained. "He doesn't hear, but he can tell when vehicles and horses are about by the vibrations. This used to be our signal when we—"

She stopped when she saw the figure standing in the open doors of the stable. Thaker was no longer a boy but a man full grown, sandy haired, wearing a leather coat and breeches and a set of filthy boots. His beard split in a wide grin.

"Am!" he called in greeting. She had tried to teach him spoken language, while together they developed a system of signs, expressions, and wild gestures by which they communicated well enough. Amaranthe held out a hand to shake, but he pulled her into an exuberant hug, then turned with an expectant smile to Mal.

"M-A-L," she signed, drawing the letters in the air. His letters had been one of the first things she taught Thaker when she arrived, and in return he taught her how to hitch a cart and take care of horses.

Thaker grinned and held up a hand, circling a finger as if with a ring. Amaranthe shook her head. *No, not my husband.*

Thaker shrugged and grinned. *Why not?*

She circled her arms in a wreath, then pointed to the big house and crossed her hands over her chest. *Who died?*

He shook his head sadly and made the motion of rocking a baby in his arms. *The lady. Her babe, too.*

"Favella died in childbirth," Amaranthe said to Mal, her throat tightening. "I should have come sooner."

"I doubt there was anything you could have done, Amaranthe." Mal rubbed her shoulder.

And Reuben? she asked Thaker, making the sign they had used to refer to the baronet, straight-armed, stomping feet.

Angry. He made a face and curved his hands into claws.

"I feared that, too," Amaranthe said to Mal. "Reuben will not be in a good frame of mind. Perhaps we should wait before we go to the house."

Thaker tapped his chest and made the ring sign again.

Married? Amaranthe asked him in delight. *You?*

He nodded, then rocked his arms again, twice.

With babies! Amaranthe signed back. *I want to meet them!*

Thaker led them out of the stables and past the gardens to a small set of cottages that had been set aside for servants. Amaranthe noticed that most of them sat empty and neglected, but one had a small flowering garden in front and ivy climbing the sides. The smell of fresh bread drifted out to meet them as Thaker opened the door and called inside. "Weh!"

"Da!" A small infant in a linen gown crawled across the floor to him with a joyful, drooling smile. Across the room, beyond a dining table, lay a warm kitchen lit with a merry fire. A woman sat in a rocker next to the hearth, nursing a baby. She drew a shawl over her bosom as they entered and gave them a contented smile.

"Wasson, my lover!" she said to Thaker, signing and speaking at the same time. "You ought to have warned me we'd have guests."

My wife, Wenna. Thaker beamed, spelling her name. He introduced Amaranthe and Mal to Wenna, then indicated the children. *The babe is Morvath, a bonny maid, and this,* he lifted the crawling child, *is Branok, my big strapping boy.*

"Da!" The boy beamed at them, drooling around a tiny white tooth.

"They're absolutely beautiful, Thaker," Amaranthe answered, signing. "Congratulations to you both."

"So this is his Miss Amaranthe!" Wenna said. "Come in, come in. I'll fix you a tea dreckly when the cheel is fed. He goes on and on about you, miss. Says you're top 'o the trees, you are." She gave her husband a saucy grin, and he signed back.

Cheeky.

"Thaker was my one friend while I lived here." Amaranthe took the seat Wenna indicated. "This is Mr. Malden Grey, who will be a barrister. Favella sent for me to be with her in childbed, but it appears—I was too late."

Her throat closed unexpectedly. She and Favella had never been close, but her cousin's wife, not much older than Amaranthe, had been her companion after her parents died and she was left alone. Though nervous and prone to bouts of the vapors, a fretsome woman who found the ill in everything, Favella had been better than nothing.

Wenna shook her head and captured the tiny fist waving from beneath the shawl. "She took to bed weeks ago when the doctor advised it." With her free hand she signed for Thaker. "But the pains started a week ago, and she suffered for days. At the last, the baronet insisted the doctor cut her open, thinking to save the baban, but 'e'd the cord wrapped fast around the neck, poor mite." She clasped her babe closer and her face was soft as she watched her older child attempt to climb his father's leg.

"What a terrible end for her," Amaranthe said. "Reuben must be devastated."

"He's howling mad, innit 'e," Wenna confirmed. "Goes on and on about his heir. You'd think that's all he cared about."

It is all he cared about, Thaker said. He hoisted the boy in one arm and with his free hand set out the things for tea. Amaranthe smiled to see her friend so domesticated. At least things had gone well for Thaker since she left.

What about Eyde? Thaker asked. He outlined a pregnant belly in front of his waist.

"She's with me," Amaranthe signed back. "Married to a Welshman named Davey—no, you'd like him!" she insisted when Thaker shook his head and huffed. "And her child Derwa is nearly six. Healthy and bright as a button."

"She's the one I was brought on to replace, then," Wenna said. "The baronet didn't want to keep me when I took up with Thaker, but the lady couldn't get any other help. Everyone here knew what himself had done to Eyde. I told him I had the pox when ee first come at me, and ee let me alone after that."

Mal fell into a coughing fit and reached for a dish of tea too. Amaranthe grinned. "I wish I had thought to do that."

Thaker put down the struggling boy to bring biscuits to the table. The child crawled to Mal, grunting, and pulled himself to a standing position using the cuff of Mal's boot.

"Da," he said seriously, regarding his guest.

"I should say so." Mal nodded in agreement, blowing on his tea.

Amaranthe's heart melted, watching Mal with the child. She liked the calm, direct manner he had with his siblings, but seeing him interact with the infant made her all soft and whimmy.

She'd never envisioned herself in a warm kitchen with babes crawling about her; her dreams involved vellum folios and inks. But a sudden, wild notion filled her. A vision of herself in her parlor, the light falling like gold leaf over her page. Her cleaning her knife and capping her ink as Mal entered with a babe cradled in his arms. Their babe, with his blue eyes and rakish smile and that fearless way he had of confronting the world.

Her vision swam, her ears ringing with a faint, high sound for a moment. She blinked to find Thaker standing before her. He pressed his hands together, then turned them open, watching her with a curious, expectant look.

"A prayer?" Amaranthe pointed to the sky. "Of thanks, that

we are together again?" She had taught Thaker the simple prayers, rector's daughter that she was.

He shook his head, giving his hoarse, high chuckle. He left the room, and Amaranthe turned to Wenna. "What do you think Reuben will do now?"

Wenna set the shawl aside and propped up the baby while she adjusted her bodice. Morvath belched, then looked about with a satisfied smile.

"Hold 'er?" Wenna rose from the chair and handed the infant to Amaranthe. "Me luv forgot the butter. I expect the baronet will marry afore his mourning is done, fixed on having an heir as ee is."

"Who inherits if Reuben does not have a child?" Mal asked. He watched with interest as Amaranthe tried first one way, then another of holding the squirming infant. Finally, she and Morvath agreed that she would hold the babe upright so she could look about.

"Joseph," Amaranthe answered. When she drew breath her head filled with the milky scent of child. A sensation she had never experienced, never thought to experience, twinged through her belly. The soft, warm weight on her lap felt lovely.

"Our father was the second son, and entail is on the heirs male," Amaranthe explained. "So Joseph is the next baronet if Reuben does not sire a boy."

Her attention fixed on Thaker as he entered the room carrying something wrapped in linen. Something the size of a book. Her breath stopped when he withdrew the covering and placed a leather-bound parcel on the table before her. She barely felt it when he lifted Morvath and cradled the baby while Wenna turned from the pantry to regard her curiously.

All Amaranthe heard was the blood in her ears. She recognized the dark leather. With trembling fingers she unwound the long straps and opened the cover.

"My book." She looked up but saw nothing at first, her eyes blurred with tears. For a moment, the signs she wanted escaped her. "You rescued my book?"

Wenna glanced at her husband and took the lead explaining. "Me luv went to the gig that day to wash it, seeing it was splashed with mud," she said. "And ee saw your book in the well. Didn't want to wet it, now did ee, so ee set it aside meaning to give to you later. Only you disappeared that day, miss—and we know now why you did—but ee didna have a chance to return it."

"You had it all this time," Amaranthe breathed. "It's safe. It's not damaged at all." Her eyes filled with tears of joy.

"We're sorry, miss, that we had to keep it," Wenna said. "Watched the mail, we did, to see if we could find your address or direction. But we never saw post from you, and when I asked at the house, it was all surly answers. We wanted to return it to you all this time, but we didn't know where you were."

"It's all right." Amaranthe laughed shakily. "In truth, I hardly dared hope I would find it again. I thought Reuben had stolen it and, I don't know—burned it out of spite."

She lifted the pages delicately. They were as fresh and beautiful as they'd been six years ago. Her first book, the cornerstone of her collection. The first in her library, back when she meant to become simply an antiquarian bookseller and not also a thief.

"Then we did all right, me luv," Wenna said softly.

"More than all right," Amaranthe said, signing to her friend with an expansive gesture. "Thaker, Wenna—thank you. I can't tell how much this means to me."

She lifted eyes blurred with tears to find Mal watching her, his expression intent. She closed the pages gently and turned the book, shielded in its leather apron, to show him the list of women's names on the front flyleaf. "Mal. It's your mother's name, isn't it? She signed it Lady Vernay."

His gaze riveted on the faded script, his throat working before he could voice the words. "But you said this was valuable. How would she have come by a Book of Hours?"

"You and your aunt both said she loved old things. Perhaps it was a wedding gift. His to her, most like. I expect your aunt sold it with some other things after she died. I wanted to ask her about it, but I had already been so pert."

She laughed, the sound a bit wild with guilt. "By rights, the book ought to be yours, I suppose. But I have a bill of sale, you see." And she didn't want to part with her book again. Not for anything.

"I won't attempt to take it from you. Only..." Mal lifted a hand and traced a finger over his mother's name, all he had left of her. "If she wrote anything else in it, I hope you will let me see."

Amaranthe closed the book and fastened the clasp, then wound the extra length of leather about it once more and bound the whole in the linen scrap. She held the book to her chest more tenderly than she had held the child. Her life had been restored to her, a great wrong made right.

"This is a priceless gift, Thaker. It makes me brave enough to face Reuben, even. I suppose it is time we went to the house."

CHAPTER EIGHTEEN

"I am very sorry for your loss, cousin," Amaranthe said for the dozenth time. She sat in the formal parlor of Penwellen, a dark and shadowed chamber, the mirrors hung with black fabric. "I wish I had been here to help her at the end. It must have been terrible for you both."

"My wife dead, and no heir." Reuben prowled the length of the narrow room, close and airless, as if the drapes had not been drawn back in ages. Perhaps Favella had stopped using the room. The funeral was done with, and the house had seen no callers that day besides them, as far as Amaranthe could tell.

"No heir. You know what this means."

He paused to glare at her, and Amaranthe tensed. Did he want to discuss Joseph? The musty smell of the house cloyed in her nostrils.

The years had not been kind to Reuben. He had gone from fleshy to portly, his face florid with signs of heavy drink, his hair greasy and his sideburns unevenly shaved. A man could be forgiven dishevelment after losing his wife and child, but Reuben's appearance suggested the neglect had gone on far longer.

"I have to marry again," he growled. "Soon."

"If you say so." Amaranthe curled her hands in her lap, pressing her knees and ankles together. She wished she hadn't left Mal upstairs, freshening up in the room the housekeeper had shown him. The surly, gloomy woman, no one Amaranthe recognized, had greeted them at the door and accepted their names as if she didn't care who they were.

Amaranthe's old room held no signs that she had ever lived there. It, along with the rest of the house, felt strange and familiar at the same time. The furnishings were the same, everything in place, but shabby and in need of care. Favella had been insistent about housekeeping, very often pressing Amaranthe to engage in cleaning herself, yet this dust and decay had been accumulating. Did they not entertain? Had Reuben no pride? What had happened here after she left?

"I won't have just anyone." Reuben continued his circuit of the room, his face flushed with anger. "Our name is too good for that."

"Of course," Amaranthe replied, paying him little mind as she looked about, wondering at the cause of the house's decline. Reuben's high opinion of his worth rested on very little basis, from what she could tell. Being a baronet put him above most of his neighbors, but there were far grander people in the world. Dukes, for instance.

She was calculating how long politeness required her to stay when Reuben wheeled on her with a sneer. "So this is why you rushed here, I take it."

"For what?" She blinked.

His contemptuous gaze settled on her bosom. Her traveling gown today was less smart than the others, but nothing of the duchess's was dowdy. Even if her figure was unremarkable—and in Amaranthe's opinion, hers was—the dress gave its own advantage.

"You're not much, but I suppose you'll do," Reuben said.

Amaranthe stared at him, her blood turning cold. "I *beg* your pardon."

He advanced upon her, his belly in its embroidered waist-coat coming first, the rest of him following after. Amaranthe scrambled to her feet. She recognized that look of avarice and lust, the face of a selfish boy looking upon something he thought belonged to him, and he meant to break it merely because he could. They were not in the stables this time, but that would not stop him. He outweighed her by several stone. She put her chair between them.

"Don't pretend to be simple. At least you share my grandfather's blood, though I can't say much for your mother. You look healthy, sturdier than Favella was. All to the good. I don't care for those dark, plain looks of yours, can tell your mother was a foreigner. But if you're here, throwing your cap at me, what else is a man to do?"

"You're lost your wits if you think I'd marry you," Amaranthe exclaimed.

"It's why you ran off all those years ago, isn't it?" He scoffed. "Teased me for years to tumble you, then bolted when I finally took the bait. And now you scramble back here the moment Favella's in her grave, looking to take her place. A slyer baggage than I ever took you for." A leer split his florid features. "Can't say I won't enjoy getting an heir off you, though. A plain woman's a beauty in the dark."

"You have a child." Amaranthe moved about the chair as he circled toward her. "Derwa. Eyde's babe."

He shook his head. "Not an heir," he growled. "A bastard can't inherit."

"She's your child nonetheless." Indignation straightened her spine. "You turned Eyde off without a character. She deserves some support from you."

"Acknowledge a by-blow?" He barked out a laugh that turned to a cough. "Worthless! Should drown them all at birth. Like puppies."

Amaranthe gasped at his cruelty. "I'll never marry you."

"You think you can do better?" He lunged toward her.

Mal appeared in the doorway in that moment, and Amaranthe exhaled in relief. What a welcome sight he was, and not only because he was big and solid and as handsome as sin. He was a superior specimen to Reuben in every way, with his brown hair unpowdered, his stockings as white as his cravat, buttons gleaming along his coat and the knees of his breeches. Everything in her leaned toward him.

"I am already contracted to be married," Amaranthe lied.

Reuben hauled himself up short. It was no easy feat, with his bulk. "What?" he barked. "To *him*?"

"Yes. To Mr. Grey." She sent Mal a wild, pleading glance. "He asked me to marry him at the inn in Tavistock. I accepted."

"You!" Reuben sent an angry, cutting glance in the other man's direction. He looked ready to lose his temper, and Amaranthe shrank back, recalling his rages. But as Mal stepped into the room, her blustering cousin retreated. He outweighed Mal also, but he seemed to sense that the other man was dangerous.

"Throw yourself away on a duke's nameless bastard? You're a bigger fool than I thought!"

"I am very honored that he asked me."

"And I, of course, am the happiest of men." Mal watched Amaranthe.

Reuben glared back and forth between them, puffing out his chest in challenge. Amaranthe went cold with the fear that she had just put Mal in a position where her cousin might call him out and shoot him.

But Mal was a better shot as well as a better swordsman.

She could guess that at a glance, and after muttering wrathfully to himself, it seemed Reuben did, too.

"Out," he snarled. "You, whore, and your cuckold. I want you out of my house tomorrow. I'd put you out of my house this moment if it wouldn't cause talk."

Amaranthe blinked, taken back that he ordered not punishment but reprieve. She knew Reuben reviled common women. He never visited brothels but preferred to defile innocents under his own roof. She could scarcely believe she might escape him so easily.

"We'd go today, if our horses didn't need resting," Mal said. He held out a hand to Amaranthe. She took it and fled the room and, she hoped, her vile cousin for the last time.

But now she had caught Mal up in her lies.

A KNOCK on her door much later, when she was already abed, made Amaranthe's heart stop, then launch into a frenzy. "Who is it?"

She was in her bedgown, covers heaped upon her. Trapped, if it were Reuben come to importune her. Mal's room was close beside hers, but she didn't know if he was in it. After a distasteful, silent dinner with Reuben brooding at the head of the table, the most sulky and suspicious of hosts, she had been grateful to retire to her room. Having visited with Thaker, there was nothing more of Penwellen she wanted to see. Nothing she would miss. She wished only to leave tomorrow, their luggage barely opened, her book cradled in her arms.

If Reuben tried to force himself on her—she looked around her room for a weapon. All she had was the Book of Hours lying open across her knees. Hardly heavy enough to knock a man out, but she would use it as a missile if she must.

"It's me." Mal's low voice floated from behind the door.

She nearly melted into the bed in relief. "I'm undressed."

"So am I. And we've shared a bed together before. Don't you remember?"

She giggled. What an uncomfortable night that had been. After that heady kiss in the parlor of the Queen's Head, feeling her awakened body humming with life and hope, she'd lain stiffly on her half of the bed all night, the rolled blanket dividing the mattress and making a barrier between them. Every breath, every movement from Mal had grated on her sensitized, singing nerves. All she could think of that night was kissing him again, and the thought recurred at least once a minute in the time that had elapsed since.

It was a terrible temptation to let him into her room. A man could be forgiven if he roamed before marriage; indeed, it was expected. But a woman could never recover her virtue once it was lost.

"Come in," she called anyway.

He looked delicious and comfortable, wrapped in a long velvet banyan robe with slippers, and she felt the inappropriate urge to press her mouth to the exposed skin of his throat. She pulled the coverlet over her hips, a layer of protection.

She wanted more of him, was greedy for more kisses, but at the same time she didn't want to rush. She was enjoying the slow, delectable simmer of attraction, the deep satisfaction of having him near. No chair in the room being available, he stretched out atop the coverlet beside her, and every nerve in her body came alive.

"I thought I would find you with your book." His smile sent heat curling through her to her toes.

"I can't believe I have it back. Intact. There's no mold, no spots, no nibbles from mice. Thaker thought to store it in a cedar chest, a cast-off from the house." She ran her hands over the parchment, feeling the light indentations the nib had made as the scholar scratched his ink into the page.

"How lucky that he is the one who found it," she marveled. "And now he is married, with children!"

"It's the way things go for many a man, so I'm told." Mal's eyes captured the candlelight and its shadows of gold. There was something deep and fathomless in his expression, as if he felt the same current that she sensed: attraction, that undeniable pull, and the deliciousness of lingering in that expectancy.

"Not for my poor cousin, I'm afraid." She giggled. "At least, not with me."

"That's why I came. I fear he might try to force himself upon you. I can sleep on the floor, if you wish."

She gave him a demure smile, tucking a pillow into the space between them. "Against the door, like a squire guarding his knight? We did well enough before, though Eyde must never learn we shared a bed. I don't care what Reuben's servants think, though."

She felt so much safer with Mal here. Outside the door, the rest of Penwellen loomed a forbidding mass, dark with shadows. Here, in the golden candlelight with Mal, they were held in an enchanted circle. She never wanted to leave.

She wanted to kiss him again.

"You can put the book between us. Better than a sword." The warmth of his smile roused a curl of heat in her belly. Her entire body hummed.

"Bea would not approve, I am sure, but I am more afraid of my cousin than of your aunt." She watched him kick off his slippers. Trying not to stare at his well-shaped feet, she fixed on turning the pages of her book, examining it for marks of damage. "And Joseph would be horrified. I wonder how he is faring with Miss Pettigrew?"

"I hope he has got as far as calling her Susannah, if not as far as sharing a bed. Only precontracted couples are allowed that, I should think." He gave her a small, accusing look.

She swallowed hard. The candle dipped in a sudden draft of air, sending a wavering light over his face, its strong lines and shadows. Warmth emanated from his big body, glazing her skin.

"I do beg your pardon. It was all I could think of to make Reuben desist in his delusions that I should marry him."

"I thought it very noble that you should sacrifice yourself to me. If he tries to coerce you, I have leave to call him out for attempting to alienate your affections."

Mal reached across the pillow and laid a hand on her hip, lightly, a question. His hand was large and warm, and heat skittered through her belly, shooting darts to her legs and breasts. She recognized the sensations now, that fire being lit.

"You aren't in the habit of fighting, are you?" The thought of Mal in a duel made her chest hurt.

"Only in practice, and not always successfully. Viktor's trounced me more than a few times." He leaned on one elbow, his eyes turning smoky. "How do you feel about kissing your intended?"

"I adore it." She leaned down to touch her lips to his, and their mouths met as if two halves of a whole. He rose to meet her, his hard chest so close, and she slipped her arms around his shoulders, only just managing not to dive her hands beneath his robe. She could not lose herself completely.

But sense lifted away when his tongue teased against her lips. She parted her lips in surprise and he swept his tongue into her mouth, and a wild sweetness welled in her core, molten wax held to a hot flame.

This was delicious madness, utterly wanton, and her whole body came aglow, like those figures in medieval illuminations surrounded by a halo of gold. He smelled rich and earthy, like warmed brandy on a winter night, and he tasted faintly of lemon. She scrabbled at his shoulders, urging him closer.

His tongue in her mouth stirred a deep wildness, a hunger inside that she didn't know dwelled there. Her hips and the tops of her thighs felt hot, his hand a brand on her waist, and her breasts tingled as his warm breath wafted over her face with his kisses.

She panted for breath as he kissed her jaw, that stretch of her neck below her ear. She recalled their last embrace, how he had almost taken her breast in his mouth, and the very thought of him kissing her *there* made her nipples grow hard and aching. She mewled like a kitten, pressing mindlessly toward him, and something about her entire collapse, her surrender, made him raise his head.

"That's enough for tonight, I daresay."

She blinked at him, dazed, as he released her, drawing back to his side of the bed. She rode on a wave that might carry her out to sea.

"We should save something for the wedding, don't you think?" His smile was warm and wicked, his lips still damp from her mouth, and that same tightness that pulled at her nipples tugged between her legs. An ache she guessed could only be relieved by his body against hers.

"I suppose so." Best not let him see how entirely she'd lost her head. She would have allowed him to do anything to her, so long as she stayed wrapped in that spell of enchantment.

She touched the corner of his mouth with a fingertip. "Mal. Is it always like this?"

He tucked a loose curl beneath her nightcap, and the tenderness in his face hollowed her chest. "It is like this with you and I."

Little wonder that women threw themselves headlong into a man's arms, then, without benefit of a priest saying a few words. She understood now. A wonder that people could go about normal lives at all when *this* awaited them in bed with their beloved.

He leaned against the padded headboard, hands linked behind his head as he studied the room, and her belly warmed at the sight of him at ease, stretched out in her bed. Near enough to touch.

Did she marry him, she would have this access to him all the time, Mal in his most unguarded moments. She would be free to touch him whenever she pleased with the possessive touch of a wife. All his steady strength, his deep loyalty, his streaks of impish humor would be hers to delight in. And his body would be hers to hold.

He had shown her companionship already. He had shown her passion. She guessed their bond could deepen into love.

And when, or if, she were discovered, he would be trapped in her lies. Realization split her warm daze like a knife cutting parchment.

She could not let Mal marry her under false pretenses. It would be the worst sort of thievery. She had to tell him what she really was, what she had done.

And then she must somehow not break from despair when all his glowing warmth went cold and he turned away from her, and she lost the chance forever to be close to Malden Grey.

She reached for her Book of Hours and pulled it into her lap. She did not have to tell him tonight.

"I've been wondering how much your mother read of her book. If she chose it for herself, or someone else did. Lady Willoughby de Broke would have read medieval French, but did your mother?"

She flipped through the pages, drinking in the neat lines of script, the images she remembered. Saints with their beatific faces and open hands, the typical marginalia of mythical creatures, the devotions for each hour of the day.

"She did love antique things," Mal said. "She had a chatelaine, one of those chains women once wore at the waist. Hers had a pair of sewing scissors and a small vial of scent. I like the idea that my father might have bought this to please her."

"I wonder how he came upon this volume. It seems strange that it might have surfaced in Bristol. Margaret Greville, the baroness, her family seat was in Warwickshire, I thought."

"There's some Hunsdon property near Wellesbourne. Though it's equally likely my father pilfered the townhouse. The first duke had no notion how to build a library and acquired whatever took his fancy."

Amaranthe slipped through the book to the back flyleaf, marveling that the volume was so intact, and as beautiful as she remembered. "That might explain how he procured the alchemical manuscript Ned showed me. It's very curious that—"

She stopped as her fingers found an unexpected bulge, pasted between the last page and the cover board. "Wait. There's something glued inside here."

Carefully she worked her fingers around the border of the cover, not wanting to tear the parchment. "This could be interesting. People often stored things in books, you know, or wrote their own notes in them. Any number of medieval manuscripts have recipes and sometimes even household accounts in the margins. On occasion someone left a last will and testament..."

She fell silent as she unfolded the document and read it. The room spun.

"I can read that script," Mal said, glancing at the page. "It's not that Gothic hand or what have you. More modern."

"Mal." She reached over and gripped his wrist, her nails

digging in. Her voice clogged her throat. "These are your mother's marriage lines."

"What?" He reared back as if she'd slapped him.

"Look. There is her signature, the same as in the front of the book. Here's your father's. And witnesses." She caught her breath, lifting her gaze to meet his. "Mal—this is a witnessed document. Their marriage was valid."

Wonder softened his face. He looked like a young boy at Christmas as he traced his mother's name.

"Then she wasn't deceived by him. He cherished her enough to wed her. I'm glad to know that." He followed the large, looping M of Marguerite.

"She must have hidden this in the midst of her fever. Your aunt said she had a spell shortly after they married. And then she couldn't produce her marriage lines, so when the duke came looking for his heir, he didn't believe they were wed."

"It would have broken her heart that she couldn't remember where she'd put the proof," Mal considered. "But that meant my grandfather could make my father marry Christine."

He hadn't grasped the implications. Not yet.

"Why wouldn't there have been a record in the parish register?" she asked.

He shrugged. "The duke didn't want his son married to a haberdasher's daughter. That might have been enough to keep anyone from looking. My grandfather was as large and terrifying as your cousin, I've been told, and he was a duke besides. Not even his son dared defy him."

"Mal," Amaranthe asked, trying to keep her voice calm. "When did your mother die?"

"July 12, 1757."

"And when did your father marry Christine?"

"The fall of 1756, I believe." He met her eyes as understanding slowly dawned.

"His marriage to Christine was not legal if his first wife yet lived," Amaranthe whispered. "It would make him a bigamist and invalidate the union. Mal—this document means you are his only legitimate child. You are the heir of the third Duke of Hunsdon."

CHAPTER NINETEEN

"I won't do it."

Mal's voice broke the vaulted silence inside St. Philip and St. James. They stood alone in the tiny church, a square stone heap that was said to be the oldest church in Bristol. It had been the home church of the Grey family, where Mal was baptized and Bea married. It reminded Amaranthe, with a familiar ache, of lovely little St. Cleer where she had grown up in Cornwall. Coming back to her home country had called up old memories with a fierce, aching clarity, as if the two split halves of her life were knitting back together.

She pushed away the sudden odd regret that her parents would never see her married. They had disliked Reuben and would have hated the circumstances that threw their daughter on his less than tender care.

They would have loved Mal, though.

"Won't do what?" she asked, keeping her voice low.

They'd returned to Bristol to yet another shock. An express from Mal's barrister friend in London informed him that Sybil, Duchess of Hunsdon, was back in the country and renewing her suit to block Mal's guardianship of the children. Mal was furious at both her temerity and her timing. He meant to depart that night, and Bea awaited them at the Green Man with a farewell dinner and fresh linens for the return trip. But he had kept his promise to let Amaranthe put flowers on his mother's grave.

Mal stared at the bronze plaque that held Marguerite's name, her presumed birth date and the all too early date of her death. The husband who had abandoned her in life had ensured her lasting memory in death with a burial vault inside the church, a coveted and protected space, and in a niche above the vault stood a beautiful plaster cast of her face and head.

He didn't lift his eyes. "I won't make that document known. The one you found in your book."

Amaranthe studied the sweetly curving lines of Marguerite's sculpted cheek and brow. A small smile lingered on the plaster lips, remote, untouchable.

Some part of her had known this was coming. Known by his careful silence on the subject during their travels back to Bristol, when he had asked her interminable questions about Reuben, Favella, Thaker, her parents, her life in Cornwall before he knew her. She'd guessed he was wrestling with something, and she knew him well enough by now to guess what it was.

Any other man would have grabbed the marriage lines from her hand and charged back to London trumpeting about his new station. Malden Grey was the only man alive who would take that evidence and bury it.

"Never?" she asked. The thought of his destroying the evidence compounded the ache in her chest. It was Marguerite's vindication that the man she loved had not lied to her. It was Bea's proof that her sister had not been completely betrayed.

"It would take everything away from the children."

He turned to face her, close enough to touch. She wished she had the right.

"It would take from them everything they've been brought up to expect is theirs," Mal said. "Hugh's been bred his whole life to be the duke—you've seen his manners, his self-importance. He stakes his life on it. Ned already knows how to play the part of the second son, the hey-go-mad spare. And Camilla—she is too young to care now, perhaps. But she'll care very much when it is time to be married and no decent man will offer for her."

Amaranthe's throat closed as she nodded. She had thought of this, too, what it would mean to the Delaval children if Mal stepped forward. "It means you remain a bastard."

"I've been a bastard my whole life. I know how to deal with it. They don't." He shrugged and let loose a short, bitter laugh. "Who would believe me anyway, producing that document after all this time? They'll accuse me of making it up. It's too absurd."

So that was the core of it. Not just the wish to protect the children, but the belief, bred into him from birth, that he wasn't worth more. Something greater. That luck had always run against him, and always would.

She gave in then to the urge to touch him. It was too much to resist: the solid bulk of him standing so close to her, his strength, the troubled look on his face, his enormous heart. He wouldn't be the man she loved if he were able to claim his birth and patrimony over the welfare of three innocent children.

She loved Malden Grey, did she?

The knowledge pierced her chest like an arrow. She meant only to lay a hand on his arm, a friendly, consoling gesture, not too improper for a church. But he turned toward her at the same instant and her hand landed on his chest, then crept of its own accord around his neck, which he obligingly bent toward her.

His kiss was sweet and hot and unhurried and consuming all at the same time. She met his fervor with her own. They plunged through tender exploration into demand, and she was just as insistent as he. Heat leapt between them as he pressed close, and she felt him vibrating with restraint as he clamped his hands on her shoulders, using his mouth to call up the depths of her passion. She leaned against his hard chest, clinging to his neck in surrender.

Her knees turned to jelly, her mind floated away, and there was only Mal, this kiss which was a declaration and a promise, beneath it the slow burn in her blood, and beneath that the deeper knowledge that this fire between them fed on more than infatuation. What had grown between them was solid and true and lasting, the kind of bond that could cleave one soul to another through life and into eternity.

The realization was devastating. When he lifted his head to stare into her eyes, his expression as dazed as hers, as full of wonder, she almost sobbed with the weight of this revelation. She closed her eyes as his ragged breath warmed her cheek.

She was his, for always, and she had just sealed that offering with a kiss in a church. In the cool quiet of the ancient brown stone, with the bars of colored light from the stained-glass windows reaching toward them across the stone floor, instead of impious their embrace felt sanctified. Holy.

"You told your cousin you meant to marry me." Mal murmured the words against her cheek, brushing his lips across her cheekbone, then below her ear and down her neck. She tipped her head to the side, helpless to resist him.

"I did," she breathed.

"Will you?" He paused with his nose at the high collar of the smart jacket that went with her riding habit, another loan from the duchess.

She squeezed her eyes shut, tears caught between her lashes. More than anything in her life—more than she wanted to start her antiquarian bookstore; more than she'd wanted Mr.

Karim to buy her copied manuscripts—she wanted to marry Malden Grey.

"Because I'll stay a bastard," he said when she made no answer. She opened her eyes to face him.

"That has never mattered to me."

His arms came about her carefully, as if she were fragile, as if he didn't dare move too quickly. "It's mattered to everyone else."

"Not to me." She pressed a firm, swift kiss to his cheek, trying to impress this upon him once and for all.

"Then what is holding you back?" he asked.

It was her perfidy that kept her from opening fully to him, not his birth. But with everything else pressing on his mind, now was not the time to discuss her dubious means of earning a living.

She straightened the neckcloth she'd crushed, pressing herself against him so wantonly. She rested her nose against one of his broad shoulders and inhaled.

"You've business to see to in London. I—I need to tell you something, but it can wait until this is settled."

He stood still, and in his embrace, with his scent and his heat and his powerful arms surrounding her, the muted light sanctifying the room, her head against his chest—where she wanted to be, always—Amaranthe promised herself that she would become worthy of Malden Grey. He had made a noble sacrifice for his siblings. She would sacrifice something as well.

She would make the *Book of Secrets* to repay Mr. Karim for his many kindnesses, and she would give the money to Joseph and his bride as a wedding gift to help set up their household since she would not be there, the reliable spinster aunt, to ease things for him and his new family. One more book, one more secret copy, and then she would be done. Only honest commissions from here on.

Mal's arms fell away. "I think I should go back to London alone," he said.

She opened her eyes. "Why?"

He stepped back, and a cold draft blew over her. His expression was shuttered, distant. He looked at the burial plaque instead of her.

"Your reputation. Your cousin thinks we are engaged, but we cannot pose as a married couple back to London, as we did in Tavistock."

She blinked in bewilderment. They had traveled together, with just the changing round of post boys for company, all the way from Callington. Why was he withdrawing from her now?

"Besides, if Joseph is to be wed, you'll want to be here, won't you?"

"I suppose." She tried to meet his eyes, but he avoided her gaze.

She had lost his trust in her. Because of her hesitation about marrying him? Or because of something else?

Without coming closer he bent and dropped a kiss on her forehead, a small, chaste kiss. It felt too much like a goodbye. She swallowed an ache in her throat as he moved toward the door of the church, breaking their closeness. She wanted to stay in his embrace forever. She wanted to stay in that moment when he believed in her. When he thought her worthy of him.

Only one book more, and then she was finished. She truly wanted to marry Malden Grey, and he was slipping away from her. She might lose him forever once he knew the truth.

"I'VE NEVER SEEN our Mal so angry." Beatrice drew the damp sheet from the wringer and stretched it to its full length. Amaranthe grasped one corner and helped her drape it over a forsythia bush in its last stage of yellow bloom.

Bea shook her head. "Can you imagine the nerve of that Sybil! Coming back to demand the estate and guardianship of the children, after she stole from them all and left like a thief in the night."

"Mal will stop her."

He'd left with the evening mail and a whisper in Amaranthe's ear. "Don't mention to Bea that you found my mother's marriage lines. I want to tell her myself, in my own time," he'd said.

She'd agreed again, as she had agreed with his decision to say nothing to the children. He wouldn't change his mind, and in truth she couldn't fault him. Claiming his own legitimacy would disinherit Hugh and make the Delaval children bastards. They'd already been left, orphaned and starving, in their own home. What would it mean to take their birthright away too?

He'd taken the document with him. He'd also given her, despite his new guardedness with her, a swift kiss, a dazzling, searing kind of kiss. A kiss that assured her, in every possible way, that the shadow of Reuben no longer had any hold on her. All she felt when Mal held her—in truth and in her imaginings—was him. His heat, his strength, and her overwhelming desire to belong to him.

"She can't have a leg to stand on, can she?" Bea fed another sheet into the wringer and turned the crank. "Even if she was the duke's wife. After all, she's a woman. And a thief, at that."

A woman and a thief, at that. Much like Amaranthe herself.

Who would believe me? Mal's face had been so bleak.

Amaranthe went to the washtub full of linens and plunged her hands into the cold water to lift out another sheet. He hadn't said anything more, but the words stuck in her head like a burr.

Did he believe the marriage lines were real?

They'll accuse me of making it up.

He couldn't think that document had been manufactured

somehow. He'd been there when she found where Marguerite had hidden the page, glued to the back cover of her Book of Hours. He'd seen her lifting the parchment. He must know that no one could conceivably accuse him, Malden Grey, of making so skillful a forgery.

But he'd seen Amaranthe's work. He knew she could mimic any hand. And if she could do that, it was not such a leap to suppose she could create a document that looked like a set of marriage lines that a betrayed woman had claimed existed but no one had ever found.

He might think she had forged his mother's marriage lines.

Amaranthe stood as if caught in the stare of a basilisk. That would explain his sudden reserve.

He might very well think that somehow, in the course of an afternoon, she had created an official-looking document and tucked it away in a book that elsewhere bore the signature of Marguerite, Lady Vernay, which would make it appear valid.

To gain what?

Why, to make the bastard, the would-be barrister who'd offered to marry her, into a legitimate duke.

He didn't believe her.

It was such a shocking discovery that she could barely believe it herself. Yet she was an antiquarian. Her field was full of stories of treasures found in the spines or margins of ancient books, of priceless volumes unearthed in the unlikeliest places. It was perhaps the one field aside from archaeology where spectacular discoveries were almost routine.

But to the outside world, of course it would look like a coincidence too wild to be believed.

Amaranthe fed a heavy, sodden sheet into the wringer. Her heart flopped painfully about her chest. Mal had left to travel alone. Perhaps he meant to withdraw his offer of marriage. Just when she understood what he meant to her, he was trying to extricate himself from what they'd shared.

The knowledge shredded her. Through tears she focused on the task at hand. What could she do to make him believe her?

"What church did you say Marguerite was married in?"

At Bea's curious glance, Amaranthe smiled. "Prying again, I know. But after getting her book back, I am more curious than ever. And I think you said the church she was married in was not the church where her memorial lies."

Bea leaned on the crank, squeezing out the last bit of water, and pushed a lock of damp hair away from her face. "St. Mary Redcliffe, that Gothic old church across the river. I think it's naught but a gloomy old wreck, but Marguerite always loved those ancient, spooky things.

"I was there, you know," Beatrice said quietly after a long moment had passed. "As her witness. Our parents were so angry about the match, it broke her heart. They knew a tradesman's daughter could never be a duchess. The high folk wouldn't allow it; they would hound our poor delicate girl to her grave. But she loved him so much, was so wild to marry him—I couldn't break her heart further by abandoning her, too.

"Signed the register with my mark, or thought I did, me and one of young Vernay's friends. I told her to bring a copy away, knowing the old duke would storm and threaten, and right I was, wasn't I? But when she couldn't find her copy, and all my searching could turn up no trace—I went to the priest and asked to see the register." Beatrice dabbed at her eye with her apron. "There was no record in it. I don't know what I signed, or what happened to that paper, but it was all a charade after all."

Amaranthe laid a hand on the other woman's arm, squeezing gently. "What of the priest who married them? Or the other witness?"

Beatrice sniffed and wiped her cheeks with the back of her

hand. "The priest said perhaps Marguerite was better off where she was. And I had to agree. The duke was so powerful, so outraged—he would have made her life a misery, and Mal's too. At least here she lived among people who loved her.

"It broke her to bits when he left her, but she had some moments of happiness in her life. I don't know if she'd have had a minute of that, had she gone with the young lord. He never returned for her while she lived, did he? She was just a lark to him. He couldn't have loved her true."

Amaranthe bit her lip to keep from blurting anything that would not, in the end, prove a solace. Beatrice believed she had done right and had come to terms with it. The proof had disappeared, and Mal wanted to go on that way.

And possibly he didn't believe the proof, because Amaranthe had produced it.

"Will you marry him, then?" Bea asked after they had stretched another set of linens to dry and the sun wheeled high above the yard behind the inn.

Amaranthe ducked her head and busied herself draping pillowcases over the bushes. It was a good day for drying, the spring sun high and warm, but the flush in her face was not due to sunshine.

"We've not settled anything."

Of course he didn't want to marry her, now that he'd had time to consider. Now that he'd seen her roots, her humble past, knew how Reuben's treatment had soiled her. He'd only proposed marriage because that man from the Middle Temple advised him to marry. The moment she'd trapped him into it, creating a ruse to delude Reuben, he'd seen the folly of his ways.

And now his situation had changed. He was likely to win guardianship of the ducal children, and that responsibility would prove his steadiness to the Benchers. He'd be called to the bar with or without a clever wife.

"But you want to." Bea snapped a sheet and the white linen leapt through the air, shading her for a moment from the sun. "Marry him, that is."

Amaranthe didn't answer, but her heart ached with a truth she didn't dare say aloud. Oh, yes, she wanted to marry Malden Grey. He had won her completely, heart and soul. She was ready to change her entire life, give up her many subterfuges for him, and he might have already moved on. The thought cleaved her like a sword, leaving her gasping. He might decide she was not the wife for him after all, and she would be left desolate, loving him her whole life, hopeless and alone.

Horse hooves clattered in the coaching yard, but without the creak of a wheeled vehicle or the blowing of a horn announcing the arrival of a coach. That meant a traveler on horseback, perhaps a wealthy one. Bea wiped her hands on her apron and straightened her cap, heading toward the covered passage that led from the back gardens to the innyard. Amaranthe dawdled, feeding another sheet into the wringer, when she heard Bea exclaim.

"Mr. Illingworth!"

Joseph, here? Amaranthe dropped the sheet, picked up her skirts, and pelted through the passage. Joseph swung down from a hired horse, his coat dusty from the road, his boots dull with dirt, his expression worn and grim.

"Joseph! What's happened? Where is Miss Pettigrew?"

"Miss Pettigrew!" He spat onto the cobbles, and the horse shied and snorted as the ostler came forward to take it by the bridle. "Miss Pettigrew," he said with a sneer, "is on her way to the Scottish border, to Gretna Green I don't doubt, in the company of Viktor Vierling."

"Captain Vierling? Mal's friend? Why?" Amaranthe cried in bewilderment.

"Why do you think?" Joseph shouted. "She's in love with

him! The whole time I was courting her, she was letting him dangle after her. He came after us on the road and walked into the chapel where I was waiting to say our vows." He strode angrily toward the common room of the inn, and Amaranthe hurried after him.

"Her family doesn't approve, of course. A Hessian? A military man, when they are people of peace? So she's gone with him to Gretna Green, and I'm the fool left at the altar in my best coat with all that money spent on a special license."

"You were in the chapel?" Amaranthe echoed. "You were to marry, and I wasn't there?"

Joseph didn't seem to hear her, nor notice how her steps checked as he strode into the coffee room. "Your Littlejohn will serve spirits at this hour, won't he? I mean to drink my troubles away." He looked around. "Where's Grey?"

Amaranthe pressed her hands to her cheeks. She felt like screaming. First, Mal was a duke but wouldn't tell anyone, and she'd said she would marry him when she couldn't, and now her brother had been left at the altar by a woman he thought an angel come to earth.

"Mal—Mr. Grey went back to London to see to the suit about his guardianship. There's been a new development."

Joseph marched to the bar and pounded on the counter to draw someone's attention. "I want to return to London as well," he said. "As soon as possible. I never want to set foot in Gloucestershire again, or anywhere near it."

"Of course," Amaranthe said, sweeping her own concerns aside. She had always done so for Joseph. Her life had always centered around Joseph, from birth, following the example of their parents. They were kind to Amaranthe, but Joseph was their son and the rock they would look to in their old age.

Their father had included Amaranthe in lessons so she might be a companion to Joseph and a help in his work someday.

Their mother had planned meals and outings and holidays around what Joseph wanted, and Amaranthe had learned to do the same. He was the elder, but she looked out for him. She had no idea how to heal a broken heart, but whatever he asked of her, she would do.

Her parents hadn't lived to see their pride and faith in their son proven, or to have him as the prop of their old age. It was her task to help him become the man he was meant to be.

"We can leave on the next stagecoach, if you wish it," she said dully. Never mind that Joseph hadn't written to tell her he was to marry, much less invite her to the ceremony. She would let him explain his reasons later, when he had his temper on a leash. At least they were returning to London, and Mal. Though she wasn't certain if Mal wanted to see her, either, considering she was the bearer of a secret he didn't want known.

Their lives had been so quiet, mere weeks ago. Steady and soothing, just as Amaranthe liked. Now love had swept through and turned them both upside down, shaking away their serenity, shattering them in pieces. And neither of them would be the same again.

CHAPTER TWENTY

B ea insisted they stay the night at the Green Man so she could cook them a farewell dinner, and that meant Amaranthe had a day to follow up on her last question. She slipped away in late afternoon with her woolen cloak, her walking boots, and the duchess's plainest traveling gown. She told Joseph and the Littlejohns she simply wanted to explore, which resulted in Bea pressing a pocket map of Bristol upon her. A quick consultation told her to continue along Old Market to Castle Street and past the old Norman keep. At St. Nicholas she would find the Bridge to cross the River Avon, and from there she need only stay due south on Redcliffe Street to find the church she sought.

Bristol was second in size only to London, and like that city, humming with trade and the commerce of the sea. Smoke from homes and the porcelain factories mingled with the scent of horses and ships and the sweet, yeasty smell of the sugar houses where cane and molasses shipped from the West Indies were baked into sugar loaves to satisfy the British sweet tooth. She saw more sailors than anyone else, all shades of brown faces mingling around the quay, those born their shade and those who had acquired it through weathering work in the sun, while here and there stood out the paleness of someone who didn't work at all.

As she neared the ancient stone bridge across the Avon, masts and ships crowded the harbor, as close as the medieval and Elizabethan houses shouldered side by side down the street. Around her swirled many dialects and languages, including the distinct Bristol accent. She heard traces of it in Mal's speech sometimes, small but clear, and the linguist in her was fascinated. Thanks to King Alfred, southwest England, including Bristol, had withstood centuries of Danish invaders until shortly before William the Conqueror arrived with his Norman armies, and so the English here had not changed in the same way as in the north and Midlands.

Of course, the Cornish claimed they had never been subject to any invaders, Roman, Saxon, or Norman. It was a point of pride. They had lived on their tiny peninsula surrounded by the sea since before Lyonesse sank into the ocean, and they defended their own ways fiercely. Perhaps that explained her stubborn streak. Even if Mal wouldn't want it known, Amaranthe needed to find out the truth for herself.

St. Mary Redcliffe had been damaged during past wars, and gaps showed in the arched stained-glass windows. The tower had been shorn of its spire, but the elaborate Gothic pinnacles still sprouted along the roof. Amaranthe could see why Marguerite, who had treasured a medieval Book of Hours so much that she hid her most precious possession within it, had loved this church.

The inside was silent save for other visitors like her roaming about, gaping at the impossibly high vaulted ceiling and the many sculpted monuments to Bristolians past, mayors and merchants and men who had made their fortune selling kidnapped Africans. Amaranthe admired the wooden choir stalls, dating to medieval centuries, and the enormous rib of a whale given by John Cabot to commemorate his voyages. She was studying the delicately painted panels of the triptych over the altar when a man in a priest's collar stepped up beside her.

"One of the newest things here," he remarked. "Commissioned by Hogarth twenty years or so ago. We have a bell that's a hundred and fifty years old and woodwork dating to the fourteenth century. One of our fonts was made in the thirteenth century, but our building was begun a century before that. Likely there was a church on this site when Christians first came to this island."

"I imagine, with so much history here, you keep very careful records," Amaranthe said. "I've been following a lively discussion in the magazines about whether Thomas Rowley, a monk in Bristol during the fifteenth century, penned the poetry that has been attributed to him."

"I am familiar with that discussion." The vicar's voice dripped with disdain. "The medieval works supposedly discovered by young Thomas Chatteron. The family have been sextons here for an age. Young Thomas ran tame through our muniments room, pawing at this manuscript and that, before he left for London. I'm afraid one can only expect such a peculiar youth to come to a bad end." He sniffed. "And what is your impression of the dubious Brother Rowley, if you have one?"

Amaranthe smiled. "I found Rowley's dialect to be like no dialect of Middle English that I know or have studied, but a strange and fanciful blend of many elements. Almost as though a bright young child had studied a Chaucerian manuscript and attempted to create a medieval dialect of his own."

The vicar's expression shifted to approval. "Very good, Mrs. —" He looked around for her male companion, no doubt to congratulate him on her cleverness.

"Miss Amaranthe Illingworth, antiquarian," she said, and

the words gave her a thrill to say them. "Indeed, I have come here in search of a record myself. But I imagine that a man of your importance would not have the time to indulge my curiosity on this matter."

"On the contrary, I am always happy to show our muniments room to those who have a proper understanding of and appreciation for ancient things," the vicar said, producing a key from his vestments. "Shall your, er, chaperone join us?" Once again he looked about in vain.

"I was obliged to come alone today, as my betrothed had business to attend to in London," Amaranthe said. "He is preparing to be called to the bar and his advice was needed for a legal matter."

"Oh, very good." The mention that she was attached to a man of gentlemanly station changed the vicar's demeanor toward her instantly.

Amaranthe saw this attitude daily in her work in London. A man could be an antiquarian as a respectable hobby or even a trade; a woman was venturing outside her proper sphere. She couldn't find it in her to feel guilty about the lie as she followed the vicar across the vast, beautiful nave to the north porch. Mal had wanted to marry her to advance his professional ambitions. It was fair play if she used him for the same ends.

Perhaps she ought to marry him after all just to see what doors would open to her as a barrister's wife. If he did not retract his offer in whole after the discussion she knew they must have.

She followed the vicar up a short stone stair. With a bit of fumbling, he opened a grilled iron door to a narrow room lined with chests.

Her heart spun a pirouette at the sight of parchments and scrolls lying about for anyone to look at. Her love of old relics and manuscripts had begun with her own dear St. Cleer, four hundred years older than the upstart St. Mary Redcliffe. But St. Cleer was a heap of granite rubble in comparison to the Gothic immensity of this church, and the miners and farmers who comprised the town's population were not much for producing literature or indeed any valuable documents.

Amaranthe harbored a small pang that there hadn't been time to take Mal to St. Cleer. It was a beautiful place of flowing rivers and ancient piled stones, perched on a rocky corner of the moors. He would have liked the holy well, her favorite girlhood refuge.

She pushed away thoughts of Mal. He wouldn't appreciate her current understanding, but just as she couldn't leave a book without reading to the end, she couldn't leave Bristol without sorting for herself this last bit of Marguerite's mystery.

"The document I seek is a marriage record," she told the vicar. "From 1747."

"A family concern?" He examined the label on a nearby chest, then lifted the lid and produced a heavy, leather-bound tome.

Her chest throbbed, and she wondered if he heard her rasping breath. "My betrothed's family, actually." The vicar wouldn't fault her for snooping, would he? A woman ought to enter marriage with full awareness.

The register was not the neat columned business of smaller parishes but an immense folio with separate pages for each entry, showing names, dates, and witnesses. Amaranthe flipped through the blur of names and happy events. There was a chunk of September 1752 missing when the calendar had been adjusted to bring Britain in line with the rest of the Western world. There were two pages for May 1747, but neither of them were for a Marguerite Grey and Hugh Delaval.

Well, Beatrice had looked and found nothing. What had she expected?

Amaranthe ran a finger down the fold, thinking for a moment of these couples that had entered the solemn institution of marriage, possibly with such high hopes, perhaps the same kind of passion she found herself harboring for Mal. She'd never be sorry, but now that she'd discovered such wild, heady desire, she wondered if she could ever be the plain, sensible Amaranthe Illingworth again.

The binding felt uneven. She ran her finger along it again.

"A page has been removed here," Amaranthe said. "Cut out, or ripped."

"You must be mistaken."

"I am familiar with how books are bound. The parchment page is folded into quires and the quires are sewn together. This is not folded but torn. The second half of the folio is missing."

"That is curious." The vicar had the same bland look she'd adopted earlier when he was condescending to her.

"It is." She turned to face him. "Particularly since the page might have held record of a rather unusual wedding between a haberdasher's daughter and the son and heir of a duke. I imagine the young lord procured a special license, rather than having the banns read for weeks. And this is the sort of marriage where a ducal father might come along later and be very displeased to find a record that such an ill-advised and unapproved marriage existed."

"We at St. Mary Redcliffe's would never choose to hide from human eyes an act sanctified and sealed by God," the vicar said. "I am sorry if you have been misled."

She closed the register, her stomach turning over. "I am sorry, too. The legal matter my intended faces has to do with settling a ducal estate. A record of the late duke's marriage might go some way toward establishing proper guardianship over his heirs. It might even save a set of young, innocent children from a usurper who would leave them—who *has* left them —abandoned and destitute."

She started for the door, disappointment a bitter weight in her chest. Marguerite's marriage lines, while they meant a world of difference to Mal's status, had little value all on their own. If the document were even admitted as evidence in a court case, a legal battle could be drawn out for years, perhaps decades, if anyone decided to challenge Mal over the duke's estates. And Sybil, she imagined, had both the resources and the determination to do so.

"I thank you for your time, Father," Amaranthe said, recalling her manners. "I have enjoyed peeking into the room that inspired young Chatterton. One might wish his forgeries and stratagems had led him to better fortune."

The poor boy had ended himself with arsenic in a London garret, about the same time she left Cornwall. Amaranthe felt an affinity for young Chatterton. She herself had more than once created a manuscript and passed it off as an ancient work, just as Chatterton was suspected to have done.

Mal had said he wouldn't claim his patrimony. He didn't want to disinherit Hugh or his siblings. Amaranthe didn't wish to, either. It was enough that they two knew the truth.

Tears veiling her vision, she turned again toward the door, fighting a tide of despair at the thought of her future. Would Mal forgive her lies if he was living one himself? Would he still wish to marry her? What kind of a life or a future would they have, neither of them quite proper nor respectable, he of dubious birth, she of a dubious trade?

She had a hand on the iron grillwork of the door when the vicar said, "Wait."

Amaranthe turned and watched as he stepped to a chest under a far window and withdrew a small box. It took him a few tries to select the appropriate key. Then he withdrew a rolled sheet of parchment and returned the box to the chest. He came toward her, his face solemn and pained, as if he had eaten something that disagreed.

"I ministered that marriage," he said quietly. "I recall it."

Amaranthe stilled, caught in a moment clear as an etching: the sweeping vaulted arches of the ceiling, the light through the paned glass, the sounds of traffic on the street below, and the cool quiet secrets of the room. Hair rose on her arms. The knowledge about to come to her, once seen, could not be unknown.

She took the parchment with trembling hands.

"The bride's family came looking," she said. "No record was ever produced."

He grimaced. "Dukes can be very persuasive, especially when they are outraged fathers. But if it is a matter of protecting children..."

She unrolled the folio-size sheet and regarded it. Unlike the hasty hand of some of the other scrawled entries, this was firm and strong. *Hugh Delaval, Lord Vernay, his mark*, clear and bold. Below it, more delicately, almost dreamily, *Marguerite Grey, her mark*. Bea's loopy letters, the scribbled dash of Vernay's friend. The same lines, the witness of a sacred act, that Marguerite had tucked into her Book of Hours.

What a strange, unhappy twist of fate to wipe Marguerite's mind with a fever, leaving her an abandoned wife thrown on the charity of her sister, and her son a scrappy bastard to grow up by his wits and his fists. Perhaps Beatrice was right and it was the work of a higher power. Perhaps her Maker had shielded Marguerite from an empty union and kept her son from knowing greater cruelty.

Mal would be a different man had he grown up like young Hugh, pampered, protected, groomed from birth to bear the weight of his own importance. He might not at all be a man she could love. She couldn't be sorry for the obstacles he'd overcome in his life, though he labored under the shadow of his birth.

But this document could make that shadow disappear.

The corners of the parchment fluttered as her hands shook. "This record would protect against an injustice, were I allowed to bring it with me. But I am not sure it is enough, on its own, to persuade a judge."

The vicar considered this. "I will send a signed letter explaining the—er, circumstances and attesting to its accuracy." He winced. "I hope you will return this page in the course of time, however. It would behoove me to restore the register."

Amaranthe gave him the precious document to hold and from her reticule produced her favorite penknife, the one she used to hold down parchment sheets as she wrote and with which she scraped away mistakes. She traveled with it as a charm and, truth be told, a sort of protection. One never knew when one would need a penknife for cutting a binding or sharpening a quill. Or to remedy a far larger mistake than a misplaced slash of ink.

"A copy for your register will be but the work of a moment, Father, if you have fresh parchment and ink."

CHAPTER TWENTY-ONE

Amaranthe had, to Mal's knowledge, been in town four days now. He knew because Joseph Illingworth presented himself on the doorstep of Hunsdon House the day after their return. The lad's eyes were bloodshot and he reeked of strong coffee and spirits, but he insisted he was prepared to return to lessons. He said little of Amaranthe but that she had begun a new project. Mal waited for her to call, to inquire about the children, or to see about her servants, who remained yet at Hunsdon House.

When four days elapsed with no note and no sign of her, Mal donned his favorite blue cloth suit with the silver buttons, pulled on his tall black boots, and set out for George Court. He was not sure how he would find her or, for that matter, how she would receive him. They'd established an unquestioned intimacy in their travels to Cornwall. She'd met and been embraced by his family. She'd kissed him until he saw stars.

She'd found the long-hidden, long-sought document that turned everything he knew about his life on its head.

And she'd agreed to marry him, hadn't she? He'd been a fool not to secure a promise from her before he left Bristol. He'd allowed worries about Sybil's return and the resurrected court case to take over his mind and had taken this rather important decision for granted.

She wanted to marry him, didn't she? She must.

Mal had learned from a long life of taunts and whispers not to let his concern show on his face. So he adopted the most care-free attitude he could muster as he turned from Coventry onto Rupert Street, lifting his hat at all the finely dressed ladies and enjoying their appreciative stares. They wondered at him, who he was, where he came from. He wondered himself. It was exhilarating and strange to walk through the world with this small but significant difference. Everything the world could know and value about him had changed, and yet he was exactly the same person.

Before, he would have inwardly laughed at these women, admiring a man they didn't know was a bastard. He would have mocked them for being fooled by a fair form and face. But he was a duke's throw no longer. His mother had been betrayed and abandoned, true, but she had not thrown herself away on an empty promise. She'd been properly wed, and it was only the weakness of her beloved—or the overbearing power of her love's father, the second duke—that had parted them.

How his grandfather, the old duke, would roll in his grave to know the marriage he'd forced upon his son, a proper marriage to an earl's daughter for the purpose of begetting a proper heir, was not legally valid. And the bastard son of the haberdasher's daughter in Bristol, a boy of low birth and only the thinnest gentlemanly façade, was the duke in truth.

Mal had no intention of making that known, of course. If Amaranthe married him, he would be called to the bar, and he was willing to work for his keep and hers. Hugh, with his punc-tilious manners and grand airs, had been reared to the dukedom. Mal needed only to glance in the library and see the lad's golden head bent over another tome of exotic travels to know he belonged in this world.

Same with Ned, gnashing his teeth and muttering as he declined Latin nouns. And darling Camilla, feet swinging from the stuffed chair as she sat side-by-side with her bosom friend, the servant girl Derwa, reading aloud and pointing to the letters. He would do whatever it took to keep them safe and sheltered. He'd failed them miserably before; he would be more careful in future.

Mal was surprised to recognize the young girl striding down the street toward him. She carried a basket of violets over one arm and, if he was not mistaken, she wore a pelisse he had seen Amaranthe wear. She gave him a saucy grin and a wink as she neared him.

"Wasson, me 'andsome?" she said, which he recognized now as the Cornish greeting.

"I saw you in St. Paul's. What are you doing here?"

"Miss likes her violets and oranges," the girl replied. "Ought to wear a spray of 'em for her, you should." She plucked a small posy from her basket and tucked it into his top buttonhole, then stood back with her palm out. "Might give 'er a smile."

"Oh, very well." Mal gave her thruppence. "You've come a long way to deliver violets."

"I's an errand girl now, I is," the girl said loftily. "Know my way about town, don't I? Rather useful party, that makes me." She dipped him a small curtsey and strolled off, whistling.

At his knock Amaranthe's door was flung open to reveal the dark-haired maid, her face flushed with fury and her apron askew. "I've decided to seek a new position!" she barked by way of greeting. "D'ye know of one?"

"What's amiss?" Mal asked, taken aback.

"That Joseph!" Her dark eyes flashed with fury. "As if Miss Amaranthe don't have enough to worry about, doing the work that supports us all! Who among us hasn't had our heart broke? But no, he must pile foolishness upon foolishness and cause us all no end of worry!"

"Good Lord, what's he done?" Mal imagined mayhem.

"He's at the Blue Posts," she snapped. "Again. Miss went to fetch him afore he rolls under a table or starts a fight as he has every night this week."

"Is Mr. Illingworth no longer a fit tutor for my brothers?" Mal asked, though he was thinking aloud.

"He ain't fit to comb a dog!" The maid stomped into the house, talking to herself in a language he didn't recognize. Mal backtracked to find a crowd gathered at the end of the court, spilling into Rupert Street, and he guessed what he'd see before he drew near enough to have his suspicions proven.

Joseph stood in the street with his fists up like a man pretending to be a pugilist, bawling insults, while a second man lunged toward him, swinging. Between them Amaranthe stood with her arms out, demanding they both stop this instant, while the crowd frothing about them offered the opposite encouragement.

Mal saw only that Amaranthe was in danger. He grabbed the second man by the collar of his coat and with a firm shove sent him sprawling onto the cobbles. He then reached across Amaranthe to grab Joseph's neckcloth and gave the lad a good shake.

"I hope you've paid your shot, Illingworth. You're going home."

The crowd objected to this, calling for a resolution to the quarrel, one that would involve one or both men showing their blood. But Mal's look, and his size, quelled the enthusiasm.

Joseph writhed in Mal's grip. "He insulted Susannah!"

"He doesn't know Miss Pettigrew from a mule," Mal said. "Miss Illingworth, if I may request your assistance?"

Amaranthe gripped her brother's arm and helped Mal haul him under the arch into George Court, where interested passersby stepped aside to let them pass.

"You!" Joseph panted, swinging an ineffectual fist at Mal. "I ought to call you out. No doubt you encouraged him! You're his friend, ain't you? And who knows what he's done to my poor Susannah!"

"What's he raising a breeze about?" Mal asked Amaranthe over Joseph's head.

Her face was set in tense lines, and she looked tired. Joseph answered before she could.

"Your friend," he howled. "The captain. Shows up in his uniform and makes her a leg, and the next thing I know she's away to Gretna Green with him."

"You're talking moonshine," Mal said shortly.

"Captain Vierling whisked Miss Pettigrew away from the chapel where she was to wed Joseph and has carried her to Scotland to be married," Amaranthe translated.

"Viktor?" Mal was astonished. "Did he even know the girl?"

"He'll know her now!" Joseph cried. "He did something to make her set her cap for him. She led me on a merry chase, but him—" He sagged between them, deflated. "She ran off with him in an instant."

Mal opened Amaranthe's door and shoved Joseph into the house, leaving her to escort her brother upstairs and settle him. He went into her parlor to wait.

The room was cluttered in a way he found appealing, with a fresh stack of parchment on one chair and bottles on a small shelf, ink waiting to be mixed. He wondered what errands the costermonger was running for Amaranthe. Shopping? Contacting booksellers? Something else?

Her Book of Hours sat displayed on a gilded stand atop a

small table, given pride of place, and a manuscript lay open on the small desk next to her chair.

It was the rather hefty tome Ned found in the Hunsdon library. Mal remembered how Amaranthe's face had transformed as she looked at it. He'd thought at the time that he'd give a great deal to be the reason that starry, wondrous look entered her eyes. He'd seen her wear that expression since, soft and dazed, as if her feet had left the earth. She'd worn it after he kissed her. He smiled to think of her bending over this manuscript with the same loving attention she'd shown her Book of Hours and drew near to see what part she was reading.

She wasn't just reading. There was a parchment page secured to her work easel by the small wooden bar, her penknife and quill lying beside it. It was a title page, heavily decorated with foliation that looked vaguely Moorish in inspiration, with many loops and swirls. *The Book of Secrets*, the title read in large, black, heavily embellished script, *or Kitab al-Asrar*. Some foreign letters stood beneath this, Arabic he presumed. *Written by Muhammad al-Razi*, followed by more Arabic letters. And in smaller print at the bottom: *Englisht by Theocratus in* 1532.

Amaranthe was making another book. But it did not have her name on it.

She appeared in the doorway of the parlor wearing a faded day gown. She'd removed her cap and gloves. Her curly hair frizzed in soft puffs about her head. Violet hollows made her eyes look huge in her face. He itched to put his hands on her, but whether he wanted to pull her into his arms and kiss her, or put his fingers around her neck, he wasn't quite sure.

"I have not seen you in days." The words leapt from him, an accusation he hadn't meant to make. He'd meant to be nonchalant, insouciant. Just in the neighborhood, passing through.

Her lips turned downward. "Joseph—hasn't been well. I

have my hands full with him when he's here, so I must work when he's away tutoring."

"The children keep asking for you. They want to hear every detail of your travels." He wanted to hear it, too. What she and his aunt Beatrice had talked about after he left. How she had fared on her return to London. What she meant to do next.

"I haven't had time for social calls, I'm afraid."

"Is it true that Viktor absconded with Miss Pettigrew?"

"I was hoping you might tell me." She stepped into the room, and her scent surrounded him. Pull her into his arms and kiss her; that's what he wanted to do.

"I haven't seen Viktor since I returned, nor heard tell of him. He may very well have eloped, though how he met Miss Pettigrew, I can't begin to imagine."

"Who she chose doesn't really matter. All that concerns us is that she did not choose Joseph." She kneaded her forehead with a wince of pain.

No, he wanted to wrap his hands around her throat and shake her. Why didn't she come to him for help? Why didn't she tell him Joseph was blue-deviled? He stepped toward her, but she drew herself up, straightening her shoulders, and he halted. He couldn't bear it if she stepped away.

"Tell me what's happening with the duchess."

"My charming stepmother Sybil—" he spat the word— "has returned from Paris with Popplewell, the once-faithful steward, trotting at her heels. She's resurrected her challenge to my father's will with the demand she be made guardian of the estate and the children. Our case is to be heard in Chancery Court on Tuesday."

She blinked in surprise. "That seems expedient. I thought cases in Chancery dragged for an age."

"This one has, but someone's taken a new interest in it. I don't doubt Sybil's been pulling as many strings as she can.

We're to be heard by one of the Masters in Chancery, nearly as good as going before the Lord Chancellor himself. I'm hoping the case will dismissed on grounds that she robbed the estate and fled the country."

She searched his face, her eyes wide and wary. "Is there anything I can do?"

Oh, so many things. Step into his arms and let him hold her, for one. It would make him feel better. But she was on her guard again, and now that he had seen her work, he knew why. An icy despair washed through him, an acknowledgement of the inevitable. He never truly expected things would work out well for him. He had too much prior experience that told him the opposite.

He wanted to believe that not every woman he knew would betray him. His mother hadn't meant to leave him; she'd been ill since before he was born. Sybil had shown signs of her own complete self-absorption from the beginning. He'd never relied on her for anything, though he had hoped she would at least prove an adequate overseer to the children.

And now Amaranthe, who had come into his life like an unbidden angel, was every bit the thief he'd been warned she was.

"You can explain this," he said in a tight, controlled voice, and stepped aside to indicate the easel and its damning contents.

She quivered, but then set her shoulders firm and straight. She lifted her chin. "I should think it obvious."

"You are making a copy of the book Ned loaned you from our library."

"Yes."

"I do not recall that Hugh asked you to produce such a copy."

"He did not." To her credit, she did not falter in her gaze but met his inquisition steadily, fearlessly. The resignation on her face told him why she hadn't allowed an embrace.

His heart tore in his chest. She was distancing herself from him. She had to, in order to do this.

"You are making a copy of this book—"

"Parts of it," she clarified. "There's a segment of notes taken from the Arabic *Book of Secrets*. A book of alchemy that details—"

"I am not interested in the contents," he snapped. "Rather the fact that, from the title page, it appears you mean to create a book that I suppose you will sell to Mr. Karim. Perhaps several copies of it. I heard him asking you for such a thing."

"That is my trade," she said in a soft, toneless voice. "I copy books."

"It rather looks like stealing. But then I am not much acquainted with your *trade*."

Up her chin went another notch. "I did not steal from Hugh. I will return the book to his library."

"After having turned its contents into other books which you will then sell for your own gain."

"That is how I support my household, yes," she said.

"By forgery."

She flinched. "That is a strong word. I would not say it applies here."

It was a very strong word. Certain types of forgery were a hanging offense. "I simply make copies of rare and valuable works," she said, "to—to..."

"To sell as counterfeits. Under a different name. No doubt letting the client believe he is acquiring a valuable, perhaps priceless original work."

She took a step backwards. "They are not counterfeits. Merely copies. Medieval scribes copied books all the time."

But books of medieval provenance were old and valuable.

"This one suggests it is a sixteenth century manuscript. Not a modern reproduction." He pointed to the title page.

He needn't say more. She hung her head.

"Tell me I have misinterpreted your intentions," he said, hoping against hope she would correct him.

A long silence elapsed. Horse hooves clopped on the narrow cobbles of the court, one pedestrian hailed another, the ruckus of traffic rose from the busy thoroughfare of Rupert Street. His breath sounded loud and harsh in the quiet inside.

"I would use different terms to describe it," she said in a small voice. "But you have misunderstood if you believe I intend to deceive anyone by my work."

"You don't think it stealing to take someone's possessions and turn it to your own use? To let someone acquire an artifact on what may be false pretenses?"

The skin beneath her eyes tightened, as if she were holding back strong emotion. He wanted so badly to be wrong. For her to give an explanation that made sense.

Her chin stayed up, but the hands crumpling the fabric of her apron revealed her inner distress. "I do not call it stealing," she said. "One cannot own knowledge and keep it to oneself, any more than one can possess art. These are treasures that belong to all men. And women."

"If I commission a portrait," Mal answered, "it is mine. If I buy a book at a bookshop, it is mine. If I author a book and register it at the Stationer's, it is mine. If someone reproduced my book without my permission or takes my property from my library, copies it under their own name or another's, and then sells those copies, they have stolen from me."

She had no answer to this. Her eyes fell to the dark rug that stretched over the floor of the room.

He gathered himself like a man trying to stuff his guts back into place after he'd been sliced open by a mortal blow. "This is why you would not agree to marry me," he guessed.

She hesitated, and then nodded. "I doubt my ability to advance your career."

Of course. Because she was a forger and a thief. A beautiful, canny liar. It was true that no one was injured by her crimes, but that would not matter in the court of public opinion. It would not matter when it came time for his superiors to consider him for advancement and boons.

He hadn't wanted her for his career to begin with. He wanted her for his heart. For his life, his bed, his drawing room. His companion on this difficult journey.

"Will you look at the time," Mal said woodenly. "I must go. I have to consult with the barrister who will argue for us on Tuesday."

"Of course." Her eyes were wide and hurt. He kicked himself for the impulse to gather her into his arms. His foolish heart had not yet accepted the ruling of his brain. The only possible path lay before him, yet he could not seem to make his feet move and take him away from her.

"Could you—would you allow me to call on the children?" Her voice sounded so small and full of despair, as if she knew what he would say.

His heart tore further, but there was only one answer he could give, as their guardian and protector.

"Given the circumstances that have already cut up their peace, I think it would be wise if they have no further associations with someone who is thieving from their house. You may have Joseph return the manuscript when you are finished with it."

That rather sounded like he was giving her permission to make all the books she liked. But he had to bar her from Hunsdon House. He had forbid Sybil the house after she stole from them, forcing the duchess to lodge with sympathetic friends. Amaranthe was stealing from the dukedom, too.

She said nothing more, but held herself very still as he stepped around her to the door. There he paused.

"Why did you not tell me everything from the beginning?"

She bent her head, and that admission of guilt lashed him more than anything else. She knew she had done wrong and covered one lie with another.

"I knew, once you found out, you would never want to see me again." Her voice that had always been so calm, practical, strategizing, and intelligent, broke with tears. "And I—very much—wanted to see more of you."

He was at the front door, exiting onto the stoop, when he thought he heard a low sob. The sound rent his heart completely.

He was protecting the children from someone who meant to steal from them. Who meant to take advantage of what the Hunsdon estate could offer. Just like Sybil. That was the only thought that finally forced him to close the door and walk down George Court, away from her. He did it, but he left his heart behind.

CHAPTER TWENTY-TWO

Tuesday promised to be a warm late spring day. In his small rooms on the Strand, Mal freshened his periwig with white powder and selected a suit that was elegant and subdued, somber enough to be in line with the barristers and judges of the court in their wigs and the black robes of office. He might be called as a witness, but he might have to rely entirely on his barrister, Rosenfeld, to make his case before the presiding judge. Whatever went forward this day was out of his hands, and Mal didn't like surrendering control to others.

He paused at his regular coffee shop to imbibe a black, bitter cup and asked the serving boy if he'd seen Viktor Vierling of late.

"Said 'e was off to Scotland to visit relatives, a few days past," the boy replied, placing a cup before Mal that steamed with heat. "What's a Hessian got Scottish relatives for, I wants to know?"

So Viktor had something up his bright red sleeve all along, Mal thought as he strolled down the Strand, hearing the lions roar from their cage in the Exchange. Mal had supposed them friends, and yet Viktor hadn't seen fit to tell him he had any interest in Miss Pettigrew, nor any intention to turn Illing-worth's expectations on their head.

Still, Joseph should take the rejection in a more manful style. No more drowning his sorrows in drink and starting mills at the pub. Take it on the chin that his lady was false. Mal had.

He couldn't think about Amaranthe or her betrayal. It felt like a bright, hot blade had sunk into his chest and lodged there.

Chancery proceedings took place in the great hall of West-minster, long the seat of British political power. As Mal strolled through White Hall and down Parliament Street, he watched the ships' masts moving along the river and the traffic roving back and forth on Westminster Bridge. This part of London, closest to the river, reminded him most of Bristol. When he stayed at Hunsdon House he felt in another world entirely, far away from his roots and what he knew.

As the tall spires of Westminster Abbey came into view, he thought of how much Amaranthe would appreciate the Gothic design and the soaring stained-glass windows reaching toward heaven. No, he must stop thinking about Amaranthe. That way lay madness and bitter regret. He'd best make a clean break, strike her entirely from his mind.

He tried to do just that as he entered the long hall of West-minster with its vast interior space and hammer-beam ceiling, a marvel of medieval architecture. Stalls selling trinkets and other goods lined the interior, and he headed for the screened-off courtroom where his case was to be heard.

"So the wastrel makes his appearance."

Sybil sat in one of the pews, advantageously close to the judge's chair and with a view of the room in whole. Popplewell perched beside her, wigged and nervous. The light filtering through the windows did not fall kindly upon the duchess. Her face was pale with lead paint, her cheeks unnaturally red, her powdered white hair piled high. She wore a flamboyant robe à la

Turque in red silk. As Mal watched she held up an enameled snuffbox, opened it, raised a pinch to each nostril and sniffed dramatically, then flourished a handkerchief and dabbed at her nose and lip. Her dainty theatrics drew every male eye in the room and made sure her insult lingered in the air.

"Sybil," Mal said, foregoing all courtesy. She was technically his stepmother, so he could claim familiarity, if not affection. "I'd heard you took flight to the Continent with a lover far beneath you in quality. What a surprise to find you here, with Popplewell in your train."

The steward shifted in his seat. His eyes, made overlarge by his spectacles, held alarm, and he clutched his walking stick as if it would provide defense.

"I'd heard *you* left town in the company of someone far beneath you," Sybil shot back. "I see the little mouse followed you here. She must be a very desperate spinster to toss her scarf at a bastard like you."

Mal turned and spotted Amaranthe in the very back pew. Her hair was unpowdered and with her simple straw bonnet and grey pelisse she did indeed look unassuming. But no one with eyes could call her a mouse.

His heart rose and slammed against his ribs in a whirl of conflicting emotions: gratitude that she was here, indignation that she was intruding on his thoughts and his life when he was determined to forget about her, and outrage that she was alone. But then he recalled a man he'd thought was Davey strolling about the booths in the hall.

Why had she come? To witness his possible downfall and defeat? To try to offer support though he'd banned her from the family? She was the only other person here who knew the secret he needed to protect. Would she expose him against his wishes, in retaliation for how he had caught her out in her ill deeds?

She met his eye with that dark, steady gaze of hers, and a

rush of warmth filled him, deeper and more layered than the rush of attraction that always kindled when she was near. He saw in her face that she had come to support him and she meant to fight for him. She could be deposed as a witness for how Sybil had left the children, if need be.

And she could testify to the documentation that made his birth legal and gave him the status of the duke's heir.

No. He refused to disinherit Hugh or the others. She was here in vain. He turned without acknowledging her and strolled to the other side of the room where the black-robed, white-wigged group of men stood conferring.

"Froggart!" he exclaimed. It was his old nemesis from the Middle Temple, a green-gilled, boot-licking cousin of a viscount who had been called to the bar before him. "You can't be representing Sybil?"

"I have that honor," Froggart said, wetting his lips in nervousness and watching Mal as if he were a snake that meant to swallow him in one gulp. But Mal was no toad-eater, which could not be said of Froggart.

His surprise was complete when he recognized the judge appointed to preside over the session. "Oliver! I'd heard you'd been made a Master in Chancery, but I didn't know you had this case."

"I took it over." Oliver pulled the queue of his wig free from his robe and arranged it down the back of his neck. "Felt I was qualified to make a good decision, and the Lord Chancellor agreed."

Mal wondered what this boded for his case. Oliver's eyes flickered to the pew where Amaranthe sat, and a light of approval entered his eyes. "I see you've brought your lady."

"She's not my lady," Mal said. Oliver's look of inquiry made him add, unable to contain his bitterness, "She proved too clever for me."

"Always a risk," Oliver said. He proceeded to the dais to take his seat and called the court to order.

Sybil's strategy emerged at once. She had decided to forego her initial line of attack, which concerned what she felt she was due her as the late duke's duchess and wife. Now she had decided to undermine Mal's claim to the guardianship with a wholesale scuttling of his worth, his ability, and his character.

Froggart began entering into the rolls, by the tactic of reading aloud to the Court, long depositions from Sybil and other witnesses painting Mal as a wastrel of the first order. Accounts were given of every time he had visited a club or private house and lost money gambling. Friends who had encouraged his most reckless acts bragged of wagers on carriage races and cock fights. Viktor Vierling, Captain in the Grenadier Horse Guards and a traitor twice over, hinted at a duel.

Mal smothered a groan. That affair had been settled at dawn without weapons on account that neither principal, nor their seconds, could recall, once sober, what the offense had been, but Froggart slanted the report to cast Mal as a ne'er-do-well. None of these peccadilloes were more than the larks that most young gentlemen in London fell into from time to time, but Froggart depicted Mal as a menace to society.

His history of reprimands and infractions at Cambridge were recounted in detail. A former schoolmaster at Winchester, the one who had liked him the least and disciplined him the most, gave an account of his character as being thoroughly irredeemable despite regular beatings. A witness from Bristol—no less than his childhood enemy, Tew—claimed that in one fight, after he'd done no more than give an accurate account of Mal's parentage, he'd feared Mal meant to kill him. Mal, arms folded, sank lower in his seat as his failures at going to sea, apprenticing to a printer, and studying for the priesthood were explored in full.

Froggart reported with particular relish the disappointments of one Sally Bly, from a family of Irish lacemakers, who had been rudely jilted by Mr. Malden Grey, of whom she had expectations of marriage. At this Mal felt the scowl freeze on his face. Sweet Sally had flirted and led him on, all to fire the jealousy of the man whose affections she really wanted, but she told Froggart Mal made promises and broke them? He looked a blackguard indeed.

And Amaranthe was hearing every word of this. Every instance of bad luck, observed; every whim or inane occupation, itemized. Mal o' Misfortune, his whole history laid miserably bare.

With the first witness Froggart called, Mal's stupefaction was complete. Mr. Thorkelson, looking more than ever like an aged Viking warrior gone to fat, took the witness stand and swore an oath to be truthful. Mal turned to glare at Sybil, who raised her brows in disdain. So she'd had both the steward and his solicitor working in her interests. He'd not given her full credit for the depth of her guile.

It seemed his lot ever to be deceived by women.

Froggart began by asking Thorkelson about how Mal had mischaracterized Sybil's flight to the Continent with the ducal income.

"Her Grace left for France with the intention of finding a house in Paris for her and the children," Thorkelson claimed, broadcasting news that, if true, he had not seen fit to share with Mal. "Since she has spent much time living in France herself, she felt it would be beneficial to their education to learn the language. When she heard that Mr. Grey was describing her as having fled the country with stolen goods, she returned at once to prove her innocence."

"Did she return the money?" Mal said loudly, outraged at

her guile. Froggart glared at him, and Oliver scowled at his speaking out of turn.

"Why should Mr. Grey go about with unfounded accusations that Her Grace had taken more than what was essentially her property as the Duchess of Hunsdon?" Froggart asked. "In addition to casting aspersions on the character of a mother who has nothing but the care and security of her children at heart."

Mal's loud snort was pointedly ignored.

"I regret to say that I believe that Mr. Grey harbors a great deal of ill will toward the duchess," Thorkelson said. "This is not the first time he has cast such aspersions on her character. In fact, it's widely known that he objected to his father's marriage most strenuously, and in the time he has been in London, he has not dined, nor very frequently visited, at Hunsdon House." He coughed lightly. "This casts some doubts, at least in my mind, about the sincerity of his wish for the guardianship of the Delaval children."

"Oh, indeed?" Froggart asked his witness. "Why do you suppose he would interest himself in these children who have no real claim upon him?"

Mal stiffened in outrage. No claim but blood, he wanted to shout.

Thorkelson coughed again, a low rumble. "I am loathe to make the suggestion, but I fear very much that Mr. Grey has interested himself more than is usual in the incomes and allowances pertaining to the Hunsdon estates. We all know that, due to the unfortunate circumstances of his birth, he has no claim to inheritance himself. A man in such a position might very well see his guardianship of the young duke and his siblings as an opportunity to line his own pockets."

Mal turned and glared at Sybil. The nerve of her, to suggest of *him* the very deed she was guilty of! She schooled her features into innocence, but a coy smile flickered about her painted mouth.

Froggart went on to paint Sybil as the picture of a bereaved mother who saw herself and her cherished children threatened and besieged by the avaricious, ruthless bastard son of her husband. What could the court do to protect this noble and virtuous woman from Mal's greedy and undeserving clutches? Award her guardianship of the children until Hugh was twenty-five, Froggart concluded, and give her the ability to direct and oversee the Hunsdon estate so she might be at liberty to support and provide for her children.

Mal's horror grew as he saw Oliver's face softening at Froggart's depiction of a duchess deprived of her proper station, her maternal impulses stifled, her very well-being at stake. Sybil adopted an appropriately sorrowful, downcast look, avoiding Mal's look of rage. How dare she even call herself a mother, he thought furiously, when to his knowledge she had never once denied herself an entertainment to see to the care of the children. She had left them in the nursery under the care of servants and spent their income on her own pursuits.

But he had not made any better a showing for himself. He had not exactly been the doting brother, either. Rosenfeld stepped forward to cross-examine the witness, and Mal felt a rush of confidence as he began questioning Thorkelson about the recent state of affairs at Hunsdon House, and the evidence that Sybil had left the children without proper oversight or care.

Thorkelson somehow contrived to blame this on Mal.

"It is my understanding that the servants left because Mr. Grey was threatening them on grounds that they felt unreasonable," Thorkelson said, looking as if it pained him to tell this outrageous bouncer. He glanced at Sybil once, and Mal saw the commanding nod she gave him in response. What hold had she gotten over the man?

"He then, I am told," Thorkelson went on, "brought in a very common person, unrelated to the family—and someone of questionable occupation as well—and installed an entirely new staff of her choosing. I am also told this woman, though she has no formal relationship with Mr. Grey, has been living at Hunsdon House, running it as if she were the duchess. Sleeping in the duchess's chambers, if reports are to be believed, and wearing the duchess's gowns."

Mal glared at Thorkelson, who looked unrepentant. Sybil gasped and withdrew a painted fan, waving it about her face as if overcome with shock.

Mal dared a glance at Amaranthe. She met his eyes with a worried look. She didn't like that Thorkelson had as much as suggested to the court that she was Mal's mistress. He could tell by the proud tilt to her chin.

But she also saw that things were going badly for him, and she was more concerned on his account than her own. Her commissions would not dry up if his suit failed and gossip circulated about her. Rather, the brief fame might drive business her way. He was the one who stood to lose everything if Oliver ruled against him. His aspirations to the law would be ended, his livelihood would be gone. He'd be cast into the world with nothing—nothing to offer a wife, at any rate—and Sybil would never let him near his half-siblings again.

His gut tightened. He had to win. He had to defeat Sybil somehow.

"One wonders how the duchess knew anything of what was occurring at Hunsdon House," Rosenfeld said mildly, "since she was abroad in France and concerned with her own affairs."

"Her Grace has many friends here, Your Honor," Thorkelson told the judge. "She is particularly intimate with the Duchess of Cumberland, the wife of Prince Henry, and the Duchess of Gloucester, Prince William's wife. They have kept her apprised of developments, especially those they feared were not in the best interests of the children."

So that was it. The wives of the royal princes, though both commoners, nevertheless held a great deal of sway over London society. Maria, now the Duchess of Gloucester, was herself illegitimate, and though she had first married an earl and now a royal duke, she would never be received at court. If Sybil had ingratiated herself with the royal family—even the less accepted members of it—she could turn public opinion as well as the court against him. Mal would be crushed like a bug under a boot. His only powerful patron had been his father, and the duke was dead.

"And since her return," Froggart continued, "Mr. Grey has denied the duchess access to Hunsdon House. He has deprived her of her own home. More than that, he has kept her from seeing her children. Your Honor, you cannot imagine the pain and distress this has caused to Her Grace's tender mother's heart. What legal protection can the court grant her, I ask, to protect this widowed mother and her helpless children from the incursions of a man who has no claim upon their affections or their estate?"

Sybil produced an embroidered handkerchief and dabbed at her eyes. Froggart turned and looked Mal straight in the eye, repeating his last accusation with emphasis. "No claim."

"No claim," Oliver mused, watching Mal as well.

He was an insect trapped in amber under their combined, condemning gaze. Even Rosenfeld had no defense for him.

It didn't matter if he were cast into the outer darkness. He'd been there before. On his own account, it meant nothing. But Hugh. Ned. Millie. Their faces swam before his eyes. The hungry, pleading looks on their faces when he'd found them in Amaranthe's parlor, like frightened birds who had found sanctuary. Their eager delight that first night they had dined together at Hunsdon House, their pride at being included with the adults, and the merry moments they'd had at dinners to follow.

Ned's look of pride when he'd unearthed that manuscript for Amaranthe, knowing he was granting her a great privilege. Hugh's correct bow to her when they readied to leave for Bristol. Ever aware of his ducal burden, the boy was unable to disguise his wish for her approval. And Camilla, who had made herself Amaranthe's devoted little shadow, clinging to her skirts and demanding to learn Greek.

In the past weeks he'd come to know his siblings better than he ever had. Before they'd been a responsibility; now they were dear. If he lost this suit, he had no doubt Sybil would bar him from seeing them. He'd be reduced to haunting Hanover Square, waiting for the children to emerge. Asking Amaranthe to ask Joseph to give him news of his own blood.

He'd lose the chance to guide the lads and teach them how a young man survived in a world that could be so cruel. He'd have no chance to make sure Camilla was courted correctly and by young men worthy of her when it came time to make her launch. Sybil would take from him the chance he'd glimpsed to have a real family at last.

But if he spoke now, he'd take away Hugh's inheritance. He'd take away Ned's chances at a good profession and Camilla's chance to marry well.

And if he didn't speak, he'd lose the children to Sybil, who would take these things from them anyway.

Mal looked to Amaranthe. He saw the urgency in her eyes. She leaned forward, clutching a package to her chest, her face pale, her eyes wide and frightened.

What do I do? He signed to her as he had seen her speak with Thaker, though he didn't doubt his gestures were inaccurate as well as foolish-looking to the rest of the room.

She held his gaze and answered without hesitation, the meaning of her quick signs clear. *You must do what is right*.

Funny that *she* would give him such counsel. But he was relieved at her answer. She trusted him to act on his own principles. And he knew that whatever he decided, Amaranthe would tell him he'd been right. She believed in him and his ability to choose the best path. She didn't see him as buffeted by misfortune or at the mercy of bad luck. She saw him as a man of integrity.

It was astonishing and undeserved, but he saw all this in the clear, steady light of her gaze. And he knew that however he'd scolded her, deserved or not, and however far he fell in public opinion or material circumstances, he could come to Amaranthe and she would take him in. She would never condemn him as he had her. She would accept him as he was, whatever his mistakes, his peccadilloes, his past behavior, and his birth. She would believe in his ability to do better, to repair his errors, to make things right.

With her beside him, everything would *be* right. As long as he did everything in his power to keep her. And keep Sybil from taking everything he loved away.

Mal stood, cleared his throat, and stepped to the edge of the cliff.

"It happens I have some claim on the estate," he said.

Froggart swept him with a freezing stare. "You are not to speak. Your barrister will argue your case before the Master. What little case you have," he added with a sneer.

Mal stepped toward the bench, beckoning to a surprised Rosenfeld to join him. "Your Honor. If you will permit me. New evidence has recently come to light that has a substantial impact upon my case."

He withdrew the precious bit of parchment from the pocket inside his coat and handed it to Rosenfeld. "I have discovered the existence of a valid marriage between my mother and Hugh Langston Delaval, third Duke of Hunsdon." He glanced from the judge to Popplewell, whose eyes were huge behind his glasses, and Sybil, whose mouth hung open in shock.

"These marriage lines make me their legitimate firstborn son," Mal said quietly. "I am not the guardian of my father's children or his estate. By terms of the entail, I am his heir."

CHAPTER TWENTY-THREE

E veryone in the courtroom surged to their feet. Amaranthe stood, too, so she could see over their heads. She strained to hear over the blood pounding in her head. Sybil was the first to find her voice.

"He's a bastard! He's lying!" she shrieked.

"Your Honor." Froggart recovered himself from this facer and scrambled to think of an intervention. "This documentation was not properly submitted during the pleadings and has not been entered into the rolls. It cannot be admitted."

"You are not in a court of common law," Oliver answered sharply. He reached down from his bench to indicate he should be given the document Mal's barrister was perusing. Once he had it in hand, the judge stared sternly at Mal. "This evidence has not been submitted during the pleadings, nor entered into the rolls."

"Your Honor, we could all withdraw back to the plea stage, and continue with deposition," Mal's barrister said.

Amaranthe liked him; he was slender, his manner unassuming, but he had a richly timbred voice larger than his frame and a gleam of intelligence in his eyes. "Or," Rosenfeld went on,

"Your Honor could consider the new evidence and make a judgment now, as it is within your power as a Master in Chancery to do."

"That document is counterfeit." Sybil's voice carried across the room. "My husband never married that commoner. His father, the second duke, rescued him from her clutches and brought him to his senses."

"My grandfather, the second duke, separated my father and mother as soon as he learned of their union," Mal answered. "But they were married in a church with a special license, with the blessing of a priest and the signature of witnesses. That makes their marriage valid in any court."

"It was after you were born," Sybil said swiftly. "So you're still a bastard."

"We can consult my baptismal record if the court has a doubt," Mal said. "It resides in the parish of St. Phillip and St. James in Bristol."

Amaranthe kicked herself that she had not thought to hunt up a copy of Mal's records while she was in Bristol as well. Would Marguerite have entered her married name, Lady Vernay, as the mother? Would she have properly named his father? It could take any length of time to produce this record, thus delaying the case further. What would Mal do while they waited, his fate in limbo? This was what he had feared: that he could produce Marguerite's marriage lines and he would still not be believed, just as Marguerite had not been believed.

She hugged her Book of Hours closer to her chest, protecting the document within it.

"I happen to have recently reviewed the record begun on Mr. Grey when he entered the Middle Temple," Oliver said. "His birth year was given as 1748. This marriage record is dated 1747."

Sybil's mouth worked soundlessly. Even in her distress, she

looked fetching. The barrister representing her, on the other hand, looked like he'd swallowed a toad. And the nondescript, gaudily dressed man sitting next to Sybil, who must be the steward Popplewell, looked about to faint. Sybil snapped open a box of smelling salts and impatiently thrust it at him.

The large blond man in the witness box, who'd identified himself as Mr. Thorkelson, watched Amaranthe.

"The document could have been forged, as Her Grace suggests," Thorkelson said. "By someone experienced in such things. Someone who perhaps took an interest in advancing Mr. Grey's position."

Here it was: what she'd feared most. Mal wouldn't be believed because of his association with her. Amaranthe willed herself to stay silent though everything in her wanted to cry out.

"It would take someone very expert to produce something this authentic looking," Mal's barrister said. "I find that accusation unlikely."

"And yet," Mr. Thorkelson mused, "the very person with whom Mr. Grey has taken up is known to be an extremely skilled copyist. I understand she can reproduce any hand and make it appear convincing. She has developed quite a reputation among the booksellers and book binders about town. If you ask anywhere for the best person to make a fair, true copy of an antique manuscript, they will direct you to one Miss Illingworth."

Amaranthe hadn't known she was so well regarded. She wished she could take pride in Thorkelson's words, instead of finding them damning. Oliver looked at her with speculation. The barristers, forbidding in their black silk robes and wigs of office, watched her as well.

"Forged?" Sybil sniffed. "Of course it's forged. But by *her*?" She swiveled to stare at Amaranthe and, like a pale shadow, the steward beside her did also.

Everyone stared at Amaranthe.

Mal looked resigned. He hadn't any other proof. All his life, since birth, he had been regarded as less than, insufficient. He didn't expect anything to change about that now.

And despite public opinion, he'd done his best to forge a life for himself. So what if there had been missteps along the way—what man did not have them in his past? He was doing his best to establish himself in a career, and now that his siblings had been cast upon Sybil's less than tender mercy, he was trying to do right by them as well. How she loved him for it.

He'd already done the worst thing he could do to her, casting her out and telling her not to seek out him or the children. He could wound her no worse. And he needed her. Amaranthe stood.

"Your Honor. I can prove the marriage lines are valid," she said.

She was surprised that her voice carried across the room, with its high vaulted ceilings, when she felt so out of breath. Shakily she opened her book and withdrew a matching piece of parchment.

She tried her best to sound calm and authoritative, though her knees quaked. "I have here the record of marriage entered into the parish register at St. Mary Redcliffe in Bristol. And a statement from the vicar of St. Mary Redcliffe, who conducted the marriage, attesting to its validity. If Your Honor will allow me."

"The court acknowledges new evidence submitted by Miss Amaranthe Illingworth," Oliver said. She was taken aback by what seemed to be a twinkle of amusement in his eye. "You may approach the bench."

"This is preposterous!" The duchess's barrister leapt forward as if he meant to bar her way. "You cannot produce more false information! This is entirely against procedure."

"Froggart," the judge said coolly, "you forget that you are in my courtroom, not yours. Miss Illingworth, proceed."

"I visited the church while I was in Bristol," Amaranthe explained to Mal as she surrendered the documents. He stepped close to peer over her shoulder at the record, and she thrilled to the sense of warmth at his nearness. He wasn't angry. Astonished, but not angry.

"The vicar produced it when I told him the situation," she went on. "The page had been removed from the rest of the register, which is why your Aunt Beatrice couldn't find it when she looked. I gather your grandfather made the vicar understand that no one who came looking was to find this document. As an enraged duke, he was extremely persuasive."

"But you found it." Mal's eyes glowed with admiration. Her sense of warmth increased.

Oliver put the two pages side by side. "These record a special license for the named parties and were properly witnessed as well as signed by the priest," he said. "Hugh Delaval and Marguerite Grey were by these lines married in the eyes of the Church, and therefore under the laws of Great Britain."

"Forged!" Sybil said shrilly. "Lies."

Mr. Thorkelson coughed into his hand. "I'm afraid the duchess may be correct, Your Honor. I have reason to know that Miss Illingworth has involved herself in forgery prior to this."

Every particle of warmth that had filled Amaranthe turned to ice.

"I *beg* your pardon." Mal's barrister turned to the witness. "Was anyone talking to you?"

"I have proof," Thorkelson said. "My firm conducted an inquiry into the Illingworth family when Mr. Illingworth was hired into the Hunsdon household. I have been a personal witness to her habit of forging rare medieval manuscripts and selling them to unsuspecting owners for a very high price."

"What's this?" Oliver turned his attention to the witness.

Sybil stepped forward. "You were the one wearing my gowns?" she demanded. "*You?*" Her contemptuous gaze raked Amaranthe from head to toe before she turned an icy stare on the blond Viking. "Thorkelson, tell them," she commanded.

Mr. Thorkelson looked at the judge, avoiding Amaranthe's pleading eyes. "As I said, Miss Illingworth is a very skilled copyist," he said. "My office is aware of at least one manuscript she was commissioned to translate, an alchemical treatise dating to the thirteenth century, whose owner, an Oxford don, thought he was in possession of the single surviving copy. Imagine my surprise when I later discovered a copy of this alchemical treatise in the library of a different client, a scholar whose estate I was in charge of. It happens my client procured the manuscript through the bookshop of one Mr. Karim, commonly known as the Moor."

Amaranthe sucked in her breath. How had he found out about her copy? That alone was enough to damn her, but Thorkelson's manner indicated he had more weapons in his arsenal.

"It then came to the attention of our office that Mr. Karim also sold, some years ago, a manuscript that bears a very close resemblance to a bestiary held in the college library of St. John's at Oxford University. And just lately Mr. Karim conducted the sale of yet another valuable manuscript, also virtually identical to a holding in St. John's College library. All of these manuscripts, he will swear under oath, he acquired from Miss Illingworth." Thorkelson's cold blue eyes bored into her.

"Forgery?" The man called Froggart gasped. "That is a capital offense, Your Honor!"

"Is it true?" Oliver fixed her with a stern glare. "You made these copies."

Lying would achieve her nothing. "Yes," Amaranthe agreed in a hollow voice. "The alchemical treatise he mentions was the *Treatise on the Spheres* by John of Holybush. I was asked by a friend of my old schoolmistress to make a fresh copy he could share with his students. I made a practice copy while I produced the fair copy, and Mr. Karim took interest in it, as the treatise draws much on the work of Arabic astronomers. The works I copied from St. Johns College Library in Oxford are the *Physiologus,* a medieval bestiary, and the more recent sale is the *Secretum Secretorum.* Also known as the *Book of Secrets,* the—"

"Yes, the advice of his tutor Aristotle to a young Alexander the Great." Oliver nodded. "I saw your copy in the bookshop, remember? Only knew it because I had to read it for my exams. And you took the manuscript from an Oxford library?"

"Borrowed it, Your Honor, while my brother was a pensioner there." She didn't add she had parted with these copies—works she'd never intended to sell—only to support first her own household, and then Hunsdon House after Sybil had robbed them. Her purposes wouldn't matter to an upholder of the King's laws. Only the fact of the crime.

It was over. With her a known forger, Mal would not be believed. It was best he had already cast her from his life, now that she was about to be thrown into the bridewell and tried as a criminal. What would happen to Joseph with a sister in prison or transported, or worst of all, hanged? What would happen to her household, to Eyde and Derwa and Davey and Mrs. Blackthorn and Inez? She'd never have the chance to spend time with the Delaval children, if they ever forgave her. She'd never have the chance to spend time with Mal.

She turned her eyes to him, lost. She'd fallen in love, firmly and truly. She'd finally found a man she could envision sharing her life with. She'd regret losing him most of all.

"So, Mr. Thorkelson, you accuse Miss Illingworth of selling, for profit, copies she has made of ancient manuscripts," Mr. Oliver said mildly. "Quite skillfully made copies, if her reputation is to be believed."

"None of that constitutes forgery," Mal said.

He wasn't talking to her but to the judge. Amaranthe blinked, her vision blurred with the tears she fought to hold back. Mal, of all people—the man who had scolded her so thunderously in her own study, before he sheared her from his life forever—he would try to claim here, in a court of law, that she wasn't guilty? She gestured at him to cease before he sank his own reputation along with hers. But he carried on.

"Was it forgery that Bishop Thomas Percy found and reprinted his *Reliques of Ancient Poetry?*" Mal said. "No. He was simply sharing antique works he had discovered that he knew would be of interest."

Amaranthe put a hand over her pounding heart. She'd told Mal about the *Reliques* in one of their conversations on the road. Its publication ten years ago, when her father brought the manuscript into their house, had enchanted her thoroughly, confirming her love for ancient writings and her commitment to rescue them for others, just as Percy had salvaged his ballads from the manuscript he'd found a maid using to light fires.

"Was it forgery if young Thomas Chatterton indeed created the Rowley manuscripts?" Mal went on. "Perhaps."

Amaranthe tried to control her shortness of breath. She'd told Mal all about Chatterton, too.

"But Miss Illingworth is not creating any works that she means to pass off as antiques," Mal said.

That was a lie. If anyone looked in the locked cabinet in her study, they'd find a whole row of books she'd reproduced for herself. Stolen, as Mal put it, just as she'd stolen the treatise on the spheres. She could and might try to sell them as ancient works, if it increased their value. She was a businesswoman as well as an artist. Besides, Mal had seen the title page for her *Book of Secrets* and guessed at once what she was about.

She ought to have burned that page as soon as he left her. She'd burn it the moment she arrived home. The manuscript Ned had given her was priceless, but she would not steal from the Delaval children. She'd find another way to share the knowledge within.

But Thorkelson was still right. All the manuscripts he'd identified had been forged by her. There was no way around it.

How bitterly she regretted now what had once seemed like her only possible means of sustaining herself, Joseph, and their household. If she did not have a protector or income of her own, a woman was forced to go into service or sell her body. Inez was proof of that.

But Inez was also proof that honest labor was better than thievery. Why had Amaranthe never chosen the straight and narrow path?

She wished Mal would not lie, here in a court of law, to protect her. Yet he pressed on.

"I have consulted with Mr. Karim himself and have a deposition that he recorded with Mr. Rosenfeld—if the court will allow me?" Mal's barrister brought forth yet another document and presented it to the judge, who took it with great interest.

"Mr. Karim attests therein," Mal said, his manner growing more formal, "that the manuscripts furnished him by Miss Illingworth, rather than mere reproductions, are special editions of her own making. He has identified several places where text has been changed or corrected, and the work in fact bears her signature, in the form of a distinctive mark. A mark in the shape of a flower of the amaranth family, as it happens, which also happens to be her given name.

"Furthermore, Mr. Karim attests that none of the manuscripts he has obtained from Miss Illingworth are works over which the original author might exert control," Mal said. "John of Holybush lived over five hundred years ago. The two other manuscripts you mention were reproduced from the library of St. John's College at Oxford, one of our greatest universities, which, if I need remind you, has been dedicated for centuries to preserving and disseminating knowledge for the good of the nation, as a matter of public trust."

Amaranthe's head whirled. Mal had spoken with Mr. Karim. He had discovered what she was about and then had gone to the bookseller to investigate the extent of her crimes. And Mr. Karim, with his sharp eye, had discovered for himself what Amaranthe was up to. But rather than shape his discovery into damning evidence, Mal had taken a position that would exonerate her and Mr. Karim both.

He was using his knowledge of the law to save her.

He was also using what she guessed to be his barrister's voice. It was low and smooth, with a rich, smoky timbre, hypnotic. She found herself nodding in response to his questions, caught up in his argument.

"Were these works entered by their authors into the Stationer's Register and thus protected by copyright?" Mal said, his voice swelling to fill the room. "No. Were they works held in copyright by another publisher? No. These are works in fact *not* protected by copyright and therefore not governed by the Statue of Anne. These works belong to the public domain and there are, therefore, no restrictions on their duplication or circulation."

He turned a steely glare on Thorkelson, then the man called Froggart. "Miss Illingworth is in violation of no known laws and cannot thereby be charged with forgery. You have made a false accusation that one may, in fact, consider libel." A chargeable offense.

Amaranthe repressed a smile of giddy relief. Mal had accused her of forgery himself, but no matter. She tried to look meek and innocent as Oliver turned a probing gaze on her.

"It does not appear that Miss Illingworth has trespassed as you say, Mr. Thorkelson," he observed. "She has broken no laws in reproducing and then selling copies of these works."

"That doesn't mean she didn't forge those marriage lines," Sybil cried. "It sounds like she very well could have."

Amaranthe drew a deep breath. Just as Mal had been deemed unworthy all his life because he was a bastard, she was deemed unworthy by the mere fact of her sex. There was no earthly reason, nor precedent, for a man of authority to listen to her.

"Your Honor," she said anyway, "an examination will prove these documents are not forged. If you will permit me to approach?"

Oliver motioned her forward, and Mal fell in beside her, his shoulder brushing hers. She reined in the impulse to lean against him.

"These documents cannot be new, because the parchment is not new," she said with quiet authority. "Do you observe this texture? These pages are some decades old. Parchment, particularly vellum, which this is, will tend to buckle as it dries. It is why medieval books are held together with clasps.

"Furthermore, I suspect both of these pages were cut from the same larger hide. There's a very distinct pattern of coloration shared by both, when put side by side. The pattern of capillaries on both suggests the hide was not scraped as smooth as could be, nor were the folios smoothed with pumice before being written upon, which means the pages were not meant for manuscript but for records that would only be seen once."

She tapped a finger on the ink. Her own finger, if the gloves were off, would have shown the ink stains from her toils that morning, but no matter. "Your second indication is the ink. Oak gall ink, unlike lampblack or India ink, fades over time. If you look at the notations being made by our court scribe there, you will see the letters are dark and black only when they are freshly laid down."

Somewhat abashed, the clerk, whose fingers were more stained than Amaranthe's, held up his most recent sheet for Oliver to inspect. The ink, still drying, immediately ran toward the feet of his letters, and he hastily turned his page flat.

"These letters have faded to a light brown." Amaranthe pointed. "The same shade of brown, as you can see. Both were written hastily, in the kind of court hand our scribe is using, but you can identify the same hand by the foot of the Y character and the use of the thorn character for 'th.' It is an archaic usage, but faster to write one character rather than two. I noticed the same usage in other records of these years when I studied the parish register."

Silence fell in the courtroom as Oliver studied the document. Mal's barrister had the sense to hold still, lacing his hands and studying the ceiling. Froggart sputtered with outrage. Sybil and Popplewell held a whispered, furious conversation. Amaranthe held her breath and stared into Mal's eyes, wondering what he was thinking as he watched the judge.

Oliver sat back. "Very well, Miss Illingworth, you have convinced me these documents are of the appropriate age. Therefore it is likely they are of the provenance you claim." He regarded her with that twinkle ever stronger in his eyes. He *did* approve of clever women. She exhaled with relief. It was a rare man who did, particularly in his profession.

"The signatures could be forged," Sybil shrilled. "We have no way of knowing if that is the same Marguerite."

"Actually," Amaranthe answered, "we do. I happen to own a book which she inscribed." She returned to the pew where she'd been sitting and retrieved her Book of Hours. It was a marvel her legs carried her, they felt so unsteady.

"I asked your Aunt Bea, Mal, how your mother came by it, and she said Lord Vernay had given it her as a wedding gift. He knew she loved old things and nothing else would delight her more. She immediately wrote her name in it. As we thought, Bea sold the book, along with some of your mother's other things, to pay for funeral expenses and save up for your schooling. Because it had first been owned by Lady Willoughby de Broke, it traveled back to Callington into the hands of Mr. Finney, and thereby to me. I have a proper bill of sale specifying my ownership," she said, with a glare at Mr. Thorkelson, "in the event you wish to challenge that, too."

Sybil crowded close to examine the flyleaf of the book that Amaranthe held open for the inspection of the judge.

"God's teeth," the duchess swore quietly. "You little—you... you!" She bit off her savage words, wise enough to recollect she should not lose possession of her temper in the presence of the judge deciding her case. Amaranthe almost wished she'd let loose. She suspected the duchess was capable of the most magnificent fits of rage. Something about Popplewell's nervous, unhappy look said he fully expected to witness one later.

Oliver cleared his throat and sat back in his chair. "Well. This evidence changes the facts of the case very much."

"Rather a change of circumstances for you, old man," Rosenfeld observed.

Froggart appeared on the verge of apoplexy. "Procedure!" he gulped, his voice high and strained. "False evidence! Not correct—no time to prepare—" He glanced at the duchess as if he expected her to open her mouth and demolish him on the spot with a breath of fire. Sybil looked as if she just might.

"I don't believe this evidence is false," Oliver said.

Everyone watched the judge, waiting. Standing next to her, Mal slipped his hand into Amaranthe's. She clung to it, squeezing. Whatever the decree, she would stand by him. And if he cast her away, she'd come back whenever he needed her again. She'd come today suspecting he might need her, ready to produce the evidence she held if he wished it. She would continue to turn up, offering whatever she could. Whatever he would accept. Whatever he needed, whether he admitted needing her or not.

"Let it be entered into the rolls," Oliver said, straightening, and the scribe dashed his quill into his ink. "The case brought by Her Grace the Duchess of Hunsdon challenging the will of the late Duke of Hunsdon is dismissed. Evidence has been submitted to the court showing that Malden Grey—named hereafter as Malden Delaval—is the firstborn son and legitimate heir to Hugh Langston Delaval, third Duke of Hunsdon, by his marriage to Marguerite Grey, hereafter known as Marguerite Delaval, Lady Vernay.

"The court confirms that by terms of the entail, entire possession of the Hunsdon estate, and the title of His Grace the 4th Duke of Hunsdon, shall pass to Malden Grey—Delaval. The estate will provide the jointure owed to Her Grace the Duchess of Hunsdon and will execute all other provisions that have been made in the third duke's will. If Her Grace has issues with these provisions, she may take her case to the common law courts.

"And furthermore," Oliver concluded, "Her Grace shall be responsible for furnishing to the Court full payment of all fees that have been generated by this case by all parties."

Sybil gave a small, smothered yelp. The common law courts moved every bit as glacially as the Court of Chancery, and sometimes with less pleasant results, being more focused on the finer points of law than the actual dispensation of justice. It would hardly be a promising avenue for any claim she wished to press.

But the worst blow, Amaranthe suspected, was being held accountable for court fees, when she had no money. Popplewell swayed in his seat, looking light-headed.

Mal's expression was calm and firm, his head bowed as he listened to the judgment. He held her hand tightly.

Oliver cleared his throat. "Now to the matter of the contested guardianship. The Delaval children—" He paused and asked sharply, "*Are* they Delaval children?"

Mal lifted his head. "My mother died in 1757," he said soberly. "Her death record is in the parish register, and her monument in St. Philip and St. James. I believe the record will show that my father married Christine, daughter of the Earl of Olforde, in 1756."

"Bastards," Sybil said in a choked voice. "They're all bastards."

"I will provide for them," Mal said swiftly. "I intend to adopt them legally. They shall be provided for."

"Young Hugh can't be your heir if he's illegitimate," Oliver warned.

Mal nodded. He knew that, better than anybody. "They will be provided for," he said again.

"And will have a true mother, I hope, rather than this harpy," Rosenfeld said. The duchess's color rose, showing through the white lead paint.

Oliver gave the barrister a reproving look. "You needn't put that in," he told the scribe. "Let the record show that by circumstances of birth, the children of the third Duke of Hunsdon by Lady Christine do not have a legal claim to the estate or title of Hunsdon, nor any of the lesser titles, holdings, or estates. Until their majority, their legal guardian shall be their elder half-brother, Malden Grey—Delaval—the 4th Duke of Hunsdon."

Oliver gathered the parchment pages and handed them back to Mal. "You'll need these to show the House of Lords, but with my decision on record, that should be all it takes. I imagine they'll want to install you before Parliament adjourns this session." His face lit with humor. "Be prepared for a great deal of toad eating. Young Hugh's been spared because of his age, but you'll have more new friends than you'll know what to do with. Fortunate that you already have a wife picked out, or you'd be besieged by hopeful mamas as well."

Amaranthe's face burned as Oliver beamed at her. "I told you to choose a clever wife. Won you a dukedom, didn't she?"

"She's no duchess!" Sybil screamed. "You can't have my clothes! I'll tell everyone—the Duchess of Gloucester—of Cumberland—they'll never allow it! I'll see that you're not received!"

Popplewell hauled her out of the room as she gnashed her teeth, wailing. "Jointure! Nothing more! Jointure, when that miserable miser—"

Mr. Thorkelson, who had exited the witness box, cleared his throat and gave Amaranthe an unctuous smile.

"How very glad I am to learn that my reservations about your work have proved groundless, Miss Illingworth," he said. "I am sure you understand that the office of Thorkelson, Thorkelson, and Son takes very seriously the honor of serving the dukes of Hunsdon as long as we have." He turned his sycophantic look on Mal. "We will be very happy to receive you in your offices, sir, or call upon you at your convenience. There will be a bit of business to see to regarding transfer of the title and so on, but we stand ready to—"

"I will call upon you to discuss who shall handle the estate in future," Mal said coolly. "Good day, Mr. Thorkelson."

The other man had no choice but to bow and lumber away.

"Ducal already," Amaranthe murmured under her breath.

Mal squeezed her hand again as he turned to Froggart. "How fortunate for you that Sybil is such an admirable, upstanding citizen, as you painted her," he said. "Considering that she now has to stand all the court fees, including your retainer."

"Grey!" Froggart exhaled explosively. "That is—er, Your Grace! Fine bit of oratory there, old fellow! You'll make a roaring good barrister."

"Barrister?" Rosenfeld rumbled with laughter. "Froggart, you bacon brain! He'll have his coronet and a seat in Lords. He'll have far more influence in Parliament than he ever could in a courtroom. With all due respect to Your Honor," he said with a cheeky grin at Oliver.

Oliver grunted as he rose. The scribe scrambled to finish his notes and blew on his parchment before he rolled it up.

"I believe Mrs. Oliver and I have earned an invitation to your wedding breakfast," the judge said as he made a grand exit. "Miss Illingworth, good day. This court is adjourned."

CHAPTER TWENTY-FOUR

Amaranthe felt a bit dazed as she and Mal left the courtroom and looked out at the crowd browsing the market stalls set up in Westminster Hall. It seemed incredible that the world outside the courtroom could have been going on in ordinary fashion all this time.

"How do you feel?" she asked Mal. He still held her hand. She made no attempt to detach herself.

"Like I parted company from my horse and took a blow to the head."

He looked down at her, his expression sober, his eyes searching. She savored the sight of him, the strong lines of his face, the arresting blue eyes, the shape of his lips. The pull grew every time she looked at him, every time she learned more of his character. Familiarity increased her adoration rather than dulling it.

Love indeed, then. Not infatuation or a passing fancy, but a deep appreciation for the man he was, and for everything that belonged to him. Love in truth.

"You will leave this hall the Duke of Hunsdon," she said quietly. "Are you prepared for that?"

"No." He studied her in return, as if he had discovered something new of her as well. Releasing her hand, he pointed his elbow toward her, and she took it. Once again that feeling struck her of pieces quietly slipping into place. Him at her side. The two of them, together. Something about it felt inevitable and delicious and right.

He held out his arm to her. That had to mean he wanted her beside him? He wasn't going to cast her off after all? Or was he only being polite?

"Will you come with me to the house?" he asked. "I have to tell the children, and I've no notion how to prepare them. It will require some planning."

She nodded. She was past pride. She would cling to him as long as he let her.

"May we stop by my house first? I must see to something."

Davey strode up to them, settling his hat on his head. "I found a scarf for Eyde and the most cunning toy for Derwa," he reported. "All wrapped up and put to bed then, miss? Mr. Grey? Saw the duchess storm out in a perfect rage, I did, so I guess things went your way? Knew the judge would see sense, I did."

"The resolution was not satisfactory for the duchess," Mal answered. "She will not be residing at Hunsdon House henceforth. We'll allow her in to collect her things, and I hope you'll watch her like a hawk the whole time."

"Davey, we will have to address Mr. Grey by his new title," Amaranthe said. "He is—"

"Let's speak of it later," Mal said, laying a hand on hers. "You will join us for dinner? We have much to discuss." He met her eyes and she nodded.

A warm thrill curled around her heart. He was holding her close. He was speaking of plans together. In the days since he had stormed from her house she had tried over and again to steel herself against losing him, against losing the intimacy and rapport that had grown so deep and strong between them in such a short time. Against losing the one man who made her come alive in his presence the way no man ever had. She had known from the start that she could not have him.

But here he was beside her, and her blood hummed with excitement and a wild, unlikely hope.

A line of carriages for hire stood in front of Westminster Abbey, awaiting the whims of visitors and tourists, and Mal crossed the street to inquire about one. Davey showed her the scarf he had bought for Eyde, and Amaranthe stroked the expensive imported lace, one made dearer by the tax.

"Davey, this is quite a fine gift," she said, though she couldn't help wonder where he had come up with the money. She paid him as well as she could, but she herself could not afford such luxuries.

"Aye, but she's serving in a duke's house, miss," Davey said proudly, and Amaranthe smarted. How disappointed her staff would be to leave Hunsdon House and come back to her quiet little corner of George Court.

"And the vails one gets in a duke's house!" Davey added. "A man come around a day beforehand asking all manner of questions about the house and the staff, who was come and gone, who ran it and such, and he gave Ralph coin for all of us, if only we'd speak with him should he come again." Davey shook his head. "Never heard such a notion, but the coin was solid enough."

Sybil's spies, Amaranthe guessed. Or perhaps someone hired by Froggart to make inquiries on behalf of Sybil's case. No wonder he had known of Amaranthe's business at Hunsdon House, though he'd put the worst possible cast on the situation.

Oliver had addressed her as if she were Mal's intended, not

his mistress. An embarrassed flush moved through her. Oliver didn't know the whole of her doings. He'd never recommend her if he knew.

But Mal had exonerated her from forgery, in the eyes of the law at least. That he had done so caused the warm tendrils around her heart to tighten painfully. Whatever he thought of her in private, he had made her doings look aboveboard to the court.

He had to do so, of course, if he wanted his own claim to stand. Associating with a known forger would undeniably call into question documents one suddenly produced proving one's legitimacy. She'd known that when she went to St. Mary Redcliffe searching one more time for the parish register and the truth. It was why it had been necessary to have the rector pen an account of why the marriage record had been hidden away. She'd known her own word would not stand, not as a woman, and not as a woman known as a copyist.

Known around London for having some skill, it appeared. She couldn't contain a thrill of pride at that.

And now Mal was a duke's heir. No, not the heir—the duke himself. He'd vaulted in an instant from an acknowledged bastard to the highest rank of nobility. The warmth around her heart seared into pain. He had not been entirely out of her reach as a duke's bastard. She could have been—she *had* been—of some use to him. But a duke? Any union between them was impossible now. He would require a bride of birth and family, and preferably some little wealth, to aid his connections, influence, stature in society, and in keeping the estate solvent.

She could be of some use to him if he had a problem finding staff, or if he found a manuscript in the library he wanted to commission a copy of. That was all.

She clutched her pelisse close about her, though her chill was not from the damp breeze off the river. Mal rolled up in a phaeton, and she took his hand as he helped her inside. Davey clung to the back, and Amaranthe relished being near Mal a while longer.

"Did you mean what you said in court?" she asked as they rolled through Whitehall, past the Banqueting House, the Treasury buildings, and the impressive façade of the Horse Guards. "About me not being a forger in truth."

"I as much accused you of it in your home, didn't I?" he admitted. He watched the traffic flowing about them, but his weight beside her was firm and steady and warm. "I regretted my hasty words, after. So I betook myself to the Stationer's Company and made a study of the Statue of Anne and England's copyright laws. Turns out there were some finer points I hadn't considered, such as the notion of public domain."

"It was stealing," Amaranthe admitted. "The treatise. The St. Johns manuscripts. And the manuscript that Ned found in the Hunsdon House. Mr. Karim mentioned he'd heard rumors of it," she said guiltily. Might as well get everything out in the open. "I did not come to Hunsdon House with entirely altruistic motives."

"Who among us is entirely altruistic?" Mal said in a mild tone. "Did you enter a contract that you were prohibited from making further copies of any of these manuscripts?"

"As you observed, the possessors might feel such a prohibition was implied in the circumstances of the commission," she said dryly. "Most certainly the librarians of St. Johns might feel a violation has occurred."

"If you did not agree to the restriction, I maintain you cannot be prosecuted," Mal said as the driver took them through Charing Cross. "And if anyone brings you to court on these grounds, I will ensure the suit drags on until we are both dead and buried. I have the resources to do it, now."

She giggled. Mal wanted to share the flush of victory with

her; that was the reason for this new amity between them. Tomorrow, or tonight after dinner, he would come to his senses and see how impossible things must be between them.

She would make the most of tonight, then.

Davey held the horses in the narrow passage of George Court while Amaranthe brought Mal inside her house. Before she had gone far Inez appeared at the top of the stairs leading down to the kitchen. She wore her cloak and carried a valise of clothes and her few other small possessions.

"Inez! You're leaving us?"

"I'm sorry, *senhorita,* but I cannot spend another night under the same roof as that man," Inez said. She held herself proudly, but her lower lip trembled. "I have imposed upon your hospitality long enough."

"You have not imposed," Amaranthe exclaimed. In truth, the girl had been a great help to her. "What has Joseph done? Has he insulted you in some way?"

"His very manner is an insult! But if you are asking *that, senhorita,*" she hurried to say, reading Amaranthe's face, "no, I cannot complain of advances. He is no more thick-headed and foolish than any man. But I have reached the end of my patience."

Inez glanced at Mal, who offered no defense for Joseph or males more generally.

"I am very sorry to see you go, Inez, and I hope you will find a position that suits you," Amaranthe said. "Please come to us if you need anything at all. Anything. I shall do my best to ensure Joseph doesn't trouble you."

The girl bobbed a quick curtsey and clattered down the stairs. Amaranthe thought her last words might have been a muttered, "If only he would," but she couldn't be sure.

Mal followed her into the parlor, looking about curiously. "We are unchaperoned," he said, his voice deep and low.

She met his eyes and saw in them a glow she recognized. An answering heat rose within her. "We have been unchaperoned before."

"But never alone in a house together. I cannot recall a single instance."

She set her gloves, bonnet, and pelisse aside on one of the chairs and went to her work easel, lifting the cover. She removed the sheet that stood there with its orderly lines of script and dark, fresh ink. From the rack beneath the window she retrieved a different page, the title page for the Book of Secrets that Mal had caught her finishing the other day. She uncapped her ink, dipped her quill, and in the small space between the elaborate border and the line crediting Theocratus for the English translation she wrote, "Prepared by A. Illingworth from the Hunsdon MS MDCCLXXVI."

"Proper credit," Mal commented, standing at her shoulder.

She recapped the ink and cleaned her quill. "No more forgery, or anything close to it," she said. She turned to face him. Her nose reached his shoulder. He smelled of wig powder and Eau de Cologne, a scent she had come to find as pleasurable as ink.

He cupped her cheek with one hand, fingers sliding into the hair around her ear. His thumb brushed her chin. She swayed on her feet, feeling an instant lift of her heart. She wasn't afraid of where this might lead. Not with him.

"In fact," she said, her voice softening, "I have been thinking I might join the Stationer's Company. At the very least, I should record my works in their register. It occurred to me, when you were so magnificently defending me in court, that if I register them myself, no one else may be allowed to copy *my* work."

He slid his second hand around her waist and stroked up her back. Heat darted from every place his hand touched.

"No more lies?" he inquired.

She bit her lip. "No more lies."

His gaze dropped to her mouth, and his mouth followed his eyes. Amaranthe lifted her lips to meet his, eager and shameless. His kiss was better than the memories she had relived for the past week. He was a wall of flame and yet solid to the touch. She wanted to wrap herself around him and hold him tightly. She wanted to hold him for all time.

She lifted her head, a thought teasing the back of her mind. There was something important—something that required attention before she could go back to kissing Mal. What had it been?

"We need to talk to the children," Mal growled, brushing his lips along her neck.

She shuddered but nodded. Somehow it did not surprise her that he so exactly shared her thoughts. He was as different from her as could be and their acquaintance covered a span of mere weeks, yet he made perfect sense to her.

He was perfect *for* her, Amaranthe realized as they untangled from their embrace. It was as though some heavenly hand, guided by divine inspiration, had shaped in every part the man who was the match for her, then breathed life into him and set him upon earth.

She'd never felt this way for anyone, and some deep, solid certainty told her she'd never feel it for another. It was he, and he alone, who could bring her alive like this.

Too bad the divine inspiration had gone ahead and made him a *duke*.

They drove in silence the short distance to Hanover Square. A small crowd of spectators had formed in front of Hunsdon House. A haphazard pile of luggage sat in the street. The front door opened and Hugh marched down the stairs carrying a small leather case.

He pitched the case atop a wooden trunk bound with brass, then turned toward the house just as Ralph charged out the door into the street and seized the small case. They both had a grip on it, Ralph earnestly pleading, and Hugh, white-faced, shouting at him. Amaranthe struggled down from the carriage and hurried toward them, a step behind Mal.

"Not my home anymore, is it!" Hugh shouted. "So I'm clearing out! Put it down, Ralph, so I can get the rest of my things."

"Why is the duke's luggage in the middle of Hanover Square?" Mal demanded, turning on Ralph.

"Because I'm not the duke anymore!" Hugh howled. He swung on Mal, dropping the case to clench his hands into fists. "She says I'm nothing, that I have nothing that belongs to me. Not even this house. Nothing."

"Who says?" Mal barked, but Amaranthe already knew. From inside the double doors, which stood open to the world, she heard a woman's high-pitched shriek.

"Sybil?" Mal snarled. "She has no say here. This is your house, Hugh. Pick up your things and carry them back inside."

"That's as what I been telling his lordship!" Ralph grunted as he heaved up the trunk, which appeared to be heavy.

"Don't lordship me!" Hugh railed at him. "I'm no grace, no lord, no nothing." His voice broke, but he held Mal's gaze with a tight, pleading look. "She says we're all illegitimate. Bastards."

There were any number of people crowding close to view the spectacle, but one could have heard a pin drop on the gravel in the sudden, awful silence that followed. The boy, shaking with anger, held his ground against the larger man. It was clear they shared blood: the same strong jaw, the same strong nose, the same blue eyes. Mal's face softened as he regarded his brother.

"Hugh," he said quietly. "While I live this is and always will be your home, no matter what. Now get you inside."

Amaranthe held her breath as Hugh didn't move and the moment spun out. Murmurs ran through the crowd, quiet now, but sure to grow and spread faster than coal smoke on a river breeze. It was not her place, but she feared these two strong-willed Delavals were at an impasse. She stepped forward and touched Hugh's shoulder.

"Come inside and we will tell you what happened at court today," she said. "Have you had your tea? I fancy a nice cream tea, and some of Mrs. Blackthorn's scones."

Hugh collected himself. His gaze swung over the avid faces of the crowd, and he flinched, then turned to Amaranthe with careful courtesy.

"I do not think I have ever had cream tea, Miss Illingworth. Please do enlighten me."

He walked toward the house beside her, and Amaranthe breathed a sigh of relief.

"There's a trick to it," Mal said, walking on Hugh's other side. "Cream tea. Something about where the jam goes, though on my life I can't recall which way is correct."

"You'll never make a good Cornishman if you don't learn," Amaranthe scolded him, and between them they got Hugh inside. Ralph deposited the trunk inside the foyer and went back for the rest. The sound of shrieking floated from the formal parlor.

"I will have this clock, you saucy wench, and I'll have your backside in the street without a character for crossing me!" Sybil's voice, unmistakably.

"Ee ain't yours, ee's the duke's, innit!" Eyde retorted. "You'll have to answer to Mr. Grey do you help yourself to anything more under this roof, and I don't care if 'er's the Queen herself!"

"I am still the duchess!" Sybil yelped. "My marriage wasn't a sham like the one that produced these miserable little bastards. I will have what I am due!"

"Hugh," Amaranthe murmured, "perhaps you would run to the kitchen for me and tell Mrs. Blackthorn we'd like those scones."

"And miss Mal taking on our stepmother?" Hugh answered. "Not for the world." He straightened his back, and Amaranthe smiled.

She admired Mal's air of command as he strode into the parlor. When he spotted Ned and Camilla in the far corner near the fireplace, a white-faced Ned holding his sister while tears rolled down her cheeks, Mal's rage became magnificent to see.

"Sybil, by God, you will not take a thing from this house but what my father gave you. And I will have your things sent to your lodgings, where you will be waiting, since you are leaving this house this instant."

"You would deny me!" Sybil lifted the heavy ormolu clock to throw at him. With alarm Eyde leapt forward and wrested it from her, cradling the ornate piece to her chest as if it were a baby bird.

"You would leave me penniless! You heard the will. You know what your father left me. An annuity, barely enough to keep a carriage. How am I supposed to hold up my head?"

"The annuity is more than enough to keep you comfortably, and if you were displeased with your jointure, you should have made that known when the marriage settlements were being drawn up," Mal said. "But you were so eager to be a duchess, I daresay you were only thinking of your immediate benefit, weren't you? You would stoop to rob Hugh's inheritance, and leave the children without money for food or fuel to run off to the Continent with Popplewell, and then dare show your face in this house? Truly, madam, your arrogance astounds me!"

"My arrogance?" Sybil stabbed a finger in his direction. "I don't know how you manufactured those documents, but you will not get away with this. Thief! Imposter! To think I thought you too witless and shiftless to ever be a bother to me, and to find you are capable of *this*." Her angry gaze swept to include Amaranthe. "And her, wearing my gowns!"

"I can assure you all your gowns will be returned to you," Amaranthe said. "I see you have need of them, since you have put off mourning already."

"I must have *something* to live on." Sybil stomped her foot.

"You should have." Mal took a step forward, his voice lowering dangerously. "The account books for both the house and the estates show that you and Popplewell have been diverting income to your own pockets for quite some time, since well before my father died. If you have not hoarded your ill-gotten gains enough to support you, I cannot find it in me to harbor any pity."

Sybil's eyes widened, and she looked nervously toward the door. "You—you're threatening me. And lying. Again."

"I have seen the books as well," Amaranthe said. "I could swear to it in a court of law. I believe even duchesses can be convicted for stealing, can they not?"

Sybil's pale face took on a hunted expression. Stealing was regarded much like forgery and punished with fines, transportation, or death, depending on the severity of the crime and the whim of the judge. Sybil had stolen a great deal.

"You," she spat at Amaranthe. "I imagine you're quite pleased with how all this turned out. Taking up with a bastard and contriving to make him a duke!"

"You will leave Amaranthe out of this," Mal said. "You will leave this house this instant. We shall not be troubled by you or your demands again, or those account books will be given to my solicitor for review. And if I hear one word—even the slightest intimation—that you have said anything ill, indeed anything at all about my brothers or sister..." His voice trailed off, the unspoken threat more daunting than anything he could have given voice to.

Camilla gave a choked little cry, and Ned firmed his arms around her. Hugh crossed the room to stand before them both.

Sybil rallied; she would not go down easily. Amaranthe had to admire her fighting spirit. "I spoke no more than what is the truth. If you're the duke now, then they're nameless bastards. They have nothing and no one."

"They have me," Mal said. "You had no right to tell them, Sybil."

She licked her lips. "Someone had to. Hugh had the right of it. It's only too bad you returned in time to stop him leaving. How can he live here, knowing—"

"Enough!" Mal roared. "Ralph, you will open the door for the duchess, and if she does not throw herself through it this very instant, she may not leave this house unscathed."

"Brute!" Sybil cried, but she picked up her massive skirts and scurried for the door. "I always knew you were uncivilized."

"Then you know better than to cross me," Mal said. "Out!"

She complied.

Mal faced his siblings, standing on the other side of the patterned rug, with a set of chairs and a small table between them. They stared back at him, forlorn.

"I—" Mal started and then stopped. Amaranthe had never seen him at a loss for words.

"I do believe it's time for tea," Amaranthe said as the cook peeked around the open door. "Excellent timing, Mrs. Blackthorn."

"Is the she-devil gone, then?" Mrs. Blackthorn brought the

tray into the room and deposited it on the small table beside Amaranthe while Mrs. Wheatley, the cook in training, and Eyde trooped in behind her.

"For now, and I hope for good," Amaranthe confirmed. "Come here, children, and I will show you how to enjoy a cream tea. The *proper* way," she stressed, "no matter what anyone else, including anyone from Devonshire, tries to tell you."

Camilla came forward first but instead of taking a seat, she wrapped her arms around Amaranthe's waist and pressed her face into her stomach. "I missed you," she said, her voice muffled.

Amaranthe slid her arms about the girl and kissed the golden ringlets atop her head. It felt natural now to touch, to embrace, to give and receive affection. The wall she'd put up between herself and other people after her parents died, after the world betrayed her, could finally come down.

"I missed you as well," she said. "It was very silly of me not to visit you as soon as I returned to town."

"Can you still visit us?" Ned looked worried. "Even if we are bastards?"

"Lord—" She stopped. She'd been in the habit of using his title, another way to try to keep her distance from the children. She no longer had a wish to keep her distance. "My dear Ned," she said firmly, "I hope to see even more of you now. You see, I stayed away because of a very foolish fear that I—well, that I would not be a very good influence for you. But your brother, I am glad to say, persuaded me to mend my ways."

"There was some concern in the court today that Amaranthe is a forger," Mal said. He took his dish of tea from Eyde, who had commencing pouring since Amaranthe's arms were full of little girl. The maid froze and stared, teapot aloft, until Mal assured her, "I was happy to lay those suspicions to rest and prove that she is not."

"By a very persuasive argumentation," Amaranthe said. "Your brother would have made a rather fine barrister, had the Benchers ever called him."

She thrilled at how easily he used her given name. She'd used his as well. She'd already stopped thinking of him as Grey, the angry stranger who'd burst into her house making wild accusations. He was Mal. Direct, unpretentious, still prone to temper, but also steadfast, loyal, and dear.

"And you are the duke," Hugh said quietly. "Our father's only legitimate child." He winced, but his hands were steady as he accepted his dish of tea.

"Amaranthe found the documents that proved my mother's marriage to our father was properly done," Mal said. "My mother hid her copy of the lines in the back of a book that our father gave her as a wedding gift. By some providential course the book made its way to Amaranthe in Cornwall and stayed hidden above the stables in her cousin's house for years."

Eyde stopped with the sugar tongs hovering over Ned's tea. "Your book, mum?" she whispered in awe.

"Thaker retrieved it and held it for me," Amaranthe explained. "It's been safe all this time."

Mal continued, passing Millie her dish. "The old duke, our grandfather, tried to pretend the marriage had never happened. He pressed our father into wedding your mother without annulling his marriage to mine, most likely because it would have been expensive and possibly damaging, or possibly because he thought my mother was dead already. But she was still alive, which, I'm afraid, made our father's marriage to your mother—"

"Bigamy," Hugh said grimly.

"And us bastards." Ned stared into his cup.

"How I hate that word." Mal winced. "It is my hope you will allow me to adopt you, so you may wear the Delaval name with honest pride. I swear to you, on my honor—no, on my life—

that you shall never want for anything I can provide you. You all shall have incomes from the estate and my support in whatever vocation you choose. And Millie, you needn't fear you won't marry well. I will see that your dowry makes up for any perceived lack."

Camilla made a face, but Ned rushed in before she could speak. "Speaking of marriage! When are you finally going to marry Miss Illingworth, Gr—" He broke off, looking baffled. A nervous look at his elder brother said he wasn't ready to address Mal as Hunsdon. Hugh wasn't ready for it, either.

"We shall all have some doing to get our tags and titles sorted," Mal said gravely. "And I will wed Amaranthe as soon as she will have me."

Amaranthe raised her cup to her lips, giving herself time to find her voice as her heart leapt wildly within her chest. "Are you asking me at last?"

"At last!" He looked confounded. "As if I haven't asked you a dozen times already."

"Commanded." She sipped her tea. "Presumed. But never *asked*."

He lowered his own cup, staring. "I didn't?"

"You did not," she confirmed.

"Well." Mal cleared his throat as the children looked at him with a puzzled eagerness. "We can settle that directly. Amaranthe, won't you—"

"Whist!" Eyde hissed, bumping the back of his chair with her elbow. "'Er'll want it done correctly, with the knee and the rest."

"I'm to go on one knee?" Mal looked perplexed.

"Well, of course!" Camilla said in exasperation. "Honestly, have you never done this before?"

"As a matter of fact," Mal said, "no."

The admission thrilled Amaranthe all the more. He'd never

wanted to marry anyone else. In fact, he hadn't thought of marriage at all until Oliver recommended he marry Amaranthe. And he'd never objected to the idea, not even in the beginning, not until he—but she wasn't a forger anymore, and never would be again. And if he meant to ask her, really and truly ask her... Her breath stopped in her throat.

Mal left his chair and dropped to one knee. "Amaranthe," he began again.

Eyde rolled her eyes. "'Ee must take her hand, sir."

"Yes, Grey—er, Mal, you go on bended knee before her," Hugh said. "You ought to hold out the betrothal ring you mean to give her, but if you don't have one, a heartfelt declaration will do."

"I haven't a ring," Mal said.

"Then you must have a flowery speech," Ned exclaimed. "Come, haven't you rehearsed one? If we'd known you needed this much help—"

"She doesn't want a flowery speech, she just wants to hear he loves her," Camilla said impatiently.

While the children argued over the best way Mal was to deliver his proposal, he crossed the rug in a few strides and dropped to one knee before Amaranthe's chair. His hand when he took hers was firm, strong, and bore ink stains on various fingers. Amaranthe smiled, her heart beating madly. He was the man for her, in so many ways.

"Amaranthe Illingworth," he said simply, holding her hand in both of his. "Will you—"

"A bit louder, Your Grace, so's we can hear proper!" Mrs. Blackthorn called from behind the door, where she stood peering with Ralph and Davey. Derwa's head popped into the opening, her eyes alight.

Amaranthe bit back laughter at Mal's look of exasperation. "Amaranthe Illingworth," he said in his resonant barrister's voice. "From the moment you came into my life, you've begun to fix things I didn't know needed fixing. You have made me aware of dreams I didn't know I wanted for myself. You have opened my eyes in so many ways to a future I could never have imagined."

She clung to his hand, hanging on his every word. His eyes were a clear, compelling blue. She wanted to fall into them forever. "Amaranthe, my dear, the most capable, astonishingly beautiful, dashedly *clever* woman I have ever met—will you do me the very great honor of becoming my wife?"

She smiled, letting her heart show in her eyes, through the sting of happy tears.

"I need some time to consider," she said.

The look on his face was priceless. "What?"

"There is, for instance, the matter of my work. I wish to continue as a copyist. I love it, Mal."

"Of course," he said promptly. "The Duchess of Hunsdon, copyist. You will start a new fashion for duchesses entering trades."

That idea was laughable, but she was not ready to laugh just yet. "There is the matter of my house. It is perfect for an antiquarian bookstore. And I have always wanted to open one."

"You have a supply of manuscripts you've begun building to that effect," Mal said. "Yes, I was listening to you chatter with Miss Pettigrew all the way to Bristol. What, I was going to listen to Joseph? Your bookstore you shall have, and as many books to go in it as the ducal estates can supply."

"Speaking of Joseph." She bit her lip. "Will he be able to continue his employment?"

"I will expect him to provide his services for free, if he is a member of the family," Mal answered. "Oh, all right, we will increase his stipend. He must follow my example, however, and choose wisely when he next decides to fall in love."

"And the children," she said.

He held her gaze steadily. "I will adopt them, my love."

"I know. I wish that as well. If—if they will have me as a mother."

"By Jove, they will!" Ned exclaimed, and Camilla clapped her hands in joy.

Mal pressed her hands, examining her face. "You are still not certain?"

She bit her lip, coming to the last and worst objection. "It won't benefit you a whit to marry me, Mal. A rector's daughter, poor, plain, barely genteel—I'm not at all a fit wife for a duke. I bring nothing to a marriage, and—"

He stopped her protest with his lips, uncaring of their audience. That kiss held everything she needed to know to make such a great and treacherous leap. She would sacrifice anything, pay any price, for the right to kiss him whenever she wanted. She slid her fingers along his jaw, ready to sink into him and that kiss forever, but he gathered his senses and drew back.

"I don't wish to rush you, and not that my posture is becoming uncomfortable, or that my tea is growing cool, but how much more time do you need to consider, my darling?"

This time she didn't stifle the small laugh. "I have made my choice."

The light in his eyes deepened, steady, bright. "Amaranthe Illingworth—soon to be Amaranthe Delaval, Duchess of Hunsdon—you are the author of my happiness and every beautiful thing that has come into my life. Say you will share it with me for always."

She smiled even as the tears spilled over. "I will."

He rose to his knees, anchored both hands in her hair, and kissed her again. Amaranthe gripped his forearms with her hands, clinging to him, laughing, crying, kissing him back.

Camilla clapped her hands over her eyes. Ned whistled and looked at the ceiling. But the others—including Hugh—cheered.

And the feast that night in Hunsdon House was the merriest yet, with the promise of many more merry times—sweet, long days and sweeter nights—to follow.

EPILOGUE

"If a man has a library in a...woman of beauty...*Aree fah*! I'll never get this." Ned tossed the shred of paper with its Latin inscription onto the library table.

Amaranthe looked up from her easel near the window and the parchment pages anchored with her wooden bar. The library at Hunsdon House had even better light than the workroom in her own little house.

"Where are you picking up your Cornish expressions, Ned? Eyde? Derwa? Or Tamara?" Tamara was the little Cornish costermonger who, with her cronies, looked after Amaranthe's house after she removed to the ducal mansion.

Ned gave her an abashed grin. "You, mum."

There'd been a happy settling of Amaranthe's staff into Hunsdon House in the sixth months since her marriage. Mrs. Blackthorn ran the kitchen with its small army of undercooks and scullery maid. Mrs. Wheatley had proved a hopeless cook but a natural born housekeeper, and she and Mrs. Blackthorn ruled their empire with wisdom and munificence. Amaranthe was allowed to make menu suggestions and choose which scents she wanted in the linen closets, and which guest to put in which room, but otherwise she was not obliged to decide on a single household issue. She found this arrangement a great relief.

Ralph, now Mr. Biggs, was the most loyal and devoted butler to be found in all of London, and his dignity was to be marveled at. Davey, first footman, enjoyed his task of instructing and advising the second and third footmen, keeping them in their place. Eyde had ascended to the role of dresser to the duchess and spent hours tending to Amaranthe's hair and gowns, carefully and with much delight building a new wardrobe for her mistress after Sybil stormed through the house and took every last glove and pin with her.

Derwa was companion to Camilla, and all summer the two had racketed about the gardens like hooligans, whooping and shouting and neglecting their lessons. Amaranthe vowed that next year they would remove to one of the country estates for the summer, but Mal had needed these months to settle into his new role.

Joseph looked up from his book. "You're switching the object with the prepositional phrase, Ned. Look at the declensions again." He passed the paper back to his pupil. Ned heaved a sigh.

Amaranthe hid her smile. Joseph had had a less blissful summer than she, but at least he had ceased drowning his sorrows in spirits.

"I'm home!" Mal strolled into the library, dressed in a beautifully embroidered brocade coat and matching breeches. He tossed his small wig into a chair and ran a hand through his shorn hair.

He had taken up wigs, following the fashion in the House of Lords, though he kept threatening to wear his natural hair. Amaranthe suspected that many other men would abandon their bag wigs and periwigs to imitate the new Duke of Hunsdon, who had caused quite a few ripples through the *beau monde* when he was formally invested at the close of Parliament's spring session and assumed his coronet and robes.

With the Lords assembling again for the fall session, Mal had taken his seat with pleasure, and found the arguing, negotiating, networks, and factions of politics his true milieu. Amaranthe smiled to see him full of confidence and self-assurance, his sense of justice and his persuasive talents put to good ends.

"What is everyone working on? I demand an accounting," Mal said.

"Latin." Ned sighed.

"Travel plans." Joseph returned to his copy of Thomas Nugent's *The Grand Tour*, the volume on France.

Camilla, without taking her eyes from the pages, raised a thick volume entitled *The History of the Decline and Fall of the Roman Empire*.

"And you, my love?" Mal strolled over to drop a kiss on her hair and glance at the pages where Amaranthe was scraping away a mistake. Her mind had been wandering of late, and she'd made two errors already.

"My new commission to make a preservation copy of the Book of Nunnaminster. It's an Anglo-Saxon prayer book from the Harley Collection in the British Royal Library. Ninth century Latin, the earliest thing I've ever worked on. I'm still astonished that the librarian would have contacted me about making a display copy for them."

"I'm not surprised at all." Mal rubbed her shoulders, working out the knot that had developed from bending forward over the fine script. "You're a duchess, and the best copyist in London. No one can quite get over that combination."

"I can think of half a dozen copyists equally good who have more need of the commission," Amaranthe murmured. "But I couldn't say no. Do you know who was first to hold and read this book? Ealhswith, wife of Alfred the Great. I'm holding a prayer book made for a queen." She reverently traced the line she was to copy next.

"A woman of beauty requires a library? Bah!" Ned sputtered with frustration. "Millie, won't you lend a fellow a hand here?"

"Not on your life." Camilla's eyes were glued to her book. "Commodus is about to be murdered by the praetorian guard, and I can't say he doesn't deserve it."

The door opened and Ralph entered, back straight as a doorjamb, his livery gleaming. "The post, Your Grace," he intoned. "And the cards that have been left today." He brought the salver mounded with letters and cards to Amaranthe, who put down her quill and picked up her letter opener.

"Viktor called? He seems at loose ends lately, as I haven't the time to racket about with him," Mal observed.

"The rotter," Joseph added from the depths of his chair.

"Come now, don't be bitter. You both share the honor of having been thrown over by Miss Pettigrew, which should make you friends," Mal said. He swiped a missive off the salver, noting the return address of Eton. "Hugh wrote! I hope the food is getting better, he's put that bully boy Southwood in his place, and he's not already asking for money."

He threw himself into a chair beside Amaranthe, already lost in the letter. Whatever Hugh needed, she knew Mal would send it at once without question. They'd gone together to deliver Hugh to Eton for the Michaelmas term, and it was clear that school was just what the boy needed to take his mind off his change in circumstances.

Mal had coached him at length about what to ignore and what to answer with his fists when he was insulted about his bastardy, and he had concluded the lessons with demonstrations of precisely where the fists should be placed. They had left

Hugh eager to fit in but also ready for battle, and Amaranthe wondered if a bit of scrapping to prove his worth wasn't exactly what the lad needed to lift his spirits.

"Will you look at this," Amaranthe said in surprise, picking up a creamy square of vellum. "The Duchess of Cumberland left a card. And the Duchess of Gloucester and Edinburgh as well. Good heavens! What do they want with me?"

"You're the newest duchess in town," Mal answered, without looking up from Hugh's letter. "Out to curry favor, I don't doubt, especially since Queen Charlotte was so taken with you at your presentation."

"If they're in league with Sybil, I rather wonder if there's some plan to humiliate me," Amaranthe said. "Ought I call on them, do you think?"

"Might as well," Mal answered. "I'm about to become rather unpopular. In our last session in Lords I voted to support the younger Hartley's patent on fire protection—it's something very clever, using iron plates—but I also endorsed the resolution he presented in the Commons, declaring that the slave trade is contrary to the laws of God and the rights of men."

Amaranthe sorted through the large stack of calling cards. "Well, it is."

"I know that, and you know that, and everyone in our household knows that. But an unpopular stance nevertheless among those making a great deal of money from slaving ships."

"I support you, however far you wish to take it," Amaranthe said. "Only think of what Mrs. Blackthorn and Mrs. Wheatley went through. And how many hundreds, no thousands of souls have it as bad or worse."

Mal passed her Hugh's letter with a fond smile. "That's my duchess. Champion of lost causes. Collector of strays."

"I don't collect them, you daft man. They choose me. And that's been my great fortune."

"As you have been my fortune," Mal returned. "No one can accuse me of ill luck any longer. Is that another letter from your dratted cousin Reuben? What is he after now, asking again for money? He didn't even come to our wedding."

Amaranthe passed him the letter. "Perhaps he's wishing us well."

Mal tossed the letter aside, unopened. "I chose you," he said abruptly.

Amaranthe paused to smile at him. "You did not," she said. "Oliver told you to marry and you cast your gaze about, and I happened to be convenient."

Mal sat up in his chair. "Did you see me married to anyone before you?" he demanded. "Did you see me pay my addresses to anyone else? No. Ergo you are the woman I chose, the only woman for me, and that's that."

"Of course, my love," Amaranthe said. She enjoyed teasing her husband about the way he had courted her, but in truth she was supremely happy with her lot. Marital relations had proved a joy beyond her wildest expectations, in every respect.

And with the conventional results. She put a hand to her belly, feeling a small movement inside. Gas, most likely. She would wait to say anything until she was quickening. Favella was her reminder of how terribly much could go wrong.

"Maria Walpole was illegitimate, wasn't she?" Camilla looked up from Gibbon. "And now she's the Duchess of Gloucester and Edinburgh."

"Yes, dear. She married an earl, and then a royal prince," Amaranthe answered. "So don't fret about what your prospects might be when you come out."

"I might decide not to marry," Camilla said defiantly. "Derwa and I might decide to travel. Or take up a trade, like you."

"Which sounds lovely," Amaranthe agreed. "In fact, I may

very well ask to accompany you if you travel. I haven't been further than Cornwall, you know." She selected a small note with familiar handwriting from the salver beside her.

"The Duchess of Northumberland invites us to one of her assemblies Tuesday next," she told Mal. "I'll accept, shall I? I do adore her assemblies."

"And she adores you." Mal chuckled. "Hasn't she promised to be one of the first patronesses of your shop, as soon as you open?"

"Which will be soon," Amaranthe said, feeling a flutter in her belly that was all excitement. "We went over today, while you were in meetings, to put up another set of shelves. And Mr. Thorkelson dropped off the consignment he promised from one of his client's estates. Mr. Karim will come Wednesday to help me catalogue and arrange them."

"How eager Mr. Thorkelson has proven to please us," Mal remarked. "I may keep our business with him after all, since he's terrified to cross me."

"The Duchess of Northumberland is a baroness in her own right, isn't she?" Camilla put a finger in her book. "And she's the one who made her husband a duke, when he started out a mere baronet."

Mal laughed. "My duchess did her one better," he said. "She made a duke out of a bastard."

"Why do you keep calling her that?" Camilla demanded, setting her book aside and crossing to their chairs, perching on the armrest of Amaranthe's.

"My duchess? Because she is."

"But that is her status," Camilla said with exasperation. "Not her *name*."

"Well, you can't call her Amaranthe, as that's rude," Mal said.

"I have it!" Ned crowed from his place at the table. "A man

who has a beautiful woman in his library lacks for nothing." He rolled his eyes in exasperation. "Bah! All that work for a love note that you wrote, Mal."

His guardian grinned. "I did. But it wasn't meant for you. Joseph set you to it, I suppose?"

"I thought it was an assignment from you." Joseph's face reddened as he passed Amaranthe the slip of paper.

"You remind me that I need to decide what to put on the sign over my shop," Amaranthe said. "Amaranthe Delaval, antiquarian? Amaranthe's Antique Books?"

"The Antiquarian Duchess," Joseph proposed.

"Hunsdon Books and Antiquarian Artifacts," Ned said.

"My Talented Wife," Mal said with a teasing grin.

"Well, I know what *I* want to call her," Camilla said, curling against Amaranthe's side. "Mother."

"One of my favorite titles," Amaranthe murmured. "In fact, it may be my favorite above all."

"Better than duchess? Or wife?" Mal affected outrage.

She smiled and reached out her hand to him. "And to think I was once Amaranthe Illingworth, orphan. You are the one who has elevated me, dear. And I wish to be no place else in the world but here with you."

ABOUT THE AUTHOR

Misty Urban fell in love with stories at an early age and has spent her life among books as a teacher, scholar, editor, writer, and bookseller. Her favorite stories take you new places, teach you new things, and end with a win. She especially likes romances about unconventional heroines who defy the odds and the unexpected heroes who woo them, so that's mostly what she writes. When she puts down the book she likes to take long walks, drag her family to new places, or hang out around water, dreaming up new stories.

Visit her at mistyurban.com
Join author's newsletter

ALSO BY MISTY URBAN

Ladies Least Likely

Viscount Overboard

The Forger and the Duke

The Painter Takes an Earl

Contemporary Novels

My Day As Regan Forrester

My Thing with Timothy Kay

www.ingramcontent.com/pod-product-compliance
Lightning Source LLC
Chambersburg PA
CBHW030236120726
47903CB00005B/1512